SHAYNA

D1114178

Kirk House Publishers

SHAYNA

A NOVEL

MIRIAM RUTH BLACK

Shayna: A Novel © Copyright 2021 Miriam Ruth Black

Paperback ISBN: 9781952976315
E-book ISBN: 9781952976322
LCCN: 2021949750

Cover Concept by Adde Russell
Cover and interior design by Ann Aubitz
Headshot by: © Susan M. Pearce

First Printing: January 2022

First Edition

Published by Kirk House Publishers
1250 E 115th Street
Burnsville, MN 55337
Kirkhousepublishers.com
612-781-2815

Advanced Praise

It's a story of the hardship of a young Jewish woman, Shayna, and her family fleeing religious persecution in their homeland of Ukraine in 1919 bound for America. Black's characters are so well-crafted that I felt like I was a member of the family. To tell you the truth, I didn't want to be part of the family, because what they go through is crushing and terrible stuff. I identified strongly with Shayna, not because I've ever endured anything like what happens to her, but there was something universal in her strength, her unrelenting quest for defining herself on her own terms, not letting the horrible actions of others define her. So in the end, I too was Shayna and deeply felt her victory. I closed the book with gratitude and a sense that what is good does win over what is evil.

—Holly Hartwell, early reader

This is a refugee story that makes all other refugee stories come to life. An unflinching portrayal of the pogroms that push Shayna's small group past borders and across an ocean to a harsh new world, and an empowering tale of the slow healing and resilience it takes for each person to find themselves again. Shayna reminds us that every refugee is a person with immense potential.

—Frankie Rollins, author The Grief Manuscript

I loved this book! It's authentic, emotionally satisfying and a compelling read.

—Bonnie Dimun, Executive Director, Museum at Eldridge Street

Shayna is one of those rare novels that grabs you on page one and doesn't let go until you reach the satisfying ending. In this tale of a spirited young Jewish woman escaping pogroms in early 20th-century Ukraine and making a life for herself and her family in America, Miriam Ruth Black establishes herself as a master storyteller. I loved every minute of reading this wonderful book.

—Alice Bloch, author of Mother Daughter Banquet

With so much fiction devoted to the Holocaust, it is refreshing to read an historical novel about the period of the great Jewish migration from Eastern Europe to the New World. From the founding of HIAS, the Jewish refugee agency, from 1880s - 1920s, millions of Jewish immigrants arrived in the U.S. There is hardly a Jewish family in the U.S. whose immigration is not rooted in that era. Few novels tell that story. It is all the more gratifying that this one, Shayna, tells it beautifully. From the moment I picked up Shayna's saga, I was captivated and found myself caring deeply about her and her family. That is the test of a good novel – and this one passes with flying colors! Kudos to the author.

—Roberta Elliott, daughter of a refugee, and former VP of Communications, HIAS

Shayna's a beautifully written novel, a story of hope, love and resilience. I did not want the story to end.

—Eva Moreimi author of Hidden Recipes, A Holocaust Memoir

Dedication

For My Father, Gershon Black

Shayna was inspired by my father's life. Orphaned at four years old after the murder of his family in a pogrom, he walked west across Europe with relatives who brought him to America. When I saw images of Syrian refugees trudging across Europe to reach safety, I saw my father as he must have been a hundred years before, a hungry, frightened and despairing child. Beyond the fear and the physical deprivation was the grief of losing his mother, a loss which never left his heart. These elements stirred within me and emerged as fiction in the novel, *Shayna*. Only after I finished did I realize I'd been attempting to give my father a better life, to replace, if only through fiction, the family he had lost.

Acknowledgments

As *Shayna* steps out into the world, I want to acknowledge some of the many people who generously gave of their time, wisdom, and encouragement to me along the way:

Katy Perry, my wonderful writing buddy from Minneapolis, whose consistent, honest and insightful feedback guided me from the beginning. Her perceptive questions led me deeper into my own understanding.

Adde Russell, my niece and artist extraordinaire, walked with me on this journey. Our frequent endless phone conversations, bemoaning and celebrating our creative struggles, nourished me as I wrote.

Meyer Weinshel, PhD candidate, Department of German, Nordic, Slavic & Dutch, University of Minnesota, the Yiddish scholar who helped me untangle the Yiddish still alive in my mind from childhood and provided proper spelling, based on YIVO standards, to my words. (See glossary in the back of the book.)

Early recognition and support from Marly Rusoff validated my belief in the importance of Shayna's story.

Winning the Hackney Literary Award, along with its generous prize, confirmed the universality and wide appeal of this novel.

Eli Andrew Ramer kindly shared his knowledge of prayer and orthodox practices.

Mary Carroll Moore and Frankie Rollins, wise teachers – Mary, who is master of the big picture and the smallest detail and Frankie, who is joyful, irreverent, imaginative and passionate about writing.

Early readers, Alice Bloch, Roz Sohnen, Elise Asch, and Ellen Melamed, blessed be her memory, fellow writers and honest critics, believed in *Shayna* and trusted our friendship enough to tell me what I needed to hear but couldn't see. Careful readings by dear friends, Lucy Shahar, Michelle Garron, Linda Garnets and Penelope Starr provided helpful suggestions and encouragement.

Joel Berman, Jane Matteson, Suze Rutherford, Dar Sumners and my beloved cousin Edie Zinman – thoughts of your enthusiasm and support sustained me on gray days.

I am humbled by Jane Yablonski Ross, my oldest friend. Thank you for always believing in me.

Ann Aubitz, of Kirk House Publishers, you believed in *Shayna* and offered her a wonderful home. It's been a delight to work with you.

Shayna's story would have remained lurking in my mind if it were not for Emmie Russell who calmed my nightmares as I wrote, listened to every word and always trusted in me when I didn't trust myself.

Prologue

The old woman's gnarled fingers brushed across the violet irises on the pillowcase she had embroidered years before. So many sets of pillowcases, blanket covers—even tablecloths—all embroidered with the Ukrainian irises her mother had loved. She remembered them exactly and gave them life on linens for her own daughters, grandchildren, and great grandchildren, as well as for David's family. Now her fingers shook. Food slipped from her fork. She could no longer hold a needle.

One set of sheets remained, where it had been buried deep in her cedar chest, wrapped for years in tissue. She hadn't known why she had saved it, but now she knew it was for today.

Her granddaughter kneeled in front of the old woman's chair. "Bubbeh, I've got a few errands. Will you be okay here alone?"

She took her granddaughter's hand in her own and held it for a moment. Not a wrinkle. Not a spot. Her fingers without knobs and bumps. She raised it to her lips and left a sweet kiss. "Stop worrying, Becky. I'm fine. I sit here in my chair by the window. I wear my diapers. You made lunch for me. I can be without a babysitter for an hour."

"David's grandson will be here soon with his new baby. They named her Sarah."

"I know. I don't have dementia yet. Here, wrap this in the tissue again and put it on the piano bench."

"Okay, Bubbeh. The phone is on the table. You've got the buzzer around your neck, remember?"

"Please. Enough. I'm fine. Wait. Before you go, fix the pictures on the piano so I can see them from here."

There, captured under glass, in black and white, dressed in her best clothes, sat her sister Perl with baby Sarah on her lap. Next to her stood her husband, with David in his arms. David, who for her would always be Dovid, her nephew, her son. Frozen there. All long dead. Even David. Here she was, nearly one hundred. The old woman stared at the picture taken over eighty years ago and thought, if only, if only, if only. But if only never happened. Another world. Another life.

"Bubbeh, wake up. Seth's here with the baby." She felt an arm on her shoulder, a gentle jostling. Her eyes snapped open, then closed and opened again. She shook her head to clear the memories away, rubbed her forehead and gathered strength.

She heard David's grandson in the hall with his wife and their new baby, Sarah. Here for a blessing. Never had she or David named any of the children after the tortured—the murdered. Yussi had said she was ignorant and superstitious, but she made up her mind. If it happened by accident, so be it. That might take away the curse, should there be a curse. Just in case.

"Come in. Come in. I'm decent."

Seth crouched in front of her chair, "Do you want to hold her?"

The old woman looked into his large, dark eyes. She nodded as she felt the baby placed on her lap and inhaled the aroma of baby powder, "What's her name again?"

"Sarah."

"Beautiful, beautiful name. See the package there on the piano bench? Take it for Sarah. You'll give it to her from me, for her wedding."

"You shouldn't."

"And why not?"

"Right. Why not? He picked up the tissue-wrapped package but didn't open it. "Was there ever anyone in our family named Sarah?"

"Maybe. Maybe a cousin. I don't remember," she lied. She lifted the baby from her lap, held her close, leaned forward, and kissed the soft hairs on Sarah's head.

The old woman closed her eyes and prayed to her irresponsible, feckless God, protect this baby from terror. Let no violent hand touch her. Keep her safe. Aloud she said, "A beautiful baby. May her life be filled with peace and joy."

נ

Chapter 1

May 1919, Obodivka, Ukraine, Pale of Russia

A thick cloud of black smoke rose from the outskirts of Obodivka, maybe a kilometer or two south of her home near the market square. It billowed like a black curtain in the sky as it moved closer. She wanted to think it might only be a farmer burning a field, but she knew better. Would they come all the way into the village? There were still plenty of us left to murder. They would come.

The rabbi hollered at her as he ran by, "Come, Shayna. They'll be here soon." Despite Yussi's plea, she didn't follow the rabbi. She had other plans—plans that even Yussi wouldn't like. He still believed the rabbi could help.

"Go tell the others I'm coming." But she didn't leave. She went back into her small house, took a knife, and picked an opening in the hem of her long skirt. She folded the paper tickets her older brother, Ulkeh, had sent from New York, eased it through the small opening, then wrapped the coins she'd earned sewing into a handkerchief and maneuvered that into another slit in the hem.

Shayna packed bread and cheese in a canvas bag. She added the only pictures she had of Papa and Mamme and her sister Perl's family. What else could she take? She glanced at Mamme's Shabbos candlesticks in the almost empty cupboard, but she could barely squeeze herself into the trunk. No room for them.

For sure no room for the linens embroidered by her mother before her death. "For the wedding night," Mamme had said. Only that morning on his way to Kiev to deliver furniture, Yussi had stopped to check on her. Would there ever be a wedding night?

She shook her head and dipped a small cloth into the water bucket, wet her heavy shawl as well, and ran to the shed where Papa had kept the horse and wagon. The horse had sold months ago; the wagon was still parked where Papa left it the day he was murdered. Shayna hoped she hadn't grown too tall to fit into the heavy tin box hidden in the shadows. Papa made it for her only a few years before, when they feared the invading Germans.

"Shayna, listen to me." Papa looked more serious than she'd ever seen him when he placed his hands on her shoulders. "You're a beautiful young woman. Never let them see you. When soldiers come, hide. Hide."

Was it the Bolsheviks? The White Russians, or maybe the Ukrainian National Army? Maybe only drunken peasants. It didn't matter. Nowhere to run. Since the Great War, no place was safe. She read the newspapers from Kiev but couldn't keep track of the turbulent politics. To the Jews in the Pale of Settlement, it didn't matter who was in power. They were always an easy target. Even after the Bolshevik revolution, when the official Pale was ended and Jews could live anywhere in Russia, there was no escape from the riots, the rapes, the murders. Shayna heard all about the slaughter in Khardorkov from her cousin, who had managed to flee. The Cossacks had chased them with horses, shot them like rabbits.

The sky to the south glowed as she ducked into the shed. Shayna tried not to think of Yussi somewhere on the road, or her sister Perl and her husband, Avrom, on the outskirts of town. Were they running? Hiding? Did they have warning? What about the baby and little Dovid? If she survived here, what would she find there?

"Shayna, Shayna. Where are you? Run!" she heard Sima, her neighbor, shriek. She crouched down into the box and pulled the cover over her head. "We're hiding in the basement of the synagogue," she heard someone yell and then only the sound of wagons and feet rushing against the dry road.

Dry. The fields crisp in the heat. They needed rain. But for what, she wondered as she twisted and turned in the box, trying to find some comfort. She held the wet cloth near her face, the smell of smoke around her now. Maybe the wet shawl might help later, but it made her shiver in the silence around her. Nothing. She twisted her head to see something—anything—through one of the tiny air holes.

The lingering smell of their horse, long gone, drifted around her. Shayna closed her eyes and tried to erase the images imprinted on her mind. Mamme thrown to the ground by a burly Cossack. Gun shots. Blood on Papa's chest. It happened in minutes. No warning. She'd gone to the market for a minute. Maybe army deserters. No one recognized their uniforms. Drunk. They stole what they could and rode away.

Here, now hidden in the tin box in Papa's shed, she could almost smell his pipe tobacco. It was as if his spirit filled the dark box. Her hand felt warm as if he held it. She heard his soft voice: "You will survive." Shayna wiped the tears from her cheeks and clenched her body against more tears. No noise. And over and over again, she mouthed the words, we will go to America. Ulkeh is waiting. We will survive.

How long had she been in the box? An hour? Two? Three? Her stomach grumbled, but she saved the food, put her fist in her mouth, and sucked. Her legs tingled as she moved them higher in the box; her back now rested against the bottom. She could hear the goat in her pen across the yard. *Bahahahah.* Bleats loud in the silence. Another few hours, it would be dark. They would be safe.

She knew the raiders by now would be drunk on blood and on any liquor they'd found. They would have loaded the wagons with everything they could steal and probably had left Obodivka. Shayna knew they were superstitious. Afraid to be on the road at night. Afraid of devils, witches, maybe even a vampire.

A rumbling sound grew louder and louder. She felt the ground quake beneath the box. Horses. Ten? Twenty? Thirty? The sound of guns. Shayna tried to recognize voices but heard only noise and rough shouting in Ukrainian: "You can't hide. All Jews outside. Now." Laughter. The neighing of horses. The bleat of the goat. Screams and then shots. Shayna coughed into the wet cloth. Not enough air holes. Not enough air. Not enough room for air.

The door to the shed creaked open. "A wagon." She heard a man's voice. "And a saddle too." Through the air hole she saw a dark shirt, gray pants, and a saber hanging from a belt. No face. Only a voice. "In here, help me." More voices in the shed and then the sound of wagon wheels against the dirt floor and the grunts of men as they pulled it out of the shed. Shadows covered the corner where she hid, but she had no illusions about her fate should they find her. Could they hear the beat of her heart?

"Please God, who has forsaken us, save me," Shayna believed the prayer was useless. Words tossed into a godless abyss. Still, after seventeen years, the entire span of her life, the habit of prayer had become a comfort. She pressed her fingers into her ears to extinguish the sound of laughter and wailing. The crackle of fire sounded close now, and then she heard horses on the road again. The box shuddered. From the street came high-pitched howling, like wounded animals. The wet shawl now cooled her. And then voices in Yiddish came from the street. They must be gone.

Shayna's hands shook as she gathered her strength and heaved. Her legs quivered as she unfolded herself and stepped out into the smoke-filled shed. Acrid fumes snuck into her lungs as she crouched down on all fours and crawled to the door and out to the back of what had been her home. She stayed on the ground, coughing, scarcely able to catch her breath. Her goat was gone. Flames still flickered in the ashes of what remained of her tiny home. Her trousseau. Gone. Mamme's candlesticks. Maybe they stole them first. Maybe they stole the trousseau too. All the linens Mamme embroidered for her. There were no tears.

She listened as people came out from wherever they hid, screams as they found husbands and sons shot in the street. Lying where they had fallen. How many dead? Who? The wet shawl dried in the heat from the fires. She threw it off. Where the synagogue had stood, now she saw smoke. What happened to the neighbors? Where was Mirtzeh, her best friend? Where was Yussi?

Shayna turned away from the sobs and the charred remains of her home. She didn't bother to look through the rubble. Instead, her legs still shaky, she moved toward the outskirts of the shtetl, to her sister Perl.

The pogroms had scorched their villages for years, and still the Jews hung on. For what? Some shtetls mounted defense, but so many men were gone already. Shayna's mind tried to find a resting place away from the sound of screams and the smell of smoke. She heard the guns in her sleep, even when there were no guns.

Shayna leaned over, felt the tickets and the coins in the hem of her skirt, straightened her body, and clutched the canvas bag to her chest. She'd walked along this rocky road near the river as long as she had memory, with her mother, her sister, and her aunts. Back and forth they traveled for holidays, for *simchas*. Yussi, cousins, and friends sang songs together as they traveled to the neighboring villages for celebrations. So many had left for America. Palestine. Even South America. She'd waited for Perl, who didn't want to travel with little babies. She'd waited for Yussi to save enough money. Ulkeh sent tickets for the family to come to New York. The babies would be old enough to leave now. They would survive. Yussi would travel with her or maybe come later and meet them.

Perl's house still stood, and Shayna took hope, lifted her skirt, and ran to the door, which hung by one hinge. No sound from inside. Mingled with the smoke coming from other buildings was the metallic smell of blood.

She pushed the door open. Chairs overturned. Broken dishes strewn across the floor. The stench of blood filled the room. With her hand pushed against her heart, Shayna tiptoed to the second room. Her sister Perl lay across the bed, bruises on her face, her skirt raised and crumpled about her waist. Blood. Her naked legs didn't move. No sign of Avrom, her husband. Shayna froze. The sight forever sealed in her brain. She forced herself to move closer to cover her sister's nakedness and stumbled before she reached the bed. Shayna looked down and saw, with arms and legs askew, baby Sarah, her face covered with blood.

She dropped to her knees, lifted the tiny, still body to her heart, and rocked back and forth. Her vision blurred and a cold sweat covered her face. Dovid? Where was Dovid?

With baby Sarah still in her arms, she rose and studied the room. No sign of him. "Dovid. Dovid. Where are you?"

She heard a tiny whimper from behind a curtain and found him in a fetal position on the floor, the stocking doll she had made for his fourth birthday in his mouth. "Dovid." He didn't respond. He smelled. Must have dirtied himself. She crouched down and touched his back. He didn't move but his body felt warm. She saw his chest rise and fall.

And from the doorway she heard, "Perl? Perl? Can you hear me?" It wasn't Avrom's voice. Shayna turned and recognized Avrom's friend, Motke.

"Avrom?"

"Gone," he told her. "The children?"

Shayna motioned to where Dovid lay curled and then unfurled her arms and held baby Sarah toward him.

He gathered the tiny broken body to himself, and as he wrapped her in a blanket, he muttered, "May God visit the ten plagues on them. Day after day. Night after night. May their wives and children be consumed by vermin."

"May God wake up and see our suffering," Shayna murmured. She turned Dovid toward herself and tried to make contact. She looked into his large dark eyes, so like Perl's, until she sensed he recognized her, then hugged him to her heart.

From a bench outside Perl's house, she sat with Dovid curled in her lap. Shayna had cleaned him and changed his clothes. His stocking doll remained clutched in his hand. Shayna didn't know where to go, what to do. Where was Yussi? So many bodies to care for in Obodivka, it had taken a long time for the burial society, the *khevre kadishe*, to reach Perl's house. Avrom, her brother-in-law, had been one of a dozen men locked in a feed store and burned to death. She felt chilled except for where Dovid's warm body touched her own.

Maybe God woke for a moment because she heard the clop of a horse's hooves and saw Yussi pull the reins and jump down from his wagon.

Chapter 2

The smell of sweat enveloped Shayna as Yussi pulled her and Dovid against his chest. It felt clumsy, new, and unnatural. They had rarely been alone together. Only that morning he touched her hair for the first time. He'd come early, even before she had time to twist her long curly hair into a braid. Her dead father couldn't protest. No one to protect her, but she didn't need protection from Yussi. She felt his lips on her forehead and leaned into him. Forbidden before marriage. Maybe there was something in the Talmud that addressed what might be permissible after a pogrom. She wondered if there were exceptions to the rules she had followed all of her life.

She held Dovid more closely. He'd made no sounds since she'd found him curled up on the floor. No whimpers, no cries. He did not sleep.

"Perl? The baby?" His voice dropped even as the words left his mouth. "Gone?"

Shayna nodded and squinted to stop her tears. Dovid closed his eyes and buried his head against Shayna.

Yussi whispered, "Avrom?"

Shayna shook her head, leaned into Yussi and heard him murmur, "*Aleyem-hasholem*. May they rest in peace."

Maybe the funeral would be tomorrow. Maybe not. So many murdered, there were not enough of the *khevre kadishe* to prepare all the bodies. Shayna knew Jewish law required interment the next day, if it wasn't Shabbos. But no matter when the bodies came to their final rest, they would always be lying where she had seen them, bloody and broken, the sight and smells sealed in her memory forever.

Shayna seemed to shrink into herself, separate somehow from Yussi, far from the world as they rode in silence. She knew he waited for her to say something, to tell him how she had survived. Tell him how Perl died. Talk to him. But no words formed in her mind. She stared out into the road, grateful that he didn't ask questions. Smoke still thickened the air and ashes drifted down along the cobbled streets. The sun did not shine on this corner of the Ukraine.

Manya Edelman waited at the edge of the road on the outskirts of Obodivka. Even from a distance, Shayna recognized Yussi's mother, taller than most women, stout, with her white hair flying from the scarf that was supposed to keep her hair covered. She moved back and forth with quick, strong steps until she must have recognized the wagon and ran toward them. The old horse knew he was almost home—must have smelled Manya and halted. Yussi jumped from the wagon and ran to his mother. Shayna could hear her sobs as she clung to her son.

Manya raised her eyes to Shayna holding Dovid. Before she could ask the question, Shayna shook her head.

"Gone. All of them," Yussi murmured.

"May God split their heads like he split the Red Sea." She spit on the ground and looked at Yussi, "It was Petliuria, the *mamzer* and his soldiers, the hero of the Ukrainian National Army. Some hero. They must have started in the countryside, near Perl's house."

Shayna thought back to the gray pants she had seen through the tiny hole in the box where she hid. Maybe that very same man had been the one who had visited himself on Perl. When Manya climbed onto the back of the wagon, Shayna heard her mutter, "May his babies drown in their mother's milk."

The Cossacks swooped in like a storm and left as quickly. They would be back to steal and murder what remained. Shayna thought Yussi would want to observe seven days of *shiva,* the official mourning required by Jewish law. She didn't need official mourning. She only wanted to flee. Maybe Yussi would feel the danger and leave with her.

From the seat on the wagon, Shayna looked down along the road through the shtetl. She could see to the end where the shul had been. Now, boards turned black by fire stuck up into the setting sun. Only a day. Only hours since Yussi had come to her early that morning, since she had shown him her trousseau, since she had a sister. Many bodies covered by shrouds lay in front of Munshik's barber shop. She didn't know why they were there, or where they should be. Pincus, the tailor, sat on a chair next to them as the *Shoymer*, a guard to honor them. Next to the bodies huddled husbands, wives, children, wailing, their clothing cut as is required by Jewish tradition. They stared into space and pulled their hair. Their screams filled the sky. Too many to count as the wagon moved by. In front of the stables, across from the shul, Khemya, the carpenter, worked with his sons to build boxes to house the dead for eternity. Plain wooden boxes and, according to tradition, without nails or metal handles.

Only months before, Shayna had stood bowed silent over her parents, whose bodies lay wrapped in simple shrouds. Soon there wouldn't be enough people left to bury the dead, nor enough linen to wrap their remains.

They reached Yussi's home, just a few meters beyond the shul. No cow in the pen. Stolen, along with her goat. Yussi lifted Dovid from her arms and stepped down. Manya reached up to help Shayna. The feel of Manya's hand in her own was odd, like a man's hand. Calloused, hard. Her grip was strong as she lifted one arm around Shayna's shoulder and led her into the small dwelling.

Her own mother's hands had been more delicate. The hands of a seamstress. When Yussi's father died just after his bar mitzvah, Manya not only sewed the upholstery for chairs, as she had always done, but took over the job of building chairs, tables, and cabinets with Yussi's help. Some of the furniture sold in the local market, but Yussi, who soon left yeshive, delivered most to dealers in Kiev or Odessa.

Yussi unhitched the horse, fed and watered him, then left to talk to the men, to learn who was now orphaned, who wounded, who killed. Manya didn't know where Shayna's friend Mirtzeh was—didn't know if she had survived. Maybe Yussi would find her. No authorities would come to investigate. Between the Bolshevik revolution and the struggle in the Ukraine for power, everyone knew the pogroms would not stop. Whatever the excuses, Jews were the scapegoats. Ukrainians accused

Jews of being Bolsheviks, the Russians accused them of not being Bolsheviks. Always they were killers of Christ.

Should they stay and be murdered? Or maybe die of starvation? Maybe go to Moscow and find work in a factory? This was possible now under the Bolsheviks. Yussi's brother Gershon and his family planned to go to Palestine to join with others to build a safe place for the Jewish people. Now was the time for Yussi to decide.

Dovid stood where Yussi placed him near the door, his dark eyes already the eyes of an old man. A little cap on his head covered his beautiful curls. The stocking doll dangled from his hand. He wore only the traditional Russian shirt, a *kosovorotke*, which hung to his skinny mid-thighs. She should have taken more clothes for him. Shayna had never been a mother, only an aunt. She knew to clean him but then had done nothing more than hold him.

Manya squatted down before the little boy. She spoke in a soft voice and told Dovid that he was safe. Was he hungry? She talked about the bread she baked early that morning. She told Dovid it was hidden. Did he want to know where? She told him it was under a board in the floor and asked him if he could guess which one. She told him there was cheese that they could have with the bread. Did he want cheese? Her voice was low, sweet. She hardly waited for answers, but just kept talking slowly and softly.

As Shayna watched Manya talk to Dovid, she felt her own hunger and remembered she had not eaten since early in the morning. She knew she still had cheese in her canvas bag, but it was abandoned on the floor at Perl's house. She'd been hungry before, lately always hungry. Hunger and fear, her constant companions.

Dovid did not respond to Manya. He stood silent and motionless, like a life-sized wooden doll of a boy. Manya tugged on his fingers once, a gentle suggestion, the same one she might make to a nervous horse. He followed her as she led him to a board in the floor along the wall. He continued standing as she knelt, lifted the board, and drew him closer.

The muffled noise of hammering could be heard from outside, accompanied by occasional cries. In the room, only the sound of breathing as they waited for Dovid to speak, to move, to reveal something. He did move closer but did not look down as Manya pulled a loaf of bread from under the floor, along with cheese and parsnips. She dipped a cloth into the water bucket and carefully washed his hands and face.

Manya sat on a bench near the table, took his stiff body on her lap, and handed him small pieces of food. Dovid did not pick them up, but when she put a bit of cheese up to his lips, he opened, chewed, and swallowed. Manya motioned to Shayna to eat with them. She wondered if Manya had more food hidden. Never an abundance of steady food, but always something. Shayna no longer had a goat, nor a tiny garden, nor a home. She had an older brother in America—one she hardly knew—a nephew, a fiancé, some in-laws. A joke from God. No one possessed anything. Without warning, in seconds, all could disappear. God gave life and even that was temporary. Should she say thank you? Blessed be He? For what?

Her shoulders sagged when she finally sat and cut a piece of cheese for herself. Yet swallowing felt too difficult. Her jaw didn't want to open.

She heard the door close, footsteps. She sensed Yussi's return. He poured a glass of water from a pitcher on the table and lifted it to Shayna's mouth. She drank, and when he fed her cheese, she chewed. They watched Manya across the table as she slowly fed and cuddled Dovid.

Yussi leaned in and whispered to her, "You and Dovid will stay here with us until we marry."

She heard the words but couldn't give them meaning.

"I talked with the rabbi from Bershad. He said to wait until after we observe *shiva* for Perl, her family, and all the others. Then he'll marry us."

So many words, moving like shadows in the wind. She couldn't catch them. She looked at Yussi, who began speaking to his mother.

"Shayna and I will marry next week after *shiva*. She'll stay here until then."

She saw Manya nod.

They talked more, but Shayna stopped listening. Her head felt too heavy for her neck, but she couldn't lay it down yet. Things needed to be decided, but no words came.

"At least two hundred dead here, maybe more." Yussi stood in the doorway now. The sun had set, only darkness lay beyond the open door. "Men are gathering for evening prayer now. Many are making plans to leave Obodivka. Most want to leave immediately."

"Who's leaving? Where are they going?" Manya asked.

Yussi knelt next to his mother. "It's not safe here anymore. It's not a life. We'll talk, figure it out. Gershon says he'll go to Palestine with his wife's family. Maybe you'll go with them, with your grandchildren, or maybe America. Germany. Anyplace away from here. Someplace safe where we can make a living."

Manya ran her fingers along Yussi's cheek. "Your father is buried here next to your brothers who didn't live past a year. I'm not going to leave them."

"We'll talk more later, Mamme. I'm going to shul."

Shayna stopped Yussi before he reached the door and took his hand. "I want to leave right away, go to my brother Ulkeh in New York. He sent tickets. No wedding talk now. I'll take Dovid. Please. Come with me now. You and your mother. Or maybe come later. I can't stay here." She pictured baby Sarah's broken body on the floor. "I must take Dovid from here. Someplace safe. Far away."

"There will be time later to make plans." Yussi kissed her forehead and left for the evening service.

Shayna reached for Dovid, who came to her without a noise. She felt his warmth against her body. What did it matter if he didn't talk? He was alive and for now she had him.

Yussi notched the wooden boards he prepared, a meter each, for Perl's baby's coffin. Coffins for Perl and her husband, Avrom, waited just outside the cabinet shop near the barn to be loaded on the wagon and taken to where the bodies lay wrapped in traditional shrouds. Not enough wood. Not enough time to make coffins for all.

At least two hundred souls massacred in a day. *Reboyne shel-oylem,* Master of the Universe, have *rakhmones* on your people, Yussi prayed as he worked. Fill the world with your compassion. Give us the strength to carry our sorrow.

Earlier, he joined the *minyan,* the traditional quorum required for prayer, then stayed and listened to the talk of preparations for the burial and preparations to leave the shtetl.

Some argued they should flee immediately. "The Cossacks will return, finish what they started. We'll all be slaughtered."

Others argued, "They're done with us. Stole everything worth taking today."

Some were too old, too poor, too frightened to leave.

And some asked, "What about *shiva?* We must first observe the laws of mourning."

His rabbi was dead. Rabbis from the neighboring villages had started to arrive to comfort the survivors, and to guide them. God always provided comfort to Yussi, when his father died, when others died in pogroms, when grief filled his heart.

But now in the shop, in the dim light of the kerosene lamp where his father had spent his life building furniture, where Yussi had come as a child to learn from his father, where he'd picked up his father's tools at fourteen after his father death, Yussi searched for God. He listened for the quiet voice to guide him. Even through the thick walls of the old barn he could hear occasional sobs of women for their husbands, of children for their fathers. But the quiet voice of God eluded him.

"Reboyne shel-oylem," he whispered, "show me the way."

The pegs entered the notches smoothly, a permanent seal between the boards that would hold baby Sarah through eternity. If Shayna left, he would go with her. As for *shiva,* he knew according to Jewish law, human life was more important than mourning rituals.

"Enough already. Go to sleep. Yussi, listen to me. Time to sleep. Tomorrow's another day."

Yussi didn't look up from the workbench. His mother's voice familiar, not only in tone but in sentiment as well. Whether he was studying before his father's death or working, after his death, Manya wanted to determine his bedtime. He felt her hand rest on his back.

"Nu Yussi, it's time for sleep. Come in the house and I'll make you a glass of tea."

"So, Mamme, if it's time for sleep, why aren't you sleeping?" The three coffins were finished. His work was done. He could sleep now, but he knew his mind would not find peace, especially with Shayna asleep only a few meters away. He wanted to keep her close to him, to hold her and keep her safe. He wanted to run his hands along her smooth skin, unbraid her hair and taste her lips. Soon she would be his.

Manya shook her head, found the broom, and began to sweep wood shavings on the floor into a pile.

"Is Shayna asleep?"

Manya replaced the broom against the bench and leaned against it. "*Az och un vey!* Such sorrow. I hope they're sleeping. But who knows? Who knows what terrible things she sees when she closes her eyes? I can't even close my eyes or rest my head on a pillow when there are tortured spirits around us."

"The souls will be put to rest tomorrow, Mamme, God will give them peace."

"Gershon says there may be peace for the dead, but none for the living here. He's taking the children, my grandchildren, to the end of the world. What kind of peace will he find there? It's a wilderness. Are there even schools for the children?"

"*Mirtse-hashem*, God willing, they'll build a life there." Yussi shrugged his shoulders, straightened his back. "Surely, Mamme, there's no peace for any of us here. Nothing will keep Shayna from traveling to her brother in New York. I won't let her go alone. We'll marry and then we'll leave. If you don't want to go with Gershon, you'll come with me."

"Marry Shayna now? Did you talk with her?"

"We're engaged. We agreed to marry. I know she wants the same as I. There is nothing for us here. Scarcely a way to make a living, even if we survive. We'll make a new life in America."

Manya rubbed her eyes, pushing back the tears, "You think I have the strength to make a new life? I don't have that kind of *koykhes*. And who will visit your father's grave if we're gone?"

Yussi studied his mother's face while she talked. Her eyes filled with tears and the furrow in her brow looked more pronounced than ever. She was almost sixty years old. Maybe she didn't have the strength, but he couldn't leave her alone.

"Mamme, God will give you *koykhes*. He smiled on you always. You were a child, lost, maybe an orphan, wandering along the road near Odessa. No one knew who you were. And God found you, protected you, and led you to safety. God saved you and he will save us now.

"You're a good boy, a good son, but what do you know about bones that ache, and muscles that cry? I've given birth to five boys and buried three. I'm tired."

"Mamme, I need you. Shayna and I need you. Who will be Bubbeh to our children?"

"I'm losing Gershon's children," Manya said. "Who knows when I'll ever see them again?" She patted his cheek, smiled, and added, "For more grandchildren, maybe I will find strength."

They walked back to the house. Silence now in the shtetl. The chaos and destruction of the day hidden by the darkness, as if it never happened.

Yussi placed his hands on his mother's shoulders and whispered, "In the morning, you'll pack what you can, whatever will fit in the wagon."

"Tomorrow, we'll see."

As he lay in his bed, likely for the last time, he wondered where he would rest his head when he slept again. Pillows? Blankets? What should they take with them? They needed to cross borders and reach the ocean, where they could find a ship to America. He murmured the nightly prayers expressing his love of God and beseeching His blessings and finally the *Shema,* the most important of all the prayers, *Hear,* O Israel: the Lord our God, the Lord is one.

But instead of the slow descent into slumber, the memory of Shayna's body as she hugged him earlier in the day lingered. For the first time, he'd kissed her neck again and again, nuzzled against her as they stood with Dovid between them. He'd felt her breasts pushed against his chest as she clung to him.

Soon they would marry and he could perform the *mitzvah* of conjugal love, the obligation to please his wife. He tried to still the yearning in his heart, the hunger of his body. An *aveyre,* to spill his seed, a sin, he knew this. *Yetzer hore,* the evil impulse, always present but forbidden. He knew Shayna was distraught, engulfed in grief. He thought about her eyes now, a faded blue, not the deep sky blue he recognized as his beloved Shayna. This was not the time. Not the time for his selfish thoughts. But his body had a will of its own. They would marry and he could take care of her, protect her.

Chapter 3

Manya lit the kerosene lamp on the table and pinched her forearm as hard as she could to remind herself to get busy. She pulled a large trunk away from the wall and began to sort through its contents, feather pillows, old quilts, and the new one she made for Yussi's wedding. At the bottom of the trunk, she found Shmuel's suit. Her husband's one suit—his marriage and High Holiday suit. Too large for Yussi's lean frame and too small for Gershon's broad shoulders. She piled cooking pots on the table, along with a few dishes and silverware. From beneath the floorboards, she pulled out the silver candlesticks. For over thirty years she used them every Shabbos, but still thought of them as belonging to his first wife. Every Shabbos he mocked her as she lit the candles but never stopped her.

"I'm sure God will come by tonight and praise you for honoring the Sabbath—not much else for Him to do."

She ignored him and lit the candles for herself and for Yussi, who shared her love for God. Her mind raced with thoughts of the work ahead but was drawn again and again to memories that filled the room. Their heavy table, which she covered each Shabbos with an embroidered white cloth that had belonged to Shmuel's mother. She must take that for Yussi and Shayna.

Pictures. She must take pictures for Yussi and for his children. Her eyes watered as she removed a picture taken after Yussi's birth from its frame. Gershon, already a bar mitzvah boy, stood beside his father while she sat holding the newborn. She placed that picture along with a few others in Shmuel's *siddur*. Yussi would surely want his father's prayer book. She'd given Gershon family pictures after he married. She wondered if her oldest son would take them to the Holy Land, or if his children and grandchildren would never know their roots.

Again she pinched herself. No time for these thoughts. She made separate piles. One for things they would need on the journey, a pan for kashe, for eggs, for soup. Another for things she would need in America: linens, her menorah, the *mezuzah*.

Her breath caught as she walked across the threshold to Yussi's room, the room where all her sons slept and three had died, taken by typhus epidemics. If she listened carefully, she could still hear the soft cries of the children, feel her own helplessness as she watched them slowly die. She and Shmuel took turns staying with them, wiping the sweat from their bodies, soothing their rashes with camphor, the bitter smell still alive for her every time she entered the room. These things she never told Yussi, who was born after his brothers died.

Nothing for me in this room, she thought. Yussi would pack his own things. As she turned to leave, she noticed a cradle in the corner. Yussi's cradle, made by Shmuel for him. She dusted it and put it with the things she would take to America.

Yussi sniffed when he came into the house. "*Kashe*? Any eggs?

"No eggs. We'll have to find them along the way."

He peeked into his mother's room, where Shayna still slept on the floor with Dovid cuddled close against her body.

"Let her sleep. All night she cried out in her sleep. She's only quiet for a short time. Let her sleep," Manya said.

While he ate, his eyes roamed across the things piled around the room until they landed on the cradle.

"What's that?"

"Your cradle."

"My cradle? Who needs a cradle?"

Manya smiled and patted his back. "For your baby."

"You know something I don't know?" Yussi smiled.

Manya shook her head. "Don't joke. You and Shayna will need it someday. You'll be happy you have something your father made for you."

"No joke. We need a cradle like a *lokh in kop,* like I need a hole in my head."

"For your children."

Yussi glanced at the piles around the room. "Mamme, there's too much. Not enough room. Take only what you really need."

Manya pinched her arm again, this time to hold back the tears. "Some things I can't leave. Don't make me." She picked up the cradle, held it close to her chest. "Your father made it for you and you lived. It will bring *mazel* to your life."

Manya watched her son's face for a sign that he understood, that he would make room in the wagon. That he would listen to her. He usually did. She watched him as he studied each pile and noticed lines across his forehead that she'd never seen before. Only twenty years old and wrinkles on his face.

"Think Mamme. We'll have Shayna's things and Dovid's. And it looks like we'll have to take at least one person with us in our wagon, maybe Charna Levinson. She lost everyone and is too weak to stay alone."

Manya knew Yussi was right. Still holding the cradle to her breast, she went to the open door, stared up at the sky and watched the sun beginning to rise. She wanted to scream, to cry, and to beg God to let her stay in her home and make it safe for them. She wanted Shmuel back and her babies to live again. She wanted a mother, the mother she never had. But Manya didn't scream or cry. She walked back into Yussi's room and replaced the cradle where she found it. She prayed an unknown mother would find the cradle for another baby and it could bring *mazel* to someone else, enrich another baby with good luck.

"I'll be in the shop if you need me," Yussi said and kissed her cheek.

What was this life? Letting go and letting go and then letting go again. Stay strong. Thank God two sons still lived. Thank God they survived the pogroms. Thank God she could leave and find a new life. Nothing else mattered.

Shayna had never slept away from her childhood home. Even after the loss of her parents, she insisted she was old enough to remain there alone until her wedding. But she no longer had a bed, nor a home.

She lay on a blanket—by smell she knew it was a horse blanket—on the floor next to Manya's cot. Dovid curled like a kitten against her chest. She wasn't sure she'd slept. Dreams still hovered in her mind. Blood flowed like a river filled with heads and faces she couldn't recognize. She woke a few times to sobs from Dovid, who clutched the stocking doll to his chest, but he didn't wake. He'd whimper for a few minutes and then drift back into gentle breathing. She feared what he might see in his dreams.

Manya's bed was empty. Shayna heard movement beyond the curtain, feet shuffling and Manya's mumbled voice. She left Dovid asleep to join her. Manya stood next to a large trunk holding a quilt. "How many quilts will we need?"

"Where are you going?"

"Yussi says we're going to America with you. Leaving right after we bury the dead. People say the Cossacks will come back. You better pack your things. Hurry."

"Things?" Shayna looked at the large trunk, bundles and suitcases stacked around the large room off the kitchen. She noticed a basket filled with kitchen utensils topped by a tin colander, the exact kind of colander her mother always used for noodles, a colander which must now be a piece of scorched metal amidst the ashes of her home.

She sagged into a chair. "Everything burned. I have no things. Only the clothes on my back"

"Go to Perl's house and get what you need," Manya said. "There's a caravan of people traveling out of Obodivka. Yussi says we'll join them. Get clothes for Dovid too."

Manya's words were like noise in the room. She needed to talk with Yussi. She needed to focus her thoughts, but couldn't remember if she'd told him about the tickets. She felt for the hem of her skirt, felt the roll of tickets while images of Perl's bloody body, the baby's lifeless limbs, the fire, the fear besieged her.

"Find a good dress for yourself, a nice dress for the wedding."

"Wedding?" She wanted to curl herself into a tiny ball and disappear.

"Yussi says you can marry today. We can't stay here to sit *shiva*. Too dangerous." Manya added another blanket to the trunk. "A rabbi from near Odessa came last night and says because of the circumstances, it will be okay. You'll be safer as a married woman. I'm already an old lady. No one wants me, but you're a beautiful young woman. You need protection."

Shayna sat, her head in her hands. She pictured the men who murdered her parents and wondered what kind of protection a husband could provide against their guns, their knives. Against their rage.

Manya continued to talk without noticing if Shayna listened or not. "Should I bring this? What about this? No music at the wedding. I wish I had time to bake some sweets for a sweet life. But there is no butter now."

She wondered if she still dreamed. Marriage? At this time? *Meshugas.* Shayna needed to talk with Yussi.

The sweet aroma of spring flowers wafted in from the open door and drew Shayna outside. She raised her hand to shield her eyes from the morning sun. A wind must have come in the night to clear the sky of the smoke that filled it yesterday. A clear sky, while on the ground she knew embers still burned.

They never set a date for a wedding. Yet she belonged to Yussi until death or a *get*. Only a Jewish divorce could separate them. She could still feel Yussi's arms around her as they were yesterday, his warmth, his strength and she wanted to to lean into him. But there could be no marriage now. Shayna tried to imagine standing beneath the bridal canopy with Yussi, but she could only see herself running away. Maybe marrying Yussi was the best idea, but her whole body, her instinct, resisted.

She heard a hacking, thumping sound from a large oak in the front of the house. She recognized the pounding of a black woodpecker, and through the leaves she could see his little red cap busily moving back and forth as it dug for ants. Lucky little bird who knew exactly what to do every day.

She used to know what to do. She would do what her mother did. Marriage. Work. Children. Make challah on Shabbos. A life. That world gone now. Everything destroyed. Ashes. Shayna stood near the road and looked toward where her house had been. She knew nothing remained, only cinders. There was only one thing she must do now. Get Dovid to safety. To America.

"Drink tea before you go to your sister's house. You'll feel better. Some bread with jam," Manya called to her from the doorway.

Shayna stretched her arms into the air as high as she could reach to ease the stiffness from sleeping on the floor. She no longer had a bed, not even a mattress. A simple thing like a mattress, maybe not simple at all. As she stretched, her eyes began to tear. So many years had passed, yet sometimes, as if her body held the memory and not her mind, Shayna heard her mother's admonition the day she nearly drowned in the river, a warning that lingered in Shayna's thoughts.

"You're not stupid, Shaynaleh. Couldn't you see the irises were too far away? You reached too far. Don't stretch farther than you can reach."

She wondered if she'd ever be able to forget her mother's anger, and the spanking even after she told her mother the irises were for a gift for her, they weren't too far. It would have been fine if the rock hadn't slipped.

"Rocks always slip. Don't reach too far. If Perl hadn't been there to pull you out, you could have drowned in the river."

"Shayna," Manya called again." There's kashe. Tea. Come in the house." Her voice interrupted Shayna's thoughts and snapped her back to the present.

"The *khevre kadishe* are preparing the burial place for all the martyrs," Manya continued. "Yussi talked to them and made arrangements for Perl and her family, so you don't have to think about that. He arranged everything so don't worry."

Shayna put down the glass of tea and stared across the room. She hadn't thought about the burials. Forgotten. Lost in her own grief. Thank God for Yussi. Her head was full of memories. She must focus her thoughts and prepare to leave.

There was no sugar cube to put between her teeth as Shayna sipped her tea, a custom she learned from her mother. No tea ever passed her lips without the image of her mother laughing when, as a child, Shayna tried to learn to hold the sugar cube with her teeth as she sipped.

"Shayna," Manya said just before she left. "Cry as many tears as you have. But the day will come when you will be happy again. You are a lucky girl. Yussi is a *mensch*. Every girl would be happy to marry him."

Shayna clenched her fists but remained silent. Lucky. No one here is lucky. Not the dead or the living. Shayna needed to talk with Yussi about the journey and about this idea of marriage before she went to Perl's. She found him in the shop but halted in the shadow at the edge of the entrance when she saw him standing motionless near the workbench, staring at a hammer in his hand. She wondered what captured his thoughts and led him to such stillness and she realized in her despair, she'd barely thought about Yussi. She guessed that he might be saying goodbye to his father, to the spirit of his father that rested in this shop, in each tool that his father held. She started to go to him, to comfort him and try to ease his sorrow. His stillness held her back. She had nothing to give him. No words of comfort.

Silently, she moved away and began her walk, a walk past the dozens of empty coffins, waiting for the bodies, the cantor and her neighbor Sima for sure. All the sons of Phishel, the cobbler. The dairy man, Eitzik. She heard five or six yeshive boys from Odessa had been slaughtered. On and on the names went through her mind as she walked. No end to the murdered people. And so many wounded. She saw Leah, the butcher's wife, walk with a big bandage wrapped around her head, carrying her daughter whose legs were covered with bandages. And Reuven, the rabbi's son, walked with crutches. He must not have been caught in the fire at the shul, which killed dozens, including his father. And where was Mirtzeh? Her parents had been found dead, but maybe she had fled to relatives in Kiev. Shayna had no address, no way to find her best friend.

Rabbis would come from neighboring villages to sanctify the dead and recite the Mourner's *Kaddish*. *"Yis'gadal v'yis'kadash sh'mei raba"* the ancient words of the Mourner's *Kaddish* repeated in her mind. May His great name grow exalted and sanctified. She'd heard that almost two hundred were murdered here. God threw away his children. Tortured them and smashed them to bits.

Yesterday she walked this road with hope, now she thought of taking revenge on this God of theirs who allowed massacre after massacre of his people. She locked her hands into fists and held them tightly against her body as she walked. She would hold this rage close.

The call of a loon drifted across from the river, a lonely cry on a sunny day. Melancholy. Manya wanted this to be her wedding day. Impossible. Only yesterday morning she'd showed Yussi their wedding linens. Her mother's delicate embroidery burned now or maybe worse. Maybe already given as a gift from a drunken murderer to his whore. The word, even in her mind, shocked her. Shayna couldn't control her thoughts as they ran like rats from her broom. Married? With no trousseau. No parents. No sister or brothers.

Each step as she approached Perl's home felt heavier and harder to take than the one before. Ahead lay Perl's home—what had been Perl's home. Only stares met her glance, empty eyes as people passed her. Broken spirits hung in the air, everywhere. Broken bodies and broken spirits crying to God. Why doesn't the *Meshiekh* come? We need the Messiah now.

Perl would not come to the door to greet her with baby Sarah in her arms. Dovid would not come laughing into her arms. She straightened her shoulders and entered. Her canvas bag lay where she had dropped it. She placed it near the door so she would not forget it again.

First she needed to collect clothes for Dovid. She stepped around the broken pottery covering the floor. Probably best to sweep it up, she thought as she searched for what Dovid might need: two shirts, pants, warm jacket, sweater, a warm cap, stockings, and shoes. She had no idea how long they would be traveling. Shayna remembered Manya telling her to find a dress, but she knew if she did marry it would be in what she wore. The same black skirt and blue blouse still sweaty from hiding in the box. She needed to wash, to clean herself before the funeral.

Not the time for heavy thoughts. There was a job to do, a task that must be thought through. Although the dresser had been ransacked for hidden money, hidden valuables, Shayna knew where her sister hid money. She guessed the tickets Ulkeh sent her sister would be hidden there as well.

Shayna knelt by the fireplace, leaned forward and reached up to the second brick, wiggled it loose, and pulled it out. She felt around but couldn't find anything. She moved into the fireplace, sat up and felt with both hands around the hole left by the brick. Her fingertips reached paper, the envelope from Ulkeh with tickets for Perl's family. Her hands were black and left marks on the envelope. Fortunately, she hadn't smeared Ulkeh's address. Shayna knew it was an address although she couldn't read it. She knew the Hebrew alphabet, she could read the prayer book, she knew the Russian alphabet, but she did not know English. She would have to learn.

Some girls were taught to read the women's prayer book, written in Yiddish, not Hebrew. They also learned to add and subtract. Her father wanted her to know more. Although deeply religious, he had experienced the secular world as a young man in Odessa, knew the world was changing and the path for girls would change as well. After she finished at the small elementary school, her father allowed her to study lessons unavailable to girls: mathematics, history, and science. She had to sit behind a curtain during the classes he taught, but still she learned and now she would learn English as well.

She found Perl's sewing thread and needle, removed her skirt, and opened the seam on the waistband where she folded the tickets, really only small, thin sheets of paper, and some rubles into a small packet and inserted it. It would lie against her belly. She tore Ulkeh's address off the envelope and hid it and his letter in another part of the waistband. Her stitches were perfect.

She didn't know if Yussi and Manya had money for the journey. Those weren't things discussed. She knew the ships that could take them to America were far away. She'd heard about trains but had never seen one. Yussi likely knew more than she because he traveled to Kiev and Odessa to deliver furniture. But he never mentioned seeing a train.

From the street, she could still hear the wails and sobs of the families as they gathered for the procession to the cemetery. She had no time for tears now. She found a blanket on Dovid's bed. The blanket on Perl and Avrom's bed had been blood stained. Blessings to the *khevre kadishe,* who must have destroyed it. She lay Dovid's blanket on the floor and used it to wrap his clothing in a tight bundle, secured with the cord she found among Perl's sewing things.

She found a bag Perl used for the market and found Avrom's kidish cup, and his *talis* and *tfilin* to give to Dovid when he was older—something of his father. She managed to remove the *mezuzah* from the door post to take to America, where she would place it on the door frame of wherever she lived, fulfilling the commandment to post the words of God on the gates and door-posts of your house. She took family pictures out of their frames and carefully placed them in a prayer book. She found room to include Perl's Sabbath candlesticks. Maybe someday Dovid's wife would have them.

She stood in front of the dresser containing Perl's clothing. The drawers hung open, blouses, underthings, stockings, everything in disarray, ransacked by the Cossacks. Shayna tried to think about what she would need, but the familiar smell of her sister lingering in the drawers muddled her mind. She would need a few shirts, another skirt, but she couldn't focus. Her vision blurred as she reached for Perl's favorite white blouse. Shayna closed her eyes tightly to stop the tears. She must hurry. Yussi would be there soon with his wagon. On the floor she found a small wooden trunk she could use and, almost without looking, she collected clothes for herself.

In the bottom drawer she found a carefully wrapped package containing the wedding dress she had designed for Perl. Her mother thought it didn't have enough ruffles, enough shiny buttons. But Perl loved the elegance of the dress—a touch of lace instead of rows and rows that would clutter the dress. Shayna pictured Perl as she stood under the bridal canopy, simple and beautiful. After the wedding, her mother admitted she had been wrong. The dress was perfect. Shayna rewrapped it now and put it in the trunk with the other clothing. She would not wear the dress, but it was too precious to leave behind.

She looked for Dovid's favorite toy, a polka dot giraffe she herself had made for him, and discovered it under the bed where Perl died. Even in the dim light, she could not miss the blood stains covering the toy. Before her mind understood, cold sweat covered her face, and the room swayed before her. She sat on the floor, her arms curled tightly around her knees until her muscles ached and her heart cracked open. She tried to hold back the sobs—there was no time—but the cries came without her permission. She cried until her eyes burned and her throat ached, until her nose ran and body shook, until she remembered that Yussi would come soon. There was no time.

Food. They would need food. She found cheese and salami high on a shelf. Pillows, she remembered. Maybe they would need pillows. She took two.

She filled a bucket with water from the pump and carefully washed her face and hands, the cool water soothing her hot skin. As best she could she washed under her arms and beneath her skirt. She didn't know when she would find water to wash again.

Shayna carried the trunk and other bundles out of the house and closed the door on her way out. With Perl's knife, she made a cut in her blouse—*krie*, the traditional ritual symbolizing the rending of the heart—and then put the knife in her pocket. She stood outside of Perl's house and waited for Yussi.

People gathered for the journey to the cemetery. Usually the entire community accompanied the coffin, but too many had died. Too many coffins. Many had been transported earlier in the day. Along with horse-drawn carts of all sorts, people walked toward the cemetery on the outskirts of Obodivka.

"See Dovid. Here is *Tante* Shayna," Yussi said as he stopped the wagon. Dovid sat next to him, still no expression on his face.

"Has he said anything yet? Did he eat?"

"I fed him," Manya said, "and then he ate." She sat at the back of the wagon, now full of bundles and packages. With her own bundles piled in, Shayna joined Manya for the ride to the cemetery.

Coffins and bodies wrapped in shrouds as far as the eye could see were lined next to a long trench, too many dead for separate burials.

They found Avrom's brother, who stood next to three coffins. Shayna dropped to her knees next to the tiny one, Sarah's coffin. She pressed her cheek into the hard, fresh-smelling wood, and tightened her eyes against more tears. She felt Manya's strong hand rub her back, but she did not want comfort. She wanted revenge. A crazy thing for a Jewish girl to think about. A maid on the brink of marriage, a future mother. Grief was natural, God's gift to his people. Revenge belonged to the devil.

On the other side of the trench she saw two men dressed in city suits, one with paper and pencil and the other standing next to a camera. Strangers. Maybe from a newspaper. She'd seen articles in the Russian paper, even with pictures of pogroms all over the Pale. Dead Jews. Jews suffering, without end. Ulkeh wrote that in America Jews were free, safe. Could there be such a place?

Chapter 4

Men Shayna did not recognize carried the coffins to the long trench. First they took the baby's coffin, then her sister Perl and Perl's husband's. Other men standing in the pit reached up to lower the wooden boxes. Soon these coffins became indistinguishable from all the others.

Yussi stood with the rabbis who had come from the neighboring villages along with other learned men. They formed a group of leaders who would guide the prayers. Shayna watched him sway back and forth as he prayed silently, his *talis* stirring in the spring breeze. For as long as she could remember she'd wanted to marry him. She tried to shut out the sobs, the smell of fresh dirt and death. But against her will, her eyes returned to the scores of rough boxes filling the ditch. A shiver crossed her body. This was not the time to marry.

Dovid's little hand was sweaty in her own. She lifted him to her chest and held him tightly. He hadn't cried or spoken. What could anyone say? She had no words.

"Don't take him to the funeral," Manya said. He's only four. There's enough horror in his mind already. Living though a pogrom, seeing his family murdered is enough for a lifetime."

Maybe Manya was right. Shayna didn't know what memories he might have as the years passed, but she believed for now he needed to stay close to her. From the beginning, a special bond existed with her sister's son. Sometimes he laughed even before she tickled him, a ritual for them every time she visited. She pictured his eyes when he used to greet her at the door. If eyes could giggle, his did. Now they were empty.

Shayna turned from the coffin-lined ditch and walked toward the main section of the cemetery. It would take a long time to lower all the bodies and begin the prayers. There was time to take Dovid to where her parents lay buried near a large cluster of oak trees.

"Can you find two small stones you like?" she said as she lowered him to the ground. "Remember Bubbeh and Zeyde?"

Dovid looked at her, no recognition in his eyes, but he did examine the ground and began collecting stones, studying them and rejecting each one until he raised two tiny round stones, one in each hand.

"Perfect," she said as they approached her parents' tombstones. She pulled the weeds that now covered their names, Sima and Velvel Rifkin, etched clearly for all time or at least as long as this cemetery remained intact. But sometimes during pogroms in the Ukraine, Jewish cemeteries were desecrated. It certainly happened when soldiers stole the headstones for their trenches during the Great War. There was no proverb or prayer etched on their headstones. No etcher skilled enough remained in the shtetl for elegant carvings, nor was there money for extras. Only their names and the year of their death, 1918, were inscribed. Neither she nor Perl knew the years of their birth.

Shayna's hand trembled as she placed her stones, one at each marker, next to the stones already there. Stones placed when she'd visited her parents' graves with Perl and her husband, only weeks ago. Dovid added his stones.

"Your Bubbeh and Zeyde are resting here. We leave these stones to let them know they will be remembered forever." She settled on the grass, took Dovid onto her lap, and wrapped her arms around him, to help manage her own trembling. He asked no questions. Made no comments. But she knew he could hear. One day he might remember the stories she could tell him about his grandparents. But Dovid wiggled out of her arms and went back to looking at rocks on the ground.

She watched him find stones, study them, reject most, but continue to find some worthy of placement along the edge of each headstone. She heard him whisper as his finger touched each stone, "*Eyns, tsvey, dray, fir, finef.*"

Shayna remembered the day her father taught Dovid to count the fingers on his hands. Dovid had been sitting on his grandfather's lap, giggling, his little hands pulling at his zeyde's beard. Her father took

Dovid's tiny hand and diverted him with numbers. So typical of her father. The teacher. Always the teacher. *Eyns, tsvey, dray, fir, finef.*

From across the way, Shayna heard Manya moan as she bent over what must be her husband's grave. All the way to the cemetery Manya sighed and muttered to herself. The sounds of the horses' hooves, the wooden wheels grating along the rough road, and the noises from many wagons made it difficult for Shayna to hear until Manya turned directly toward her.

"*Es tut mir vey.* It hurts me. Everywhere I turn, I hurt."

"What's the matter? Are you sick?"

Manya nodded. "Yah. I'm sick." She pounded her chest. "In the heart. My son Gershon follows a dream to a wilderness, a wasteland. He takes my *eyniklekh* to the end of the world, fleeing to Palestine with my precious grandchildren. They'll die there in the desert. If I go with him, I lose Yussi, my baby. No matter where we go, there are only strangers. If I stay here, I'll be murdered or starve to death. If I leave, I abandon my husband, may he rest in peace, and my babies who lie buried by his side. Who will visit their graves?"

Shayna could think of nothing to say. She had taken Manya's gnarled hand in her own and held it all the way to the cemetery.

"You didn't know Shmuel, Yussi's father. He would be happy to have you as a daughter-in-law. He would love you. Yussi came late in our lives. A surprise, if you know what I mean."

Shayna blushed. She guessed what that meant.

"We lost three babies. Not counting the one I miscarried. My oldest son, Gershon, *borukh-hashem*, lived. But three little boys died before they reached one year. One after another. Then Yussi came. A gift from God. A blessing. I said his life should be dedicated to Torah, to be a scholar, to serve God. Maybe become a rabbi."

"But my husband had different ideas. 'The world is changing,' he said. 'Let him study with the rabbis, but he must also learn to work with his hands.' So Yussi helped his father. He learned to build the chairs and tables that fed us. Choices. Our son needed choices. He wanted Yussi to study with your father, modern things: mathematics, history, and geography. 'A man must be ready to change to survive,' he used to say. My husband only went to shul to please me. I knew that, but in his heart he was a free thinker. He used to say, 'Live in this world not in the next.'

Shayna remembered Yussi from her father's classes. Three evenings a week after her father returned from teaching Torah, students came to him to study the subjects *goyim* studied. Her parents agreed to let her hide behind a curtain when he taught. Although Shayna absorbed her mother's lessons—cooking, cleaning, and working at the market selling the skirts and blouses her mother made, even becoming an apprentice seamstress to her mother—she was always hungry to learn more. As she sat behind the curtain three times each week, more and more often her eyes drifted from her father to the boy who was always ready with the right answers.

She would sit on a hard chair with a tablet on her lap, a small opening in the curtain so she could see the board where her father wrote the numbers and the words and she could copy, but the boys couldn't see her. Never, not if she ever wanted to find a husband. Who would marry such a girl? One who wanted to study, to read and write, beyond what was needed for the marketplace? That's when she first loved Yussi. For although the other girls admired his good looks and his intelligence, she felt behind his eyes, there was a *mensch*, a true heart.

One day, after many weeks, a few of her father's students spied her behind the curtain and laughed. The boys berated her. "Girls can't learn—you have the wrong kind of brain. Live to comfort your husband, your children."

But Yussi never teased her, and he stopped the others. First he asked them to stop, and when Moshe Pinkler didn't, Yussi hit him straight on the nose. It bled. Maybe Yussi was twelve and she was nine. But she never forgot the look on his face after he hit Moshe. He turned to her and smiled.

After his father died, Yussi came to study with her father less and less. She saw him only from afar, at shul or sometimes he waved to her in the market. By the time she was fifteen, Shayna looked for opportunities to spend a minute with him, at least to offer a greeting without arousing the gossips.

Then one day, when she reached sixteen, her mother began to speak about a *shadkhn*.

"Velvel." Shayna remembered the day her mother interrupted her father's study. "Velvel, it's time for you to talk with the *shadkhn*. Ask the marriage broker to find Shayna a *mensch*, someone with *seykhl*, smart. And one who can make a living. Time for her to marry. Before she gets stale on the shelf."

"Nu, Shaynaleh." Her father removed his glasses and looked up from his book. "A good idea?"

Shayna shook her head and looked away from her father.

"Nu Shaynaleh, and why not?"

From the moment her Mamme said *shadkhn* Shayna realized how much she wanted Yussi, but hesitated to say that out loud. Instead she said, "I want to choose. I'll spend the rest of my life with this man. I need to choose."

"So we'll wait," her father said.

Mamme stood with her hands on her hips, her chest jutting forward. "Velvel, you spoil her."

"Her life. She has plenty of *seykhl*. A smart girl like Shayna will not end up on the shelf. She'll make a good choice," her father said and winked at her just as her mother turned her back and left the room.

She never got to the shelf to grow stale because only a few months later Yussi asked her father for Shayna's hand in marriage and she agreed immediately.

The whole community gathered to celebrate their engagement. No one could know that in the midst of such a wonderful *simcha*, both of her parents would be murdered within the month by drunken deserters from the Ukrainian army. She tried to conjure up pictures of their celebration, of tables full of delicacies, the *tagelakh* and the tall sponge cakes, but the pictures that came were gray, without joy.

Everyone considered Shayna blessed, lucky to have such a *mensch* as a groom. Even though he did not come from a family with *yikhes*, he achieved his own high status in the community for the quality of his learning. Not only could he recite Torah and Talmud, he could read and write in Yiddish, Russian, and Ukrainian, not to mention the sacred Hebrew language. But he was also a carpenter, able to make his living in the world. And he was tall and strong like his father. She blushed when the other girls joked about Yussi. "*Shtark*, strong, like a bull." They laughed and said he would make her pregnant from looking at her.

That was then and this was now.

Shayna and Dovid walked back to the mass burial site with Manya, and as they approached they heard a melancholy voice, a cantor's voice she did not recognize. "*El malay rakhamim,* God full of mercy, who lives on high." Hundreds of people surrounded the ditch.

One by one, the survivors filled a shovel to throw dirt over the wooden boxes, a painful custom. Only holding Dovid's hand and smiling at him from time to time kept her from collapsing on the ground. When it was her turn, she filled the shovel with dirt and walked to the edge of the trench. Dovid followed her to the edge, his head directed down into the pit. She quickly emptied the shovel and took his hand again. She knew he needed to be connected, to belong to something living, something other than wooden boxes and dirt where his mother now lay buried. They both needed connection, to belong to something living.

Even though she knew the burial gave peace to the dead, gave them the opportunity for resurrection, she felt they all participated in covering up a crime. The trench stretched as far as she could see. Every Jew left alive in the region stood there to honor the dead. There was no thunder. No lightning. The heavens did not weep.

Beyond the sound of the birds in the trees, the only sound she could hear was the steady clop of dirt onto the coffins. Would there be headstones? Would any Jews be left here to place a small stone of remembrance? A massacre like this could not go unnoticed, but no one would be punished. The pictures would be in a newspaper in Moscow, in Kiev, used to wrap fish in the market. If it wasn't for Dovid, she knew she might jump down among the coffins and beg them to cover her with dirt.

"Shayna, Shaynaleh," Could that be the voice of a living person or was it her sister calling to her from the grave? "Shayna. Look at me." She felt Dovid being lifted away from her. A calloused hand took her own and led her back to the wagon. She recognized Manya's skirt in front of her, the embroidery along the hem was Shayna's own mother's work. A gift from one mother to the other in honor of the engagement.

Yussi now waited near the wagon with a rabbi she recognized from a neighboring shtetl. All in black, the rabbi stood, his eyes shaded by his hat. And then she realized what was expected from her.

Shayna's head began to shake, back and forth, like a pendulum. No. Not today, not now. Yussi took her hand and led her away from the wagon. "Better we should marry now before we leave. It's the only choice if we travel together."

"Only choice? God always gives choices." She needed to make him understand. "My sister and her family are barely in the ground. Don't you see? Should we dance on their graves?"

Manya came up behind them and whispered near Shayna's ear, "Take happiness where you find it. Tomorrow is a new day."

A new day, as if she could turn the page and unsee everything she'd seen, unfeel what she felt. She searched her mind for words to say to Manya, but the only words that came to her were angry, vicious. Not words she could say.

Yussi motioned his mother away and put his arm around Shayna's shoulders. "How I feel has not changed, Shaynaleh. Eventually we'll marry. So why not now, before we begin the journey."

Shayna looked at his face, a face she'd watched since childhood. He seemed a stranger to her now. A man with deep-set dark eyes and thick eyebrows, a sharp nose, full lips obscured by a mustache and black beard. Yussi. The Yussi she loved as a child, the man who would be the father of her children. But now no pulse in her body connected to him.

The days after her parents were murdered, it seemed as if her very *neshome* withered, her very soul dying like flowers after an early frost. But then she had her sister Perl. Shared memories. Even laughter watching baby Sarah's first steps. Hope. The days that had blurred into nothingness had slowly begun to take shape again. Now, like the nothingness of creation, only emptiness swirled within her. There was no sign of God hovering. Only a hollow void. Maybe someday Dovid would giggle again.

Maybe she would feel Yussi's devotion. Maybe someday. But no marriage today.

Her eyes pleaded with Yussi to understand, and when Shayna said, "I must take Dovid to safety. Come to America with us. In time we will marry, but not now," Yussi simply nodded.

When Manya again began to insist, Yussi stopped her.

"*Mamme, zol zayn shah,* be quiet now," he said. "Shayna will tell me when she is ready."

Chapter 5

Shayna listened to the arguments around her. Everyone had an opinion—many people more than one. All agreed the safest place to cross the border would be Brody. Although Odessa was closer, the Russian customs agents might stop all the men from emigrating. On the spot, they might be conscripted into the Bolshevik army. Odessa was out of the question.

Menakhim Levin, the blacksmith, argued that agents from Jewish organizations waited in Brody to help refugees. Sara Rokhel, the midwife, said the Russians had driven them out early in the Great War. Brody was destroyed, she claimed. Back and forth they argued. Everyone agreed it was best to stay together as much as possible. If God watched over them, if they were attacked, Cossacks and bandits might only steal their meager goods and let them live. But Shayna believed God was busy elsewhere, too far away to hear their prayers.

A half-dozen men arrived on horses, some of the organized Jewish militia. Small groups throughout the Pale of Russia had trained to use guns and sabers and were scattered throughout the region to help fellow victims of pogroms. Far too few to make any difference against the Ukrainian National Army or renegades of all sorts, yet their presence instilled confidence among the refugees.

Shayna recognized Yankel, who stood off to the side, beyond the main group. She hadn't seen him for several years, an outcast now without *peyes*, clean shaven, dressed like a Ukrainian peasant. She remembered him from her childhood, a young boy who came to her father for lessons. Gossip surrounded him. She knew he had been born to a Jewish mother and father—maybe the mother was a loose woman, or maybe she ran off and lived with a *goyishe* farmer. Shayna had no idea what happened to the father or anything about Yankel's current life, only vague memories of the past. A saber hung from his waist and he held a rifle. Friend or enemy?

With a horse and wagon, the road to Brody would take at least two weeks, maybe three or four depending on the roads. If the rains came, mud would slow them. The carts and wagons were old, the people worn and frayed. Bones were visible on the few horses and mules. Some people brought carrots and parsnips; others had bread or herring. Some had cheese and smoked fish. But they would all need to find more along the way. They'd need to find safe markets where a few kopecks could add to their stores.

They would camp on the outskirts of Obodivka, on the edge of the forest, a group of almost a hundred souls, some going to America, some to relatives in Western Europe, even some to Palestine. All prayed they could cross the border at Brody—prayed the trains to the west and the south still operated, prayed someone would be there to help them buy the tickets they would need.

Yussi's ancient wagon, built to deliver furniture, had four large creaky wheels. The horse, old and tired, replaced another horse stolen in an earlier pogrom. But he pulled the wagon. Yussi would drive with Dovid seated next to him while Shayna walked alongside. Yussi complained about all the things on the wagon—"Too heavy"—but his mother insisted she'd sacrificed enough already.

Manya pulled out a large pot, filled it with water, and carried it to the fire being built by other women. Someone had parsnips. Someone added a few potatoes. Manya added a cabbage. Dovid sat next to a tree near the fire. Shayna wrapped her shawl around him. Although the days turned warm, the spring nights carried a chill. Dovid remained silent. She helped Manya gather more wood until Yussi returned from the evening prayers. So far there were plenty of men for a *minyan,* but what would he do when their numbers dwindled as they gradually began their separate journeys?

"Walk with me?" Yussi reached his hand toward Shayna. There were many women already preparing food. She wasn't needed, he said.

The light from small fires reflected on the faces of people she'd known her entire life. Menakhim. Sara Rokhel. Yenta and her baby and so many more fleeing from the Ukraine and Russia. Shayna wasn't sure who else was going to America. She knew many had relatives there. Some hoped to reach Palestine. She heard Pincus, the tailor, had relatives in South America. All now refugees. Homeless.

Shayna walked hand in hand with Yussi along the edge of the forest beside a grove of birch trees, their white bark still visible in the dusk. Shayna inhaled the earthy smell, wanting to hold the familiar scent in her memory, a smell of her homeland.

Yussi drew Shayna to him, wrapped his arms around her and held her close. She relaxed into his warmth for a few moments before her body stiffened and she pulled away. Her heart felt heavy. She'd heard people use that expression, yet she hadn't realized that sadness had an actual weight, weight that she now carried.

"Shaynaleh, why do you turn from me?"

Shayna shrugged, walked to a nearby tree, and removed a peeling strip of birch bark. "Look, Yussi. Small enough to take with me, to keep with me, something real from home."

"Take what you want. But stop ignoring me. Even before the pogrom, since your parents died…"

Shayna pointed at her chest. "My parents died? She turned her hand and pointed at Yussi. "Your father died. He died in his bed surrounded by his wife and children. My parents were murdered. Murdered. They were murdered." She threw the birch bark on the ground. "I want nothing of this place."

"Shaynaleh, look back at all the people gathered around the fire. Everyone has suffered. Everyone there still suffers. But we go on. To spite the anti-Semites, if nothing else."

Shayna looked toward the camp, waved her hand into the air. She didn't want to hear. She took a deep breath and inhaled the rich loam, the smell of the forest. She thought of all the things that would only exist in her memory, like the irises along the riverbank, the bustle of the market, the sound of her goat. And her family. Never again would she see

Mamme carry a freshly baked challah to the Shabbos table or Papa on the floor playing with his grandchildren. And Perl. Perl. Gone forever.

The sound of accordion music drifted across the field. Getzel must have brought his instrument. Shayna wondered what he'd left behind in order to carry the accordion.

As they walked back toward the encampment, Yussi began to hum along with the accordion's tune and sang when the words became clear: *"Libe ken brenen un nit oyfhern"*—love can burn and never end.

Shayna reached for Yussi's hand and joined him on the next line of the verse, "A heart can yearn, cry without tears. Tumbala, Tumbala, Tumbalalaika."

"Dovid! Dovid!" Shayna recognized Manya's voice. She'd forgotten all about him! Many other voices calling Dovid's name echoed through the forest. She saw Yankel, Menakhim Levin, his wife, Yosseleh from the fruit stand, and many others following Manya as she ran. Shayna pulled Manya to a stop. "What happened? Where's Dovid?"

"I don't know. I watched the soup. He sat by a tree, like a statue. One minute he was there and the next, he was gone. I don't know how long. May God strike me down if something happened to him."

Trees as old as time grew thick and tall in the forest, home to mushrooms growing in the dark, and criminals hiding. A scary place which often appeared in dreams and nightmares. Some people said bears lumbered between the giant spruce and oak and maybe even tigers. Dovid had disappeared. Rumors flew around the shtetl that babies could be stolen, given to a childless couple. Dovid, a poor orphan, lost forever.

"Dovid! Dovid!" Shayna rushed deeper into the woods, close to sunset now, barely any light as she moved carefully around the heavy undergrowth, Yussi beside her.

"Dovid!"

Adding to the sound of voices, leaves crunching, and branches breaking came the sound of wings flapping as the birds rose from trees, agitated by the commotion. She repeated every prayer she'd ever learned, a plea to a God she knew no longer listened. Yet she prayed as she studied the ground, moved downed branches out of her way. Deep in shadows to her right, she knew Yussi walked and Manya next to him.

What a fool she'd been. God blessed her with the life of Dovid—out of the bloody massacre, a sweet soul survived, and in her selfishness, she'd forgotten, neglected his precious life. She had barely thought about him. Let Manya take care of him or anyone else who was willing to help.

"Dovid, Dovid!"

No light filtered down between the leaves. They needed a lantern, but Shayna wouldn't go back. Their eyes tried to pierce the darkness. Manya returned to the wagon for a lantern.

A moan came from somewhere, impossible to tell directions. They stopped talking. Everyone stopped moving to listen to an almost silent moan—the sound of a wounded animal. Louder and louder it grew, as if the trees cried out their pain. A howl filled the forest.

"Dovid? Dovid, is that you?"

The howl, now a scream, "Mamme! Mamme!" After his long silence, cries for his mother rent the air around them. Huddled down, his head nearly buried in leaves, his small body shook.

Shayna knelt by his side, her knees landing on sharp branches. She wanted to pull his body to her but instead touched his back. At her touch he curled up and rolled away.

"Dovidel, it's me, *Tante* Shayna." Again Shayna reached out and touched his back, a soft caress down the length of his spine. "Dovidel, it's me, *Tante* Shayna." Inch by inch she drew closer to his body, coiled as small as he could. She wound her own body around his without touching except to continue moving her hand along his spine. His cries now whimpers interspersed with hiccups.

"Just pick him up, Shayna. Take him back to the wagon," Manya whispered. "Everyone's gone back. I have a lantern. You can't stay here. Pick him up."

Shayna didn't answer, only continued her tender touch on his back. *Barukh Hashem*, she thought, God has not forsaken us. God has given me a lesson about my selfishness. Dovid rolled back toward her. She still couldn't see his face, but she felt him snuggle into her body.

"Pick him up and we'll take him back," Manya said.

Again, Shayna ignored her. As Dovid huddled closer, she adjusted her body around his so she could see his face. "*Tatele*, it's okay. *Tante* Shayna is here. I'll keep you safe." Shayna waited until he focused on her. His tear-stained face was visible in the dim light from the lantern. She concentrated on his large dark eyes until she sensed he recognized her. "Sh *tatele*, you're safe. I'm here."

When Dovid's breathing calmed, with Yussi's help, Shayna raised herself to her knees. She carried Dovid's body tightly to her own, while Yussi lit the way through the forest. Manya followed.

Manya had prepared blankets under the wagon where they would sleep. Just before Shayna crawled under, Yussi stopped her, raised her face to his own, and kissed her on the lips.

Black smoke drifted around Shayna. She smelled it around her but couldn't see the fire. Any moment it would engulf her body as she held Dovid. She twisted to escape the bindings that held them in place. But she couldn't move. A sharp object hurt her back, pushed against her shoulder blade. She blinked and opened her eyes to the light of dawn. Only a dream. This time.

Dovid slept in her arms. He hadn't moved at all. There was actual smoke, but it came from the morning fire. The breeze must have carried the smell toward them under the wagon. Manya no longer lay next to her. She must have awakened and begun to prepare tea and kashe.

Yussi came back from *davening* the morning prayers with the other men. They had laid *tfilin* outside and prayed their observance of all the laws and precepts of the Torah would lead to a reward, here or in the world to come. Amidst the prayers always was the acknowledgment of divine retribution should the people disobey. Maybe the pogroms were His retribution. But as hard as Shayna thought, she couldn't imagine what human sin would cause God to inflict such devastation. Her thoughts did not bring her comfort.

They wanted to start in the cool of the morning. Shayna had never been beyond Obodivka in her life. She'd dreamed of travel to faraway places, but here was no joy or excitement in this journey, only a hunger for peace. A heavy sorrow hung over the caravan. As the few wagons began to move toward Brody, those on foot followed.

At the back of Yussi's wagon sat old Charna Levinson, who could scarcely walk. They knew she had relatives near Brody. She'd lived with her son, who had been murdered along with his young wife. No one was left in the shtetl to care for her. They all had heard about Ellis Island, the Island of Tears, which must be crossed to reach America. They knew no one crippled was allowed, no one sick could find a home there. And in the wagon ahead, Yenta Lowen held her one-week-old baby, now fatherless. Both mother and child were weak and needed to ride.

The sun rose. The few horses that pulled the wagons raised dust along the dry road, covering the black mourning clothes in a fine powder.

Chapter 6

June 1919 - On the road To Brody

Manya rolled to her side under the wagon, careful not to wake Shayna and Dovid. Above the treetops near the clearing where they camped, a light pink edge rose into the blackness beyond. She glanced back at Shayna and the boy, their faces barely illuminated. Shayna's brow creased as if worries penetrated her sleep. Even during the day as she walked alongside the wagon, Shayna's occasional smiles never reached her eyes.

Each muscle in Manya's body ached as she rose to her knees and then stood. The creaking of her bones was so loud she feared it might wake everyone around her. After five long days of walking and five nights asleep on the hard ground, she wondered how long before her body refused to work.

Old Charna Levinson still slept on the spot Yussi had cleared for her among the bundles in the back of the wagon. Her gray, wizened face showed little emotion when Manya helped her each day to relieve herself. No expression even when Manya fed her as if she were an infant. Everyone believed she would die before they reached Brody.

With her shawl tight around her shoulders to ease the morning chill, Manya leaned against the wagon, gathering strength for the day. Dew covered the ground, carrying the scent of the evergreens surrounding them. Muted voices were audible as the refugees began to awaken. On the opposite side of the camp, men began to move: the single men, like Yussi, as well as the men who left their families to make their fortune in America. Soon many would form a *minyan* for morning prayers. Yankel kept himself separate. She wasn't sure where he slept, but she knew he carried his own food and water. No one knew why he traveled with them.

Yussi would come after prayers for something to eat; they still had herring and bread. She couldn't even boil water. The defense guard who still traveled with them insisted it was too dangerous to light a fire. Deserters from the Ukrainian army still roamed the area.

She walked to the trees behind their wagon, her knees aching as she crouched. Later in the day the sun might ease her arthritis. Manya stood for a while in the stillness of the trees, breathing the silence into her body. Thank you God for these days of peace.

When she returned, she saw Yussi sifting through their meager food supplies. He lifted out the bread and handed it to Shayna, who sat on the ground, her back against the wheel, her braids loose and disheveled. He reached for a knife to cut the remaining herring and lowered it to the plate Shayna held on her lap. It appeared as if her son was serving Shayna, who let him wait on her like he was her servant. Shayna's mother was dead. She had no one to teach her how to be a wife. How to be a mother. She liked to play with Dovid but often left his food to Manya's care. Even after she almost lost him. Maybe grief was making this young woman careless about her duties, but Manya guessed she was too independent. Shayna had studied sometimes with the boys. Too much freedom was not good for a girl. They should marry as soon as possible, she thought, then Yussi could control her better.

Only the other morning when the men stood around after their prayers and discussed the problem of crossing the border, Shayna embarrassed Yussi in front of all the men—all the ones who gathered every morning to *daven*. Menakhim Levin, a blacksmith, traveled the road to Brody many times and said it would take two weeks to reach the border, which was now controlled by Poland. His boy, not old enough for a *bar mitzvah*, said there would be no guards at the border. Munshik, the barber and his younger brother with the pimples, contradicted the boy. Pincus, the tailor, always wearing a jacket that didn't fit around his belly, said it would take three weeks and not two to reach the border. He could tell by the clouds that rain was coming and it would make mud. Travel would be more difficult. Yashe Yaroslavsky insisted he knew a back road that avoided the border.

Chaim Bernstein, the socialist, raised his booming voice above the conversation. "If we all contribute, we can hire a guide to smuggle us across the border."

"How much money will we need?" Shayna, without an invitation, had pushed herself among them and opened her mouth as if they waited to hear from her. She stood straight and tall, her long hair uncovered, not terrible since she wasn't yet married, but Manya was afraid people would say she was too proud, showing off her beautiful hair.

Chaim looked down at her as if she were a bug, then looked away as did all the other men.

Shayna looked at Yussi for an answer, but he too looked away.

Manya pulled the girl back toward their wagon and tried to be kind. "It's not seemly for you to mix into the affairs of men. You're just a girl, not even married." The rest of the women busied themselves repacking the blankets and food supplies. They would have their say privately to their husbands, not shame their men.

"You must manage from behind, not from the front. That's the only way men listen." The girl needed a mother to help her know the right way to behave. Shayna would be the mother of her grandchildren. Manya could tell Shayna wanted to argue with her. The girl's face reddened and she looked down, as if she were ashamed, but Manya was no fool. She prayed that God would teach Shayna to be humble.

She reminded herself to get busy. Sara Rokhel, the midwife, swore a village lay a few hours ahead where they could buy food. She wanted to find milk for Dovid and maybe some farmer's cheese for Yussi. She knew she could find noodles cheap and maybe some eggs. No meat. No way to get kosher meat. As they walked she often heard stomachs grumbling, an orchestra of terrible musicians.

On the tenth morning, Shayna lay under the wagon, Dovid snuggled close to her. He usually started every morning walking next to her, still carrying his stocking doll, but his short legs never lasted very long. He'd reach up for her to carry him, and cried when she could no longer hold him. Eventually he settled down next to Yussi as they traveled along the side roads, where they felt safer from random attacks. The armed guards traveled back and forth along the line of refugees.

The dust from the road had gathered in Shayna's hair and itched. She should brush and rebraid it, but it was still unpleasant to touch. Water in the barrel was precious, and she could only wash her face and her hands. Two times they had come to rivers, their currents swift after spring rains. Women who traveled on wagons filled their water barrels. Then some of the women stripped down and walked hip deep into the water. Her mother had been modest, always covered, only her neck bare— and even that was often covered with a shawl. But Shayna wondered what her mother would do after days without washing. These women did not hesitate to show their swollen legs with varicose veins and drooping breasts.

Manya stood in the water along with Menakhim Levin's wife and Sara Rokhel. Chana was there too. Shayna tried to reconcile the image of the Chana she remembered from the synagogue, the woman who read the prayers aloud for the women who couldn't read, with the woman who splashed water now at Manya, long skinny wrinkled arms reaching deep into the water and aiming at Manya's smiling face.

"Come in Shayna," Manya yelled to her. "It's a *mekhaye*, makes life worth living."

Shayna shook her head. She felt her face redden. Some day she would have to dip herself into water, to purify herself in the ritual bath, the *mikve,* just before her marriage and do it in front of another woman, or maybe even show her body to her husband, but it wasn't something she could do now.

"Come, I'll help you wash your hair. It'll feel good." Manya mimicked scrubbing her scalp.

Shayna shook her head again, filled another container with water and walked back to the wagon. She did want to wash her hair, to make herself clean. She remembered the sweet smell of her mother leaning over her to dip Shayna's hair in the lukewarm water left in the tub, the strength of her fingers rubbing soap into her scalp, massaging it, and then her mother's strong arms holding Shayna's head while she rinsed her long hair. But she barely knew Manya. She could not make herself naked with the others.

They had stopped in a few market towns and cautiously made small purchases. Manya found milk for Dovid, more cheese and fresh bread. The little boy loved noodles, especially with cheese, so whenever they could build a fire, Manya boiled noodles and added a bit of cheese.

One day they came upon a freshly harvested field of onions, and Menakhim Levin sent his children to skirt the edges and pick a few of the overlooked ones. Shayna ate one as if it was an apple, moist and fresh. But there was never enough. She tried not to think about the constant ache in her belly. She kept her list of complaints to herself. Everyone suffered.

Smoke from the morning fire drifted under the wagon. The guards must have thought it safe enough for a fire. Shayna stretched her arms carefully, trying not to wake Dovid. As she began to slide out from under the wagon, her sleeve caught on a metal strap hanging loose. She reached her finger to feel and pulled back quickly from the sharp edges of wood. Something had broken.

She rolled out and told Manya, who crawled under to look. "*Oy vey. Tsores.* We don't need this trouble," Manya said. "Maybe it's not too bad. Maybe it will hold until Brody."

They waited for Yussi to finish morning prayers. He took off his jacket, crawled under, examined the crack, and lingered there while other men joined him to study it. Menakhim, the blacksmith, crawled under, then Munshik's son, who claimed he was an expert, also crawled under. Yankel stood apart, leaning against a tree not far away while everyone else gathered around their wagon.

Shayna grew restless as they all talked. She already knew they weren't interested in her opinions. She looked down the dusty road, the sun rising now. They expected another hot day. Periwinkles and bachelor buttons bloomed through the meadow where they camped. Dovid watched as Menakhim's children searched the grass for frogs. Each day he stood closer to the other children, but he had not, as yet, played or laughed with them. Shayna wanted to pick some of the lovely wildflowers, especially the deep pink hollyhocks, but there was no vase, no water to waste on keeping flowers alive.

"Leave the wagon. Take only what you need, we'll take what we can on our wagon. We'll take Charna. We'll make room," Munshik said.

"You won't be able to fix it here. You'll need tools, wood," piped in Mendle, the butcher.

"It didn't look so bad to me. It won't break so fast. Maybe it's been that way for a long time. Just keep going until it really breaks."

"It will take too much time. We can't stop here in the middle of the road. It's too dangerous," someone said from back in the crowd. More opinions pro and con.

Yussi maneuvered out from under the wagon. "I don't want to take chances. I should be able to fix it. I have tools here." He motioned to his mother and Shayna to remove everything from the wagon bed. Munshik carried Charna Levin to his wagon. He carried her as if she were a pillow and just as heavy.

"You should have a guard with you. One of the men with a horse and a gun should stay with them," Sara Rokhel suggested to the crowd and then everyone began talking at once.

Shayna tried to make out what people said. Amidst the noise she heard agreement and disagreements. Chaim Bernstein, the socialist, tried to get order and said they were all in this together. Everyone should stay and wait. Back and forth it went until Yankel moved away from the tree, holding a rifle and with a saber hanging from his waist. Shayna noticed everyone seemed to take a few steps back.

"I'll guard them while he fixes the wagon." His deep voice silenced the others. Although the words he spoke were in Yiddish, they sounded stiff, as if his tongue was unfamiliar with the sounds.

No one knew what to say. No one knew why he traveled with them. For a moment all she heard were quiet mutters. Shayna remembered the gossip about him, his *proste* family, vulgar and disrespected. But her father had accepted him as a student. She didn't know who else knew something about him. She wanted to ask him why he traveled with them. Someone had to. She would know from his answers if he was a friend or a secret enemy. She began walking toward him but felt Manya's firm hand grab her arm and pull her back.

"Not for a girl to talk to a man like that." Manya waved her index finger at Shayna. "Stay away from him. Leave it to Yussi."

They looked odd standing next to each other. Yussi was as tall, but leaner, dark in his black suit, black yarmulke, black beard, and his pale face. Young. So very young, especially compared to Yankel, his face weathered and clean shaven. He stood broad, his shirt sleeves rolled up, browned by the sun, his head bare to the heavens.

Everyone waited while the two men walked away from the group and stood near a large spruce. The smell of spring sap intense around them. The other refugees clustered in small groups and watched. Yussi didn't want to accuse the man of being a spy, a troublemaker, or a thief, and his heart told him Yankel was none of those things. The man wanted to help. He must have a reason but refused to explain. Did his motive matter? Kindness for the sake of kindness. Yussi struggled for a way to test the man without offending him. He closed his eyes and prayed God would guide him to a good decision. The seconds moved slowly.

Not a muscle flinched on Yankel's body. No fingers twitched, nor did he crack his knuckles. No movement. Yussi couldn't recognize nervousness or concern.

"Are you a Jew?" the question slipped by his lips without planning.

"What is a Jew?" Yankel in his calm voice waited for an answer from Yussi, then added, "Give me your yarmulke and I will be a Jew."

"So, if I take off my yarmulke, are you saying I'm no longer a Jew?"

"Do me a favor, take off your yarmulke and then tell me if you're still a Jew."

A question for a question, thought Yussi. He must be Jewish. "Nu, what's in this for you? There's some value in helping poor Jewish refugees?"

"What do you think? You think I like getting no work done on my farm, that I like leaving my wife alone?" Yankel smiled and his eyes twinkled. "*Nu*, you want my help?"

Yussi felt the crowd restless behind him. They wanted to continue on their journey. He knew Yankel must have reasons, but he wasn't talking. Yussi believed evil was not in Yankel's heart. He passed the test God sent for him.

"We're fine." Yussi nodded to the people still waiting. "Yankel will guard us. We'll catch up to you later today." He watched as the friends of his childhood, his life, his world, moved away to hitch their horses, gather their things, and organize for the journey ahead. Once they all moved away from Yussi's wagon, Yankel spoke again.

"Shayna's father taught me to read and write when I was a child. It's nobody else's business. My family was not their business." He spoke quietly and then walked away. Nothing more and Yussi didn't pry.

A cloud of dust blurred the end of the line of refugees as the horses, wagons, and those on foot moved toward Brody. Yussi and Yankel collected what they'd need for the repair, but Shayna and Manya stood long after the cloud of dust was visible. Everyone said, "We'll see you soon," but Shayna knew she might never see any of them again.

"I lifted you from your mother's womb and watched you grow," Sara Rokhel had said just before she left. "From that first moment, your mother loved you, was proud of you. May God cherish and protect you." Shayna could still feel the kiss Sara Rokhel left on her cheek. When would they see a friendly face again?

For days they'd been surrounded by noise, wagon wheels, voices, prayers, cries, the clop of horses, and the banging of pans. Behind her, Shayna heard Yussi and Yankel's quiet conversation, beyond that was silence. Stillness in the trees, no wind to wave the branches. The birds resting now in the heat the day. Shayna saw Manya pinch her own arm; a permanent black and blue mark showed the spot she returned to day after day. She watched Manya rummage through the food stores, probably to prepare something for Dovid to *nosh*.

Their belongings rested against a tree in case they would have to tilt the wagon. Shayna decided she could consolidate their belongings, maybe make more room on the wagon bed and save her shoes, the soles nearly worn through.

Yussi had taken off his jacket, rolled up his sleeves, and still sweat dripped from his forehead into his eyes. With only limited movement under the wagon combined with the repetitive motion of his arm as he hammered and sawed the wooden beams, heat gathered around him. He hurried to finish the repair. It would hold at least until Brody and then he could have it properly fixed. So much time in the morning wasted with discussions and arguments. And then the goodbyes. As if they might never see each other again. So much time with limited tools to make the wagon secure again. The sun was high now in the sky. He doubted they could catch the rest of the caravan before nightfall. They would have to camp alone somewhere. He'd sent Shayna and his mother further into the trees to gather firewood, to be ready for the unexpected. They'd promised to stay close.

Yankel, a strange one, said little. Yussi knew he stood guard near their horse, tied to a tree, his rifle ready to stop any bandits or deserters who still straggled in the forest.

All that could be done was done. Repairs finished. Yankel reached out to help Yussi from under the wagon.

"Where's my mother?" He looked around the clearing. "Shayna? Where's the wood?" He rubbed the sweat from his forehead and ran his hands through his damp hair. He adjusted his yarmulke and looked around again as if they had appeared. "They should be back already." Yussi caught his breath and felt his heart began to race. "Did you hear anything while I was under the wagon?"

Yankel shook his head, whispered, "Sh," and pressed his finger to his lips.

Yussi froze when Yankel unclasped the saber on his belt, prepared his rifle, and headed toward the trees. For a moment, Yussi couldn't move, a silent *Shema Yisroel* came to him: Hear, O Israel, the Lord is our God, the Lord is One. Then he too moved toward the trees.

Manya went in one direction, her apron slowly filling with kindling. Shayna walked deeper among the trees, cooler there in the shade. She could see Dovid carefully selecting small branches for kindling. She looked for larger pieces that might be chopped into smaller pieces to serve the fire.

Shayna heard the crunch of footsteps behind her and looked around, expecting to see Yussi, who must have finished repairing the wagon. Then a crash, and a loud thud followed by a growl like a large animal. She saw Manya on the ground a few meters away. Motionless. A tall man with shaggy blond hair wearing a tattered soldier's uniform stood above her. He hadn't seen Shayna, which enabled her to duck beside a tree and look for Dovid. She spotted him crouched behind a large boulder. Good for him. He knew what to do. Shayna wanted to rush to Manya's aid, but knew there was little she could do against a man of his size. The blond man searched Manya's jacket pockets; all were empty. He unbuttoned his pants and relieved himself on Manya's prone body. Shayna couldn't stop an intake of breath. The blond man looked around for the source of the sound. She crunched down low.

"Look what I found," a loud voice boomed directly behind her. Before she could run, or even turn around to see, she was hauled up like a sack of potatoes and thrown across thick shoulders. The wood she carried in her apron fell as she was lifted. Blood rushed downward to her head as it swung back and forth. "Borys," the man who carried her yelled to the blond man, "leave that hag. Look what I found." He threw Shayna on the ground.

She knew she couldn't reach her knife. No prayers came to her, only icy fear as she tried to shift back and away. The blond peasant moved from Manya's body, lifted Shayna's legs, and pulled her closer as he unbuttoned his pants.

"I found her first." An obese bald man grabbed her from the blond, pushed him aside, leaned over Shayna, lifted her skirt, and ripped her underthings. Again she tried to crawl away, but he hit her in the stomach, raised her legs to his shoulders and laughed as he opened his pants. She managed to free one leg, but he grabbed it again, and suddenly an enormous pain pierced her body. She screamed, then a heavy hand landed on her throat. The pain did not stop as he continued to pound into her. Drunken breath, stale sweat, and pain as if her body was being torn in two, cleaved apart.

"Another scream and you're dead."

Shayna gasped for air when he removed his hand. Suddenly the blond man ripped off her shirt and exposed her breasts, "Look at these tits." His rough hands clutched at her breasts and squeezed. She moved her head toward his arm and bit down as hard as she could. He howled and then she saw his arm move toward her, his fingers curled into a fist. Her head snapped back as it smashed into her jaw. She tasted her own blood.

"Bitch," he snarled, and a searing pain pierced her shoulder. She couldn't turn her head, but she smelled blood. He raised a bloody knife in front of her face and laughed.

"Idiot. No knives yet. I want her alive a little longer," the massive bald man said between loud grunts and jerky moves. The blond pinched her breasts and continued to laugh.

"My turn."

Then it stopped, her legs dropped to the ground but the pain remained.

"Move away from her." She recognized Yankel's voice. The hands stayed on her body and then she heard a shot. Neither man fell to the ground.

"That's a signal to others. They'll come with guns," Yankel said. "You can wait for them to kill you, or I can kill you now."

"What's this? A Yid with a gun? You don't look like a Yid. You can have her when we finish." He laughed and walked toward Yankel. Another shot and the bald man clutched his thigh and fell back.

Shayna tried to lift her head, but even the slightest movement intensified her agony. Nothing was in focus, all seemed blurry before her, and then nothing. No sounds. No Dovid. No Yussi. No Manya. Nothing.

Chapter 7

"Reboyne sheloylem, Lord of the universe, all powerful, she's burning up with fever, suffering here in this wagon. Have *rakhmones,* pity this orphan girl, relieve her pain," Manya prayed as she stroked Shayna's forehead. Manya's own body ached everywhere. The bastard had thrown her hard against the ground. She thought her skull would crack open. No position was comfortable for her to sit as she watched over Shayna, who was still unconscious. Shayna's temperature had risen over the last day and night as they bounced along narrow roads on the way to Yankel's farm. Yankel knew roads that didn't know they were roads. Paths for deer, not wagons. Each bump sent pain along Manya's back. Her head pounded like a hammer against an anvil. So far they hadn't seen other people, but Yankel was convinced the bastards would try to find them again.

Shayna hadn't opened her eyes. Manya was convinced God protected Shayna from the memories. But Yankel said it must be the wound near her shoulder, likely infected from the knife that stabbed her. He wouldn't let Manya wrap a bandage around her shoulder to protect the cut. He brought vodka stored in his pack and poured it on the wound. Shayna's body shuddered, but Yankel said it was necessary to keep the wound clean. More pain before the poor girl could heal. She knew that to be true, in life. But maybe it wouldn't heal. Maybe Shayna would not recover. Manya's mind drifted to her son, but there was nothing she could do to help them. No way to make what happened disappear. Maybe Shayna's forehead wasn't as hot now. Manya couldn't be sure. Black and blue bruises spread across the girl's swollen face, across her body, her clothes bloody and torn.

Manya's own clothes smelled of urine, but there was no evidence that she *pisht* from the shock. She didn't know what happened, couldn't let herself think about it. She wanted to wash herself from head to toe.

Yussi was still in shock. Manya tried to talk with her son, told him she was fine, only a headache. Why should she tell him every bone in her body cried to God for relief? She told him Shayna too would be fine, but he couldn't look into her eyes. As she leaned back against the side of the wagon, seeking a comfortable corner, Manya closed her eyes, tried to lock out the memories that wouldn't go away. The sound of the rifle still reverberated in her mind, the smells, blood, urine, and vomit. She still could hear her son gagging and smell his vomit. *Barukh Hashem,* God put Yankel in their path to save them. The Lord's instrument. A miracle. Manya could still hear his deep voice yelling at Yussi to rip off her stinking apron and help her to the wagon. Yankel himself carried Shayna and held Dovid's hand as he followed.

The vipers ran. Yankel let them live. He should have destroyed them. Outlaws. Animals. Put bullets through their hearts. She prayed their *shlongs* would be devoured by maggots, their bodies thrown into vats of lye. There were not enough curses in Manya's mind. No punishment great enough for their sins. Her curses fought in her mind with her prayers to God for help, for Shayna's recovery, for a place of safety for them all.

Yussi sat next to Yankel on the driver's seat, too stunned to drive. Dovid hadn't said a word. Still silent. His eyes didn't leave Shayna's face.

Shayna's eyelids fluttered and her tongue ran across her lips. Manya patted a wet cloth to further moisten them. Tears filled Shayna's eyes when she saw Yussi's mother. Manya hadn't witnessed the worst with her own eyes, but she knew what must have happened to the girl. *Az och un vey,* a terrible misfortune, but God, in his wisdom, kept her alive, saved her, saved them both.

"Dovid?" barely audible, only a scratchy whisper from Shayna as she looked at Manya, who nodded. "Dovid?" Shayna repeated and the little boy curled his body close to her. She looked at Manya again, "Yussi?"

"Barukh Hashem, Thank God, everyone is saved."

Shayna woke in a strange room covered by a sheet. She thought for a moment that maybe she lay in her own shroud. The intense pain between her legs suggested that she was still very much alive. Another of God's gifts. Later she learned that Yankel insisted they get off the road to Brody and hide because the bandits would regroup and return.

Shayna reached her hands down along her body. She wore no clothes, only a large bandage between her legs and another wrapped around her shoulder. An emptiness filled her heart, a despair so deep it went into the earth and all the way to the ocean. She turned her head to the wall.

"Shaynaleh, it's me, Manya." Shayna heard a chair pull up next to the bed where she lay.

"Manya? Where are we?"

"Let's see your face. I think the swelling on your face is going down."

"Where are we?"

"Yankel took us to his farm. He has his wife here. Let me see your face."

Shayna twisted her whole body toward the wall, then felt Manya's hand on her shoulder, and she was pulled back to face Manya.

"Look at me."

Shayna closed her eyes and prayed Manya would disappear.

"Look at me." Shayna opened her eyes. Manya's face was black and blue, a bandage wrapped around her head. She'd forgotten Manya had been the first victim.

"Shaynaleh. Don't turn away. God gave you life and kept you alive. You will rise from this. The shame is not yours. Do not cling to it." Shayna closed her eyes and turned away.

"You must listen to me. Open your eyes and look at me. You are as innocent as the day you were born. This skin will peel off of you like a snake." She leaned over and kissed Shayna's forehead. "Remember they are pestilence on this earth. May God send leeches to suck their blood until they are dry. The shame is not yours."

Shayna shook her head, closed her eyes, and motioned Manya away. She pictured the snake that Manya described and knew her skin was just as empty. Nothing left inside of her. Pain, but that would diminish with the bruises. Shame would never leave.

She had readied herself with a knife and when the time came, she could do nothing. Her knife. Her skirt. The tickets. Her money. Where were her things? Where was Dovid? It didn't matter how she felt. Dovid must live and she would get him to his Uncle Ulkeh in America. This she had to do.

Later that afternoon, Inge, a lean blond woman, Yankel's wife, brought her clothes. Her shirt, jacket, and underthings were totally ruined, but Inge managed to save her skirt. Cleaned it as best she could. Shayna felt the hem and waistband for the tickets and money. She knew that Inge must have discovered it as well, but she had not unsealed the hem. She also brought fresh undergarments and a blouse. Yankel's wife didn't speak very much, but her face spoke of acceptance and caring. Without comment, she handed Shayna the knife that had been in the pocket. Shayna couldn't remember exactly but she thought she forgot about it in the moment of attack. Never again. She would think carefully of how to prepare for the ship, the journey to the ship. Manya was right about one thing: she would rise from this. Not the same person, but still *Tante* Shayna. Ulkeh would never know. Yussi would never marry her now. He shouldn't.

She knew nothing beyond the room where she lay, slept. She tried to plan but her thoughts hurried back to where it happened. His face hung before her; wherever she looked she saw him. The beast. The animal. She wished she had died, but then Dovid would be alone—no family, a child alone. She had to stay alive.

Yussi came to see her, his eyes cast downward, his steps timid as he came into the room. She pulled the sheet tight up to her neck, her right eye hardly visible beneath the swelling on her face. He knew there were bandages. He knew about the shoulder wound but could only guess where else she may have been hurt. Her beautiful braid lay twisted and filthy. He held Dovid's hand and they stood a few feet from the bed. Dovid's head was lowered but his eyes raised until they caught her own. She smiled as best she could and he smiled back.

"Dovidel, *tatele*," her voice cracked. But he came toward her and touched the bruise on her jaw with his finger.

"What color is it?" she asked.

"Blue and black too. And yellow on the side by your ear." Shayna realized he talked. When had he started to talk again?

"It will disappear soon and I'll be fine. Soon we'll meet your uncle in America. You'll like him."

Inge had told her she'd been out for two days and that Dovid had spent many hours with their puppies in the barn. Maybe the puppies had given him back his voice.

"Tell me about the puppies."

"Yankel said I was a big help. I watch them. Every day I bring them water."

Yussi looked on as she tried to smile at the boy, but there was no life in her face, only the vivid bruise surrounded by pale skin. She looked up at Yussi with a message that Yussi didn't understand, as if she was pleading. Did she want them to go? He needed to talk to her, so he ruffled Dovid's hair and sent him out of the room. After pulling a wooden chair closer to the bed, Yussi lit a cigarette and took several drags. He wanted to touch her, to comfort her, to say something that mattered. Her arms remained modestly under the sheet. Yussi guessed she might be naked beneath it.

Although sun flowed through the open window and a light breeze cooled the air, a dark spirit hovered somewhere. He couldn't be sure, didn't know where, couldn't see anything, and only felt the presence of heavy sorrow weighing on them both.

His mother told him not to visit yet—that Shayna wasn't ready. As he sat in the stiff chair, he realized he wasn't ready yet either. Even as he mumbled some words of comfort, "You will heal, soon we will marry and you will forget, God will bring you comfort," he heard hollowness in his own voice. Not lies, but not truths either. He searched for guidance, for God's gentle voice to help him find the words to heal, but he heard nothing. Shayna's eyes remained closed.

"Are you tired now? Do you want to sleep?" Yussi asked.

Shayna nodded and turned to the wall.

He took another drag of the cigarette, snuffed it out with his fingers and saved the stub in his vest pocket. "Yankel wants me to help with some repairs to the barn, so I'll come back tomorrow," he said as he stood close to the bed, leaned down, and kissed her cheek. She twisted away.

Chapter 8

"Careful. Don't spill," Shayna said as she watched Dovid walk from the pump to the front porch with a bowl of water for the puppies.

"I won't spill. I bring them water every day."

"I forgot. You're a big boy now."

Dovid blushed, puffed out his little chest and managed to lower the bowl without spilling a drop. "My job. I give the puppies water."

Dovid got down on all fours, crawled close to the water bowl where four tiny puppies jockeyed for a place, wiggling his *tukhes* as he went. Shayna noticed Dovid's tongue quickly shoot in and out, imitating the dog's licking behavior.

"What are you doing Dovid?"

"Why do they drink with their tongues out?"

"They don't have hands to hold a cup."

"Why not?"

"God gave them hands to walk on."

"Why didn't God give me hands I can walk on?"

"You're walking on your hands now."

"Can the puppies ever use their hands to hold a cup?"

Shayna shrugged. "We'll have to watch them carefully and see if they can do that. Where are you going now?"

"I need a cup of water" and he ran into the house.

From the porch where she and Dovid played with the puppies, Shayna could hear the ongoing argument between Inge and Yussi. Yussi paced near Manya and Inge while they washed and hung laundry. Morning sun cast shadows around them, but their raised voices carried across the yard. The same conversation circling around them all for days.

"I mean no disrespect to you, Yussi," Inge said, "but you're not listening to what I tell you. You may know books, but I know about crossing the border. You must shave your beard, cut those things hanging by your ears. Your hair is too dark, thick, too Jewish. Maybe we should lighten it."

"Lighten it? What are you talking about? I am Jewish. Why should I cut my *peyes*? Hide my yarmulke? Erase the signs of God, signs that light my life?" Yussi's finger waved in Inge's face as she hung a sheet on the laundry line.

"Your beard will grow back." She waved her index finger back at him. "I hear you're not a stupid man, don't you understand? No country wants Jews to enter, no refugees, no penniless people. It's easier to sneak across the border from the forest, not at the official checkpoint. I can get you across. If you're caught crossing as a Jew, as a refugee, without papers, there's a terrible danger. They ignore people like me, but never Jews, not without heavy bribes, beatings, or worse. You all must pass as normal, regular Ukrainians."

"Don't tell me I'm not normal. Who made you the judge of what's normal?"

"Does your son have a hearing problem? Manya, maybe he'll listen to you." Inge shrugged her shoulders and turned away from Yussi.

Manya lifted her hands from the washboard and looked back and forth at the two who had sparred for days. Yussi, breathing heavily, his face red, turned and walked toward the barn. Manya shook her head and went back to washing clothes, Yussi's, Dovid's, her own and even Shayna's. She didn't listen to Shayna's protests. "You're still weak," she insisted.

"I'm doing the laundry for the family. We're all *mishpokhe*, the same family." Maybe sort of a *mishpokhe*, but not exactly a *mishpokhe* that Shayna recognized as her own.

The runt of the litter cuddled on Shayna's lap now, a chocolate-colored puppy with a white patch on his face. His warmth seeped through to her legs and his fur was like silk against her hands. The arguments would end soon, Shayna knew. Yussi in the end wouldn't be a fool, but Shayna knew he was afraid. They all were. Afraid of all the changes, afraid of the unknown that lay ahead.

Three weeks had passed, enough time for Shayna to heal. Enough time to replace the hastily repaired broken parts of the wagon. For the first week, Shayna drifted in and out of a restless sleep. Manya slept on a mat next to her bed and comforted her each time she woke screaming. Inge washed and cleansed Shayna's wounds daily, and changed the bandages. Both hovered over her, fed her and anticipated every need. She let them because she had no energy to stop them.

Yussi brought Dovid in every morning and every evening before bed. She forced herself to look at the little boy, smile and think of something comforting to say. She knew he needed connection but even the smallest effort exhausted her.

By the second week, she could stand, then dress, then eat with the others. Inge and Yankel took to Dovid as if he were their own. Inge invited him to help her bake cookies and feed the chickens. Yankel placed him on a horse and led him around, but mostly playing with the puppies gave new life to the child.

She tried to remember who she was before, to pretend to be that person, but she couldn't remember. Could only act like everyone expected, pretend her soul healed as quickly as her shoulder. But inside, she was *shmutsik,* filthy, a girl covered with the stench of her attacker, a stink that would cling to her forever. A lie, like a housewife who wears a clean white apron over a filthy dress.

By the time the swelling on her face disappeared along with all the black and blue marks, Dovid wanted to stay with her, to sleep with her. Every night before they slept she taught him songs, songs of the alphabet, the Yiddish alphabet and the Russian. And she sang her mother's song to her as a child, a song she knew Perl had sung to Dovid since he was born.

"Puptshik, du bist mayn lebn. Ikh hob dikh lib." You are my life. I love you. She knew Yussi listened on the other side of the door as she sang. He used to love her voice. His eyes studied her now, with hunger, but she could not feed him, could give him nothing. She would live now only for Dovid, because he had no one else. She would buy an English dictionary when she got to Brody and learn the new language herself by teaching Dovid. The loss of her dreams didn't matter, nor did her pain. Getting Dovid safely to America mattered. She could never be able to erase what he had seen. Never erase the loss of his family. But she would care for and protect him. She would do this for her sister.

Yussi wished he truly remembered what he looked like only a month before. His rational mind told him the man in the mirror was the same one who left Obodivka after the pogrom, but he knew the man in the mirror was not the same person, didn't even look like the same person. He knew dark gray never before circled his eyes. He remembered fleshy cheeks on his face visible beneath his facial hair. Now he saw only bones jutting out above his beard. He remembered the mirror on the wall in the kitchen of his home in the shtetl where, as a young man, he watched the stubble grow slowly into a beard, where he saw his *peyes* grow darker over the years, darker and curlier.

Inge won the argument, insisted he cut his beard.

"Look at Yankel," she said, pointing at her husband who sat at the table with a cup of tea.

Yussi noticed Yankel's face reddened, but he didn't say anything.

"That's why my husband survives. They know he was once a Jew, but he doesn't rub it in their faces. It will all grow again. Leave your black coat here and those things hanging from your waist. Since Yankel wounded one of the bandits, they will look for Jews to kill. You must be invisible to them and to the guards at the border."

Hide who he was. Hide the Jew part of him. He ran his hand along his beard, a familiar gesture recalling the hours watching the rabbis studying the ancient texts, leaning forward as he listened and asked questions.

In imitation of his teachers, he grew into the habit of rubbing his own beard as a secret step before understanding came.

Inge prepared a scissors, a long razor, shaving cream, and a bowl of hot water with a cloth. She spread some old material under where he would stand in front of the mirror to collect the hair as it fell. She volunteered to do it for him, to steal away his manliness, he thought. No woman could touch his beard, even though he knew she only wanted to help. This beard was not his manliness, was it? A question he had never before asked himself. Manliness. Everyone said after his bar mitzvah he was a man, but he had no beard then, little body hair. Did waking up with wet nightclothes make him a man? He couldn't stop it from happening at night, maybe that made him less of a man.

A son looked to his father for answers, but his father was long dead. And his brother was a *nar*. Could you ask a fool questions? Maybe he was the *nar* for wondering. No one asked the rabbis these questions, as if the body did not exist, should not have needs. Maybe not a man at all.

The picture of Shayna on the ground, her skirt raised, legs bloody, blouse torn and her full breasts covered in red scratches flashed across Yussi's mind. Yankel had picked her up and held Shayna to his chest as he carried her to the wagon. Yussi rubbed his eyes, tried to wipe away his memory, the memory of him emptying his guts while Yankel rescued Shayna.

Yussi picked up the scissors and cut through the bottom of his beard. He pulled on the remainder and made another cut. Was there a blessing to be said before cutting hair? He couldn't remember. He snipped at the hairs along his jaw and his cheeks until it was time for the razor. His skin stung as he moved the razor along his cheeks. The pain oddly satisfying. A stinging sensation that he deserved.

He needed help to cut his hair. It looked like a wild bush. The long curly hair had to go. Inge wanted to help but he would ask his mother. It would make her happy to help him, as if he were her little boy again.

"He's old enough to comb his own hair. He's old enough to dress himself. He can tie his own shoes." Yussi could still hear his father's deep voice, feel the tension that lived in his chest when he was a little boy. Every day there was something. His mother's voice, thick with tears,

"Should I let him go naked, trip over his shoelaces? Ignore my own child? How many children should we lose?"

Yussi stared at the strange face looking back at him from the mirror. Naked skin. A chin he hadn't seen for years. An Adam's apple bobbed in his throat. Could he pass now for a *goy*?

Manya moved a chair closer to the window to get the best light and wrapped a cloth about him while she worked. She ran a hand through his hair, then insisted he go wash it before she cut.

"Munshik, the barber, I'm not, but your hair is too dirty, too oily to do a good job. Nu, go wash it at the pump."

No memory came to him of the last time he washed it. Days ran into each other. Everything more complicated. Decisions no longer his own. The pump water poured forth cold on his head and the soap smelled of too much lye.

Manya tilted the mirror so he could see. He watched her face while she combed and cut. Tightness around her eyes and gray skin made it seem that little blood ran through her body. The bruise was still visible on her head.

"Does it hurt you?" Yussi pointed to his own forehead. "You have a headache?"

"Life is a headache. Don't move. I don't want to cut your ear."

"Make it much shorter," Inge said from across the room. "Much shorter, close to his scalp. If he's almost bald, it won't look so dark." Manya mumbled something under her breath but continued to cut. Yussi felt her fingers, gentle against his head, comb, lift some hair, and snip, comb and snip. He remembered the feel of her fingers pinching his shoulder when he was a child to stop his wiggling while she cut his hair. Now he sat still while she worked, the skin on his face still burning. His hands rested on his lap. Motionless. Patient. Waiting.

Yankel prepared their wagon for the trip to the border, constructing a false bottom to cover luggage that would identify them as refugees. Yussi's old horse would never finish the journey to Brody, so one of Yankel's horses would pull the wagon with Inge holding the reins. She knew the border area; her large family spread across both sides of a border that shifted between rulers over the centuries. The Austro-Hungarian Empire's border now belonged to Poland, unless more recent changes had occurred.

Inge prepared food for their journey, likely to last at least a week. Mostly vegetables from their garden, carrots, turnips, and parsnips along with smoked fish and pickled herring. She also packed noodles and cornmeal. She wanted to add dried beef to the stores, but Yussi asked her to bring only enough for her own use because it wasn't kosher.

Inge and Yankel devised a plan to sneak them across the border without passports. Disguised in traditional Ukrainian festive clothing, they would pose as locals on their way to a wedding. Only Dovid did not speak Ukrainian; the others were fluent. Inge had traditional Ukrainian clothing, some her own and some her mother's. With slight alterations they would fit Shayna and Manya. Yussi was smaller than Yankel, but men's clothing was worn loose. It would work.

The bed of the wagon could not contain all their belongings. Only wedding gifts and baskets of food should be visible. This decision precipitated a crisis for Manya when she and Shayna found Yussi in the barn, sorting through their belongings. Already the stink of the cows, the horses, the chickens wandering in and out drifted over her precious bundles. Manya hoped to buy another trunk in Brody for travel on the ship. One look at Yussi pulling her things apart told her there would be little left for another trunk.

"Don't do this to me," Manya said. Don't leave me like a beggar, with nothing."

Shayna understood they would no longer have the wagon after Inge left them in Brody. They must carry their belongings. There was no choice. She noticed Manya rubbed the bruise that remained on her forehead. She claimed her head no longer ached. Shayna guessed the pain joined the other blows of Manya's lifetime, deep inside her heart.

Yussi paused, reached his hand to his beard to think of what to say, but found only stubble on his cheek. No more beard and no answers that his mother wanted to hear. Only the truth.

"Mamme, do you want to stay here? Keep our wagon, our horse, and find a way to live here, among the *goyim* if they'll let us. Is this what you want?"

"Don't mock me." She reached into the pile of linens and pulled out the quilt she'd made for his wedding. Yussi, you'll find room for your quilt. Where are my *Shabbos* candlesticks? The *mezuzah*? The picture of your father? His *kidish* cup? For you, for your son, your father's cup to bless the wine on Shabbos. You'd leave it here?"

Shayna put her arm around Manya's shoulder. "We have—"

"Don't get between me and my son," Manya snapped. "If he disrespects me, he'll disrespect his wife."

"You talk to her." Yussi shrugged and stomped out of the barn.

Manya's eyes followed him, her jaw tight as she muttered, "I can still teach him to be a *mensch.*"

Shayna thought about trying to talk to Manya, but instead knelt to study her own belongings. She removed everything from the small wooden trunk and spread the contents of the bundles on a blanket. Yankel said there would be no room for any trunk. None of it made sense to her. Nothing seemed to matter, except what belonged to Dovid. She took the pictures of their family, clothes, and his father's *talis* and *kidish* cup and carefully placed them, along with Perl's candlesticks, in an old satchel Inge found for her. She looked up and saw Manya watching her as she tried to sort the other things.

"Take the wedding dress, Shayna. Soon you'll be a bride. Yussi will make room for the dress and for your wedding quilt. But we'll take my Shabbos candlesticks. You'll use them every Shabbos, long after I'm gone. The family candlesticks."

Manya and Inge cleaned the kitchen after dinner the night before their departure. The smell of fish still lingered in the room. Inge breaded and fried the carp Yankel caught in a nearby lake and served it with boiled potatoes and carrots from her garden. Even the Jews ate carp, which made Inge happy. When they first came, she noticed Yussi's hesitation about eating from her dishes. Yankel explained to her that the dishes themselves were *treyf* if they'd had pork on them, or any meat that wasn't kosher. They were forbidden no matter how much they were washed. After a few days, Yussi ignored thoughts about *treyf* dishes and focused only on the food, regardless of on what dish it was served. Yussi never neglected to mumble prayers before and after their meals. Shayna and Manya would say Amen as needed while Inge and Yankel waited in silence for him to finish.

They heard the door behind them open and they turned to see Shayna emerge.

"Perfect. A beautiful young Ukrainian woman. Blue eyes. Look at you. Fits you perfectly." Inge adjusted the embroidered headscarf. "Tie it in the front. Not like your babushka." She hung three strands of red beads around Shayna's neck.

Shayna did not look toward Yussi, but rather toward Inge. He called her name, but she didn't respond. He scarcely recognized his Shaynaleh in the woman who stood before him. The colorful costume brought life to her pale cheeks, and the headscarf accentuated her long neck and high cheekbones. The red vest hugged her body and outlined her bosom, always invisible in the unshapely dark clothing she usually wore.

"I can't take these things from you." Shayna ran her hands along the heavily embroidered red vest, which matched the embroidery on the skirt. "They are too beautiful, too rare."

"Keep them. "You'll remember us."

"You've done so much. How can we thank you?"

"No need."

Dovid would dress in a heavily embroidered *kosovorotke*, the traditional Russian shirt, and another for Yussi. Manya was given a simple Ukrainian widow's headdress and darker, less elaborate clothing. When Inge was satisfied with their disguises, she carefully packed the clothing in a basket, ready for use when they approached the border.

Yussi would sit next to Inge as she drove. The others could sit in the back next to baskets of food and presents for the imaginary wedding they planned to attend in Galicia just across the border. The city of Brody, virtually destroyed in the Great War, had again become a haven for Jews escaping from the pogroms. People on the caravan insisted there would be refugees' aid organizations in Brody to help them find their way to America.

In spite of Shayna's plan to act as if she were fine, she found it almost impossible to look anyone directly in their eyes, especially Yussi. But she needed to thank Yankel. She knew he told Yussi that her father had been his teacher, but that seemed to Shayna to be a very inadequate reason for all the kindnesses. Yankel saved her life. Every time she broached the subject with him, he lowered his head, looked away or distracted her.

On the morning of their departure, with tears in his eyes, Dovid brought a bowl of water to the puppies in the barn. In spite of the strong breeze that splashed the water from side to side, no water spilled. Inge surprised him with small box of cookies as a thank you for his help. She told him the puppies would always remember him.

The gray sky and steady breeze suggested rain might interfere with their journey. Inge secured the gifts and boxes of food with a light canvas. With the wagon bed raised for a compartment to hide their belongings, the sides were shorter, leaving less room for Manya and Dovid. There was scarcely room for Shayna to sit in the back of the wagon. Before she jumped up into a corner, she asked Yankel to talk with her for a moment.

She stopped a few meters away from the wagon where the others waited, her hands against her legs to prevent her skirt from flapping in the wind. Yankel stopped near her, folded his arms across his chest and looked away. She followed his eyes to the large stone barn, probably built a century before, probably built by Inge's ancestors. Nothing in Shayna's life experience led her to guess what life path led Yankel from the shtetl to this farm, to a wife, to a *goyeshe* life, which seemed to suit him.

"Don't look away, please." Her words rushed out quickly before he could move. "You saved us all. Truly a *tsadik*, a righteous man. I cannot repay you enough."

His eyes opened wide as she spoke. His head shook back and forth, and he began to turn away. Shayna reached out and said, "I owe you my life."

"You owe me nothing." His arms were no longer folded around his chest. "I owed you. A debt to your father. I've looked for a way to repay him."

"Debt?"

"When I heard your father was murdered, and your mother, then the pogrom, I came. I heard about your sister. I looked for you."

"A debt to my father?" The words made no sense to Shayna.

"You don't know?" Yankel looked surprised "I thought your father would have told you." He shrugged, "Maybe not much to him, but to me…everything."

"What does my father have to do with this?" She looked back at the wagon, where everyone waited for her. But now Yankel looked directly at her. His words grew louder as he talked.

"They treated me like dirt. A joke to everyone. My father the *shiker*, drunk day and night and my mother the *zoyne,* the whore they snuck to in the dark. And I their child, garbage to throw away."

Shayna had heard gossip about his parents, but little conversation about their son.

"They thought I was too *proste*—too vulgar because of my parents and I would infect their children. Wouldn't let me near the school when it was time for me to go. Only your father. Only your father. He found me on the street, took my hand and walked me into the *kheyder,* No one would sit near me, but he smiled at me," his voice broke. "Your father patted my head. I remember he touched my head, like I was a good boy."

Shayna held her hand over her heart. Her father. She blinked several times. Yankel went on, his voice moving down to a whisper.

"Without him I would not read or write. You owe me nothing." He reached into his pocket and pulled out a small, carved horse. "Dovid is Perl's son. His grandson?"

Shayna nodded.

"Give this to Dovid. Your father carved it—gave it to me when I was Dovid's age. 'So you'll have a friend in school,' he'd said. Take it Shayna. Give it to Dovid. Something from his grandfather."

Chapter 9

July 1919

Other than play with Dovid, Shayna hardly spoke as the gray days crawled by. When she passed Yussi, she lowered her eyes and turned away. She could tell he wanted to speak to her about what happened, but she did not give him a chance. She watched him *daven* and lay *tfilin* each morning and in the evening stand by the wagon for afternoon and evening prayers. He was a Jew alone, without a *minyan*. There were no other voices to help him carry his voice to God. She hoped his prayers were strong enough to reach heaven.

Inge drove the wagon and Shayna could hear Yussi reciting portions of the Torah in a quiet singsong voice, like an incantation. Shayna wondered if this recitation was a way for Yussi to prove his faith despite the loss of the outward Jewish symbols that pronounced his identity, his *peyes*, his beard, the *tsitses*, and the yarmulke. Inge also insisted he shave every morning. Maybe reciting portions from the Torah distracted him from the world around him, from the suffering. She wondered if perhaps that was what it was always about. The dedication to study, the commitment to the laws, the rituals, the traditions, the stories of the Jews through history would be enough to soften the ache and strengthen the hope for a better world hereafter. She wondered if she had ever believed any of it.

"Walk with me?" Yussi asked after they ate kashe, an apple, and herring for their evening meal. He said the blessings and then took her hand.

"I have to watch Dovid," Shayna said and tried to pull her hand away.

"My mother's watching him." His grip tightened a little. His hand felt firm and vibrant in contrast to her own. Her arms, her legs, everything felt lifeless, weak, without substance. It was as if he sensed her distress and wove his fingers through hers—sent his strength into her. But little changed. Empty as she walked along the river, next to their camp, they watched the sun set in the cloudy sky, watched the trees become silhouettes against the red and pink streaks across the sky.

He stopped walking and caressed her cheek. "We can marry when we get to Brody." His words came unexpectedly and shocked her. Marriage was no longer an option for her. "The rabbis there will help. They'll have the paperwork. We must marry before we get to America."

"I don't want to hear it," she whispered. "Let's just walk." Shayna removed her hand from his and turned toward a thick grove of trees. She tightened her shawl against the advancing evening chill.

Yussi followed her, "It will be good Shayna. I know you are worried, but Jewish law tells us—"

She didn't let him finish, stopped walking, and whipped her head toward him, her eyes filled with rage. "The law. Tradition. The rabbis. What do they know? I see these wise men as they smooth their heavy beards, searching the air for God's words. Then they nod. God spoke to them, she should marry, bear children, and forget what happened." Shayna walked deeper into the woods for a moment, then looked around and saw only darkness. Daylight had disappeared, but Yussi stood behind her.

"No one asks you to forget. But to believe it was not your fault." He placed his hand gently on her shoulder. "You are innocent."

"Innocent? Don't talk like a fool." She turned and pushed against his chest, moved him away from her. "What do the rabbis know? Evil came into me. Into me, you hear? Filled my body. How can we marry now? You are not a *nar* Yussi; don't talk like a fool."

"Shaynaleh, it will take time. God will give you comfort. Don't turn away."

"Comfort? God will give me comfort? No. No comfort. God made a fist and squeezed me out." She pulled her shawl as tight as she could around her shoulders. "Let God suffer like I did and tell him that it will be all right." She backed away from him, her face twisted. "And inno-cent. Innocent? I'll never be innocent again. Ruined. To myself. To you. Find someone else." She turned and walked back to the camp.

On the third day, it finally rained. Soon after dawn, clouds came from the east, then short drizzles and then a downpour. Lightning filled the sky so they could not seek cover under the trees lining the road. By the time they scrambled under the wagon and unloaded as much as they could to put under it, they were drenched. Inge pulled a heavy woolen blanket from the wagon, and they tried to wrap themselves to stay warm. They could not risk going to any nearby farms. Shayna held Dovid on her lap. Manya and Inge on either side.

Yussi sat at the very edge under the wagon, his body away from the women. Although he rode next to Inge every day, he still sat as far from her as he could. But here on the road, Yussi watched Shayna from a distance, watched her skirts sway as she walked. Shayna felt his eyes on her whenever she tilted her head to hear the birds singing, or bend to smell a flower. She knew he listened to her voice as she sang to Dovid. It was as if a magnet connected him to her and she couldn't disengage it. A strong force used to pull him to her. She had felt his body alive in a way that she knew was prohibited. She knew her body responded. Com-pletely unwelcome now. She knew he wanted to hold her, comfort her, other things as well. She turned away from him, refused to connect with him. That part of her life was over.

By nightfall, the rain slowed and stopped. Crawling out from be-neath the wagon, all their muscles ached. Dovid had wet himself again and Shayna could see he was ashamed when she asked him to remove his pants.

Anxiety mounted as they neared Brody. Their progress was slow because they only chose the side roads, muddy now after the rain. They had to stop often to clean the horse's hooves and pull the mud off of the wheels.

Inge had relatives in Brody, cousins on her mother's side, and had often visited as a child. She claimed she knew how to cross the border without doing it officially. She claimed they always crossed unofficially because one never knew who was at the border. The wars had made everything confusing, so she insisted they sneak across.

The Jewish grapevine told story after story of Jews being sent back to Russia only to be killed—or worse, conscripted into the Russian army for life. There were too many Jewish refugees in Brody already, no room for more starving refugees. Yankel sent a few bottles of valuable Horilka, Ukrainian vodka, which would be a typical wedding gift. It could be a useful local bribe. But Inge was afraid to take the risk of crossing at the official border. Yankel had made her swear to get them safely across.

They'd heard that different organizations were in Brody to help. The question was how to get there without passports.

Inge had gotten them this far. They trusted her. From the small road they turned onto an even smaller path, like a deer path through the forest. They stopped shortly before where Inge thought the border might be. Maybe there would be a local guard stationed there, not a whole garrison. Hopefully it might be one of her cousins or someone she knew from her childhood. They stopped to dress again in the festive Ukrainian clothing that Inge had arranged for them, and then prominently displayed baskets of presents for the alleged wedding they were attending.

Things had changed since Inge's last visit. Now there was a small fence built between two trees where one armed soldier stood, maybe German, maybe Polish. No one could keep track of the politics.

Dressed in Ukrainian festive clothing, they headed to a celebration. Inge stopped the horse.

"Papers?" said the young guard. He spoke Ukrainian.

Inge laughed. "Papers? Who needs papers?" She leaned back and pointed to the baskets of presents. "We're just going to celebrate a wedding."

"You need papers."

"My family always crosses here." Inge sounded perplexed. "We never needed papers before."

Shayna held Dovid on her lap and teased him with his little carved dog. Manya smiled while they played in the back of the wagon.

"Since the revolution you need papers. We must guard against the Bolsheviks."

"Of course. True, true." Again, she pointed at the baskets. "Look at all the presents. We are already dressed and ready to celebrate."

He looked at Yussi. "And your papers?"

"What papers? To go to a wedding?" His Ukrainian was flawless. He felt exposed, naked without his *peyes*, without his black coat, no yarmulke on his head. He slid down from the wagon, kept his hands visible and motioned the young man to the side.

"The ladies will be upset to be late. As it is, they're tired and you know how nasty women can get. I have a gift for you, in honor of the marriage, let us spread the happiness." He reached back into the wagon and handed two bottles of Horilka to the young soldier. "Maybe these will help the time to pass. Have a drink in honor of the young couple."

"Are you trying to bribe me?"

"Absolutely not. Only to share our celebration."

They stayed on the dirt road for a few kilometers after the border until they reached a small clearing where Inge stopped. Their ordinary clothing quickly replaced Inge's Ukrainian festive costumes. Inge insisted they finish the remaining food. She could easily get more. The mud along the road had slowed their progress, added days to their trip. The original abundance of food dwindled quickly. No milk for Dovid for a few days. His large eyes, circled by darkness, stood out in a face that grew thinner as the days passed. Shayna wondered if her face looked as hollow. There would be food for them in Brody, she prayed.

The city had been a safe haven for refugees leaving the Pale of Russia for many years. Although they'd heard the Jews of Brody also suffered bloody pogroms during and after the war. They hoped the refugee organizations from America and Western Europe might still be there to help.

Shayna knew that Yussi felt strange without his *peyes* and beard, although the yarmulke was back on his head. He looked shorn and appeared to walk differently, hunched and awkward.

Inge pulled her identity papers from the secret compartment along with their things. She would have no trouble crossing back into Ukraine at the main border gate after she took them closer to Brody. "Go with God," Inge said as she departed.

They walked for a kilometer before reaching the outskirts of Brody, where they rested on the side of the dusty road surrounded by their belongings. Many carts filled with produce traveled toward what must be the market. There would be food here for them.

Refugees lined the way. They sat under trees, exhausted and disheveled. Sad-looking children dressed in rags clung to adults. Shayna wondered if they looked the same but knew the days at Yankel's farm had helped them. Yet all were survivors of the pogroms. Homeless. Stateless. She looked for *landslayt,* for people from Obodivka who left the same day, but she recognized no one. Maybe they already moved on, maybe to Germany to reach ships to America, maybe to France or Italy. Maybe some left for Palestine. Shayna had no idea where. Maybe they had met violence again and not survived. Thrown to the wind.

They followed the carts to the market and found milk, kashe, cheese, potatoes, and herring. Enough for now. They also found the information they sought and learned there were volunteers in Brody from Jewish organizations in America and Europe who staffed an office to aid victims of the pogroms. No one they talked to in the market knew exactly who they were or what aid refugees might receive, but within an hour, their stomachs were full and the flicker of hope was kindled.

They spent the first night in Brody outside, under the eaves of a large building, Dovid, clutching the wooden dog from Yankel, huddled between Manya and Shayna. The stocking doll had disappeared somewhere along their journey, but Dovid didn't seem to care. The heat of the day lingered through the night. Dovid slept, his breath steady. Manya slept as well, but Shayna stayed alert. She couldn't see Yussi, although she knew he was across the road outside of a shul that was partially destroyed but still standing. Small sounds continued through the night. The scuttling of rodents, the snore of people huddled near her. The smells of unwashed bodies. The town was overrun with refugees all seeking a safe haven. She heard matches lit, smoke exhaled, coughs, the cries of babies. Since the evil that had befallen her, her ease in the world, her confidence, had transformed into vigilance, caution. If she was attacked again, there would be no Yankel to save her. Could Yussi? His body thinner now, could he protect her? Maybe. Maybe they should get a gun. Her knife still lay hidden within her skirt.

Dovid whimpered in his sleep. "Shh *tatele*," Shayna whispered and gathered him closer. She kept her eyes closed but did not sleep.

Today they would search for more food, find fresh milk for Dovid, and maybe find a place to cook *lokshn* for him. Perl used to say he would turn into a noodle, he loved them so much. The high prices at the market shocked her, even for bread and milk. Everyone blamed the war, or the Bolsheviks. She didn't care who or what was to blame, only worried that their money might not last.

As soon as they passed the border, Yussi had replaced his yarmulke. From across the road, she heard the men begin the morning prayers. They would look for water to wash. Dovid smelled as she must. Mud clung to her shoes and her body itched; she knew the sun had burned her face. Flies now explored any uncovered skin. Her face. Her hands. She didn't have the energy to swat them.

Dovid finished the bread that remained and they gathered their bundles and walked along with scores of other refugees to the large building at the edge of the square, where a line had already formed. Yussi joined them. Shayna wondered what he felt, what would become of them. In the dirty, thin man who walked with them, she could not recognize the boy she had loved. Loved? Who knew about love? Her fiancé. What did she know of love? Who cared about love? Let them find peace and safety. Food. Shelter.

They stood out in the sun for hours as the line slowly moved. Jews from shtetls as far as Kiev stood with their possessions wrapped in blankets, tied with belts. Some carried suitcases. The women wore *sheytls,* others with scarves covering their heads. Unmarried, Shayna was not required to cover her hair. Dovid clutched the wooden dog in his little fist. He leaned against her, creating more pressure on her tired limbs.

Chapter 10

Seated on a stiff wooden chair with Dovid on her lap in front of a small table covered with papers, Shayna waited for the woman of middle years on the other side of the table to finish writing and help her. The woman wore no *sheytl*, nor kerchief to cover her auburn hair worn in a casual bun. It shone in the light from the glass bulb that hung from the ceiling. Shayna had heard about lights that lit themselves, but she'd never seen them. This must be it. She and the woman sat in a circle of light and its glow reflected off the woman's large glasses so that Shayna couldn't really see her eyes. In Yiddish, the woman asked, "Name?"

"Shayna Rifkin," she answered and then asked, "Who are you?"

"Sorry, my name is Evelyn." The woman smiled and added, "I am here to help you. I work for a Jewish rescue organization. We get funding from the United States and Europe, especially from the Baron de Hirsch, a German Jew who created a foundation to help victims of anti-Semitism, like yourself."

Shayna formed her mouth into what she thought would be a smile but couldn't think of anything else to say. The woman must be Jewish. Spoke Yiddish. But she'd never seen a Jewish woman look so elegant. Shayna studied the cut of her shirtwaist, looked for the seams, the buttonholes. It looked seamless.

"Middle name?" Evelyn repeated the question, drawing Shayna away from dreaming about making such a beautiful garment.

"Rokhel"

"Age?"

"Seventeen." Evelyn dipped her pen in the inkstand and wrote on an empty page in a large book. Many pages of the book appeared used, although some looked untouched.

"Where were you born?"

"Obodivka"

Her pen raised, still questioning.

"Ukraine, Russia."

She pointed at Dovid. "Your son's name?"

"No. Not my son. My nephew. Dovid."

"Dovid?"

The woman turned to a fresh page apparently just for Dovid.

"Dovid Lev Goldfarb"

"Age?"

"Four." Embroidered leaves ran along the edge of the button placket of the woman's dress. The deep green color and precision of stitches made Shayna almost think they could be real. Shayna prayed a time would come when she could again sew, maybe even create beautiful dresses. She wondered about her *meshugene* brain, to think such thoughts. But when she thought about dresses, about making something beautiful, she had reprieve from the images in her mind. She wanted to ask the woman to stand so she could study the way the waistband came together. Maybe there were pockets in the skirt.

"Also Obodivka?"

"What?"

"Is your nephew also from Obodivka?"

Shayna nodded.

"And his parents?" Evelyn's dress disappeared in front of her eyes, and instead she saw Perl's skirt lifted over her legs and Sarah's broken body.

"Gone."

"Gone?"

Shayna nodded. "Gone. I don't know where. Murdered. Dead." She tried to stop but didn't. "Dead. Yes, dead." She shook her head, trying to erase the memory of her sister splayed out on the bed. Dead. Then she remembered Dovid, who sat quietly on her lap. "Sorry. I am sorry." She kissed the top of Dovid's head, leaned forward. "I'm sorry."

Evelyn ignored Shayna's outburst and made more notations in the journal. She'd heard that and much worse many times before. "Where do you wish to travel?" Evelyn turned back to what must be Shayna's page.

Shayna wondered who owned this information, who wanted it and for what reason, but she was afraid to ask, afraid not to answer.

"To America. To my brother. His uncle."

"Are you traveling alone with the boy? Any other family."

"No more family. My fiancé and his mother travel with us." She pointed behind her, where Manya stood with Yussi, in line, waiting.

"Do any of you have travel documents?"

The question that they all dreaded.

Shayna shook her head and looked down. The woman's mouth had tightened into a straight line. Yussi had been listening, and he and Manya moved up closer. She felt their presence behind her.

Shayna closed her eyes and images of Obodivka filled her mind, as if she stood now in front of the burned remains of her home, the sound of fire crackling, the smell of smoke, men laughing, guns, horses. She leaned in close to the woman to make sure she would be heard over the voices around her, the crying, yelling, and mumbling of other refugees. So many lines, so many people in the lines, so many little tables.

"What papers? Who has papers?" Shayna asked. "Do you think we never had papers? That we weren't born? Everything was burned. Even death certificates burned." She hissed the last words, took a deep breath and added, "Do you also need proof that someone is dead? Maybe proof that we're alive?" She stuck her hand across the table. "Touch me. See I exist." She touched her face, her hair, and wrapped her arms around Dovid. "We do. We exist."

Evelyn put her pen down, folded her hands on the table, and for the first time looked directly at Shayna.

"Do you think I don't know? Do you think I care if you have papers?" Evelyn's voice dropped to a whisper. "The police care. The conductor of the train will care. The border guards will care. How will you get to a ship?"

Shayna covered her face and sank back in the chair. She felt a hand on her shoulder. Yussi? Manya? She didn't know—only knew she had to talk to the woman. Maybe there was hope. "Tickets. We have tickets to a ship. From someplace called Antwerp. Where is Antwerp?"

"You have tickets?" Evelyn's shoulders relaxed, the straight line of her mouth turned back into a curve. "Good. Very good. We'll be able to help you. Antwerp is far, but since you have tickets, we can help. I will be able to arrange visas. Show me the tickets."

Shayna thought of the tickets rolled carefully into the hem and waistband of her skirt. "Can I bring them to you later?" She hadn't given Yussi his tickets yet. He and Manya would use two of the extra ones. "I don't have them with me now, but I can bring them back very soon."

Evelyn nodded. She folded her hands together over the book, her head titled to one side. "How else can we help you?"

Tsedoke, charity, certainly existed in the shtetl. A chicken for a widow on Shabbos, some kopecks to rebuild a roof destroyed by fire. This she understood, but she marveled at a heart that must be so big that it reached all the way to the Pale to save them. A heart so large matched with a purse so large.

Evelyn repeated her question. "How can we help you?"

Yussi approached the table and asked, "Is there a place to sleep while we are in this city? How do we get to the ship?"

Evelyn looked up. "Please sir. Wait your turn. I'm talking with this girl now."

"He's my fiancé," Shayna snapped. "We are traveling together."

"I'm sorry. Really sorry, but we have our rules. When you are married, we can talk to you together. To the whole family. How would we know if you weren't in danger from this man?" She looked back at Yussi. "Step back please."

Yussi's face turned red. He did step back, but Shayna could feel his shame. Her own shame. Who was this woman, a Jewish woman to be so rude to a man? Was he nothing?"

Maybe a reason to get married, Shayna thought.

The woman asked many more questions. "Can you read and write? What languages?"

Shayna felt proud to tell this strange lady that she could read and write in three languages: Yiddish, Russian, and Ukrainian. The woman seemed surprised, but she must have believed her because she wrote it down. Shayna wondered if you have to read and write to get to America.

The woman told her there was no longer a train in Brody. The tracks had been destroyed in the war although they were being repaired, no one knew how long it would take. There was a rumor they could reach a train junction after a three or four day walk.

"We can also provide you and Dovid with a room and a small stipend for food until we run out of money. Maybe a month, maybe two or three. It depends on how many refugees come through Brody and need help."

She had the tickets in her skirt. There were rubles too—rubles that she'd gotten from Perl's fireplace and some kopeks of her own, from sewing. She'd never discussed money with Yussi. He had paid for some of the food along the way. Or Inge had given it to them. They needed to talk.

She didn't think she was selfish, but she held on to that money as if it mattered. After they crossed the border, Yussi had exchanged his money to local money. She would have to change her rubles too, otherwise they had no value. Maybe those rubles mattered because they belonged to Perl. Maybe they mattered because they were familiar and she had so little.

She waited by the door for Yussi and Manya to join them. She and Dovid were given a room, but no others were available. A place to sleep. Maybe a place to wash. Dovid's neck was striped; sweat lines dripped through the dust gathered there. Manya would sleep in the room with them. Yussi would have to fend for himself.

He accompanied them as they searched for the address on the small piece of paper. Gathered on every corner were other refugees. Everyone looked for answers, but there were none. Shayna carried Dovid until her back felt like it would crack open. Yussi took the boy from her. No one talked as they wandered through the streets of this strange town.

The address matched a large wooden building near the railway station, maybe once a factory or warehouse. They could see the railroad tracks twisted in large hunks of metal strewn about the road. It would take forever to rebuild the tracks. Couldn't God at least provide a train? She wondered why God provided bandits, rapists, murderers, and hunger, but no train.

The smell of unwashed bodies surrounded them as they entered. Children ran up and down the halls. A frazzled American man, who spoke Yiddish with a terrible accent, asked for a room voucher, which only Shayna had. They all followed him through a maze of halls to a small room, no window, only a metal frame with a thin mattress, folded sheet, blanket, and pillow. Across the room they saw a table, two chairs, a bench, and assorted kitchen utensils. He pointed to his right, down the hall toward the water closets and then to the left, where he said they would find a kitchen they could use.

"This is the best we've got now. I'm sorry. I wish I could help you more, but all the facilities built for refugees before the war were destroyed. I was here in nineteen ten and there were proper rooms to help refugees. Now most of the Jews of Brody emigrated or are homeless as well."

"There are cots on the top floor for bachelors," the American said to Yussi. "There's a staircase somewhere around here." Before they could ask other questions, he hurried away.

After climbing three flights of stairs, Yussi reached a large dusty room under a pitched roof, its ceiling so low he could only stand upright in the center. Simple cots filled the room, lined beneath the slanted walls. Dim light came through two small windows. Wooden boxes separated the cots. Most held suitcases and other bundles, while a blanket and pillow rested on a few empty cots.

Yussi chose the first empty box and adjoining cot. He saw two men in silhouette near the windows, their heads close in conversation. They passed a cigarette between them, its smell mingled with the stale smell of unwashed bodies. The men looked up briefly when they heard him enter but turned back to their own conversation.

Leaving his suitcase on the cot, he approached them: one an old man, no beard or yarmulke, the other younger and also clean shaven.

"*Sholem Aleykhem*," Yussi greeted them with the traditional greeting, "Peace be unto you."

"*Aleykhem sholem*," the younger one said. "Peace be unto you as well." He turned back to their conversation.

"You have a cigarette to spare?" Yussi interrupted.

This time, the old man answered, "If we had an extra, we wouldn't be sharing this one." Again they turned away from him.

Yussi stood for another moment, but the men continued their conversation as if he weren't there. From their accent in Yiddish, he knew they were *Litvaks*, Jews from Lithuania, and could easily make out their words. They talked about someone's sister, or daughter, he couldn't tell—a terrible story of misfortune. He could have been a statue as far as they were concerned. Slowly he walked back to the cot he'd claimed.

There was no way to lock the box next to the cot or even cover it. Any thief could just reach in. He thought about sliding his suitcase under the cot, but even in the dim light he saw large balls of dust and what looked like rodent droppings. Instead, he placed it in the box. If someone took it, they would come away with nothing but a few old clothes, books, *tfilin, talis*, and what was left of his father's tools. Almost everything else had to be left with Yankel. He sat with his back against the wall, the top of his head scraping the slanted attic roof.

The room assigned to his mother, Shayna, and the boy provided only slightly better accommodation. Still, it was a place to rest, safer than sleeping in the streets. His stomach grumbled and he needed a cigarette. What kind of Jews were these who scorned a fellow Jew? Maybe they hadn't scorned him, maybe only busy. He thought about Shayna and his mother somewhere downstairs and wanted to join them.

Soon he would meet Shayna outside and they would go to the market. He wanted to get her alone, someplace where she wouldn't run from him, a place where he could convince her not to be stubborn and stupid, words he couldn't use. He wasn't a fool but didn't know what words to choose—what words to remind her of the promises they made to each other. He wanted her to know they needed each other, they would find peace together. She needed to trust him.

His face itched, only stubble now. He needed to find a shul, soon. Maybe these men knew, but would they answer him, if they knew?

As was his custom, his eyes drifted closed and he began with the *Shema*, the holiest of prayers, to bring God's presence into his heart. God used to come easily to him; even in his father's cabinet shop with the smell of wood around him, he felt His presence, His spirit. Each day away from his books, his rabbi, his shul, his home, God drifted away. Foolishness, he knew as he continued his prayers. His memory, always good, hadn't failed him. God hadn't abandoned him, never would abandon His people.

The voice of his father intruded, like a drip of water, steady and relentless as it slipped through his prayers and opened his thoughts to memories. His father's mocking voice, "Tell me *khokhm*, if you're so wise, why doesn't God stop the Cossacks? Explain this to me. What do the rabbis say at your yeshive?"

He saw his mother's face, her jaw tight, her fists curled as she turned away, careful not to provoke his father. Yussi never saw his father hit her, but he often saw her body cringe with the slam of his humiliating words.

"Go pray, kiss the hem of the rabbi, but don't be a *nar*. Only a fool believes the rabbis—lazy people, stupid weak people. Go, pray. See if it will help you."

Even as a boy, before his bar mitzvah, he'd tried to explain to his father the feel of God's presence in his soul, the strong connection that brought light to the drab world of the shtetl. To chant the prayers with the men, their voices joined together, yearning, searching, reaching, and finding peace, like heaven on earth.

Now alone, his voice, often silent, meager, struggled to reach the heavens.

No *takhlis* in these memories, no value at all.

As they walked through the warehouse district on the way to the market, Shayna listened while Yussi talked of the room where he would sleep, his need to find a shul, and the kiosk where he bought cigarettes. He talked of the destroyed train tracks and the choices before them to get to America. Rarely did he chatter, but Shayna felt his mouth working disconnected from the rest of him, while his spirit lingered around her, demanding, pressing into her. She couldn't explain the pressure she felt, there were no words, but if the invisible could be made visible she would see tentacles reaching out from him to surround her. He didn't mention her, or his desire to marry, which relieved her. Maybe he accepted she no longer was a suitable wife. Yet, she couldn't ignore the invisible cords that pulled at her.

They came to a small cobblestone square surrounded by what must have been large apartment buildings before the war and now hollow shells. Yussi drew Shayna to a wooden bench, still intact amidst the rubble and shaded by a large oak. He insisted she sit and rest. Shayna sensed it was an excuse for him to remain close, minimizing her movement and her ability to ignore him and his yearning to marry.

"You're still weak, tired," Yussi said. There is no hurry. No rush. Don't shake your head at me. Listen to me."

Shayna's knuckles tightened around the handle of the empty string bag and she sat on the edge of the bench.

"Lean back. Get comfortable. Rest. My mother is watching Dovid and fixing the room. We'll get food. No hurry." Yussi stretched out, reached his arm along the top of the bench, and pulled her toward him.

She shook him off, her back rigid.

"Shaynaleh, please."

"Please what? What do you want from me?" Her eyes followed a small squirrel as it raced across the cobblestones and leapt onto the thick bark of another oak. She watched it as it disappeared among the leaves.

"Look at me." Yussi took her chin and twisted her face toward him. "It's me. Yussi. What did I do? You look at me like I'm a stranger to you."

She glanced at him and couldn't miss his dark eyes filled with confusion. Her fingers wanted to run across his forehead, smooth his frown, but instead she tightened her grip on the shopping bag.

Again he pulled her toward him, this time with his hand at the back of her neck. She knew the movement, remembered when it thrilled her those few times when they kissed. Now she shook him off, pulled away. "You're not a fool, Yussi. Why act like one?"

He pulled back, clasped his hands together and looked around, his eyes searching the deserted buildings. Shayna didn't know what he might be looking for and only felt relief that he withdrew his pressure.

She leaned back, loosened her grip on the bag, closed her eyes and raised her face to absorb the sun. She tried to find the place in her heart where Yussi used to live, to feel the excitement she used to feel when he touched her. Innocent touches. His hand accidentally touching her hand as they walked in the shtetl. His kiss behind her house after their engagement.

She could barely hear him when he turned to her again and whispered, "I don't know what I did to you that you should look through me as if I was a chair in a room. You used to smile when you saw me. I am the same man."

A wall of glass separated her from him now. She wanted to feel the warmth of his arm around her, wanted him to fill the emptiness in her. She knew he didn't understand she was not the same girl, not clean, not pure, not deserving. She should have used the knife. She shouldn't have been so far from the wagon. She should have died rather than surrender. And even if she let herself believe him, let herself believe Manya that she was innocent, she was now and likely forever too broken to marry.

"Come. The food will be gone before we get to the market." Shayna rose from the bench and waited for Yussi to join her. Instead he lit a cigarette and continued to sit, stubborn, like a child, she thought. She sat again.

Yussi balanced his cigarette on the edge of the bench and again reached toward her. She pulled away and moved to the far end of the bench, sliding easily over the worn wooden slats.

"We're betrothed, you must..." Yussi stopped himself.

Shayna believed he would never understand her feelings. Defiled. Violated. Polluted by evil. She turned to face him but saw only his profile, his gaunt cheeks, and scruffy stubble as his beard grew.

"You are betrothed to me, in the presence of your parents..." Yussi ground his shoe into the butt of his cigarette but didn't look at her.

He was trying to act like a man, strong and decisive, but in that moment, Shayna heard the pain in his voice, the doubt, the confusion. He was as broken as she, all of them wrenched from the soil where they had grown, strewn about without care.

"Yussi." Shayna moved closer. "I am not ready." She doubted she would ever be ready but continued, "I will marry you, but not now." While Shayna waited for his response, she stared at the abandoned hulks around her. She wondered who had lived in these apartment buildings. Could anyone have survived the heavy bombing? The same bombing that must have demolished the train tracks. Shayna waited another moment, then turned to Yussi, "Remember, the trains are destroyed here. We must have a plan to reach Antwerp. Let's have a plan before anything else."

He showed no sign of having heard, or agreeing. They sat in silence until Yussi rose and motioned to her to follow. Had she ever known him? Maybe it was impossible to know anyone. The world was inside out now, like an old garment, with torn seams and dangling threads. She was not the same girl who eagerly agreed to marry him.

Chapter 11

Smells drifted toward them from the market as they walked. Shouts in many languages boasting of fresh rye bread, slaughtered chickens, fresh vegetables, and pickles mingled with the voices of women haggling for better prices. A cacophony of languages that drowned out Shayna's thoughts and Yussi's voice. A city market coming to life again after the ravage of the war. Crops had been devastated and animals confiscated by armies as they gained and lost ground, yet goods appeared along with shoppers desperate for food.

All the meat was *treyf*, nothing kosher for them, so they looked for good prices on herring, cheeses, noodles, and bread. Shayna bought milk for Dovid and an orange to divide among them all.

Yussi took their purchases back to Manya to give Shayna time alone to search for fabric. She wanted to replace Dovid's stuffed animal. His favorite was splattered with blood the day of the pogrom. She'd left it in Perl's house. Many of the stalls were empty. They looked as if they had been empty for a long time, but next to a shattered building sat a woman whose face resembled the crumbling walls beside her. A few barrels surrounding her were filled with old clothing. Shayna didn't let herself think about whose clothing or how it was abandoned. She found a blouse with circles, not polka dots, but still good enough to remind Dovid. Dark stains covered the sleeve, but enough material remained clean, she decided, until she brought the sleeve to her face and sniffed. Blood. Could it be blood? Did the smell cling even after washing? Her stomach clenched. Maybe this blouse had been taken from a martyr in a shtetl like her own. She dropped it back into the barrel.

She walked further into the market and eventually found a sapphire blue scarf, the exact color of the Ukrainian irises her mother had loved to embroider. The same shade of blue as the embroidery on her lost trousseau. With a few kopecks, she bought that and a few other pieces that might work. Among the belongings she carried from Obodivka were Perl's sewing scissors, along with a spool of thread and a needle. She'd also taken a handful of embroidery floss. Her heritage. She bought tiny buttons for eyes and decided she would embroider the mouth a deep crimson. Off to the side, she found a pile of tiny scraps that she could shred into stuffing.

When Shayna returned, Manya had organized the little room. Even the old mattress looked inviting, covered with Manya's quilt. She'd hung some clothes on a hook, as if they planned to actually live there. No one knew how long they would occupy this dismal room. Manya boiled water in the small kitchen at the end of the hall. She added milk to it and stirred in kashe to serve for their dinner along with farmer's cheese and fresh bread.

Dovid sat in a corner conversing with his wooden dog, which seemed to frequently occupy him. His little cap was pulled down over his ears. He'd never worn it that way before. Shayna pulled it way down to cover his eyes and asked, "Where's Dovid? Did anyone see him?"

"No, haven't seen him for hours," Manya said.

"*Oy vey*," Shayna laughed. "Where could he be?" she said as she picked up the little boy and twirled him around. "Maybe this sack of potatoes knows where Dovid is. Do you think these potatoes can talk?" She lifted up his cap and asked again, "Hey little sack of potatoes, where's Dovid?"

"I'm not potatoes."

"Sounds like Dovid. Could these potatoes really be Dovid?"

"I'm not potatoes!" Dovid insisted.

"No, you're not potatoes. You're my sweet *tatele*." She covered his face with kisses. "Right?"

"Right," he giggled and snuggled close in her arms.

Yussi sat on the floor, reading a newspaper he found. "No one knows when the train will come. No one knows when they will fix the tracks." His voice got louder. "It's all in the hands of the government, but no one knows what government. No one knows who is in charge." He mumbled as he washed his hands, "It's not safe here. We have to move on."

Before he left the room he looked directly at Shayna, ignoring his mother and Dovid, "While I'm at shul I will also pray that you find some common sense already. If we were married, we would have a room for all of us."

The thin walls of the room rattled when he slammed the door. No one spoke. She did not want to think about him, or a wedding. She wished he would find some common sense. Finding a room where he could be more comfortable was not a reason to marry.

Soon Shayna heard Manya's snores, familiar to her after so many nights together. She liked this time alone: time to dream, to think. She no longer recognized her life. The only thing she knew for sure was that she had to save Dovid, keep him alive. Give him a life. Maybe the wise thing would be to deliver Dovid to Ulkeh, his uncle, who probably could provide a better life for the boy. She herself was empty, with little to give a child and surrounded by questions without answers. Would they find the ship? Were the tickets still good? What would happen in America? How could she help Yussi find someone else? Why did he pray so much? Why did she feel nothing? Questions like a flooding river filled her head, and there was no dam to stop the flow. Maybe it was good that Yussi prayed all the time. Let him pray for all of them. So ridiculous. Prayers flying off to an empty heaven.

She busied herself with the small pieces of fabric, shaping floppy ears and a long tail for the stuffed dog. She tried to close her brain to all the questions. Evelyn from the Jewish charities gave them information about Antwerp, in the country of Belgium. Germany and many other countries still stood between Brody and Antwerp. Between this dismal warehouse and the even more frightening ship. The ocean was completely beyond her imagination. Her mother used to say you can't eat the cake before you bake it. Shayna only needed to take the next step, what-ever that was.

She sat on the bench and rested her head on the wobbly table. She felt the tension in her neck, reached back to rub the stiff muscles, so tired and no place to rest. No safe place anywhere. Her body still felt like a stranger's to her. The limbs moved, the eyes opened and closed. She ate. She slept. She talked. But the Shayna who grew up in Obodivka, beloved child of Velvel and Sima Rifkin, had disappeared.

In the morning, Shayna opened the hem of her skirt and the waist-band and pulled out the tickets, folded and stiff. She feared they might tear. Carefully she opened each one. She wondered if she should give them to Yussi to hold, to ask Yussi to show them to Evelyn at the Jewish agency, or maybe Manya should do it because she was the oldest. Who was in charge? Who decided? Manya was tired and old. Yussi's head was in the Talmud. He wanted her, but could he help her? Could he help any of them? No one to tell her what to do, what rules to follow.

But she knew she shouldn't be afraid to trust herself, not since the day she'd been embarrassed by the old rabbi's wife for answering too many question when she was only five or six. She remembered being comforted that day by her father. The *rebetsn*, an ancient woman in a stiff, black dress, taught a small class of girls every Shabbos. Shayna used to watch the skin under her chin shake as she talked. Mirtzeh sat next to her and they had to be careful not to laugh. But Shayna always knew the answers to every question, about the Garden of Eden, or Abraham and Sarah, simple bible stories that her father taught her. One Shabbos, the *rebetsn* asked who gave Joseph the coat of many colors. Shayna's hand went up before anyone else had a chance to think.

The *rebetsn* walked to the little table where Shayna sat, looked down at her and said in a loud voice, "Such a show-off. Girls should be modest. You should learn not to show off all the time. Give other children a chance."

Without letting anyone see, Mirtzeh took Shayna's hand and squeezed it hard. Shayna felt a flush on her face and tears climbing up ready to come pouring out, but she tightened every muscle on her face and looked away.

"You are perfect the way God made you," her father had said when he heard the story. "God gave you a brain to use, not to sit in your head like a tree stump."

That made no sense to Shayna then. Why a tree stump? She still did not understand exactly, but she did know that her thoughts and opinions mattered.

She refolded the tickets and placed them in the pocket of her skirt. There actually were seven tickets—three extra. She might tell Evelyn about the extras, or maybe not. Maybe they were worth money, which might help them on the journey to the ship. She'd seen rivers, but never anything like an ocean. She heard there was a sea on the shores of Odessa—her father had come from there and told her about it—but she herself had never seen such a thing. She understood that even a sea was like a tub of water compared to the ocean they would have to cross to reach America.

Shayna wanted to look presentable when she took the tickets to Evelyn. She washed as best she could. Although her hair needed a good scrub, she couldn't count on the water actually coming out from the pump in front of the building. She wondered if there was a *mikve* in Brody, if it had survived. Maybe there she could become clean. She changed to the other blouse and skirt she carried with her. Maybe Evelyn would know if there was a place in Brody where she could wash clothing.

All night, as they tried to sleep in the small bed, she scratched and could hear Manya and Dovid scratch as well. There must be fleas in the mattress. But at least there were no Cossacks.

She still carried Perl's wedding dress, carefully wrapped. Maybe she would wear it if she married, a way to ensure her family's presence. She'd designed the dress when she was only thirteen. Her mother wanted her to sew something traditional, but Shayna had a different vision. She'd sewn a delicate border of lace along the neck and far fewer ruffles than was the custom. She certainly couldn't wear that to meet Evelyn.

At least she should be clean. Neat. She wound her long braid to resemble the way Evelyn wore hers. In truth, she had so little. Thread and a needle. Her canvas bag. Everything else had burned during the pogrom. She'd rather go naked if Perl could still be alive.

Evelyn remembered her, and although she still had to wait in line, Evelyn smiled at her and Shayna felt it mattered to this woman, that she mattered, that this fancy woman might be able to help them. Evelyn's Yiddish was stiff, like it was not her native language, but Shayna was sure she was Jewish; she had a Jewish *neshome,* her soul was Jewish. Shayna was sure of that.

Evelyn studied the tickets, looked over each one and smiled. "Perfect. With these it will be easier for me to get you the visas you will need."

"A visa? Like a passport? Will you give us passports?"

"Not exactly." Evelyn shook her head, but she was smiling. "With this kind of a visa, you'll not need passports. It's an official document that allows you to travel until you reach Antwerp. It gives you permission. It is not as good as citizenship papers, or a passport, but it is a legal way to travel. I see you have seven here. Who else is traveling with you?"

"Only those you met yesterday. Four. My parents and Dovid's family were murdered. Three extra now." Shayna had tried to read the thin sheets of paper, but the tickets were written in English. She needed to learn that immediately. Maybe she could find a book in Brody. She could read the numbers, the price, but she had no idea about the exchange rate. "Is there a problem?"

"There's no name on them. Anyone could use these tickets." Evelyn brought one closer to her eyes and studied the small print. "I see you still have several months to reach Antwerp. Did you know that?"

"My brother wrote the information but…" Shayna's eyes drifted around the room, filled with people of all ages, but all with the same desperate look in their eyes. "I forgot what he wrote." The last months had disappeared in sorrow. They would have to hurry.

Evelyn stacked four tickets together, made the edges all meet squarely and then folded her hands together on top of them. "These are the tickets you'll need." She pointed to the ones she'd placed on the side. "Do you know anyone who might need them?" Evelyn's voice was casual, but Shayna could tell her answer was important.

She wasn't sure about the right answer, so she told the truth.

"No one. No one left."

"The tickets your brother sent to you are valuable. Hide them. Keep them safe." She slid four tickets into an envelope and handed it to Shayna. "Guard them carefully. Don't show them to anyone else until you reach the ship."

"What about the others?" Shayna asked.

"They're valuable. If you wanted to sell them here, I could help you." Evelyn opened a drawer and brought out a chart with many numbers. Evelyn explained the chart to her, explained about exchanging money, about inflation since the end of the war. Although Shayna could read and write in three languages, she did not understand exchanging money or inflation. Evelyn asked her questions about their resources.

"How much money do you have? How much does your fiancé have? How much will you all need to get to Antwerp? To America?"

Shayna wore a gentle smile to cover her shame, her confusion and ignorance. She nodded her head slowly, giving an impression of thoughtfulness, as if she understood.

Evelyn continued, "Each of you will need twenty-five American dollars to enter America. Will your brother pay for you? For your nephew? For your fiancé and his mother? Does he have enough money for all of you?"

Shayna wished she knew the answers. Maybe Yussi was right. Maybe they should marry, and maybe he should handle these decisions, decisions about money. Who would be in charge when they married—if they ever married? Her own mother always managed the money. Her father never touched it. A scholar, a teacher. All their family money had come from her mother's sewing, or the little left by her grandfather. At the least, she must talk to Yussi and Manya about these matters. Maybe they had money. Maybe they would need the money from the tickets. With this thing called inflation, maybe it made more sense to sell the tickets near the ship. But she knew she would not allow them to decide for her.

She thanked Evelyn, reached for the extras, and said she would be back. She didn't go directly back to their room but instead sat on a wrought-iron bench that looked across what must have once been a city square, a jumble of buildings surrounding it, some with solid walls and windows and others only empty shells. Grass grew between cracks in the bricks that once must have neatly filled the square. Indifferent to the war, it grew nourished by the sun and rain in its own familiar soil.

Chapter 12

She couldn't hear over the clatter of the train wheels—a loud, steady whoosh, and then a loud clang—making conversation almost impossible. Two days had passed since they boarded the train at a crossroads, a three day walk from Brody. They used some of the money earned from the sale of the extra tickets to hire a guide. Although the guide stayed drunk during the trek, he did manage to get them to a train going west. There'd been no stops, no place to buy fresh food, no milk for Dovid.

Evelyn told Shayna once they boarded the train, the Germans wouldn't allow refugees off the train as they passed through that country. The government restricted immigration and feared hordes of refugees begging on their streets. With the visas Evelyn arranged, they could get on a train, but they could get off only after they reached Belgium. Evelyn gave her a little book of English expressions. The Russian-English guidebook made little sense to Shayna. First she had to learn the alphabet, which was in the front of the book, but she would need a teacher. Manya also wanted to learn. Yussi said he knew already what he needed to know, the holy language of the Torah and the Talmud, the language God understood. And he knew Yiddish, Hebrew, Ukrainian, and Russian. Shayna didn't argue with him. She understood Yussi held tightly to what was familiar to him, but she knew by the time they reached New York, Yussi would be hungry to learn the new language.

He sat with several yeshive students, away from Shayna, his mother, and Dovid. Their singsong voices carried through the train car as they recited Talmudic passages and discussed them. Strangely, there were no actual *landslayt* in this railway car, but she'd seen the Rosenblatts from Obodivka in Brody and thought they would be on the train. A friendly face, maybe a story about a shared acquaintance, maybe some information about Mirtzeh—something to connect her with the world that had disappeared behind her. As if it had never been. Most of the people crowded onto the train were Jews, survivors of pogroms or survivors of poverty and oppression. There were others; she'd seen them on the train platform, Ukrainians with their beads and embroidered dresses. All seeking a better life in America.

They could not escape the smell from the toilets that filled the car. No one cleaned them. Shayna waited as long as she could before she went there. Any day she expected the curse to arrive. Without rags, how could she manage? She lost track of the time, the number of days since her last cycle. She thought maybe the rape might have stopped the flow of blood. She couldn't stop thinking about what she would do if the blood came and she had no way to manage it. Manya might know, but embarrassment stopped Shayna from asking.

The smell from the toilets mingled with the smell of unwashed bodies and the garbage piled in the corner. The waste can overflowed. The official from the train promised they would stop soon, and although they could not disembark, the toilets would be cleaned, the garbage taken away. They would be able to buy food. But the smells circled around her; she felt them cling to her body. And since the attack, the image of the bald man's sweat-covered face hovered around her. She swallowed the bile that rose in her throat, closed her eyes, and waited for it to pass. Dovid slept now, cuddled by Manya's warmth. He slept through Manya's snores, the babble on the train, the clacking of the wheels.

Shayna wanted to take down her hair, brush it through or, even better, wash it and let it dry by a warm stove. She imagined her mother's strong fingers massaging her scalp. She'd sing to her, the unforgettable scent of her mother, and Perl at the other end of the tub, waiting for her turn. Shayna could almost feel the sharp sting of the hard bristles as her mother worked on the snarls, then brushed her long curly hair, the pull against her scalp as she braided her hair each week in preparation for Shabbos.

She distracted herself with thoughts of Evelyn's dress, the one she wore the third time Shayna met with her. A shade of gray that she had never seen, the gray of a bird's feather—alive, not the dead gray of ashes. She yearned to touch it, to feel the fabric to test if it was a soft as it seemed to be, not heavy and stiff like the wools she knew. But she didn't think it was wool. She'd never seen anything like it, had no name for it. The dress had no sleeves, and Evelyn wore a crisp ivory blouse underneath, so the sleeves of the blouse showed. She imagined herself sketching out a pattern and sewing it.

A shriek jarred her from her thoughts. Not a human shriek, she thought, then realized it was the train. As it slowed for the first time, she leaned over Manya and Dovid, still asleep, to look out of the window and saw many other trains. Beyond the trains she could see very tall buildings, taller than she had ever imagined. She had no idea where they were. She heard honking noises and saw scores of automobiles. She'd seen a few in Brody but was stunned by the numbers and variety stopped in a long line, apparently waiting for another train to pass.

They were someplace in Germany, not allowed to disembark, nor could they open the windows. Some fresh air came into the compartment when soldiers or police officers, she didn't know which, entered and walked through the crowded car without talking, inspecting each passenger from head to toe. Dovid and Manya awoke. Shayna took Dovid's hand and squeezed it tight. Directing her eyes downward, she held her breath until the officers passed. They were followed by a thin man in a pinstriped suit with small glasses perched on his nose.

"*Mach shnell*," the man snapped and pointed at the pile of garbage in the corner. He motioned to a woman, dressed in gray with a heavy scarf covering her head who was already on her knees cleaning the toilet room.

"Fresh bread, hardboiled eggs, cheese, salami, drinks!" shouted women with baskets of food. They spoke in German so similar to Yiddish that Shayna had no difficulty understanding.

By the time one reached the bench where Shayna sat with Manya and Dovid, Yussi had joined them. He pointed to the salami and asked if it was kosher.

The woman laughed as if Yussi had told a very funny joke. The woman refused their Russian kopecks. Evelyn was right. All of those coins were worthless to them now. She had the money Evelyn exchanged for them and tried to bargain for better prices, but the woman laughed and started to move on through the train car. Shayna worried they might starve before they reached America. They bought only bread, cheese, a few hardboiled eggs, and a herring. And one apple because it was dear but big enough for all of them to have a good taste.

The peddlers had salamis with them as well, which some of the other Jewish refugees bought. She could smell the spice, the fat, and almost taste the salty meat. Yussi shook his head when Shayna reached toward one.

"Just for Dovid," she said. Dovid needed meat.

"He doesn't need to eat *treyf*." Yussi rumpled Dovid's hair. "Right, Dovid, you don't want to eat *treyf*, do you?"

Shayna was sure Dovid, at four years old, didn't know the difference between *treyf* and kosher, but she had no energy to argue with Yussi.

Dovid was already eating some fresh bread and cheese and looked satisfied.

Yussi leaned over them to see out of the window. "This is Berlin," he said. "One of the men davening in the front, Moshe Lebowitz, from Kiev, told me he has a cousin here. He'd get off the train in a minute, he said, and find him if he could get off. Thousands of Jewish people live here. Maybe more. It's a much better life than in Russia."

"He can't go to his cousin?" Manya shook her head. "Why not? Who cares?"

"They don't want any more Jewish refugees from Russia here. People without papers. Without money. Moshe knows an uncle that got smuggled across the border, but the army controls the trains. That's why they won't let us off the train."

Yussi continued to lean over them as he looked out at Berlin. Shayna felt trapped by his body even though he didn't touch her. Between Manya and Dovid, she could scarcely move on the bench. "I need to get off the train for a few minutes. I need to walk. I want to see the sky. To breathe real air."

"They could put you in jail," Manya said.

"They wouldn't let me visit you. Stay here. Soon we will be in Antwerp." Yussi smiled at Shayna, a wonderful familiar smile. She missed that smile. It had been many days since she had smiled, and many days since she'd even looked at him. Really looked.

It seemed like only moments before the soldiers disappeared. The thin man in the striped suit must have left the train along with the cleaning women and the food sellers. She heard a loud bang when the door slid shut. The noisy click clack of the wheels returned and drowned out Yussi's voice. The engine gained strength as it rolled out of the station. Shayna twisted herself so she could take a last look at the tall buildings, the automobiles, the vastness of this city, Berlin, where Yussi said Jews also lived.

She wanted to sit by Yussi, but each day since the attack the distance between them grew. Could she ever regain the tenderness, the closeness she once felt with him?

Shayna didn't know how long they would have to stay on this train, how many more days. Her body ached from the hard wooden seats, her mind ached from the noise, the smells, although it was better now that the trash had been cleaned. She knew it wouldn't take long before it would stink again. She noticed as soon as the cleaning people left a long line grew outside of the toilet. Strange men went into the toilet room as well as strange women. Modesty was impossible. The rules about men and women, about *treyf,* about Shabbos. She couldn't even remember if it was Monday or Tuesday—if they were waiting for Shabbos or if it had been Shabbos. Would God forgive them their infractions?

She tried to picture America, to picture where she would live. Her brother, Ulkeh, had a wife now and children. She remembered him as someone tall, but she had been a child. She couldn't remember if his eyes were blue like hers or dark brown like the rest of the family. She remembered he used to *daven* with their father. They'd go to the shul together every morning for prayer. She wondered if God went to America too. He came and went in the shtetl; maybe He came and went all over the world. Maybe she could eat *treyf* when she thought God was still in Russia. Stupid thoughts, she knew better. Probably there was no God to worry about what she ate.

The sweet, cool juice of the apple filled her mouth and she forgot about God, forgot about worrying. The bread was lighter than she was familiar with, lighter and without taste. The cheese was cheese. So far, she'd had no meat, eaten no *treyf*, but her skirt hung loosely from her hips. She needed more food; they all did.

"Don't play with him." Manya's loud whisper drew Shayna out of her worries. Manya pulled Dovid back onto the seat from down the aisle where he played.

"What's the matter?" Shayna leaned out to the aisle and saw another little boy run toward the other end of the train car.

Dovid's face scrunched up until his scream filled the car, then another scream.

"What happened?" Shayna demanded.

Dovid struggled to escape from Manya who held him by the arm.

"Dovid, listen to me," Manya said. "That boy was sick. You can't play with him."

"What are you talking about?" Shayna asked as she dried Dovid's tears and lifted him to her lap.

"Did you see his eye?"

"No. Who?"

"He came from the back of the train car and wanted Dovid to go play with him."

"Why didn't you let him?" Shayna lowered her voice, as her eyes glanced around them. People were listening. Everyone heard everything. After three days, they recognized each other's snores.

"His eye."

"What about his eye?"

"You didn't see?"

"No. I told you I just saw his back."

Dovid's screams had subsided to sobs now. Shayna reached into her pocket for a small piece of apple she'd saved. "*Es, tatele.*"

"His eye, only one eye, was red, runny. Maybe it's the eye sickness. They stop everyone with the eye sickness from coming into America. They send them back from Ellis Island. Didn't you know?"

Shayna watched Manya's eyes, surrounded by dark circles, slowly fill with tears.

"Shayna." Manya leaned in closer. "They would send us back on a ship. Where would we go? What would happen to us?"

"Manya, we are in God's hands. He will protect us, help us. He's kept us alive. For a reason. You must be calm." She repeated these words by rote, nodding her head, even smiling. She looked across the car and saw Yussi's head inclined in conversation with the other scholars. This was his mother, not hers. His problem, not hers. But she knew when they married, all of them might depend on her. Yussi, Dovid, and Manya too. How would they live? Would her brother take them all in, support them? Would he respect Yussi, let him continue to study Torah?

Shayna searched her mind for peace, for a spot to rest. She thought of her father's kindness, of Yankel and his quiet confidence. She could find that in herself. Inside Shayna's mind her own screams were louder than Dovid's had been, but there was no one for her to cry to. Only herself. At least until she met Ulkeh. Maybe an older brother could be like a father. Useless to pray for that.

Shayna reminded Manya of the scarf for Yussi she'd begun at Yankel's house. "Maybe time to knit. Yussi may need it on the ship." From her own bag, she pulled the yarn for Dovid's scarf. She tried to breathe through her mouth, to control the smell from the toilet that already filled the car. Soon she would have to find the courage to enter the toilet room herself.

Chapter 13

Antwerp, Belgium, August 1919

"Thirty minutes until Antwerp. Thirty minutes until Antwerp."

"Finally we'll be rid of this *farkakte* train," Manya muttered as she began to gather her belongings.

Shayna organized her things and Dovid's. Yussi stood near their bench with his suitcase. The countryside they passed through all day reminded her of the land around Obodivka. Farms. Trees. Grass. Now brick buildings replaced the open land, more and more buildings, bigger and bigger as the train slowed. She looked around the compartment where they'd spent so many days and nights. Everyone stood clutching their bags; a combination of fear and excitement ran through the car. Shayna noticed tags hanging around the neck of each person and then she remembered Evelyn's instruction.

"*Oy vey*. We almost forgot the signs we're supposed to wear." She reached through her canvas bag to the tags Evelyn prepared for them. Written in heavy dark letters were the words, S.S. Finland. The name of the ship that would take them to America.

"Don't forget," Evelyn had said. "It maybe the most important thing you have to do. Someone will come to the train station to find you and take you to a place where you will stay until the ship sails. Hang these tags around your necks. Make sure you take all your bundles with you." Evelyn explained.

Antwerp in the country of Belgium. Both new names for Shayna. New words, new names, new ideas filled her mind. Dovid looked pale and thin. Manya quiet. Yussi's beard looked more like a beard and his *peyes* reached along the edge of his ears. He looked a little more like himself. He smelled now, as they all did. Evelyn promised there would be a place to bathe, to sleep, and to eat until it was time to get on the ship. Evelyn didn't know when the ship would leave or how much time they would have to wait.

Shayna tried to read the tags people wore to discover if anyone would be on their ship. She knew the Yaroslavskys, a car away from them, would sail on the same ship. She wondered who else. She struggled with the English alphabet and couldn't make out the names of other ships.

They all fell backward when the train stopped suddenly. She lifted Dovid to stand on the bench as soon as they regained their balance. People shoved against them, pushed their bags aside. Yussi stood to shield them but was caught in the crowd and shoved along to the door before they could follow him. Like animals, Shayna thought.

She felt tears fill her eyes as she finally stood outside of the train, Dovid holding tightly to her hand. Manya searched the crowded platform for Yussi until she saw him waving in their direction. They followed the other people who disembarked at the same time. Tired, smelly people with tags around their necks. Fancy people stared at them as they walked through the station. Shayna raised her chin rather than let anyone see the shame that surrounded her. No one would know what happened to her.

They joined the Yaroslavskys, also from Podalia province in the Ukraine. Not exactly from the same village, but close. A mother with four daughters and an old man, maybe her father. Also wearing S.S. Finland tags were two brothers from Poland, young men—barely men. Shayna thought they probably didn't shave yet. Their *peyes* and *tsitses,* and *yarmulkes,* like Yussi's, marked them as observant Jews. Would they be safe in Antwerp?

They stood together with the other S.S. Finland passengers at the edge of the station. They all waited. And waited. Manya held Dovid's hand. Would not let go. He wanted to run and inspect the train station, a miracle for him. For all of them. There were more people around them than Shayna had seen in her whole life. Women in silk dresses and high-heeled shoes. She could see their ankles. Some men wore work clothes, familiar to her, but others had top hats, like pictures in books she had seen. She didn't know what language they spoke. She understood nothing, nor did she recognize the words on signs all over the station.

Yussi wanted to go to the food wagons they saw parked across the thoroughfare. They could see fresh fruit, apples, and oranges. They smelled bread, but Shayna insisted he wait. What if the man from the S.S. Finland came and he wasn't there? Maybe they would leave without him. Now Dovid wanted a toilet, but she had no idea where to take him. She and Manya stood behind him while he peed against the outside wall. The Yaroslavsky family had seen them. What did it matter now?

Shayna didn't know how long they had been traveling. The pogrom had happened in May, in the spring, and now she could tell by the length of the days that it was the middle of the summer. So at least two months, maybe three. She couldn't exactly remember. In her memory she saw the pogrom, the burial, and Perl's house. She remembered walking and walking. But when she closed her eyes, she often could only see the bald man, his mouth open as he breathed heavily over her, his breath the smell of alcohol. "With time," Manya told her. "With time you will forget." Maybe a lifetime it would take to forget.

She'd heard nightmare stories about the ships also. They shoved all the poor people, third class, Evelyn called it, together in the bottom where it was damp, no windows, and the food, what little they gave them, was said to be disgusting. So many stories and no way to know what was true. Maggots in the soup, the soup was only water with a few vegetables, smelled like garbage. Evelyn told her to buy what they could in Antwerp before they left. Save money so you have money for food for the trip. Save money to get into America.

"*Borukh-Habo*," they heard a man's voice coming toward them. "Welcome, welcome. I found you." A young man, with a well-trimmed beard, without a yarmulke, dressed in a suit that must have belonged to someone else, someone much larger many years before, reached them and held up a sign that read S.S. Finland. He bowed politely and said, "My name is Stefan. I work with Jewish charitable organizations. Yes, the same people that helped you in Brody. I will help you get settled."

Shayna recognized that he spoke Yiddish, but he spoke with an accent that made it difficult to understand all his words.

"Come, follow me." He looked around. "How many are you?"

He counted in a language she didn't recognize, looked around and said in Yiddish, "Twelve all together. Good. Streets are crowded. Stay close to me."

They followed him around the station and through a dim tunnel to a large opening into the bright light of a summer's day. Overhead the sky was glorious to Shayna, the color of light delphiniums back home. The hot sun leaned to what must be the west. They walked in that direction, first crossing a large thoroughfare.

Cars came toward them as they ran after Stefan, who dodged between the oncoming cars. Shayna's suitcase banged against her leg as she ran, her scarf slid from her head. She'd grabbed Dovid's hand, but he struggled to escape and run fast. It had been so many days, weeks since the little boy had been able to run, to move, to be a child. And he was ready to go.

It felt good to walk, even to rush, to be in motion after days cooped up on the train. Stefan raced along the streets, indifferent to the people behind him struggling with their suitcases and bundles. The Yaroslavsky girls marched right along, stayed close to the young man, but the old grandfather fell behind, as did Dovid gradually. His short legs could not maintain the pace. Yussi reached down, scooped him up, and they hurried along.

Smoke from the back of the cars on the street increased the discomfort Shayna felt. They passed a huge building with statues behind big glass windows. Statues of women dressed in elegant gowns and fancy dresses. Shayna slowed to get a better look. The skirts came up almost to the calves and they wore very high-heeled shoes. One particular dress caught her eye, but Stefan yelled at her to hurry and she left with the image of a mauve dress with a soft collar that drifted down across the bosom.

A rotten-fish smell permeated the streets, adding to Shayna's discomfort. The smell from many cars of all sizes, streetcars overflowing with people, trucks filled with crates forced her to cover her nose as she walked. They followed Stefan down narrow streets lined with small shops. Through their grimy windows Shayna could see merchandise she'd never seen before, green shiny statues of a fat man, fans that looked to be made of paper, odd wooden statues of animals or people, she couldn't tell which. In the distance she began to see smoke rising, not the smoke of fire, but what she later learned was smoke from steamships in the harbor.

A quick turn into a broader street brought dozens of ships into view; some looked larger than a village. They floated on a wide river alongside boats of all descriptions. Maybe the S.S. Finland was among them. The port. A gathering place. A gate to a new world. They were like ants crawling on the face of the Earth. Refugees. Exiles. Unrecognized and unknown in the midst of thousands of people.

Stefan stopped in front of a large building. He read the sign to them: "Red Star Line. This is the company that owns the S.S. Finland."

"This is a boarding house for passengers waiting to board Red Star Line ships to New York, to Brazil, to Cuba, to many ports around the world. Housing is provided for passengers at a very small fee. The foundation pays it. Stay close to the building. Safer. People in Antwerp don't want refugees roaming the streets. My job was to get you here. They hire me because I speak Yiddish. I bring the Polish people here too and the Russians. Somebody else brings the Turks. There are many people who bring other refugees from the train station to the ships."

They were met at the entrance to the building by a very tall man; maybe he only looked very tall because he stood at the top of a flight of stairs that led to the building.

Shayna noticed his shoes first: shiny like black glass. His suit was also black and he wore spectacles.

"Mr. Andriessen is in charge of this building. He will take care of you," Stefan said and hurried back down the stairs.

Finally they got to lower their bags to the floor. Shayna's shoulders ached. Mr. Andriessen stared at them, then said simply, "Tickets," and held up a sample. He spoke in German, which resembled Yiddish, as he told them to follow him to an office. Stacks of papers covered every surface in the small room. Again, he said, "Tickets." And when they hesitated he added, "No, I won't keep them. I just need to check off your names."

"When will the ship come?" Manya asked. "When can we leave for America?"

"I don't know," he answered. He clearly understood Manya's Yiddish. "The ship is docked for repairs in Germany. In the meantime, every family gets a room. You will get breakfast here and another meal late in the day. In case you are Jewish, you should know the food is not kosher. There is a market not far. There is no place to cook but you can get water at the pump in the back. One floor up there are rooms for families, and when I check your name I will give you your room number." He smiled and again reached for their tickets.

Shayna could tell he thought they were a family: husband, wife, mother or mother-in-law, and child. Yussi looked at Shayna, as did Manya. Someone should say something.

He took Yussi's ticket first and checked his name off one of the sheets of paper. "Your family will use room two hundred ten." He checked off Manya's ticket and then reached for Shayna's.

"You have a different name. Is this your wife?" he asked Yussi. "Your child?"

Yussi shook his head.

Shayna heard the Yaroslavsky's began to whisper.

"We don't allow such things here," Mr. Andriessen said.

Yussi's face turned red. He opened his mouth to explain, but the man said, "The women can stay in room two hundred ten. You can find a cot with the other bachelors."

"I didn't plan to stay there," Yussi said.

"You acted like you did."

Again Yussi thought to explain, but he let it go.

Mr. Andriessen checked off Dovid's ticket and they left the office together.

"Take your bags upstairs then come down. We must talk." Yussi spoke to Shayna like she was a small child, as if she had done something wrong.

Upstairs they found laundry hanging across the halls and children yelling and running around, speaking languages they did not recognize. Eventually they found their room. One large bed, a table, and four chairs crowded into a small space. A light bulb hung from the ceiling. The window that looked over the street did not open. The room was hot, stuffy. Shayna knew what Yussi thought must be discussed. Marriage. He wouldn't let it go. They were still engaged, promised to each other. She owed him respect.

A prayer entered Yussi's thoughts as he leaned against the outside wall of the boarding house waiting for Shayna—a bedtime prayer he'd learned as a child to seek protection during sleep. The melody hummed along in his mind while the sun still hung in the sky, reaching for the horizon on the west. Not bedtime, but yet a time for protection. A time to reach to God for shelter, for refuge.

B'sham Hashem, In the name of Adonai, the god of Israel, May the angel Michael be at my right, and the angel Gabriel be at my left, and in front of me the angel Uriel, and behind me the angel Raphael, and above my head the Sh'khinah, the divine spirit.

It seemed strange that he would seek God's messengers now, three months after the pogrom, when they were safe. No Cossacks. No marauding renegades. He should feel secure with a roof over his head, food to eat, tickets to America, and a place out of the storms.

Still he felt compelled to call the angels to protect him. He closed his eyes and wrapped himself in the comfort of the angels. Brought them forward in his thoughts. In the background he could hear voices of other men, others who came outside with their cigarettes and their conversations. He heard Russian, German, and even Yiddish, but when he opened his eyes he couldn't determine who the Jews were. No *tsitses* visible. No long beards, or *peyes*. No yarmulkes, although many wore hats. He wondered if his soul was safe here among so many strangers.

He lit a cigarette, inhaled, and let the smoke out slowly. Watched it float into the air until the edges faded and nothing remained.

If he walked around and stood closer to each group, he could discover who spoke Yiddish and he would find a place to be. Never before was this a question in his mind. He always knew where he belonged, knew his future as much as God let any man know. Foolish. No one knew. No man who walked the face of the Earth knew.

For years he imagined he would walk into the future with Shayna by his side and over time, children would join them on their journey. Now the man in the office talked to him like he was a *paskudnyak*, a lowlife, a rotten vulgar man who would take advantage of Shayna. Use her. Disrespect her. But what was Yussi really worth? Again he saw Shayna as she lay strewn across the ground, blood over bare legs and across her chest. Was the rapist made in God's image too? Yussi stopped these thoughts. They brought him nothing. No *takhlis*, no value.

Soon he would find the nearest shul. They might be in Antwerp for many weeks. Maybe he could find some work, some way to make some money. They'd need money to leave Ellis Island, money to make a home in America. His savings were almost gone and he did not want to depend on the little that Shayna had or, worse yet, charity from her brother in New York.

But first he had to talk with Shayna and convince her it was time to marry. Her head was full of crazy ideas, as if the attack was her fault. Or worse yet, that he could not love her because another man stole her virginity. A man should not be embarrassed by words, by truth. A man did the right thing. Soon they would marry. He needed to act like a *mensch*. For many years since his father's death he worked. Earned money. Helped his mother. He did what was expected of him. This was not a time for questioning. It was time to grow into his shoes.

She joined Yussi outside the building and they walked in silence along a crowded street until they reached a long boardwalk stretching along the water. Shayna let him take her hand, yet she wanted to slap his away. She knew that was crazy. Yussi had nothing to do with what had happened to her. The smell of fish filled the air. Again she felt bile rise in her throat. She must have eaten something along the way that disagreed with her.

Her limbs felt heavy, tired. She needed to rest, but the fresh air felt good after so many days on the train. They stopped at a bench, sat silently staring at the ships before them. Gray birds landed around them. Her father told her about the birds by the harbor in Odessa. She wondered if these were the same kind of birds: seagulls. They tottered close to her feet, not afraid of people. So much courage in such a small body; maybe stupidity and not courage.

"Here we will find a rabbi." Yussi's index finger was raised to make a point. "It's time. Before we leave for New York. You must stop making a joke of me. We must marry."

"Making a joke of you?"

"We are engaged and yet you will not marry me. What am I? Garbage that you throw away?"

Shayna concentrated on watching one of the seagulls as it lifted its wings, hopped once or twice, and flew away.

"Are you listening to me?"

She nodded. "I'm listening. How can you talk to me this way after what happened to me?

"I don't care about that. We are engaged, we made promises before God and the congregation. You will be my bride. I am nothing like the *mamzer* that attacked you. Shayna, you know me. I will be gentle with you."

Everything he said made sense, but it didn't make sense that she felt the insides of her body pull away from her skin. She needed to rest. She wanted to run but had nowhere to go. She glimpsed another seagull out of the corner of her eye. It sailed off the railing, free from Earth. She could barely lift herself from the bench. Her heart heavy.

Shayna remembered her mother on the day of their engagement. When she closed her eyes she could almost smell the *tagelakh*, the sponge cake, the blackberry wine. Her mother's smile of pride that her daughter would marry such a wise young man. Not only a scholar, but one who could also make a living as a carpenter. Ulkeh would expect them to be married. He knew they were engaged. What would he say that they had traveled all this way and not be married? If there was a chicken for Shabbos, her mother made it, if there was fish, her mother made it. If there were only turnips, she cooked them. Her mother did not look backward or forward, only accepted what came. How did her mother do that? Never complained or whined about anything. She did what she had to do. Shayna's mind whirled.

Good? Bad? It didn't matter. She was betrothed before God and her parents. Although she doubted God paid attention, her parents had. She didn't know if she would be cooking turnips or a chicken, only that marrying Yussi was inevitable for her.

Shayna took his hand. "Before we sail, we'll marry. You'll find a rabbi?"

Chapter 14

"Better than a rabbi. I found a *rebetsn*."

"A *rebetsn*?"

Yussi nodded, his face flushed with excitement. "Yes, the rabbi's wife. She wants to make the wedding for us. There will be a *klezmer* band."

Shayna looked up from the floor where she played with Dovid. He'd found a small ball outside and they rolled it back and forth across the floor.

"Rabbi Weiss. Where I've been *davening*. Every day he talks to me. He likes having a young man who knows Torah in his shul. He talked to his wife about us and after the morning prayers, this morning, he tells me she wants to make our wedding.

"Make our wedding? Why should they do that?"

"I don't know. Don't care. It's a gift from God."

Shayna couldn't remember the last time she had seen Yussi so excited.

"She wants us to come there for dinner on Shabbos and talk with her. And we'll talk with the rabbi who will prepare a marriage contract for us."

"*Barukh Hashem*," Manya said. "See. What kindness. Always kindness. No matter what else. People are good."

Yussi and his mother began to discuss other details. Should they invite the Yaroslavskys? Would the congregation come? How much would it cost? He needed a suit.

They didn't notice that Shayna still sat on the floor with her back against the wall. She listened but couldn't make sense of all the words.

After a moment, Yussi knelt by her side, "Did you hear? Shaynaleh? The *rebetsn* will help us. The whole congregation will come."

His eyes sparkled and she saw a smile like she hadn't seen for months. There was joy on his face and she understood in a flash that she must move forward. They were promised to each other. They would marry. She would put the ugliness deep into her heart in a secret compartment and lock it up. As if she had never been violated. No matter what she felt.

She dug deep into herself and tried to find her old smile. A smile from their history. She could make it live again. "*Barukh Hashem.* It's time."

As they approached the rabbi's house, Shayna recognized the poverty that sucked the life from the Jews of Ukraine had not touched these Jews in Belgium. It was a two-story brick home, with dozens of glass windows and a wrought-iron fence surrounding it. Flowerboxes filled with violet hyacinths graced each window, and beautiful bushes lined the path to the door.

"*Gut Shabbos, Gut Shabbos,*" said woman who opened the door. "Welcome. Welcome Yussi. This must be your mother," she said, taking Manya's hand. Shayna stood back in the vestibule, unable to take her eyes away from the tall, stately woman. She wore an emerald-green silk dress with long narrow sleeves, decorated with light-green embroidery. Although there was no scarf on her head, Shayna guessed that she wore a *sheytl*, a rich auburn wig styled with elaborate curls. No one could have hair that looked so perfect.

"Shayna, meet the *rebetsn.*" Yussi said,

This was the rabbi's wife. Impossible. Such a *rebetsn* Shayna had never seen before. She pulled her eyes away from admiring the woman's dress and blushed when the *rebetsn* said, "Certainly a *shayna*, pretty as can be." She tried to keep her arm over a large stain in her blouse that no amount of scrubbing had removed. The edges of Shayna's sleeves were folded inward and stitched to hide the unraveling that happened over the months on the road.

"Call me Freide," the *rebetsn* said. "You must be very tired. Such a long journey. So brave, such courage." Then she saw Dovid peek from behind Shayna's skirt, "And who is this?"

"My nephew Dovid." Shayna tried to bring him forward, but he stayed near her back and clung to her skirt.

"Poor thing. So thin. Come eat." The *rebetsn* reached for Shayna's hand. Her fingers were soft, smooth, and delicate. Hands that Shayna knew had never scrubbed clothes or harvested vegetables. Never washed dishes.

Freide led them into her home, where the rabbi waited to greet them. Dovid was the only child, so Shayna stood against a wall and held his hand while Yussi talked to men he knew from the shul.

Shayna overheard two women talking. "A *mitzvah*," one said. "Such a good deed. The *rebetsn* is always pulling refugees off the streets. We donate money whenever we can to help, but who wants them with their fleas in the house?" Their conversation stopped when they realized Shayna may have heard. If they didn't want her to hear, why did they speak Yiddish?

She knew her face turned red. She felt the heat as it spread across her cheeks. Maybe they wore silk dresses, but they were no different than the worst *yentes* in the shtetl. The more withered their souls, the bigger their mouths, her mother had taught her. She wanted to approach them and tell them she had no fleas, that she was educated, that her father was a learned man. But what if she did have fleas? What if she had no education or was a *mamzer* and had no father? When the Cossacks came, they didn't care. Someday they might come for these women as well. Even in Belgium. In a moment they too might be driven from their homes, murdered in the streets.

Shayna hoped the *rebetsn*, unlike her friends, was truly compassionate. She was ashamed to be the one receiving *tsedoke*. She preferred to give charity. She would ignore them and keep her head high.

First the *rebetsn* lit the Shabbos candles. Through this ancient tradition, she invited peace, warmth, and light into their home. Shayna closed her eyes, locked her heart so it couldn't break open the memories that swept over her. She saw her mother gently moving her hands over the

Shabbos candles, as she welcomed the Sabbath, every Shabbos of Shayna's life until her mother's death.

The glow of the candles reflected off the crystal goblets. The dishes so thin, almost transparent, she wanted to lift her plate from the table and test it. Her father told her of wealth in Odessa where the dishes weighed not much more than a feather. The rabbi and *rebetsn* owned such plates, *fleyshek*, dishes for meat meals. Shayna wondered if they had the same kind of plates for dairy meals. Wallpaper with deep purple flowers decorated the walls in the dining room. The wooden floors were shiny like glass. Yussi sat with the men gathered around the rabbi, Shayna and Dovid at the women's end of the table. When the men finished the Shabbos blessings and a maid appeared carrying steaming bowls of chicken soup with *kneydlakh*, the rich aroma filled the room, the smell of Shabbos, at once familiar to Shayna and yet alien at this table so far from her roots.

At first she heard only the slurping of soup, but gradually as the platters of food continued to arrive, the men's voices got louder. She could hear Yussi tell the other men about the pogroms, about the fear, the violence, and their helplessness. Shayna focused on Dovid, helped him cut the chicken into small pieces. She didn't want to hear stories about death and destruction or about the politics of the Jews in Russia. She didn't want their pity. She knew there was no reason she should feel shame, yet she did. She expected to feel shame about the attack on her, about which they knew nothing. But oddly she also felt shame for failing to protect her parents, her sister, even baby Sarah. A victim. Helpless. Needy. At the same time she was grateful for all the help they had received. Shame and gratitude struggled in her mind. She prayed for a time when she wouldn't need anyone's help. When she would be strong. And when she would be safe.

After the closing prayers, the *rebetsn* took Shayna into a sitting room to discuss the wedding. The *rebetsn* indicated Shayna should sit on a small sofa and she immediately sat next to her and took Shayna's hand.

"It's always an honor to help those less fortunate," she said. Shayna felt like a worm on a hook: stuck. The *rebetsn* wanted Shayna to be weak, so she could be important, so she could rescue her. The food she'd eaten soured in her stomach.

As they discussed the date for the wedding, Freide asked about Shayna's cycle. Shayna didn't know what to say. She couldn't remember the last cycle. Must have been before the pogrom because there had been no blood since they left Obodivka. Maybe the rape and the agony had stopped it. She'd heard of such things before but could not ask, nor could she mention a monstrous thought that flitted in and out of her mind. "Before two weeks," she lied.

"Did your mother ever talk to you about congress? About how babies are made?"

Shayna wanted to run from the room but nodded instead. Perl had told her some things. Told her it was pleasure to have sexual relations with her husband. Whenever she thought about it now, she saw Perl stretched out on her bed. Worse yet, she felt the stabbing pain of the attack.

Freide went on. "Yussi, such a *mensch*. He'll know what to do. To help you. Don't be afraid."

By the time of the wedding, Shayna managed to sew new pants and a jacket for Dovid, which he proudly wore. But he would not abandon his cap, nor the carved dog, his gift from Yankel that he kept with him, hidden in his pocket. He also wanted to carry the stuffed dog that Shayna had made for him, but Manya drew the line.

"You need to be a big boy now. You will carry the ring. After the ceremony, if you still want, you can have the dog. I'll keep it safe for you."

Manya also insisted that Shayna wear the wedding dress she had designed and sewn for Perl. Before they left the shtetl, Shayna had packed the dress carefully, in the hope that someday she herself might wear it, but now she was indifferent to what she wore. Shayna knew she should feel blessed, but instead she felt cursed.

Before the ceremony, the *rebetsn* came to wish her well and was stunned by Shayna's gown. "Where did you get this dress?" Freide walked around Shayna, inspecting it.

"I designed it for my sister's wedding. My mother helped me sew it."

"Impossible. Impossible." The *rebetsn* clicked her tongue against her teeth. "That's a couture gown. I'd swear to it."

"Couture?"

"The highest fashion. Dresses worn by queens and princesses all over Europe. The fabric, it's not so fancy, but the style. Chic. Very chic. Who taught you to think of such a gown?"

"My mother. Mostly she made alterations, skirts, blouses, but she had been to Odessa and bought magazines with pictures of clothes. Sometimes I saw such picture magazines in the market. Sometimes when someone had silk, or cashmere, Mamme became a genius."

"I can't believe my good luck. I heard there's at least a month before your ship is repaired. You'll sew for me, won't you? I have silk from China. I'm thrilled. A new seamstress. A brilliant designer. And from the Ukraine. Who knew Jews from the shtetl had such talent? Other women from the congregation will be jealous. Maybe you'll make them a few things. They'll pay you. Charge them a lot. I'll arrange everything.'

"I have no sewing machine."

"My maid has a machine. So you'll have a machine to use."

"My honor," Shayna said to Freide's retreating back. She watched as the *rebetsn* rushed around to tell other women of Shayna's skill. Complimented and insulted in the same breath. Of all things to thrill her about her wedding, she never expected to find work, to be able to design and sew elegant dresses and to use rich materials, silk from China. Maybe she would make enough money to buy fabrics to make warm clothes for Dovid and for Yussi.

"Your mother would be so proud of you. You look beautiful. They are here in spirit. I know it. I feel it," Manya whispered to her as she walked Shayna to the bridal canopy where Yussi already stood. Shayna smiled, a smile that reached deep into her eyes, when Yussi turned to her. She could not ignore the joy in his eyes. Let it be catching, she thought.

The Belgian rabbi began his sermon, speaking for their benefit in a combination of Yiddish and Hebrew, instead of his native Dutch. Shayna, confused by his unusual accent and feeling weak, was unable to clearly follow his sermon. Both she and Yussi had followed tradition and fasted all day before the ceremony, which likely contributed to her discomfort.

The rabbi talked about marriage according to Maimonides, a Jewish scholar from hundreds of years before. "Most important," he said, "the wife must respect her husband, look up to him, admire him. And the husband must cherish the wife and protect her." She heard him start on *Eishes Khayil,* telling her she must be a woman of valor, responsible for creating the Jewish home. She hoped he would stop talking soon.

Wishful thinking. She couldn't concentrate on the rabbi's words. She felt sweat on her face but a chill through her body. She tried to look interested, keep her back straight, and prayed he would finish soon.

Finally, the rabbi finished his sermon and talked about the marriage contract, written in Hebrew, which they would sign after the service, making her commitment before God to Yussi. Her name would become Edelman, no longer a Rifkin. The rabbi motioned for her to circle Yussi seven times. She knew there must be a reason, but she couldn't remember. It was expected. Then Yussi broke a glass in memory of the destruction of the second Temple in Jerusalem. The rabbi yelled, *Mazel-tov.* Everyone yelled *Mazel-tov* and it was over. Married.

The *rebetsn* started to clap and sing, *"Tate Mame Makht Mir khasene."* Strange timing Shayna thought at a wedding, a song about asking your parents to arrange a wedding. They'd sung it in their shtetl at every wedding and now here in this strange city, they also sang it. Everyone sang with the *rebetsn* as they walked to the tables filled with food in another room.

"You look pale," Manya said. "Sit for a few minutes. I'll go find Yussi."

To Shayna the honey sweet smell of the *tagelakh* filled the room. Hard to breathe. She swallowed hard as she felt bile rise in her throat.

I'll just sit for a minute, she thought, but before she could she felt a heaving in her belly. She rushed out to the yard in the back of the shul where she hid behind a large tree and vomited. Lately smells made her sick. Shayna was convinced that from the moment she saw her sister's violated body, the smell of blood clung to her insides and made everything else disgusting. As if a poison entered her body and was destroying her from the inside.

She wiped the sweat from her face with the lace handkerchief the *rebetsn* had given to her. She shivered, the chills unexpected in such a warm afternoon. Shayna held on to a strong branch. She thought she might faint, something she had never done. Or maybe she had fainted after she was attacked. Maybe she was becoming insane hiding behind a tree in Belgium trying to decide if she had ever fainted.

"Shayna? Shayna? Are you outside?" Yussi's voice came closer to where she hid. She couldn't let him see her hiding, so she stepped out and pasted a smile on her clammy face.

"I couldn't find you. Everyone's asking for the bride. He noticed her pale face. "Are you sick?"

"Not really. Just too much excitement."

"There will be more excitement when we can finally be alone." She tried to match the big smile on his face. She knew Manya and Dovid would stay with the rabbi tonight. They would have privacy.

Shayna's already pale face must have whitened more because Yussi asked, "Are you nervous?" Without waiting for an answer, he said, "I am nervous too." He leaned in and kissed her lips gently and then pressed harder.

"Were you sick Shayna? I smell vomit."

"I'm sorry." She nodded. "Forgive me. I am fine now. Just too much excitement. I am fine now. I must wash my mouth."

Yussi put his arm around her shoulders and led her back to the house. "And you must eat something. Come inside. There is more food than we have seen for months."

Yussi held her hand as they walked back to the room provided by the shipping company. A cold breeze came from the harbor. She was glad they would be leaving soon, before winter came fully. People said that the winter crossing was the worst, especially with third-class tickets. Steerage they called it. Dirty. Smelly. And sometimes storms struck unexpectedly. The ships bobbed and rolled and sometimes people fell overboard.

Yussi and Shayna talked about everything except what they could not say aloud. Shayna knew the little that Perl had told her about sexual relations she must now experience. Her married sister told her she found it thrilling and fun too. It brought the husband and wife closer. It was a comfort to be held afterward. She trusted Perl and knew that in the months before the pogrom, she felt desire for Yussi. Every time he looked at her in that special way, when his eyes darkened and a slow smile spread across his face, she felt warmth between her legs, a softening in her belly. Perl explained that was desire.

Since she was attacked, she felt nothing. Did he stop looking at her? Smiling at her? She didn't know. Maybe Perl lied to protect her from the truth. Shayna thought only of the pain, the violence. The shame of violation. She could not talk to Yussi about this. Maybe it was on his mind as well. The rape. A word she could never utter aloud and barely think. She wondered if he pictured her as she must have looked spread out with her skirt raised and blood flowing between her legs, just like the image she carried of her sister Perl.

As a girl helping her mother in the shtetl, she often overheard the conversations of women as they prepared for celebrations. As soon as she learned to use a knife, she became her mother's best helper. Slice the almonds. Cut the apples. Smaller pieces. Chop the walnuts. As if it happened yesterday, she could picture her mother, in the steamy kitchen, lift her apron to wipe the sweat from her brow. She could almost hear the laughter as the women talked. The biggest wedding in the shtetl was the marriage of a young distant cousin, a girl without a dowry. A girl without hope. But a successful marriage had been arranged for her with a widower, an old man with four grown sons. He paid for everything. The *klezmer*. The wine. The special hall. He even paid for her dress and clothes for her impoverished parents.

"She's a lucky one. He'll buy her whatever she wants."

"He's so old, she'll probably have to feed him soon."

"Worse. She has to get into bed with him."

"*Oy vey*," someone said. "Poor girl. Why does he need such a young one? For babies? He already has four sons."

"To *shtup* her. If he still can. What else does that old cocker want?"

"She'll learn soon to close her eyes. It will be over soon."

Close her eyes. It will be over soon. Sentences she heard often. She wondered if her mother would have given her that advice. But in her heart she knew that the marriage of her parents, although arranged, had grown into love. She saw them at the table on Shabbos, a glow on her mother's face as she lit the candles and love flowing from her father as he admired her.

Had anyone given Yussi advice? His father died long before their engagement. Maybe the rabbi talked to him. Maybe. Most likely not. Maybe the boys told each other stories, but everything was forbidden until marriage.

She couldn't say these things, so instead she asked Yussi why the shipping company provided them with such a cheap place to live.

"They make a fortune transporting refugees. Competition. All the companies want the business so it's an extra, something special to get more travelers."

Usually men stood outside in front of the building smoking. Often Yussi spent time with them. A young local boy came by a few times every day to sell single cigarettes. But on this night, no one witnessed their return. Married now. Shayna glanced up to as they entered the building. She wasn't accustomed to seeing the glare of electric lights through the small windows at night. She missed the soft glow of the gas lights at home.

Yussi pulled the chain to turn on the light bulb in their room. Shayna stood in the bright room, saw the wine and two glasses Manya must have left, then stared at the floor. Yussi took off his jacket and poured them each a little wine. He mumbled the prayer over wine, but before he said anything more, Shayna abruptly turned, grabbed a towel, soap, tooth powder, and ran out of the room.

The women's bathroom had two stalls and one shower, which was new for Shayna. Until she came to Belgium she'd never seen a shower. Back home, only on special occasions a metal tub would be filled with water from the pump heated on the stove, but mostly they washed with a bucket of water, soap, and a washcloth. Now she could stand under water that came pouring down on her body. Sometimes there was hot water but mostly lukewarm. She'd been to the *mikve* the day before the wedding, so her hair was clean, but she needed to cleanse her mouth from the taste of vomit, to wash her face, to cool herself, to calm herself. Since the attack she felt vile, dirty, something she could not explain to anyone, especially Yussi.

Shayna forced herself to look into the cracked mirror that hung over the sink. Manya had braided her hair for the wedding and wrapped it like a crown on her head. Her blue eyes looked pale and bigger than ever, staring out from a face she scarcely recognized. Her plump rosy cheeks now sunken and gray. Even her nose looked alien, narrower and longer. Her lips, no longer full. No longer a *shayna*, no longer a pretty one.

She closed her eyes and prayed for her mother. If only she could come from wherever she was in the other world, to come quickly, to reach out and hold her. To make her safe again, but only silence surrounded her. She would never smell the sweetness of her mother, feel the strength of her arms, the tenderness of her touch. Never hear the wisdom of her mother's heart.

She gathered her things and returned to the room where Yussi waited.

Chapter 15

Candlelight created a soft glow around where Yussi sat on the bed. He must have taken a few of the Shabbos candles they'd purchased in the local market and placed them on a small table near the bed. His thoughtfulness moved her but frightened her even more. He had expectations. Hopes. She came to him with self-disgust and fear.

Yussi motioned to her to sit beside him. She followed his direction but felt her shoulders tense when he placed an arm around her back. He quickly withdrew it. To Shayna the tension between their bodies resembled the tiny filament she saw in electric light bulbs. Tiny, tiny shivers. She wanted to find the ease they used to share, the excitement and desire she used to feel as a young woman.

"Lie down beside me and let me hold you."

Again Shayna followed his direction. His arms came around her back and pulled her close to his body. She smelled cigarette smoke and sweet wine on his breath.

"You're trembling."

"I'm sorry."

"Maybe you need more time but we must fulfill our marriage. We must cross this barrier." He reached back and began to remove the pins that held her braids in place. "I'm sorry too."

"What are you sorry about? Sorry you didn't marry a virgin? Am I disgusting to you?"

"Oh Shaynaleh. Never think such thoughts." He finished removing the pins and began to place tender kisses on her forehead, her cheeks, and her nose. His freshly grown beard scratched her face.

She felt a hardness between his legs as he pressed closer. She jerked away. "I'm sorry."

"Stop being sorry."

"I'm sorry," she said before she could stop herself. She blushed and laughed.

Yussi smiled at her, the smile she recognized from before, the smile that spoke directly to her heart. His face rested closer to her than ever before. For the first time she noticed a crooked tooth and then his long eyelashes. She watched his long delicate black lashes as they flickered on his pale skin with each blink, as light as butterflies landing on a flower.

Yet out of nowhere, images began to slip into her consciousness. She closed her eyes and saw sweat dripping from the bald man's forehead, his toothless smile, and she could almost smell the foulness that surrounded him as he attacked. Quickly she opened her eyes and focused on the sweetness of Yussi's face as he looked at her. She noticed a thin hazel line circled his deep brown eyes, which she had never noticed before.

"Are you frightened?"

She moved closer into his body, her head cuddled on his chest.

"I won't hurt you," he whispered as he began to unbutton the placket on his pants.

Shayna could feel the movement of his hand near her stomach and tried not to move. She knew this was something that had to happen. Yussi pushed his hips into hers, "Do you feel how much I want you?"

Shayna sensed he meant the stiffness she felt nudge between her legs. She nodded.

He raised her skirt and pulled off her bloomers while she lay still, her legs held tightly together. She felt what must be his penis touch her thigh and then felt his weight on her as he raised his upper body over her. She tensed in anticipation of pain. Yussi poked her near her sex, then began to pump up and down, pushing at her faster and faster. Panting and mumbling, he yelled and then fell on her. A hot liquid ran across her thighs. His breathing slowed and he rolled off of her.

He didn't say anything until he moaned, "I am a fool. An idiot."

"What happened?"

"What happened? I'll tell you what happened. You married a boy, not a man."

"I don't understand."

"Shaynaleh, I'm sorry." He lay back and covered his face. "Too excited. I couldn't wait, lost control. I've dreamed of you for so long." The words so muffled, it was hard to understand him. Then he reached for a cigarette. She watched as he lit it, inhaled, stared at the ceiling and began to speak, his voice clearer, but he did not look at her.

"I gave you no pleasure. I failed to consummate the marriage. I did not enter your body. I lost control."

Shayna didn't know what to say, what she thought, what she wanted. She really didn't understand. She stayed in the same position and waited, although she was very uncomfortable in her wedding dress. It was no longer Perl's wedding dress. Forever now it would be hers. She waited, comfortable now in the silence between them. Yussi finished the cigarette and ground it out in a dish on the little table. The candles, the cigarette on the edge of the bed, even a place to extinguish the cigarette. The little details told her of his planning for the wedding night.

Now they lay on their sides, facing each other. Shayna's wedding dress was tangled around her legs. The stuff that dripped on her legs began to feel sticky. But she didn't want to take the dress off, to do anything but wait to see what would happen.

"Shayna, *zise*, my sweet one." He slid a curl back from her face and pushed it behind her ear. "Did you know the Talmud teaches all about sexual relations in a marriage?"

"I knew about some things, about times of the month when relations are forbidden."

"There is a lot more. We studied it in the yeshive, but tonight I realize I know nothing about a woman. Sex is a *mitzvah*, a good deed, my religious duty as a Jewish man. It's my responsibility to give you pleasure. But I don't know how to do that. I learned words in a book. Only words. Not life. I failed. I am a man, not a beast to jump on you and lose control. I am not like those men." He rolled to his back and stared at the ceiling again and in a very quiet voice he said, "Tell me what pleases you. You need to help me. Maybe we need to help each other."

She couldn't answer. Didn't know the answer.

He jumped out of the bed, wet a small towel, lifted her dress to her waist, and carefully washed his semen off of her legs. Then he brought his lips to her legs. She felt tender kisses along her thighs. Over and over he roamed across her skin with his tongue and his lips. Shayna felt a softness spread in her belly, but when Yussi reached upward and began caressing her breasts, the sensual warmth she felt very suddenly transformed into rage. It moved quickly, like a storm through her body. She tried to lie still, but without thinking she shoved him off and screamed.

"Don't touch me! Get your hands off of me!"

"Shayna, it's me. Yussi. I won't hurt you." He reached to comfort her, to sooth her shaking body.

"Get your hands off of me! Please. Please. Stop!"

"Sh, you're safe now." He moved to the other side of the bed and continued to reassure her. "I won't hurt you. You are safe. I love you. You are safe. *Zise*, sweetheart, time will help us. I won't hurt you. You are safe." He repeated the sentences quietly over and over until Shayna's body stopped trembling. He got off the bed, pulled a chair close to the edge and waited.

The candles were out when Shayna awoke and saw Yussi asleep in a chair on the side of the bed. His features looked different in sleep, softer, as if in sleep he got reprieve from all of their troubles. She hadn't been thinking about his concerns. He was no longer a yeshive *bokher*, and hadn't been since his father's death. Yet he still hungered to study Torah. He was a gentle man. A good man. Would there be a place in America for him? How would they all live? Would he be a carpenter? She'd never talked to him about these things.

"Yussi," she whispered. "Yussi."

His eyes opened slowly and found hers immediately.

"How are you?" he asked.

"I'm fine now. I'm so ashamed. Not the wedding night you imagined."

"Don't be ashamed. You have no reason to be ashamed. You've done nothing wrong. I am the one to be ashamed."

"Should we have a competition? Maybe we could ask the rabbi. Who should be the most ashamed?"

"Would that help Shayna? Do you really want to talk with the rabbi?"

Shayna smiled. The old smile.

"You're teasing me."

She nodded.

Yussi shook his head. "You always catch me when you tease."

"Some wedding night. Not what we imagined."

"Not what we imagined," Yussi said. He stretched and stood. "God willing, we'll have many more nights together, many more nights to figure out who should be most ashamed."

Chapter 16

When Shayna opened her eyes to the ceiling, she saw the same cracks that had been there the day before. A fissure ran from one end of the room to the other. Maybe just dried paint and maybe the whole building was coming apart. Other than the ceiling, everything felt different. Dovid wasn't curled up with his head on her belly; instead, a heavy arm lay over her belly. Yussi. Her husband. Maybe that arm would lie over her until the end of her days.

An arm that held her down, or did it protect her? She had no idea what the future would bring. It would be nothing like her past. A new country. A new language. A place without her beloved family. A place with a brother who was a stranger. And now she had a husband. In the shtetl, she would have known the way of husbands, but her imagination could not lead her into visions of this new world.

She rolled to her side and realized that she wore a nightgown, then blushed to remember they had dressed in night clothing, standing with their backs to each other. She'd wanted to peek. To see his body. To learn how he was different. She wondered if that would come in time. She knew her parents had always undressed in private, as much as possible in their small house.

Shayna felt bile rise in her throat and knew she needed to get out of the bed. She must have a flu or maybe the bit of the chopped liver she tasted at the wedding reception was too rich. But it was the same feeling that she experienced after the wedding ceremony, before she had eaten anything. And if she was honest, she knew the feeling was the same as she experienced on the train. Last night was the first time she lost control. She prayed it was not the Spanish flu or typhus or any other disease that might keep her from America. She prayed it was not something more terrible. She must keep silent. No one could know.

She lowered her bare feet to the floor, and before she could stop herself, she felt the bile surge and as she grabbed for the tin soup bowl on the table. A chair crashed. Yussi began to wake.

Again she lost control. Sour. Bitter as her stomach heaved and tears came to her eyes.

Now he was fully awake and she could not hide.

She tried to turn away so he wouldn't see, but he sat next to her and rubbed her back until the spasms stopped. He took the bowl from her and she fell back unto the bed.

He brought a wet cloth and wiped her mouth, then gave her water to drink.

"I didn't know you were a nurse." Shayna tried to smile, to change the subject, but she knew she wasn't likely to succeed.

"I'm a great nurse. I cared for my father when he was dying."

"I'm not dying."

"Did I say you were dying? You won't get rid of me so fast."

"Even if I'm sick?"

"Not even if you're sick. He smiled and sat at the edge of the bed and felt Shayna's forehead for a fever. "Two days in a row. This is not normal. Maybe you ate something bad."

"Maybe."

"But maybe not. Perhaps something else."

"Probably nothing. I'll be fine in a minute. The rabbi will expect you for morning services. You better get ready."

"A wife for less than a day and you're already nagging?" He kissed her forehead and placed his hands over hers. "This could be something we can't just tease about Shaynaleh, this may be something serious. There will be doctors at Ellis Island. There are also examinations before we can board the ship. We must make sure you are not sick."

She started to argue but realized that he was right. They needed to know. In the shtetl, when anyone was sick, after the doctor left for America, they knew to see Sara Rokhel, the midwife, who also knew about medical matters. But here in this strange city Shayna was lost. All the wisdom that filled the tiny streets of the shtetl spread like pollen from the aspens, carried away by the wind. Disappeared forever.

"There's a doctor who comes to shul every day. Very *frum*. Deeply observant. I'll ask him this morning.

"It's not necessary. Let's wait a few days and see what happens."

"No. Shayna. I insist."

Shayna raised an eyebrow.

"Yes. I insist. What if you have something that is catching? Something Dovid will catch. You must see a doctor."

"Don't think you can start ordering me around now."

"It's not a joke, Shayna. We must discover why you're sick. It's better to know."

"Promise me you won't tell anyone else. No one should worry. Wait. Before you leave, think a minute. Careful how you talk to the doctor at shul. What if someone hears you and tells the people from the ship?"

"I'll be careful."

The doctor's house took up half of a block. Shayna never saw anything like it. Her father described houses like this, houses he saw in Odessa. Two stories of bricks faced the street proudly. Many windows reflected the morning sun. Trees and flowers filled the yard. Beyond the cost of such a home, it spoke to Shayna of safety. That here in this city, in this foreign country of Belgium, Jews would not be attacked, their property destroyed or stolen. They could live in peace.

The home of the rabbi and his wife was not nearly so fine, but still with windows and two floors. Carpets on the floor and many comfortable chairs. The ship would not come for at least a month, and she would have time to sew for the *rebetsn*, to make some money. Since she'd come to Antwerp, as she passed women in the streets, she gathered ideas for other dresses, for skirts, blouses, and jackets. She knew Ulkeh made a living from sewing; maybe she could help, and maybe she would find a way to create dresses like she'd seen. The women wore fabrics she could scarcely imagine. Sometimes she passed a woman and had to hold her hand in to her waist to keep it from reaching out to feel the texture. Colors and designs drew her eyes. Beautiful fabrics, silks and satins, and dozens of unique buttons.

She herself looked shabby, poor, and needy. No matter how hard she tried to keep her clothing clean, it was impossible. Little soap to spare and the clothes would not dry completely. The winds from the ocean brought too much moisture. At least in the shtetl, she could hang her clothes outside to dry. Here she knew whatever was left outside would be stolen. Many of the refugees were desperate. At least she escaped with a few belongings. Whatever sickness she felt now would not last. Someday she too would be safe.

Once inside the doctor's house, the wonders increased. Paintings hung on the walls and rich carpets covered the floor. Light reflected off the polished furniture. To Shayna it felt like walking into a picture book. But the man who opened the door was familiar to her. His suit was finer. His shoes shined. But the *peyes*, the beard, the kind smile nearly brought tears to her eyes. He resembled the men of the shtetl.

"Dr. Feldman, my *vayb*." Yussi looked at her after he said, *vayb*, his wife, the first time she'd been called a wife. She wondered if the title would ever feel comfortable. Now it seemed like a dress that didn't quite fit properly.

The doctor nodded at Shayna, "Pleased to meet you," then shook Yussi's hand. "A beautiful wife. *Mazel-tov. Mazel-tov.* A long life to you both."

The doctor addressed his questions to Yussi, who also did not refer to Shayna. Together they discussed her condition. When Yussi finished, the doctor pointed to a small room next to the salon where they stood. Shayna could see a high narrow bed covered with a sheet. He motioned to Shayna to follow him. She hesitated, looked to Yussi to follow as well.

"You'll come alone. My wife will join us. Another woman will be in the room during the examination. Yussi will wait here."

Narish for Yussi to insist she come here. Foolishness. She wondered if they would have to give the doctor money, money they couldn't afford. She was healthy, strong. She thought about stomping her feet, jumping up and down like a child and refusing to go with the doctor. He may have looked familiar to her, like any old Jewish man, fancier, but still a *Yid*. Although she should trust him, she didn't want to. She didn't want him to put his hands on her. Wife or no wife in the room. Nor did she want him to find anything wrong with her.

Dr. Feldman noticed that Shayna was not following him. He and his wife stood near the door to the examining room and waited for her. She stood frozen, her head down, her fists locked.

"Shayna." the doctor stood before her. "Look at me."

Shayna raised her head.

"I will not hurt you. This is Yetta, my *vayb*. We have three daughters. She will watch over you. You are safe." The doctor's wife put her arm around Shayna and led her into the room.

Dr. Feldman asked her several questions and then asked, "When was your last cycle?"

"I don't remember. Maybe in May. Maybe before the pogrom."

She noticed the doctor and his wife looked at each other, a look that stopped Shayna's heart. It couldn't be, she thought. We just married and nothing happened.

"I'll examine you now and we'll discover what's been bothering you." He motioned for her to sit on the tall table.

Shayna followed his directions to remove her bloomers before she jumped up on the table. She turned her mind off, closed her thoughts, thoughts that were too terrible to think. He told her to lie back and relax, then lifted her skirt above her waist and raised her legs into a strange embarrassing position. The doctor's wife held Shayna's hand as he examined her private parts. She felt a cold, sharp, stinging sensation for moment, then nothing.

"Relax. All finished," the doctor said as he readjusted her legs and lowered her skirt. "Wait here." Then he left the room.

Shayna didn't wait. She jumped off the table, adjusting her clothing. Before she could reach the door, the doctor's wife tried to hold her back.

Shayna shook her off and opened the door. The doctor stood over Yussi, who sat with his face buried in his hands.

"What is it? Am I dying? What's the matter? Talk to me."

The doctor knelt in front of Yussi's chair. "Don't despair. It is not the worst sin. Yussi, you must be realistic, you were betrothed and now you are married. After what you've been through, it is no *shande*, no shame."

"Yussi, talk to me," Shayna yelled. "What is he saying?"

The doctor turned to look at her, a smile on his face, "*Shah,* you're going to be a mother. *Mazel-tov.*"

"A mother? We just got married. Yussi, what's happening here? Talk to me."

Yussi looked up at her, his eyes appeared buried in his face as if someone had died.

"Yussi?"

"Shayna, didn't you hear me?" The doctor stood directly in front of her. "Look at me. You're pregnant. Almost three months." Shayna watched his mouth open and close but knew he was crazy. A gold tooth shone in his mouth. Something she didn't notice before. Must have cost him a lot of money. She wondered how such a crazy doctor made so much money, to have a gold tooth and to live in such a big house.

"*Meshuge.* Yussi He's crazy. Take me from here."

Yussi grabbed the back of the chair as he stood to steady himself.

"You should be happy," the doctor's wife said. "A baby is a gift from God. *Mazel-tov.*" Her voice started strong, but as she began to truly look at the young couple, her voice dwindled to a whisper. *"Gotenyu.* Oh God."

Shayna didn't know how long the silence lasted. No one moved. No one said anything until the doctor dropped into a chair, looked at Yussi and said, "*Nu?* It's not your baby?"

Yussi didn't answer. Shayna's eyes darted around the room, wishing she could fade away like smoke from a fire, never to be seen again on Earth. Yussi just stood and looked at her with an expression she'd never seen before. Maybe it was pity.

"But Yussi. How could this be?" she whispered.

She watched him swallow. Scratch at his short beard. He opened his mouth to say something, but nothing came out. He reached for a cigarette in his jacket pocket, then looked to the doctor for permission to light it. Shayna smelled the smoke and jerked away. Again there was silence until Yussi cleared his throat.

"We can't hide from *tsores*," he said. "This trouble will not go away, Shaynaleh." She felt his arm come around her and he pulled her close. "Shaynaleh." She felt his kiss on her forehead. She heard him say to the doctor. "She was attacked when we left Obodivka."

"No. No. Yussi. Couldn't be." She pushed him away, rushed toward the door and tried to open it. It didn't budge. Must be locked. Where was the key? She reached up to the edge of the door and felt for a key. This made no sense. Why would they lock the door?

Yussi came up behind her. "Shayna, sh, calm down. We'll go now. It will be all right." He put his arms around her, but again she pulled away and turned to him.

"All right? All right? It will never be all right again." She raised her fists and looked around the room. The doctor and his wife stood back by the examination room, their eyes averted. "What did I do that God hates me so much? Tell me."

The doctor's wife approached her, reached for Shayna's hand.

"God doesn't hate you. You'll see, a baby is always a blessing. Sit down here at the table. I'll make some tea. Some strudel. You'll feel better."

She shook her head, tried to respond. She should say thank you. She should say something, but could only plead with Yussi, "Open the door. Please, take me away from here."

She heard Yussi mumble something to the doctor and shake his hand. Strangers, the doctor and his wife. They knew her shame. She must not let them pity her. Yussi opened the door. It hadn't been locked after all.

Her body trembled as he took her arm. "We'll find a way Shayna. *Mirtse-hashem*, God willing, we'll find a way."

Chapter 17

"I have the flu," Shayna said and moved toward the bed to lie down.

"Dovid, you need some fresh air. Go play outside." Yussi's voice sounded shrill. Manya's face turned toward her son, the unusual sound of his voice drawing her attention.

"What's the matter?"

Shayna heard Yussi say, "I wish she had the flu," before she buried her head in a pillow. It muffled the sound of Yussi's voice as he told his mother that Shayna was pregnant. Then silence. No voices audible, until Shayna heard a wooden chair creak and Manya's footsteps as she approached the bed. Shayna felt Manya's hand slowly move across her back, but she could not lift her head.

"I'm going to for a walk," Yussi said. "You must rest." He threw his words toward Shayna as he hurried from the room. She knew he would go to the shul, back to the room the rabbi had converted to a dormitory for refugees, for men who spent most of their time studying. Since Manya and Dovid needed a place to sleep, Yussi would be back on his own. Marriage or no marriage.

A chill slipped through her body, as if she stood outside in a winter storm. Shayna curled into a ball, clutching her arms around her knees. Manya continued to stroke her back, but neither woman said anything. Eventually Manya leaned over, kissed her forehead, and then covered Shayna with a blanket.

One day passed and then another and they found few words to speak. Manya at first managed her shock by preparing remedies for Shayna's morning sickness. She prepared hard crackers with salt for Shayna to eat before she arose, then tea with ginger, which helped. But the fennel seeds Manya insisted Shayna chew triggered more intense nausea.

Shayna went to work at the rabbi's house. The *rebetsn* had placed the sewing machine beneath a large window overlooking a garden. A profusion of fabrics filled a massive table positioned in the center of the sun-filled room.

"I've brought out some of the fabrics I've collected over the years," Freide said. "This I got in London, this tweed will be good for a winter suit. What do you think?" Without waiting for an answer, Freide pointed to a deep purple silk. "What about this for Rosh Hashanah? I see a three-piece suit, maybe use lavender for the blouse."

She thought of the rabbi's wife in Obodivka, a bent wrinkled woman when Shayna knew her, exhausted from years of giving to others. Eight of her own children, not counting orphans in her care. Always in a black dress, with a dark kerchief on her head. A bright silk dress for Rosh Hashana? Who thought of such a thing? Shayna remembered her father's description of some of the Jews he met in Odessa, people who did not live in poverty, people who could raise their heads in the world, and people who lived comfortably, elegantly. But to see it for herself was shocking. She wondered about this God who gave some people mud and others fresh flowers.

The *rebetsn* continued to talk. "Batiks from Indonesia." Maybe this was a country, or a store. She didn't know and had never seen colors melting into each other like the sky at sunset. Lace. Linen. Crepe de Chine.

"You'll draw some designs, maybe get ideas from these French magazines." With great fanfare, Freide pointed to a drawing tablet with pencils and charcoals.

"Why don't you draw some things and when we have lunch you can show them to me?" Then she was out of the room, gone.

Shayna fell into the nearest chair, her legs shaky, and tried to slow her breathing. She'd never drawn designs; she only felt them, saw them in her mind. A fraud. She sank deeper into the chair, ran her hand over her belly, still flat. She knew if God did exist, he had abandoned her. No more evidence was needed. Orphaned. Pregnant. Not her husband's baby. Soon she might be discovered. Soon she might be dishonored and tainted.

Her eyes drifted to the stack of magazines waiting for her on the large table. French magazines, the *rebetsn* said. French magazines, the words echoed in her mind, calling forth a fragment of lost memory. A French magazine. She studied the drawing of a gown on the cover. Her fingers recognized the feel of the slick paper. She'd seen the title before: *La Mode*. Although she didn't understand the words, they were familiar. She'd seen magazines like these, held them, studied them, years before in the shtetl on market days.

Mirtzeh, her best friend, saw them first and pulled Shayna to the bookseller's wagon, maybe when they were nine or ten. Danya, the bookseller, she still remembered his name, so old there was no space between all the wrinkles on his gray face. Danya, who called to the two little girls who lingered near his small portable store, filled with books, mostly used books with stained pages and torn bindings, but books, in Russian, Ukrainian, Polish, German, probably even English and French. Hidden in the midst of the deep wrinkles was a smile as big as the sun, as he beckoned to the little girls.

"Don't be afraid. You can look," Shayna could see her mother's stall from where she stood and could rush over if someone stopped to shop.

"You won't believe it," Mirtzeh chattered, always chattered. "I couldn't believe it. The most beautiful clothes. You have to see. So many beautiful dresses. And shoes. And umbrellas. He said you can look." Mirtzeh glanced at the bookseller for confirmation.

He nodded and handed one to Shayna. She remembered her hands trembled as she held it and turned page after page, amazed by what she saw. "Take a look whenever you want."

And she did. Week after week and dreamed of making such dresses. Every Tuesday, market day in Obodivka, he let her look at the magazines until the day her mother found her there, took the magazine from her hands, and gave it back to the bookseller, took Shayna's hand and led her back to her own shop.

"Shaynaleh," her mother had said, "You're too old for such *narishkayt*, only *narishkayt*, foolishness. No *takhlis*, no benefit in dreaming. How many times do I have to tell you to keep your head out of the clouds? You're growing up now. Not a little girl anymore. Remember what happened when you reached too far for the irises in the river?"

"Mamme, that happened one time. I don't go near the river anymore."

"God gave you a life lesson. If you reach for the clouds, you'll fall on your face."

"Mamme. It has nothing to do with this. I just wanted to see the beautiful designs."

"You stretched out too far to pick flowers, yes beautiful irises, and a present for me, but you landed face first in the river. Ruined your shoes. Almost drowned. Cut yourself on branches. You forget too soon. No one buys fancy clothes here. It's a waste of time. Who can afford such things? No one wants them here. Learn to sew what we can sell."

Maybe *narishkayt* in the shtetl, but foolishness no longer. The dreams that had lain dormant for so many years came to life again, here in the *rebetsn's* sunroom.

Shayna began to flip through the pages, noticed the lowered waistlines, draped fabrics, and deep colors. The models looked like statues frozen in a pose. She walked around the table, touched the tweed, the silk, felt the softness of the crepe de chine. Then she picked up the tablet and a piece of charcoal. Maybe Freide would kick her out, send her away, but until then, she would imagine. She pushed thoughts of rape and pregnancy into a corner of her mind and rose to the challenge of creating beautiful garments.

On her way home after that first day, Shayna felt a lightness in her step. The *rebetsn* chose three of her ideas, three of the twelve styles she created. Ideas came from nowhere into her mind and straight to her hand that held charcoal, as if they were stored, waiting in a line until she called on them. Freide especially loved the suit Shayna designed for the blue silk fabric. A simple Ukrainian embroidery design emphasized the flowing lines of the deep shawl collar on a rather long jacket with cuffed sleeves. Matching embroidery edged the button placket of the blouse. They agreed on a hemline that landed just below the calf, which shocked Shayna but made the *rebetsn* happy.

"I want to be modest but also modern. This is perfect for me."

Shayna suggested using the batik fabric for an evening dress cut on the bias, flowing but modest, and also an everyday outfit of a wool A-line skirt with an embroidered middy blouse. Shayna embellished each costume with a different embroidered design, which thrilled the *rebetsn*.

"So original. My sister Bluma will love you. She'll be here after Shabbos. Taking the train from Paris. No, she doesn't live in Paris. She lives in New York."

Shayna knew if she stayed quiet, the *rebetsn* would give her more information, so she didn't say a word.

"Her husband owns a big department store, Silvers, that's his name—many branches, in different cities. He's very rich. Everyone was shocked when she agreed to marry him. The belle of Vienna society and she married a coarse American. Bluma will love your work. And she lives in New York. You're going to New York, aren't you?"

Shayna nodded and waited.

"She works. Doesn't need to, obviously, but she works. In the store. Shops for fashions in Paris and London for the store. She hires designers. You'll show her your drawings."

Words cluttered together in Shayna's mouth. Full sentences to tell Freide. She wasn't really a designer. Only a seamstress. A good one, but the only dress she ever designed was Perl's wedding dress. She held her lips tight against the words ready to flow out. Her father lived by the great Shammai's simple maxim, "Say little and do much." Shayna always thought that was a strange sentiment for a teacher, but in his class the students talked as much as he did. All along she believed he knew every answer, but maybe he too pretended sometimes. Maybe she could be a designer. A designer in this new world. Nothing had been as she'd anticipated since the day her parents were murdered. Not Perl's death or baby

Sarah's or the attack that left a foul seed planted in her belly. And wasn't it true that if the *rebetsn* paid her for designing and sewing clothes, she was indeed a designer?

As she walked back on this first day of her job, she swung her arms, cookies for Dovid in one hand and a bag of sliced corned beef for Yussi and his mother in the other. She smiled and hoped her mother and father could see her with her light heart as she walked to the big warehouse. Large oak trees lined the streets where she walked, just beginning to show the golden leaves of autumn.

On the fourth day of her employment, Freide sent the maid to the workroom to invite Shayna to tea. She followed her to a room in the back of the house with doors open to the garden, where Shayna found Freide seated at a small table set for three with flowered china dishes and real silver flatware. Next to her sat Bluma. She knew it must be Bluma because the woman resembled Freide—everything similar, the almond eyes, the straight nose, the high cheekbones—but it was as if God got tired before he reached Freide. Bluma was perfection, Freide less so. Maybe it was the stylish clothes, the slight gardenia aroma lingering around her, maybe the almost invisible make-up, something that elevated Bluma Silver and gave Shayna a glimpse of a world she never imagined. Freide herself was a different sort of woman, a kind of *rebetsn* she'd never seen before, but Bluma made Freide seem regular and common.

While they sipped tea, Freide sent the maid to get Shayna's design sketches, which Bluma then studied carefully. Shayna sat at the edge of her chair, her breathing shallow and her heart beating rapidly.

"Very ethnic," she said. Although Shayna didn't know what that meant, it seemed to impress Bluma. "Original." The conversation, which was mostly between Freide and Bluma, ended when Bluma said to Shayna, "Let's see what you can really do." She handed the sketches to Shayna. "My measurements are the same as my sister's. I'll have fabric delivered to you in the next few days for the suit you designed. Here, this one," she said and pointed to the same design her sister selected. "Freide will pay you. She'll mail the suit to me. Do you have a sketchbook for more ideas?"

Shayna shook her head.

"Freide, give her a sketchbook. Something small. She's going to travel." Bluma took Shayna's hand. "And you, you write to me when you get to New York and we'll see what we can do for you."

The sisters soon left the room and the maid led a dizzy Shayna back to the sewing room. A dream, she thought. A dream sent by the devil to tempt her to want, to hunger for a foreign world, a world of strangers. Woven into the fabric of her fear were delicate threads of joy, threads of hope.

Yussi was still at shul when she came home. Dovid was outside playing with other children who waited to depart for America. Manya poured Shayna a cup of tea. Without waiting to hear about her day and without shame, Manya said, "An abortion. Shayna, you'll probably have a miscarriage, but just in case, an abortion is a good idea. The doctor should help you. If he doesn't, the rabbi will know a doctor who will."

Shayna's stomach tightened. She couldn't catch her breath. She stared at the cracked walls around her, the flimsy furniture and meager clothing that hung from hooks. She shook her head. "Not now. Please. Manya. Please. Let me breathe. Don't say a word to anyone."

She watched Manya's mouth open and close but heard nothing, as if her ears filled with cotton, only a buzz audible, like a fly she wanted to swat. Instead, Shayna curled up in the bed and buried her face in a pillow.

With Dovid in tow, Shayna at work, and Yussi gone to collect information about their ship, Manya set off to find the synagogue where she knew she would find Rabbi Weiss. He would know what to do. No need to mention her intentions to her son and his wife. Neither of them truly understood what was at stake. Yussi always tried to be a *mensch*, to do the right thing, but sometimes a *mensch* could be a fool. This thing growing in Shayna's belly should never take a breath, never be born, never be alive. The rabbi could help. In the shtetl she knew what to do, who could help, but here in a strange city, she was helpless.

Another's man's child growing in Shayna's belly. A *shande un a kharpe,* a shame and a disgrace. Thoughts circled her brain, around and around they flew, and no matter how much she tried to hide from it, she couldn't. *Az och un vey!* A terrible misfortune. The only answer was an abortion. To rid Shayna of the abomination. To rescue Yussi from a life of misery.

She stood outside of the synagogue, larger and even more imposing than the synagogue she knew from her days in the orphanage in Odessa. She made out the Hebrew letters etched in gilt, *Bayes Tikvah*, House of Hope. Manya prayed that here she could find help.

She rested on the steps leading up to the wooden doors and wiped the sweat from her forehead with a clean handkerchief. Dovid, also tired from the long walk, sat quietly and played with his carved dog. She adjusted the scarf covering her hair, wiped dust from her worn shoes, and despite the heat, wrapped herself in her black shawl. It would cover the stains on her blouse. She looked as respectable as possible.

Their footsteps echoed along the long dim hallways as Manya and Dovid wandered in search of the rabbi or someone who could direct her to him. Maybe the quiet was an omen that she shouldn't approach the rabbi. Maybe an *aveyre*, a sin to interfere in her son's life, maybe a sin to try to end a pregnancy—although she didn't think so. Life began at the first breath, and if there was no first breath, there would be no life. Manya did not think of herself as a *yakhne*, a troublemaker, a busybody, but someone had to seek justice, to seek a solution.

She heard voices coming from the left side of the building and walked in that direction. She recognized Rabbi Weiss, but none of the other men who sat around the long table covered with books of all sizes and shapes. The singsong melody of their voices reminded her of her childhood in the orphanage when she cleaned the yeshive in Odessa, the sounds of study, of learning Talmud.

She stood quietly by the door until the rabbi noticed her. He smiled, rose, and motioned to the students to continue without him. It seemed to Manya that he recognized her. She knew he spoke Yiddish. Nothing stood in her way except her own fear.

"Manya, and Dovid too. What a surprise."

No words came to her. She nodded at the rabbi but couldn't open her mouth. She felt a buzzing in her head and thought she might faint.

"You look pale. Manya, are you all right? Did something happen to Yussi? Shayna? Sit down a minute." He directed her toward a bench along the wall.

"I'm fine. Maybe just a little water," Manya said.

"Can you walk a little further? Just around the corner to my office."

Manya nodded and followed the rabbi to his office, where he poured a glass of water for Manya and one for Dovid. The room was bright, with lamps and an electric light in the ceiling. Manya sat in a heavy wooden chair next to a large desk covered with books and studied the rabbi while he moved volumes to another table.

She couldn't see much gray in his hair. No long beard and no *peyes*. Only a goatee and a yarmulke. They had dinner at his home on the Shabbos before the wedding, so she knew he was observant. Yussi told her the rabbi was something called modern orthodox. If he was kosher enough for Yussi, that was fine with Manya.

"Maybe I should to talk to Shayna about this," the rabbi said, "but since you're here now, maybe you can decide, at least for now." He placed his hand on Dovid's head. "He's old enough to be in school already. Old enough to learn to read and write. Don't you want to learn to read and write?" he asked Dovid, but didn't wait for an answer. "Why waste the weeks here in Antwerp while you wait for the ship. Let him join our school, right here in the synagogue, for little boys." He knelt down in front of Dovid. "Do you want to go see the other boys?"

Manya nodded since she didn't want Dovid to overhear her conversation with the rabbi. An excellent solution, she thought, at least for now. But Dovid didn't budge. Didn't take the rabbi's hand. Instead he moved to sit on the floor next to Manya's chair.

"Don't you want to learn with other boys? Has he ever gone to school?"

"I think he went to the *kheyder* in the shtetl. But I'm not sure. That was a long time ago."

"Is this why you came to see me today? To help Dovid?"

She shook her head and stared down at her hands twisting on her lap. She didn't want Dovid to hear what she had to say, but she didn't have the heart to send him away, even to a room full of boys down the hall.

Rabbi Weiss took his chair behind the desk, folded his hands, and waited.

"It's something else completely. Advice. Help. Just between us." She touched Dovid's shoulder, and when he looked up, she smiled. "Dovidel, wait for me just outside the door. It won't take long."

"Please," she said, and when he didn't move, she added, "I'll tell *Tante* Shayna what a good boy you've been today. You can see me through the glass in the door. I won't leave without you." She led Dovid to a bench in the hall and returned to her chair. Maybe the rabbi was irritated with her already, but he didn't say anything. Just waited. She knew he probably wanted to get back to his students.

"*Nu?* How can I help?" the rabbi finally asked.

Enough time wasted, she thought, but her throat felt tight. Her words locked up in her mind. She closed her eyes, took a deep breath, and blurted out, "Can you help me get an abortion?"

"An abortion?" Manya heard the shock in his voice when he asked, "Are you pregnant?"

She felt her face turn red. "No. No. Not possible. Not me. Not for me. Shayna."

Manya watched the expressions on the rabbi's face shift quickly from concern to shock. He composed his features and she sensed he must have remembered that Yussi and Shayna just married. But still, the baby would be born in wedlock. He didn't see a problem.

"This is not Yussi's child," Manya whispered.

The rabbi leaned forward, his eyebrows lifted. "Not Yussi's child?"

"No. No. Not what you think. Shayna's a good girl." She raised her hands to her temples and pressed her fingers into her head. The sounds of Shayna's screams still reverberated in her mind. "Not what you think."

The rabbi waited. She could hear Dovid in the hall talking with his little dog. She needed to say the words, but they were locked away. Too awful to ever repeat.

The rabbi leaned back in his chair. "Did it happen in the pogrom?"

Manya nodded. "Just after. We were gathering firewood. They came from nowhere."

"Did Yussi see?"

"Not until after. He was fixing the wagon and didn't hear. She didn't know when they married. Didn't imagine. Couldn't imagine the *hartsveytik*, the heartbreak."

Again the rabbi waited.

"So, can you help her?" She didn't know if the rabbi could hear her over the pounding of her heart.

"Is this what Shayna wants? Yussi? Did he send you?"

"No. No. They don't know I'm here."

"Oy, Manya."

"You don't understand." Manya rose from the chair, put her hands on the desk and leaned close to the rabbi. "This could kill her. Maybe her body would survive, but her *neshome* would die, her soul would perish." Her legs trembled beneath her.

The rabbi stood, "I do understand, Manya. I wish I'd never heard a story like yours. But I've heard it. More than you can imagine. I've heard it from other refugees from Russia, Poland, and the Ukraine, from wherever women suffer." He walked around to where Manya stood and put his hand on her shoulder. "I need to talk to Yussi. It's complicated. Against the law in Belgium. Catholics here."

"What about Jewish law?"

"Complicated. Not simple either. I must think. Study. Yussi must bring the question to me. Yussi or Shayna."

"Don't tell him I told you."

"No. I won't. But I think, now that I know, I can encourage him to talk with me, to ease his heart."

Manya raised her hands together in supplication. "Rabbi, have *rakhmones*, pity on Shayna and Yussi. Help them. I beg you." As she spoke, she noticed a faraway look in his eyes, as if he took himself away from her pain. Study. He would study. They didn't need study. They needed action—help. She didn't know where else she could turn. Maybe this was *bashert*, God's will. Maybe she shouldn't try so hard to fight destiny.

"Please don't tell him I told you. Please," she said as he led her to the door.

"I won't," he mumbled as he turned back to the classroom where she'd found him.

Her legs still trembled as she took Dovid's hand. It would be a long walk back to their room.

"*Ikh darf pishn*," he said, pulled away from her, and looked around the hall.

His request startled her for a moment. "Of course, of course, me too. Let's find a toilet. They must have a toilet in this big building. Don't you think? Maybe even two toilets." She looked both ways along the dim hall. "Which way should we go?" He smiled, a little tilt of his lips, which eased the pain in her heart. It wasn't the giggling smile she remembered from the shtetl whenever she'd see Dovid in the market with his mother, the little boy who always had a twinkle in his eyes. But this beginning of a smile gave her hope. The hollow-eyed little boy was beginning to disappear. She must remember that from frozen ground, flowers grow.

At first Shayna didn't know. Manya didn't tell her, but Yussi found out because the rabbi shared the situation with the scholars in the synagogue, with all the men who came regularly to study Talmud with the rabbi. Yussi immediately recognized the situation the rabbi described as his own, but he remained silent. And each day Shayna worked in the *rebetsn's* sunroom cutting, sewing, and fitting the rebetsn and her friends with garments she designed. Waiting for her shame to be known, waiting for someone to say something. No one did.

Yussi returned to Shayna each day with reports from the discussions. The rabbi acknowledged it was not a new question. The woman in question was not the only Jewess raped. There was nothing unique about her situation. But abortion was illegal in Belgium, so the rabbi knew it would be difficult, if not impossible, to arrange.

According to Rashi, the great scholar of the Talmud, a fetus was not a person until it took its first breath. So Manya thought they would help Shayna, but, of course, as always, there were other concerns beyond the mother's wellbeing. For Shayna knew for a fact that she could not survive the birth of this child, this aberration. This horror that God had allowed. Shayna could not concentrate on Yussi's words as he tried to explain how rabbis would assess the health of the mother, about the difference between secular law and religious law. If the state said it was a crime, Jews would have to treat it as such, regardless of biblical law.

Shayna didn't know who made her angrier. Yussi, who repeated, *mirste-hashem*, God willing. If God wills the destruction of this fetus, it will happen. If this fetus comes to breathe air, then that is the will of God.

"Are you saying God wanted me to be raped? What kind of a God wants to inflict such evil on an innocent woman? God planned that that beast would *shtup* me?" She saw Yussi flinch as she spoke these words. "Who is this God of yours?" She could not get him to budge. She imagined Yussi held on to his faith, maybe for the same reason he had grown his beard and *peyes* back immediately. Who would he be without God?

What right did Manya have to tell everyone their *tsores*? For it must have been Manya who told the rabbi, making Shayna a subject of pity and shame.

But it was Manya, ironically, who gave Shayna a solution of sorts, at least a hope.

"With my first pregnancy, I had a miscarriage. Don't worry. You too will have a miscarriage. With such a bad diet, with all the turmoil, God will help you. Relieve you of this evil. Most of the women in the shtetl lose their first babies. It happens all the time." Manya would clasp her weathered hands together, nod her head up and down. "Not to worry, Shaynaleh, you will miscarry. Surely with the rocking of the ship, you will miscarry."

Chapter 18

October 1919

From her position in the crowded line of third-class passengers that wound down the street flanking the S.S. Finland, Shayna craned her neck to watch the first-class travelers as they strolled along the ramp leading to the top deck. The women wore elegant dresses, high-heeled shoes, and furs. The feathers on their wide-brimmed hats waved in the autumn wind. Some carried small dogs. A few held hatboxes. The men wore top hats, their arms unburdened while men in uniforms, maybe servants, or ship employees, followed them up the ramp carrying heavy trunks and suitcases.

Shayna thought they had come early enough to avoid a long wait, but scores of other immigrants must have spent the night on the side of the ship, all third-class steerage passengers. One hour passed and then another. There was no place to sit and rest. No water. They stood next to the ship, like ants and as important.

In the market, Yussi had found a small wooden trunk, which took the place of the many small bundles. Along with clothing, his *talis* and *tfilin*, it held the religious books he replaced in Antwerp, a few tools from his father's cabinet shop, and the blankets and pillows the *rebetsn* had given them. He carried the box on his shoulder, supported by his right arm. In his left, he held a suitcase with Dovid's clothes, Perl's candlesticks, and Dovid's father's *kidish* cup along with another bag with food for the trip. Manya carried her things in a large bundle, which she sometimes held tightly to her chest and sometimes secured to her back by a shawl wrapped around her body.

Shayna's shoulder ached from the weight of the other suitcase. She shifted it from one side to the other, careful to never let go of Dovid's hand, watching that he held on to the basket he carried. Twice already Yussi had lowered the box, the suitcase, and the bag, hunched himself, and struggled to light a cigarette in the wind. He inhaled a few times and then snuffed it out with his fingers. All of them worried that the line would move suddenly and they might lose their places.

Shayna tightened the scarf around Dovid's neck. The cold winds foretold an early winter, a bad omen for crossing in October. Winter brought storms to the North Atlantic. Usually, October was still a safe month to travel, well before the onset of the most turbulent weather. The jackets Shayna had sewn should protect them against the fierce chill.

The line remained orderly despite the mix of old and young, big and small. Nobody pushed their way to the front of the line. Shayna suspected the men in uniform who walked along the row of immigrants prevented potential fights. No one wanted to be refused passage. Some families dressed in clothing that appeared strange to Shayna. Some people wore clothing similar to the Ukrainian festive wear, although Shayna noticed it was far more elaborate, heavily embroidered vests, jackets, and skirts. Some women wore dozens of necklaces and bracelets. Others dressed in black with no ornamentation.

Shayna averted her eyes when she noticed rigid geometric patterns tattooed like frames around the eyes of a few men. She knew the Torah banned stains on the body, but she knew *goyim* could have them. But to see them on faces spoke to her of something primitive and dangerous. Some wore huge fur hats that stood tall on their heads. Some carried babies and others musical instruments. Like Noah's ark, they were ready to board the ship. All the species of God's human creatures.

The steerage passengers were subject to medical exams and interviews before they could board the ship, which had arrived in Antwerp harbor more than a month after their own arrival. Men in uniforms sat at long tables outside of a small building next to the ship. She heard a whistle and the line began to creep toward the officials. The sun was high in the sky when they finally reached the end of the line.

"Edelman," Yussi said as they reached the table. A tall bald man with glasses looked down at a list in front of him and made a check. Shayna realized she was no longer of the Rifkin family. Married barely a month, she stood stunned when she realized that now and forever she was an Edelman. Everyone from the shul in Antwerp had called her Shayna, never a last name, until now. Neither the man who sat at the table in his navy uniform with gold buttons nor anyone else would ever know that all her life she had been Shayna Rifkin. It seemed like a technicality when she watched an official change her name on her visa and her ticket after the marriage. But she now wondered if Shayna Rifkin was lost forever.

She stood by Yussi's side as they waited for the next step. Her mind drifted amid the strange words around her, the cries of babies, the sounds of papers shuffling. She shut her mind to the thing in her belly, shut her mind to memories of her parents at their table on Shabbos, and shut her mind to the sound of her goat in its pen as she ran to the shed to hide from the Cossacks. She closed her eyes to the image of Perl ravaged on her bed. If only her memories could disappear along with her name.

"Shayna, Shayna." She felt a pull on her arm as Yussi's voice penetrated. "We must answer their questions."

Several translators stood behind the tables. Shayna, Yussi, and Manya understood the Yiddish the translators spoke despite their slightly unfamiliar accents. After their travels through Europe, they recognized that Jews from Western Europe sounded different than Yiddish speakers from Russia or Poland. But the language was essentially the same.

First they were asked standard questions: name, address, nationality. Can you read and write? More probing questions followed. Are you healthy? Any diseases? Ever had a disease? Ever been to prison? A poorhouse? Are you an anarchist? Shayna wondered if anarchists confessed, announced themselves. The official in charge of their interview, a grayhaired man in a navy uniform, wanted the names of everyone they knew in America. He wanted to know if they had money with them, money to leave Ellis Island. He looked up at them over the metal frames of his glasses.

"America doesn't want beggars. Who wants beggars? Do you have twenty-five dollars? If you don't, they'll deport you."

Yussi looked bewildered for a moment, but Shayna nodded and told the official their tickets had been prepaid, they had money, and her brother waited for them. When Shayna showed the official Ulkeh's letter, he stamped their tickets and checked their names off a long list.

Shayna, still holding Dovid's hand, followed Yussi and his mother toward another line to wait for a medical examination. A more thorough exam would occur at Ellis Island, but here before boarding, the ship's doctors could refuse passage to anyone who might be rejected by the Ellis Island doctors. The ship's company did not want to be responsible for the financial burden of returning a sick person to Europe.

A small brick building had two entrances, one for men and one for women. Dovid entered the building with Shayna and Manya but was led away immediately by a nurse in white who indicated children were seen elsewhere. Dovid looked back, screamed, wiggled away from the nurse, and ran to Shayna. Everything in his basket fell to the floor. The nurse tried to grab him, but Shayna lifted him. Her eyes shifted around the room, sought a translator, but none were visible. The nurse reached again for Dovid, but Shayna shook her head. Dovid continued to cry while Manya picked up his clothes and toys from the floor. Another woman dressed in the same kind of white hat and dress quickly reached for Dovid's arm, raised his sleeve, and poked a needle into his tiny arm. His screams increased, but the nurses looked satisfied and left them.

Shayna had heard about these needles, about shots that they must have to prevent diseases, but she didn't know what diseases. So many things she didn't know. She could barely hold Dovid now, she felt exhausted all the time. Manya said it was typical when one carried a child. She tried to take one step at a time, but sometimes she didn't have the strength to do that. Other days, she had a lot of energy. Her life was upside down.

They motioned her to a doctor who leaned in to listen to her chest in the front and the back. She thought of the pregnancy. It didn't show yet, and no one mentioned it. She too had a shot and tried to smile at

Dovid when she saw the needle. She didn't want him to be afraid of the new experiences. There would be many.

The doctor spent more time with Manya, listened with careful attention to her heart. He told her to take deep breaths and cough. Shayna's heart stopped. What if they kept Manya back? Was she sick and no one knew? The doctor made a mark on their tickets and waved to a nurse, who guided them through another door where they waited for Yussi to join them.

Another line formed, and when there were a few dozen travelers, a young man, with S. S. Finland printed in large letters across his jacket, led them up a ramp and helped them down a steep ladder to a room crowded with bunks along two sides. A long table lined by benches on either side dominated the middle of the room. Shayna looked around for windows someone might open to relieve the musty smell, but the room was windowless. The dim lighting came from three bare light bulbs. Shayna felt like they entered a cave carved into the ocean.

Other passengers were already seated at the benches, pulling food from baskets. Many of the bunks were piled high with bundles and packages, and the young sailor directed Shayna, now carrying Dovid, Manya, and Yussi to the left side of the ship toward some bunks that were still empty. Each bunk held a straw mattress covered in faded white canvas, a thin blanket, a tin bowl, plate, and eating utensils. Nothing else. All their belongings would have to remain on the bunk. There were no lockers, dressers, closets, or hooks, no place to put a suitcase or a bag. Since Dovid was short, his bunk got the majority of bundles. Manya and Dovid sat on the lower bunks while Yussi and Shayna were assigned to those above Dovid and Manya.

The young man wanted to show them the washroom, but they were afraid to leave their belongings unprotected. Manya stayed with Dovid while Shayna and Yussi went with him to view the rooms with sinks and toilets located down another dim corridor. The women's bathroom had eight toilets and eight sinks.

Shayna wanted to ask how many people used the facilities. She wanted to ask who cleaned the facilities and how often were they cleaned. She knew Yussi had the same questions, but they stood mute. The sailor guiding them spoke only in Dutch, and although similar to German and therefore similar to Yiddish, it was not similar enough to understand each other. Shayna hated the feeling of helplessness, of being unable to get basic information. She thought the official behaved toward them as if he thought they were stupid. Shayna hesitated to even try to ask. People had warned them not to stand out. Don't be a troublemaker. They can punish you by giving less food, less water, and less access to fresh air on the upper deck. Be careful.

The ship was scheduled to depart at dawn the next morning. This dank cavernous room would be their last stop before America, that is, before Ellis Island, which was the gate to America.

These days, although Shayna went through the motions of paying attention to her life, her whole being was focused on only one thing, one single prayer. No matter where she was, how hungry, satisfied, tired, or awake. When she played with Dovid, or sewed for the *rebetsn*, or counted the coins she made as a seamstress, or bought fabric and sewed for her family. Even when she made a man's shirt, a beautiful white shirt for Yussi so he could be presentable when he met her brother. Even when she studied the English book and practiced remembering words, her mind drifted into the prayer, maybe an evil prayer, a terrible prayer. She asked God to lift the baby from her belly and take it to heaven. She prayed that God would never breathe life into this thing she carried in her own body.

Over and over Shayna pleaded with God and reminded Him that this baby had been planted by an evil act and might have evil sewn into the fabric of its little life. The world needed no more evil. The thing growing in her had been planted in violence and brutality. Would its little soul, if it had one, be draped in the same? Would the very existence of this creature, this soon to be life, always be a reminder of the evil that had befallen her? Of the evil in the world? Could anyone ever love this child?

Now on this evening before departure, she sat on the bunk while Manya organized their food and prepared a small meal for them. As the doctor predicted, Shayna's nausea passed. But in its place came exhaustion and little appetite. They had been told that two meals would be provided to steerage passengers, but the food was not kosher, and what was there was never enough. Rumor was it also tasted terrible. Everyone told them to prepare what food they could. Fresh water would be scarce. Maybe the motion of the ship, the difficult circumstances of their living conditions would cause a miscarriage. Twice her own mother had lost babies. It happened to Manya once as well. Maybe God would recognize the wrong to her and repair it.

Shayna curled up on the lower bunk that would be Dovid's. There was room here for her as well and they could load all their bundles on the upper bunk, make everything more difficult to steal. More and more people came into the large room. She heard Yiddish spoken, Russian, what sounded like German to her, so much like Yiddish, but still different. Many languages beyond her recognition. Babies cried. Dishes rattled. Laughter. Tears. She must cover herself she thought, and couldn't believe she lay on a bed in midst of a room full of people. Men as well as women. She needed a curtain, something to protect her modesty. But no one seemed to notice. Not even Yussi, who immediately went to search for Jewish men to form a *minyan*. Plenty of Jewish refugees. But so many others. Strangers. *Goyim*. All going to America. Would there be pogroms there too?

They were called "stewards," the men in uniforms who rolled carts into one end of the room. She sensed everyone move toward them. "Supper," they said in English. She recognized the word and heard it repeated in many languages as people moved forward holding the tin bowls and other utensils provided to steerage passengers. She smelled only unwashed bodies.

"Come, Shayna, get in the line. There will be nothing left for you," Manya said as she took Dovid's hand. Dovid looked to Shayna. Always looked to Shayna before he moved. She nodded at him. "No place to sit at the table if we don't hurry."

Many people already returned balancing bowls and plates to sit on the long benches. She wondered if she would make a friend here on the ship among all these strangers. But everyone blurred into one mass. She focused only on Dovid, Yussi, and Manya. She could not absorb anything else. All the people around her were simply colors, movement, smells. Noise. She looked for Yussi. He stood nearby with a large group of men praying. He'd found his *minyan*. All was right in his world. Talking to God, sending prayers into thin air.

Chapter 19

"*Tante Ikh darf pishn.* Wake up." Shayna jumped at the sound of Dovid's voice, almost drowned out by pounding, screeching sounds all around them. She shook her head, tried to orient herself while Dovid pulled at her. Manya's bed was empty, and when she looked, Yussi was gone was as well.

She slept in her clothing, so she took Dovid's hand and started toward the bathroom. Her first step was steady, but then she felt a jerk and a roll. Suitcases and shoes slid across the floor. The noise was intense. *Pound. Scrape. Hiss. Pound. Scrape. Hiss.* This must be the steam engine. The ship moved. She tightened her grip on Dovid's hand, and with her other hand she balanced herself along the table until she reached the hall, where she discovered a long line in front of the toilets.

"Hold it, *tatele,* just a few minutes. I know you can do it," Shayna said as she watched him twist his thin legs together. She wanted to hit something, to scream, to push other people away, to yell emergency and rush to the front of the line. None of these things were possible. Instead, she smiled and soothed Dovid. She herself felt an urgency and understood that from now on she would have to rise early to make sure they got to the bathroom before the line formed.

Two children, a boy and girl about Dovid's age, came to stand in the line with their mother. They spoke Yiddish and smiled at Shayna and Dovid. The woman introduced herself.

"Faigl Belensky, from Kiev, on the way to New York, United States of America."

"Shayna Edelman." Faigl looked older than Shayna, maybe thirty. Not religious, she wore no hair covering. While Shayna abided by the head-covering tradition, she had not shaved her head, as was often the custom after marriage, nor could she afford the purchase of a *sheytl*, a wig that many righteous Jewish women wore. A head scarf suited her preference.

"My husband sent us tickets. He has a good job in New York."

Dovid clung to Shayna's skirt but kept peeking at the other children. She prayed that maybe they would play together and a path might open for Dovid to find his way back to childhood.

"And your husband, is he in New York too?"

Shayna shook her head but didn't have to say more because they reached the room with the water closets and separated. She wondered if Faigl might know English, or how to pronounce the letters in the alphabet without a terrible accent. She needed to learn, to prepare to manage in a new country.

Silvi, the *rebetsn's* daughter, studied English in the university in Belgium. Shayna had never seen such a thing. A university that took Jewish students, even girls. Too busy with her studies to spend much time with the dressmaker, a poor refugee, she'd agreed to go through the alphabet with Shayna and teach her some important words. Not enough, but still something. As soon as Shayna had learned the letters as best she could, she taught Dovid. Silvi had also given Shayna a book of English expressions, which she hoped to study on the ship.

She felt the steady, relentless pound of the engine: *scrape, hiss, pound, scrape*. It never stopped. She fell asleep to it and woke to the sound. A few hundred people filled the cavernous damp room, one of three such rooms squeezed between decks next to the massive steam engine. The only fresh air came when they were allowed to climb a ladder and crowd together on a deck. No place to sit, only directly on the floor, which was cold, as was the air. The weather held for three days. During those days, a routine developed: Rise early, trip to bathroom, try to wash with the cold water that came from the faucets. Then breakfast. The porridge served on the ship wasn't terrible and they ate it, all of them. Dovid began to play with Faigl's children, and Shayna began sewing a dress for herself, a blue shirtwaist, something to match the importance of coming to America. She suffered from a deep fatigue, which Manya said was caused by the pregnancy. Usually she fell asleep after breakfast while Manya fed Dovid and cared for him.

Shayna couldn't tell if the constant slight nausea she felt was from her pregnancy or from the endless rolling of the ship. Although another refugee, a self-proclaimed expert on steamship travel told everyone the waters were exceptionally calm. "Smooth. Very smooth," he said and proceeded to tell all who would listen about the terror of a storm at sea, not in first class, he added, but steerage, *Oy vey*, don't ask.

Yussi studied with the other men of the *minyan*, at least ten men from different parts of Eastern Europe who quickly discovered each other in steerage. They spent each day discussing Talmud and traded stories about their rabbis, their yeshives, their learning. Although Yussi's yeshive education ended when his father died, he continued to study on his own.

Since the day at the doctor's office in Antwerp, Yussi had not touched her with desire. She felt him watch her from across the room, but there had not been private time as husband and wife since their wedding night.

Dinner, always a thin soup with pale, soggy bread was definitely not kosher. They saw chunks of some kind of meat and only took the bread. Someone said it was pork, but Shayna didn't look closely. *Treyf* was *treyf,* and she didn't want to be tempted. Fortunately, the *rebetsn* had helped them fill a bag with cheeses, pickled herring, vegetables, smoked fish, and even salami. Much of their food was salty, which made them thirsty. Water was scarce and there was no milk for Dovid.

Shayna yearned for more time on the deck, even though there wasn't much room. The cold breeze made them huddle together. But it also dispersed the smell of unwashed bodies and unwashed clothes. Shayna continued to sleep in her clothing, as did many others. From the lower deck where the immigrants clustered, Shayna could see into the upper decks, where the rich people walked. Like looking from hell into heaven. Maybe hell was too strong, certainly better than subject to the Cossacks and the violence, but Shayna felt shame at her dirty clothes, dirty hair. Her fingernails, despite trying to wash carefully every day, remained dirty. Occasionally, elegant women in fantastical hats leaned over the railings to looked down at the immigrants. She would not look away, would not show shame. She only saw them from the waist up and wished she could study the flow of their skirts, the length of the skirts, but she was able to see the sheen of silk and satin on the bodices, the rich colors, deep reds, and purples. Someday she would make such dresses and sell them.

"Your mother-in-law," Faigl nodded at Manya, "tells me you're expecting a baby. *Mazel-tov.*" Faigl smiled, a mother-to-mother kind of smile that made Shayna truly want to vomit. To vomit on Manya who sat on her left. She wanted to turn to Manya and slap her. Over and over Manya opened her mouth, and no matter how often Shayna asked her to stop, to protect her privacy, Manya talked. She told everyone in Antwerp that Shayna was pregnant, humiliated her. Everyone knew she and Yussi had just married, and now she was pregnant. "It's important to tell the truth," she would say, or she would say, "I only told the rabbi." And then she'd add "And the doctor already knew. It's not my fault that the rabbi told other people."

Shayna believed Manya didn't mean to make trouble. Maybe it was just Manya's way to make a connection with strangers. Her oldest son, Gershon, traveled now to Palestine. Likely she would never see him again. Her husband had died, her friends, murdered or gone to who knew where. They all suffered, ripped from their roots and living on hope.

Now, here on the ship, Manya continued talking about things she shouldn't. What else had she told people on the ship? Yussi couldn't control her either. He'd told Shayna to remember, *sholem bais*, peace in the home. So Shayna remained silent like a dutiful daughter-in-law, but it had to stop. She knew this was not the time to say anything to Manya, so she nodded to Faigl and placed a smile on her face.

"You're so thin. Skinny, I couldn't tell."

Shayna nodded again. Faigl was a fine woman, not a *yenta* at all, but this was not a conversation that she wanted. She turned her attention back to the last stitches she had made in the seam of the dress and realized she'd have to pull them out. They were crooked and too far apart. She needed to concentrate.

"Have you sewn any baby clothes?" Faigl asked. "You're so talented with the needle, your baby will be the best dressed baby in America."

Yussi stood with other men by the railing and Faigl yelled to him, Yussi, "*Mazel-tov* to you."

Yussi paled and nodded at her. They hadn't talked beyond Yussi's constantly repeated phrase, *mirtse-hashem, mirtse-hashem*. God willing. As if God was paying attention to them and had an opinion about this thing growing in her belly. Yussi had faith. Nothing gave him doubt, at least nothing he would admit.

For Shayna, God came and went like the weather. And was just as reliable. Soon they would have to have a real conversation about the possibility that she wouldn't lose the child. They would have to lie to Ulkeh, say they married before they really did. Never tell him about the attack. Never tell her brother that she was soiled, stained irrevocably.

Faigl was trying to be friendly, but it was none of her business. Manya, like a *kokhlefl*, a big spoon that stirred the pot, talked when she shouldn't have. Neither intended any damage, but these days Shayna was on the edge of irritation constantly.

She bent and picked at the improper stitches.

"So, *nu*. I'd love to see the clothes for the baby that you've already made. Do you expect a boy or a girl? I know you don't know, but what would you like? Another boy I bet."

Everyone assumed Dovid was her child and she let them.

"I'm superstitious," Shayna answered. "It's too soon. I don't want to tempt fate. There's time. Maybe it's not well planted in my belly and I'll lose it. I understand it happens often."

Faigl started to tell stories of women she knew, failed pregnancies, surprise births, the stories that women told each other. Manya joined in, as did a few women sitting near them.

"Maybe you should stay on the bed," an old woman sitting next to Manya piped in. "Don't move, don't cause yourself to lose the baby. I see how you climb up the ladder. You might fall. Be careful."

She stopped listening. No one noticed. Manya kept the conversation lively. As Shayna bent over her sewing, she prayed that God would take this thing from her belly, that her breasts would lose their sensitivity, that she would stop being nauseous, that she would see her monthly blood flow again, that she would be happy to see it each month for many years to come—without interruptions.

In the midst of her thoughts, she heard the women begin to laugh. She looked up and saw Dovid and some of his new friends next to the men, who had formed a circle and started the afternoon prayers. The men stood next to the railing, their prayer shawls wrapped around them, swaying back and forth, typical in men's prayer. Dovid, along with several other boys, stood behind the men and bobbed back and forth, copying their movements. Shayna could tell the women thought it cute, but it was not cute to her. She realized she didn't want that kind of life for Dovid, a life of blind faith and disconnection from the world. No one could judge anyone else's faith, she knew that. But watching Yussi over the months gave her a sense that parallel to faith and dedication to God was escape from the suffering of the world. Yes, it might give comfort, but it also provided an excuse not to face difficult choices. God's will. Always God's will.

The little boys began to laugh as they pushed away the few girls who had joined the group. They swayed back and forth, following the custom of men at prayer. The men heard the laughter and nudged all the children away. Innocent. All innocent. Shayna knew she read too much into the men praying, but it annoyed her. Maybe because she, as a girl, was excluded, just as the little boys understood to exclude the girls.

Being a girl didn't stop women from praying. They could gather and make their own circle. Their prayer books were in Yiddish, not in Hebrew, the holy tongue, in which the men prayed. Less than. God's plan. She had no words for these feelings, only a strong resistance. And a resistance to raising Dovid in that same tradition.

As she watched Dovid giggling with the other children, she recognized a look on his face that she had not seen for months. It was as if his heart opened again, embraced being alive. Dovid looked over at where Shayna sat and waved at her as he ran along with the other children. She wanted to shout at him, tell him to slow down. Be careful. Don't run so fast. Watch where you're going. Her mind raced with admonitions, but she kept silent. She knew the other mothers also paid attention and the children would be safe. Then she realized she was beginning to think of herself as Dovid's mother, not his aunt. If not his birth mother, then his mother in life.

Suddenly, it became harder to see across the deck, as if the sun had set. She looked up and saw ominous dark clouds now filled the sky. The men near the railing held their hats against the wind. Suddenly, one of the ship's officials called to them, motioned them all back toward the hatch that led to the steerage compartments. "*Shnell!*" he yelled in German and something else, which must have been English. She saw Yussi call to Dovid, grab the little boy up in his arms, look toward Shayna, and motion her to the ladder. She took Manya's hand and they ran to the opening that would lead them to the dim, dank, cavernous room where they would hopefully survive the gathering storm.

All the immigrants on the deck surged toward the small hatch where they could descend, but there was no order. Shayna was jostled back and forth as everyone tried to reach the ladder quickly. Elbows in her chest, feet stomping on her own. Large men rammed their way in front of her and she couldn't see much, caught a glimpse of Yussi who held Dovid tightly to his chest. The ship began to pitch, at first gradually and then toppling some people as the wind increased. Shayna and her family were in the middle of the crowd, but those on the outside hung on. Screams were heard as people pushed forward. Shayna lost Manya's hand as people shouldered between them. In the midst of the danger and fear, Shayna welcomed the chaos. She believed the pushing and shoving would put an end to the growth in her belly. She saw Yussi descend the ladder with Dovid, and miraculously Manya's head was visible as she went through the hatch.

But Shayna was caught in a bottleneck with people pushing on both sides until she finally stood before the ladder and was pushed through the entry. She grabbed the rungs of the ladder to keep from falling through. For a moment, she hung precariously until she felt someone grab onto her legs. She looked down and saw Yussi, who held on to her as he lowered her body into his arms. Truly he was a *shtarker,* strong and not afraid. Her body trembled as he carried her back to the bunk and lay her down. He moved in next to her, holding her tightly. An odd thought ran through her mind as she leaned into him. She must still mean something to him, to carry a woman and to move next to her, even his wife, in broad daylight in the company of hundreds of people. He must care. Even now.

The ship pitched, jerked back and forth while thunder seemed to blast through every crevice of the ship. The gentle rolling they previously experienced had transformed into a rapid, almost explosive up and down jerking of the entire ship. Clinging to the metal structure of the bunks kept them from falling out and rolling along the floor. Suitcases, bundles, dishes, and clothes crashed to the floor and slid along with the heave of the ship.

The sounds of retching and sobbing filled the room as the ship rocked violently from side to side. Shayna, clutching the metal rod supporting her bunk, leaned over the edge and looked for something that might contain the vomit that spewed from her mouth. She was not alone. She saw Dovid, seasick in Manya's arms. But she too could not contain the bile. Only Yussi seemed to withstand the roiling of the ship. They could hear huge waves bash against the side of the ship. The steady *pound, swish, pound* of the engine did not stop. Thunder boomed overhead. Fear filled the steerage compartments as the immigrants imagined the ship overturning. They would have no exit, no way to escape.

Carefully, clinging to the metal bars and the walls, Yussi grabbed their towels and worked his way to the washroom. He found galvanized buckets stacked there, apparently the ship's authorities knew a storm was imminent. With two buckets and wet towels, he managed to dodge flying suitcases until he reached his family.

Shayna remembered little after the first several hours of turmoil. She lay on her bunk, scarcely able to move. She must have slept or passed out. Yussi came often with a wet towel for her forehead and left an emptied bucket each time. She felt his cool hand on her forehead, a caress as he brushed her damp hair back away from her face.

"Dovid?" She tried to rise from the bunk.

"*Shah*. He's doing better than you. Don't worry. My mother watches him."

Later. No idea how much later, as time blurred, as she lay spent on the now damp bunk, she heard Yussi sing a lullaby to Dovid. His voice tender, sweet as he sang the Yiddish lullaby, "*Rozinkes Mit Mandlen.*" Melancholy and yearning for a lost world. His voice carried her back to her home in the shtetl, to her mother's voice as she sang the same song to Shayna as a child. Shayna couldn't remember the exact words, but some of them drifted into her consciousness as Yussi sang. "Raisins and almonds, you will at some time be scattered throughout the world, remember this lullaby."

She could still hear rain pound the deck above them, but she no longer heard thunder. The wind must have died down, Shayna thought as she managed to sit up in her bunk. She didn't know how long the intense storm lasted, only that the ship wasn't rocking as much. When she looked around the cave-like room, she saw it was uninhabitable. It stank. Pools of vomit scattered around the slippery floor. The only hope was to reach Ellis Island. She clung to the hope that her brother would be waiting for her there, at the Kissing Post. That's where relatives met, at the place they called the Kissing Post, where they kissed and hugged. She prayed that he received her letter from Antwerp and that he would come and save them.

Yussi woke to the smell of vomit and human waste. His back ached from the pressure of the metal bed frame. He didn't want to move and wake Dovid, who finally slept peacefully in his arms. In the lower bunks Shayna and his mother slept as well, along with most of the other steerage passengers. A few people walked around dazed. He still heard the sound of rain from the deck above, but no thunder now. The steady *thump, swish, thump, swish* of the engine could be heard again. He didn't know how many days since the intense storm began. Night and day blended into one long nightmare of cries and moans.

He shifted the sleeping child to the bed, still damp from Dovid's pee and the sweat of the little boy's body where he lay for at least two days. Yussi didn't know if the ship's steward would give them clean sheets or how long it would be until they reached America. The stewards had come infrequently during the storm and left porridge or sandwiches, which no one could eat.

He looked around the room to locate the men who usually *davened* with him, but no one was visible. He was alone with his prayers.

Maybe it was the smell, maybe the moans, but during the storm he was haunted by the memory of his father's death. Along with the vision of his father's shrunken body, his bony hand as he held Yussi's, his whispered voice were the memories Yussi carried of the prayers chanted in shul for his recovery. He could still see the faces of their neighbors, of Mordecai, Munshik, Yitzik, and all his father's friends, their voices raised in the ancient prayer of *Mi Shebeirakh avoteinu*. The same prayer he uttered silently as he stood over Shayna's bed as she convulsed with nausea.

May the one who blessed our ancestors, Abraham, Isaac, and Jacob, bless and heal those who are ill. May the Blessed Holy One be filled with compassion for their health to be restored and their strength revived. May God swiftly send them a complete renewal of body and spirit, and let us say, Amen. Over and over as he held a bucket for her, wiped her face with cool cloth, or when he raised her head so she could sip water, the *Mi Shebeirackh* whispered from his lips.

His mother and Dovid had simply vomited and slept, but Shayna's nausea continued hour after hour. The other prayer in his mind was an ugly one, maybe even evil. Maybe one that God should never hear, but Yussi prayed that along with the contents of her stomach, the contents of her womb would empty. This thing growing in her should never take a breath.

He knew the passage in the Talmud where Rashi, the great scholar, wrote that it was not a living thing until it came into the world. Couldn't it be removed before birth to save the mother? And wouldn't Shayna's life be destroyed, should it be born? Their life together, destroyed. So was it a sin to pray for Shayna's life?

She slept quietly now, his prayers for her recovery heard. He touched her more during the storm than he had ever touched her before and in ways he never imagined. Like a nurse, until his mother was well enough to help and took over her more private care. He'd seen all the parts of her body now, and it was nothing like his dreams in the shtetl when he knew she would become his wife. Even on the wedding night, he hadn't dared look.

What a *nar* he was, like a foolish child living with a *bubbeh-mayse,* a fairy tale. Pogroms were all around them, her parents murdered, poverty everywhere, and yet he imagined once they married they would be safe. *Meshuge.* He was hungry to hold her, care for her. Nothing in his imagination had prepared him for seeing her lying ravaged on the ground. He knew how he should think, how a *mensch* would think, but in his heart he felt only disappointment and shame. He offered her no protection. No safety. What use was he? And he lied to her. He did not want to raise a child that was not his own. Give his name to *goyishe* offspring.

And so his thoughts wandered along roads with no end. He prayed to God to keep his mind clear and not let him get lost in despair. Man dreams and God decides. Yussi knew his happiness depended on trusting the Divine, trusting in wisdom beyond his own. How easy this was before the death of his father when he sat with learned teachers at the yeshive studying the holy books all day. Some days he stretched his mind even more and relaxed into an even deeper peace with Shayna's father's lessons. His mind replete with learning.

Even before his father's last breath, he could no longer attend yeshive. His brother Gershon had a family of his own to support. His mother could not manage the cabinet shop by herself, although she insisted she could. Yussi had to fill those shoes—uncomfortable, but his to wear.

In whispered conversations just out of hearing of the dying man, Manya had said, "Your father taught me, maybe not the fancy things, but how to use the lathe, clamps, all his tools. I helped him. Since the beginning. Way before you were born. I'll find someone to drive the wagon, to deliver the chairs to Kiev. I can make simple furniture to sell. You must stay at the yeshive."

"Papa taught me to work with my hands for a reason. He wanted a *bal-takhlis* for a son, not just a *bal-Torah*, a practical man, not just a scholar."

"You will not work with your hands," Manya had told him. "*Seykhl* like yours shouldn't be wasted. You were born to serve God, to study Torah. I'll manage."

They took turns sitting with his father, caring for him during the weeks he lay dying. But little work was finished. Manya often refused to leave her husband's bedside, so Yussi would sometimes go to the cabinet shop, sit next to the workbench, and look around at the boards piled against the wall, the pile of already shaped legs, and his father's tools. He didn't know where to start, but he knew he couldn't go back to the yeshive.

More movement now in the bunks around him. No *takhlis* in thinking these thoughts about the past. Yet he couldn't rid himself of what could have been. More and more as they neared America, he understood there would be more mouths to feed. Shayna. Dovid and his mother. Most likely a baby. He would seek work in a cabinet shop. Did they hire immigrants? He must learn English. Amidst all the questions without answers was the one that picked at his brain the most. How would he keep his soul nourished in this foreign place? Would he ever find a way to study Torah?

He needed to cleanse himself before morning prayers. He walked around the compartment and looked for men to join a *minyan*. Morning prayers would ease his spirit.

Chapter 20

A morning fog covered the ship's deck so Shayna could scarcely see Yussi standing just feet from her next to the railing, the small trunk balanced on his shoulder. If America was there, it was invisible in the fog. The ship's horn sounded over and over as it moved forward in the haze. Shayna tightened the shawl covering her hair. In one hand she clutched the suitcase with all of the tangible memories of her family. Dovid held a straw basket with his clothing with one hand and clutched Shayna's skirt with the other. A shawl wrapped around Manya secured a large bundle along her back.

"Are we here?" she heard Dovid ask, and Manya answer, "Yes. Soon. This morning we will come to America."

For days no one had discussed it. Shayna knew they all waited for it to lose its grip and never live, that the bad blood would extinguish itself. But all of the jostling, pushing, hunger, fear—nothing had taken it out. Each day, Shayna waited, prayed for relief from this burden. But her prayers remained unanswered.

For days Shayna stayed in her bunk, too exhausted to move except to line up twice a day for the meager food the ship's steward served. The seasickness she experienced during the storm, combined with her pregnancy, left her drained. Many of the other immigrants, including Faigl and her children, all half-starved, thirsty, seasick, and frightened, remained near their belongings in the unbearable stench of the room. But tomorrow would be the last morning on the ship.

Neither Yussi nor Manya talked about it, but it could no longer be ignored. As she lay in the bunk, she wondered if she could find a doctor in America to take the thing from her, but without the language or the money, she knew it would be impossible. She barely remembered her brother and she didn't know what was in his heart. She didn't know his wife or what they would think. She did not want to be an object of pity or scorn.

"Tomorrow you will clear all your belongings and prepare to disembark," the ship's steward said in German as he distributed the thin soup. Only Dovid ate it for the bit of nourishment he might get even if it was *treyf.* There were several people who began translating as the news passed through the long line of people waiting for food. Dovid and Manya sat at the table with Faigl and her children.

Yussi motioned Shayna away from the long table where they often ate and motioned to her bunk. They each had a slice of white bread that tasted unbaked and the last pieces of the now-dried salami. She wondered what kind of life they would have in America, with Ulkeh. Would there be enough food?

Every day Yussi asked Shayna the same question. "Any change?" he asked even though, if there had been, he would recognize the relief on her face immediately. Every day she shook her head no—the seed still clung to her. He took her hand in his own and squeezed. On the day before they landed in America, his touch gave her confidence to say the words she barely said to herself.

"This thing in my belly may one day take a breath and be a living baby. It seems now there is a good chance it will be born. God has not taken it from me, despite my prayers.

"Shaynaleh, we don't have to talk about it now."

"Yes we do. Yussi, we have to decide. It has survived, at least so far." She moved away from Yussi to the farthest end of the bunk but continued talking. Yussi had to lean in closer to hear her almost whispered words.

"It has a strong will to live. It is of me as much as it is of the beast that planted it. As I feel this baby grow within me, I think of all those I have lost, of all we as a people have lost. No one can take the place of Perl, of my mother, my father, baby Sarah. All the others. But once there is a birth, there will be life. And it carries my blood, my family's blood.

Can you ever accept this child, if it is born, as your own and give it your name and your blessings?" She didn't look at him as she spoke.

She knew he must have thought about it since the moment they discovered she was pregnant. He didn't speak much, but she knew his thoughts were deep. They sat quietly and watched the people mill about the room, starting to gather their belongings. She didn't know if he heard her, didn't know if he even wanted to answer.

Manya poked her finger toward Dovid's hand without moving her eyes downward. She inched her finger closer. With his eyes directly on hers, he reached out quickly to slam her finger on the table. She escaped his attack, provoking a giggle from the boy. Again, she slid her finger along the table. Again, he tried to catch her.

"My turn!" he yelled. Manya made herself comfortable on the bench, as comfortable as she could. She rested her hands on the table and watched as Dovid slid his finger toward her.

"Look at me," he said and poked her hand. A much louder giggle this time along with a big smile from Manya.

He loved the finger poke game almost as much as he loved the game he made up with his little wooden dog. He moved the carved figure between Manya's gnarled fingers and barked, trying to scare Manya into retreat. Back and forth they played.

"Today's the day," Manya said. "Tomorrow we land in America and we must cut your fingernails."

Dovid shook his head and sat on his hands.

She'd waited for Shayna to take care of him, to make sure he cleaned his teeth, washed his hands. She didn't want to take over. Manya didn't know if it was her hunger to care for another little boy, or if indeed Shayna neglected, or had no idea how to care for a child. The little boy's nails were long enough to hold a lot of dirt. They might send him back.

"You go hide and if I find you, I get to cut your nails."

"You won't find me," Dovid said as he slid under the long table and crawled between the legs of people finishing the dinner. She counted to ten and pushed up from the bench, her joints stiff from sitting.

Yussi sat with Shayna on the lower bunk. Manya recognized her son's nervous habit; he twisted the strands from his *tsitses* around and around as he talked with Shayna. Manya wondered if his eyes stayed on Shayna's face or dropped to her belly, already visibly pregnant. Would anyone notice at Ellis Island? Did it matter? Most miscarriages happened before the fourth month, but it still could happen any day. Manya pinched her arm as she bent to seek Dovid under the table—pinched herself for evil thoughts. None of her prayers had been answered. The baby would live, maybe live to destroy their lives. She knew her son would never be able to accept this child as his own. Would Shayna be willing to give it up for adoption? Crazy thought. What would Shayna tell her brother?

Manya kept her eye on the little boy as he crawled around. She had been Dovid's age when the soldiers found her wandering the roads around Odessa alone. So young. She knew nothing of her parents. They must keep the memories of Dovid's parents alive. Like Manya, he was an orphan. She wouldn't wish that on her worst enemies.

She glanced at Shayna and noticed the buttons on her blouse pulled against her growing breasts. Her pregnancy more visible. Manya always thought her own parents had died, not that they abandoned her. But as she watched Shayna, a new idea stole into her mind. Maybe she too had been a child of rape and no one wanted her. No one took her. Only the orphanage. The soldiers brought her to a Jewish orphanage because she only spoke Yiddish and there she stayed until she was given in marriage to the widower Shmuel.

She pinched her arm, no need to dig up old memories. Where was Dovid? She saw his curly head peek out from under the far end of the long table. He ducked in again when their eyes met. Several children now crawled with him along the very dirty floor. Stupid game, she thought. She tried to remember the games she played with her little babies before they died, but a steel door slid down to cover her memories of them. None of the three she lost ever reached four years old.

Yussi's arm now held Shayna close. Manya saw him kiss her forehead. He would never tell his mother what they talked about, what secrets they told each other. She thought maybe her son was foolish enough to think he could raise this abomination.

Yussi took Shayna's hand, raised his arm over her shoulder, and pulled her close, "I told you from the beginning, *mirtse-hashem*, if God wills it. If there is a birth, I will be the baby's father. I will give the baby my name, everything I would give to my own. *Mirtse-hashem*. If this is God's will, I believe it is right." Even as he said the words he knew Shayna wanted to hear, Yussi questioned his ability to accept the child, to love the child.

"You have this kind of faith?"

He nodded and kissed her forehead. "It's always been in God's hands."

Shayna covered her face, her thoughts tumbling over each other. She knew there was something else she needed to say, but she was even more afraid to voice the words.

"Can you also live with a wife who does not love this God of yours? Maybe once when I was a child, I had faith, but now there's only a *bubbeh-mayse*, an old wives' tale. From childhood I had the habit of praying, but I know no one is listening, no one is there. And if there is such a thing as a God, he is a reckless God who throws away his people. A God I cannot love."

"But then, why do you always pray?"

Without thinking, Shayna answered, "Do you have a better idea?"

Shayna expected him to get angry, to shame her for being an *apikoyres*, one who does not believe. Instead he laughed and ran his fingers along his beard. He reached the end of it quickly and seemed surprised. It was slow to grow into its full length. Soon Manya and Dovid would finish eating and return. They needed to finish this conversation in private, very difficult to do in their short married life. Only alone together one night.

"Remember the story of Jacob—Jacob who wrestled with an angel, or maybe wrestled with God. The rabbis do not agree on what this story means. I don't know myself. But you remind me of Jacob, fighting always, struggling. If you had no faith, why would you struggle?"

Shayna was too tired to decipher what he said, but then he added something very simple that she did understand.

"I don't know if any rabbis would agree with me, but I believe that God lives deep inside each one of us. All of his children. Even the most evil. *Yeytser-tov* and *yeytser-hore*, the urge to good or evil. We choose again and again. Conflict with God doesn't matter, what matters is how you behave. Shaynaleh, since I first saw you as a child, God shines from you. He is always in your heart."

His words came to her like dawn comes to the sky, bits of color rising in her heart, but before she found any words, Manya interrupted.

"Yussi, help me take down these bundles. We need to have everything ready for the morning. Tomorrow we come to America." She stood between them and reached toward the bundles piled in the upper bunk.

Shayna realized there was something more she had to say before they got off the ship, before they landed in America. "Sit a minute Manya. Dovid, you still have a little time to play with your friends before we pack up everything and go to sleep. See if you can find them. I'll call you when it's time." She kissed both cheeks and tapped him on the nose. Yussi gave him a quick *patsh* on the behind.

"One year ago I had parents, a sister, a family. All was taken. For everything you have done to help me, I am in your debt."

"I made trouble for you in Antwerp. I talked too much."

"Yes, you do," Shayna said. "But I think you mean no harm. You're always good to me, to Dovid." She closed her eyes for a moment and then added, "I have a favor to ask of you, something very important to me. If God has not taken this thing from my belly before we meet my brother…"

Manya interrupted, "It's as stubborn as you, a real *akshun*. You'll have this baby in America."

Shayna clasped her hands together and looked at them both. "I want us to lie to my brother and his family."

Manya looked at Yussi. Neither said anything. The cacophony of sounds around them filled the space. Loud voices, crying children, dishes clacking, and always the thump of the engine. For a moment no one talked. Yussi chewed on the nail of his index finger, which Shayna learned meant he was desperate for a cigarette. Manya's eyes roamed around the large compartment but focused nowhere.

"I don't want my brother and his wife to know what happened to me," Shayna whispered. "They can never know."

"It was not your fault." Manya patted Shayna's knee. "You must never forget, you did nothing wrong." Shayna ignored Manya's words, which might be true. But in Shayna's heart, forever she would feel the stain of that day. She leaned in as close as she could get.

"I was seven when Ulkeh left. I don't remember much. I don't know what kind of a man he is. I know nothing about his wife or her family. The risk is too great. I don't want their scorn. I don't want their pity." Shayna put her fingers over her mouth and was quiet for a moment. "More important, I don't want this child to ever know about what happened. The shame is mine, not the baby's. No one must ever tell the baby."

"But you're married now." Manya looked confused. "There is no problem. I won't say anything." She looked at Yussi for confirmation.

He nodded. "Shayna's child will be our child."

Manya placed her hand over her heart. "If this is God's will, this child will be one of my grandchildren."

"If they ask, we say we married before we left the shtetl," Shayna added. She looked directly into Yussi's eyes and waited for him to nod, then to Manya and waited for her to agree.

She wondered what sorrow would come from a life built on lies. Would they ever find peace of mind? As she rose to find Dovid, she thought about her mother, who always accepted what came before her. She'd say, "Why pull your hair out with worry? You'll need it to keep your head warm," which never made much sense until now.

The horn blasted again, louder than before, and someone yelled in Russian, "We're almost there!" Out of the fog, a huge statue appeared, a graceful arm reached toward the heavens. Shayna recognized it from the pamphlets that flooded the countryside in Russia. Come to America advertisements from the ship companies. The ship's office in Antwerp had a picture of the statue as well, along with a poem, which Shayna hoped to read one day.

She knew it must be the Statue of Liberty. A symbol of their hope, a symbol of sanctuary. Shayna's hands were full, and she couldn't wipe away the tears that gathered. She felt them slide along her cheeks and tasted the salt as it hit her lips. Gradually the fog lifted and a vision appeared: buildings that reached into the clouds, hundreds of buildings each climbing taller than the next. New York.

"Make a line. Make a line. Don't push," the ship's officer yelled in German, so much like Yiddish they had no trouble understanding. But no one seemed interested in forming a line. Everyone got as close to the railing as they could, their eyes raised to the magical sight before them.

Doctors and officials in uniforms came aboard, but they walked directly to the upper decks. The steerage passengers waited in the chilly autumn air with no information about the next steps. Someone said the rich ones never wait. They would disembark quickly after only a few questions. Someone else said that the ship's company just took money from third-class passengers and then dropped them someplace else, maybe in the wilderness somewhere, and left them to die. Someone else said they had to stay on the boat for many more days in order to reach Ellis Island.

Shayna tried to manage her thoughts, to wait quietly. Soon she would see Ulkeh and everything would be good. He would be waiting for them. Luckily, she did not mention the wedding, only that Dovid was with her, and Yussi and Manya also. She didn't say who they were, only names. He would help them; they were family. But maybe America had changed him. Maybe he would not be able to help. He had sent the tickets, he must have some extra money. Would he find a place for them to live, food to eat?

Lunchtime passed with no food served to them on deck. The rich people started to leave the ship. The immigrants on the steerage deck were restless and angry. Shayna worried there might be trouble.

Dovid started to cry. "Shah, *tatele*." She dropped her suitcases and took him from Yussi's arms. "It's going to be all right. Soon, you'll meet your Uncle Ulkeh. I think maybe he has some children. You'll have cousins to play with." He rarely cried, but Shayna knew what must have happened. He had wet himself again. It had been too long since he went to the toilet. He was not the only child crying.

A man they hadn't seen before in a uniform blew a whistle and spoke in what must have been English. She recognized a few words and had learned the numbers. Word passed through the crowd that a barge would come and take them to Ellis Island. The last hurdle.

Ellis Island must be an island, because they called it an island, but it was like a castle from the outside the longest, most beautiful building Shayna had ever seen. Sunlight reflected off the many windows, like a glittering dream. But once inside, the story was different. Carrying their luggage, they climbed a long staircase into a huge room, a room larger than her entire shtetl. From below, the noise assaulted them: shouts and cries, feet stomping, doors closing, and the sound of a thousand languages being spoken at once. Many ships must have arrived, because there were more people in the massive room than she'd seen in her lifetime.

Orders came from men in uniforms, in a language she could not yet understand. She didn't know if they were police or soldiers, nor did she know if danger was imminent. Nothing about a man in a uniform felt like America to her. No one said police arrested people or soldiers might shoot them at Ellis Island, but everyone looked away from where the men in uniform stood. Shayna felt the fear of everyone around her, no matter what language they spoke.

As she walked up the stairs with Dovid, she noticed men in white coats made chalk marks on people's clothing. She stayed toward the middle of the staircase and kept her eyes downward. The chalk marks had been discussed on the ship. She'd overheard a Russian woman explain to another Russian that she'd been to Ellis Island before and got a chalk mark on her jacket. The men in white coats had noticed her limp and she'd been sent back, deported without reaching America. But her children had been allowed in, along with her husband. Now she had special shoes that helped her walk straight. Every day on the ship she practiced. They would not catch her this time. Shayna lost track of her in the vast crowd and didn't know if they caught her again.

She was grateful for the new jackets she had sewn in Antwerp and the attempts they had made to make themselves clean and presentable. She knew their smell was strong, but other people looked much worse; some were dressed almost in rags. They sat for a long time until they heard their names called. They stood and walked to an official and were comforted to see other people they recognized from their ship gathering in the same line. Without explanation, the officials separated the men and the women, and before Shayna could catch her breath, someone stopped her. She recognized a button hook in his hand; he came close to her and quickly lifted each eyelid without saying a word. She remembered Manya's warning on the train. This must be the inspection for eye diseases. She turned and could no longer see Yussi. He'd been taken with the other men. She felt her heart race. She wanted to run and find him, ask questions, seek explanations. Instead she remained silent, did not draw attention to herself. She knew they deported people, sent them back to Russia or from wherever they'd come.

More doctors checked her heart, her ears, and her throat. Manya came behind her in line. No chalk mark on her or Dovid. More directions in English, more lines. Whenever she could, she held Dovid in her arms, sang to him, laughed with him, anything she could think of to help him not be afraid. Manya helped her with the luggage, but by the time the women finished all the medical lines and were directed to another huge room with long tables, with dishes and silverware, she thought she might faint.

No idea where Yussi was. No idea when they would see him again, nor where she could find Ulkeh. He knew the name of the ship. He'd bought the tickets, but would he know on what day she might come if her letter hadn't arrived? She knew more hurdles awaited. Their papers had to be verified and questions asked. Many of the same questions the shipping company asked, but everything would depend on their answers.

Food was distributed. Some kind of meat between slices of white bread. Dovid shoved it into his mouth immediately, didn't wait for permission. A long yellow fruit was on the table, called a banana, which no could figure out how to open. But there were apples and cheese and bread without meat that she and Manya ate. There seemed to be no end to the food that was distributed in America.

As they ate, she realized a large group of men entered the dining area. She recognized Yussi. Without thought she stood on the bench and yelled his name until he saw her and smiled, a smile as filled with joy as her own. They were not lost to each other.

This time Yussi came with them when they entered another large room, the registry office, where they sat on long benches facing tables where men in uniforms sat.

"Edelman family," someone called, and Shayna remembered that was her family name now only when she saw Yussi and Manya rise. The Edelmans. A Yiddish translator stood by their side as they were interviewed. First Yussi. Next Manya, and then the questions were for her.

Yes, Shayna confirmed the information already on the papers from the S.S. Finland. Yes, Shayna Edelman was her name. The man showed her the spelling of her name in English, which she had learned from Freide's daughter, Silvi, in Antwerp. Yes, she was seventeen. In truth she was by now eighteen, but there was no reason to correct the record. Yes, she was married. Yes, she was born in the Ukraine. Yes, she was Jewish. She showed her visa. There were more questions about her politics. Shayna had been told they might deport Bolsheviks. She didn't know much about politics. Yes, she could read and write. Yes, she had money. She expected Ulkeh to help them with the money, but she didn't know where he was. Fortunately, when they insisted on seeing their money, she was prepared. Children accompanied by adults didn't have to prove they had funds. From the extra tickets they'd sold in Brody, the rubles they'd converted, the money she'd made sewing for the *rebetsn*, they were able to show the money they needed. The rabbi in Antwerp helped them convert their money into real American dollars. She was prepared.

No one guessed in her belly there clung another immigrant, one who was not noticed, probably because her clothes hung on her scrawny frame. No need to tell the officials. Shayna answered for Dovid as well. She tried to tell the man that her nephew's name was Dovid. She even knew how to spell it in English, but the man wrote David and so he became David Lev Goldfarb.

On the ships and in pamphlets all over the old country, there were stories about Ellis Island, so most of the immigrants knew what to expect. But there was no preparation possible for the tension in the building, the anxiety that built as they faced each new obstacle. At each station, people had been stopped. People she recognized from the ship, whether by chalk marks or something else. Everyone saw people being taken out of the lines and sent to another room to wait. To be tested more. One woman fainted when the doctors listened to her heart and men came with a stretcher to carry her away while her family tried to follow, crying and screaming.

And then as she watched, the official stamped their visas. Stamp. Stamp. Stamp. Stamp. "Welcome to the United States," he said.

Chapter 21

New York City, October 1919

"*Ich darf pishn.*" Shayna recognized the signs, Dovid's tense jaw and his face paler than usual. The same look he had when Perl taught him to hold his little penis and aim. She smiled, remembering the *mayse* Perl always told about the time Dovid miscalculated and sprayed her skirt. No time now for memories as he pulled at her hand. Why hadn't he told her in the registry office, where the toilets were easy to find?

Manya and Yussi followed her as she maneuvered through the jostling crowds waiting for loved ones to claim them as they exited Ellis Island. Where was Ulkeh? Maybe she wouldn't recognize him among all the strangers.

She searched for the WC symbol but wasn't tall enough to see over the heads of men as tall and thick as walls. Yussi yelled and pointed to something and they all headed in that direction.

"*Tante,*" Dovid whined as his fingers pulled at her arm. She wanted to swat him away, pick him off of her body, like a leech from the lake. Instead she smiled down at him.

"Shh, *Tateleh*, soon. Such a sweet boy." She patted his head, ran her fingers through his hair as they waited in a line, imitating his mother's touches. In the tiny cubicle, she pushed his fingers aside as he struggled with the buttons on his trousers.

"Look at you, such a big boy now." He truly was a good boy, a sweet boy, quiet, and obedient. She could manage him, but what about the thing growing inside, bulging up her stomach so the protrusion stuck out for all to see? Her brother would notice.

Maybe in the time it took to take care of their business and return to the Kissing Post, where families reunited, Ulkeh had left. She couldn't see him. All of Europe gathered in that hall, although all the languages were different, the hugs and kisses, the tears spoke the same language. She watched as men knelt and kissed children, as an old couple bowed their heads to an even older man. With a scream, a girl jumped into the arms of a well-dressed man. Shayna and her family stood in the midst of the tears and laughter and searched for her brother. They lowered their bags and waited.

"Is this America now?" Dovid asked.

"Barukh Hashem." She nodded and knelt before him. "This is the door to America. As soon as we find your uncle, he will take us to where we will live in America, to your new home."

Shayna remembered Ulkeh as a tall young man who resembled her father, the same dark beard and deep-set eyes. He would be older, but she thought she would recognize him. Yussi and Manya only vaguely remembered him, but as they scanned the room from one side to another and back again, no one seemed familiar to them. Maybe he hadn't received her letter. Or maybe he had already left.

Around them were dozens of men advertising themselves to be guides, to take immigrants to any address for a small fee, to take them to trains, to sell them lunch boxes, to offer drinks at bargain prices. Shayna felt she was back at the market in Obodivka, an experience that taught her not to trust easy offers.

Shayna could see the exhaustion on Manya's face. Dovid was pale and on the edge of tears. She recognized the look that had become familiar to her on Yussi's face, his lips tight, eyelids lowered, and knew he was holding himself awake. She knew the same signs must be on her own face. She certainly felt the ache in her back and the rumbling in her belly.

They walked around the edge of the large room, full of posts, but at none of them did she see anyone who looked like her brother. She did see several people, old ones and young ones holdings signs with names on them. She studied each name, some in Russian or Yiddish but most in the alphabet they used in America. Many of the people holding signs were also tired, may have been waiting for many hours. Some of them leaned against the wall and when Shayna approached they stood taller and held their signs out. A young boy, maybe ten or eleven, held a sign in English and the words were clear "Shayna Rifkin."

"I am Shayna. Shayna Edelman now."

A smile burst on the young man's face. He removed his cap and bowed low. "Welcome, welcome to New York," he said in Yiddish. "Call me Max. I'm Jack's special messenger. He sent me."

"Jack? Where's Ulkeh?"

"You're brother, Jack." His eyebrows went up, his face tilted. "Your brother is a very busy man, very important." He pulled some money from his vest pocket. "This is money for us to take the ferry. To bring you to him."

Shayna continued to look bewildered.

"So important he can't meet his sister who comes all the way across the ocean?" Manya asked as she looked at young Max from top to bottom. She started with his scuffed brown shoes, then the long socks tucked into his knee-length trousers and ending with his once white shirt, obviously too large for him, and now visible under a thin jacket. "Some special messenger he sent."

"He must have an American name now," Yussi added. "Ulkeh is now Jack."

"Yes, Jack, Jack Rifkin is very busy, very busy. But he trusted me with money for the ferry." Again he showed them the bills. With that, Max slapped his cap back on his head, turned, and motioned to them to follow. He did not pause to help them carry any of their bundles.

They boarded another boat, called a ferry, which was much smaller than the ship from Europe. Packed from side to side with other immigrants, it chugged toward the giant buildings which, from a distance, appeared covered with spots. Could they be thousands of glass windows? Shayna recognized some people from the medical line, others from the S.S. Finland, and some from the registry office. Dreams in their eyes, as there must be in her own. On her right stood the Statue of Liberty, tall and clear in the light of dusk. A proud welcome. She tightened a scarf around Dovid's neck, held his hand tightly, and pulled her own shawl over her jacket. She could feel winter in the air.

"Battery Park." Max pointed to the trees around them as he hustled them off the ferry. The park was the first thing Shayna noticed that was familiar to her: grass, birds, trees. She left home when spring buds opened and now here the branches were bare. Couples strolled along the paths arm and arm. Children ran between the trees laughing. The people wore winter coats, many in styles she had never seen. She wanted to sit for a while and catch her breath, rest while she watched the people and studied their clothes. But Max hurried them along the path until the trees were gone and they were surrounded by buildings five and six stories high. Automobiles raced along the streets along with streetcars, similar to those she'd seen in Antwerp. Everything moved fast past her as she struggled to keep up with the young boy.

"Stop," she yelled to Max when she noticed Manya weave from side to side as she walked. "We can't walk so fast. We're exhausted. Wait," she yelled again. This time he stopped and looked back at all of them now leaning against a building.

"Our feet don't work after so many days on the ship. The street is rolling beneath us."

Dovid raised his arms to Shayna for her to lift him, but she shook her head, "Just a little longer, *tatele*." She looked at Yussi but his eyes were closed.

"Jack didn't give me money for the streetcar; we have to walk. Please, just a little longer and we'll be there."

The buildings blocked out the sun. She could tell it was setting, but couldn't see the sky, only the tops of the buildings, which got shabbier and shabbier as they walked. Laundry hung in the small spaces between some of the buildings. People were everywhere on the streets, many sitting on the steps in front of buildings, others pushing and shoving along the crowded sidewalk. Fewer cars drove by, but more people, hundreds of people hurrying. Men pushed carts with fruits and vegetables, carts laden with clothing, pots and pans, more things than she'd ever seen before. These people spoke Yiddish, and the signs on many storefronts were in Yiddish or Hebrew. A kosher butcher. A kosher bakery. She couldn't hold all the commotion in her mind, like a confused dream, like a shtetl, transported to America.

Max darted through a doorway and left them to stand near a store-front window. They huddled with their bundles to avoid the push of so many people. Old and young hurried by, intent on the tasks driving them, oblivious to the new immigrants. Overpowering the noise and the commotion was the smell of horse manure, exhaust fumes from automobiles, rotten fruit lying in the street, and a smell she knew came from her own body as well as the people rushing, the smell of sweat and unwashed bodies. Through the window she could see dozens of young women, their heads bent over sewing machines. Max talked to a stout man of medium height who looked up and saw them through the window. No *peyes*, almost bald, but familiar to her. Ulkeh. He pushed the young boy aside and rushed outside. Max followed close on his heels.

"Shaynaleh, Shaynaleh, Shaynaleh, *zise!*" Tears filled his eyes as he stood back and looked at her. "Beautiful, beautiful, just like Mamme. Shayna, just like Mamme." His embrace engulfed her. Her body sank into his, like it was her father who held her. She knew it was her brother even though he looked like a *goy*. Clean shaven. Not even a yarmulke.

"You need a bath," he said as he turned away from Shayna and bent to look at Dovid. "And you must be Perl's son. Let me look." Although Dovid clung to Shayna's skirt, Ulkeh jerked him away and lifted him high while he stared at him. "He looks just like me. Such a handsome little boy. Looks intelligent too."

Yussi and Manya waited to be introduced, but Ulkeh ignored them and continued to swing Dovid back and forth, "You'll love New York. You'll love the business." Dovid wiggled to free himself. "My nephew, my son. Rifkin and Son. No more Dovid, you need an American name. David. David Rifkin. You'll be so happy."

"Ulkeh," Shayna touched his arm. "His family name is Goldfarb, Dovid Lev Goldfarb. That's his name, given to him by his father, Perl's husband, *olev-hasholem*. May he rest in peace."

"Not a problem. I'll adopt him. I have two daughters; I want a son. We'll change his name. Right David? You'll be my son."

Meshuge, Shayna wanted to say but kept silent. She looked at Yussi and Manya, all of them bewildered. Although Ulkeh spoke in Yiddish, she didn't think Dovid had any idea what Ulkeh meant. She'd never considered someone could take Dovid from her. The idea never came to her mind. Even when she was too tired to care for him, she never imagined letting go of her sister's first born. Was it possible? She was his aunt, but Ulkeh the uncle. Now that Yussi was her husband, did he have the right to an opinion? She never thought to ask.

Her thoughts were interrupted by a scream from Dovid as he wiggled to free himself, *"Tante, Tante* Shayna."

At first Ulkeh didn't let go of the boy. "I can see already he's spoiled. He'll learn to behave. In America, you'll be a good boy, right?"

Dovid's face grew even paler. Shayna noticed sweat on his forehead and suddenly, without warning, Dovid heaved and began to cry as he vomited on Ulkeh, who dropped him immediately. He lay crumpled on the cement sidewalk, his face covered in tears. Shayna bent to lift him and cradle the crying boy in her arms.

With a white handkerchief taken from his pocket, Ulkeh wiped the bile off of his head with slow precision. He stared at Dovid clinging to Shayna, shook his head, and turned back to the factory. At the door, he snapped at Max. "Take them to 412. Clara left food for them."

No one said anything, nor did they look at each other. Manya and Yussi divided Shayna's bags between them while Shayna carried Dovid, who hid his head on her shoulder. Max led them up a dim staircase. The only light came from dirty windows at each landing.

"Before you know it, you'll be up there," Max said as he raced up the steps. Yussi went first, then Manya, with Shayna following carrying Dovid. The walls smelled stale, musty, and the stairs creaked. City smells. Alien to her. They stopped at each landing to catch their breath. Shayna knew in the past these steps would not have been a problem, but after months of travel, two weeks on a ship, a long walk and a near starvation diet, not to mention the thing in her belly, she didn't think she could make it without pausing on each step. Dovid's face was white, but she had to lower him to the stairs.

There was no air in the hall as they mounted to the fourth floor. Max waited for them by an open door after reaching up to pull the string on a light bulb that hung from the ceiling in the main room.

Manya and Yussi followed Max into the large room. Immediately, Dovid curled up on a sofa near the door, his whimpers quieter now. Shayna sat next to him and smoothed damp hair from his forehead. She watched Manya across the room, her mother-in-law's dress hung on her once full frame, her back bent, and yet, despite her age, she had managed the long walk from the ferry and four flights of stairs. A woman to admire.

"So this is America?" Manya asked as she walked to a small alcove where a single window looked down at the street. "I didn't see any of the streets lined with gold, did you?"

"Maybe no gold in the streets, but look at this great apartment," Max said. "Ulkeh remodeled the building when he bought it."

"He owns it?" Yussi asked.

Max nodded. "Yes he does." Max leaned in toward Yussi, "And the word is he owns another building too. That's what I heard."

"Is there a shul near here?"

"I don't know. Likely," Max said. "Lots of Jewish people here." He turned to Manya, "Really lady, you should have seen this place before. You have your own sink and a stove. Jack furnished it for you. Look at these open shelves with dishes, pots and pans for cooking. Everything you'll need." Next to the alcove was a partial room with a bed and chair. Shayna thought they might enclose it more by adding a curtain. Max pointed to the sofa where Dovid now slept. "That turns into a bed. You don't have to start from scratch like some of the greenhorns." A wooden table with four chairs stood in the middle of the room.

Manya examined the chairs, "Look Yussi. Like they were put together in five minutes. No cushions on the seats. We always added a cushion even on the cheapest chairs we made, right Yussi?"

"Mamme, *zol zayn shah,* be quiet now. Everything is good. Jack prepared it for us."

Manya shook her head and went to examine the large bed behind the curtain.

"Clara, Jack's wife, left soup for you on the stove."

"Is it kosher?" Yussi studied the contents of a pot.

"Likely. Likely. That's what they sell around here. I need to hurry. Follow me, I'll show you the water closet. Jack will kill me if I don't hurry."

Shayna joined them as Max led the way along the dim hallway to a room with a sink, a toilet, and a bathtub. She covered her nose as she went into the room. Almost as bad as the WC on the train to Antwerp. *Shmutsik*, filthy.

"Who uses this?"

"Everyone on this floor."

Shayna wanted to ask Max questions: who lives here, who are they, from where, how many, who cleans the WC. Too tired. Later she would find answers.

"Mamme, sleep on the bed with Shayna tonight. More comfortable for you. Dovid and I will take the sofa. Now I'll go find a shul. Time for evening prayers. Where are the keys? I see a chain lock but no keys. There must be a key." He left without waiting for an answer.

Shayna lay still in the bed next to Manya, who immediately began to snore. Her mind whirled. At least they weren't buried in a mass grave somewhere in the Ukraine. Ulkeh had helped them. Soon there would be a baby. Everything mixed up in her head, and as tired as she was, sleep did not come easily.

Y'hi ratzon milfanekha, Yussi prayed as he left the building and wandered alone along the strange avenues before him. May it be your will, Lord, our God, and the God of our ancestors, that you lead us toward peace, guide our footsteps toward peace, and make us reach our desired destination for life, gladness, and peace. Unlike the journey from Obodivka, across Poland, Germany, all of Europe, he was safe now, physically safe. No Cossacks charging through streets. But what of his soul? He prayed for a good end to his search, to find a *minyan*, to find a congregation of people from his own village, to find *landslayt*, to find the touch and taste of home. To find a place to study the holy books. Maybe he could find others who'd left before the last pogroms, maybe a few families who'd also survived the recent pogrom. In the chaos of their flight from Obodivka, he hadn't thought about names or addresses. Fischel Malinsky, his father's close friend, should be here somewhere in New York. Surely he would be a leader in a synagogue. People would know him. Chaim Gluzman and his two sons also left with the caravan. Wouldn't they be in New York? *Frume Yidn*, very observant Jews, there would be a shul. All around him as he walked, he saw street signs he could read, some in Yiddish, some in Hebrew. The words spoken all around him were familiar, yet everyone was a stranger. Maybe from Romania, or Belarus. Who knew?

They spoke the same language, but so many of the women walked around without their hair covered, men without yarmulkes. Crowded. Dirty. Carts overflowing with clothing, fruit, vegetables, tables, a collection of things. The old market in Obodivka, like an empty closet compared to the riches here. Where did they study? Where were the yeshives? He stood on a corner, looked at the buildings on his left, on his right. He sounded out the English, Broadway Street.

He saw boxes of cigarettes in a window. His first purchase in America. Twelve cents. Maybe he should buy six oranges for twenty-five cents. But Shayna and his mother would buy food. His mother and his wife. Managers. Shayna even more than his mother. He'd watched her through the mass burials, rape, border crossings, hunger. From each agony she moved ahead. They all did, but she was the driver. He was not ashamed to admit it. Where did she find the courage?

Yussi knew that God lived in Shayna's heart, although she denied it. He knew all strength comes from God. He stopped and moved back against a brick wall, inhaled, and watched the smoke drift off toward the people still crowding along the street as the sun set. And his own thoughts drifted to what would happen if he did find *landslayt*, people who knew Shayna, his mother, her family. They would ask questions. The lies would begin. He'd accept their *mazel-tov* on his marriage to Shayna. A baby so soon. *Mazel-tov*. Congratulations. An American baby. Blessing on your first child, who was not his child at all.

He'd noticed Hebrew signs that indicated shuls and saw men *davening*, maybe not *landslayt*, not men from his village. But no one there would ask hard questions.

Chapter 22

Shayna thought perhaps Manya's snoring woke her, but when she glanced at her mother-in-law, she heard no sound from that direction. Instead, she recognized the sound as a soft knock on the door. The filtered light coming through the grimy bare window hadn't woken any of them. Yussi must have heard it too. From across the room she saw him rise, open the door, and step back as a woman entered carrying a basket. Yussi quickly covered himself with the blanket, leaving Dovid uncovered but still sleeping on the sofa bed, the little carved dog propped at the edge of his pillow.

"You must be the husband," the woman said in Yiddish. "I'm Jack's wife, Clara." She brushed by him toward the kitchen area, where she emptied her basket, placing a fresh loaf of bread, butter, a jar of jam, and a bottle of milk neatly on the table.

"*Borekkh Habo.* Welcome. Welcome." Yussi stood in the corner holding the blanket over his nightclothes. "Wake up. Time you were awake," she spoke to no one in particular. "I brought food. I told Jack, people need to eat. Nu? Wake up."

Shayna was grateful that the nightdress the *rebetsn* in Antwerp had given her for a wedding present covered her body, kept her modest. She had a moment to study her new sister-in-law before she rose. The bright purple dress Clara wore, a terrible color for her sallow complexion, had so many ruffles on it, Shayna thought she might be able to fly.

"Oh, Shayna. You must be Shayna. We are blessed to have you here with us in New York. Jack made it happen. Such a man." She pulled Shayna toward her chest, engulfing her in a rather large bosom and a distinct fragrance.

Shayna couldn't help sniffing as she pulled herself back.

Clara noticed. "You like it?" She lowered her voice. "Called Le Jade. Very new on the market. You should get some. You'd love it." She didn't stop for a response from Shayna, but continued, "Eat something. Maybe walk in the neighborhood. Rest. Whatever you want. Tomorrow you'll work. But tonight I'll make you supper. You'll come to us."

"Are there *landslayt* near here? Anyone else from Obodivka? A shul? Is there a shul here, someplace to *daven*?" Yussi's question hung in the air. Clara looked about the room as if the walls might have an answer.

"Don't know. Ask on the street. Maybe someone knows. Or rest today. Whatever you want. We're downstairs on the first floor, the white door, you'll see."

Again she engulfed Shayna in her arms and smiled, "Then you'll tell us about what happened, about Obodivka, the family." Just before she walked from the room, she whispered, "May they rest in peace."

Shayna waved her hands back and forth to dispel the lingering aroma. She dropped into a chair, rested her head on the table. A sister-in-law. A stranger. With nylon stockings so early in the morning. No *sheytl*, No scarf, no hair net. Nothing to cover her head. She wants to hear what happened, asking like how's the weather. Shayna imagined telling her about each murder, one by one. Not enough Le Jade in the world to cover the horror.

"At least they didn't leave us up here to starve," Manya muttered as she rose. She tore off a hunk of bread and covered it with butter and jam. "You'd think she might have brought some cheese." She licked crumbs from the edge of her mouth and reached for another hunk.

"Mamme, No *brokhe?* Since when do you eat without thanking God for his blessing?" Yussi washed his hands and recited the blessing over the bread.

Shayna mumbled the blessing because Yussi wanted that from her, at least that she could give him. In her own mind, she wasn't interested in thanking God, let alone for a bit of bread.

That evening they walked down the four flights of dark, narrow steps. Shayna told Dovid to keep his hands off the walls. In contrast, the door to Ulkeh's home, to Jack's, was indeed white, painted bright shiny white, and when they entered, light filled the room. Shayna felt like she walked into another world. Heavy, stuffed furniture, many chairs, a large maroon sofa, with wooden tables at each end, polished so they shone. On each table a lamp glowed, a soft light, like a dream. They met Ulkeh's daughters, Flo and Millie, nine and ten, who immediately invited Dovid to their room to play. Ulkeh, she couldn't think of him as Jack, although she tried, showed them around. His apartment was next door to the factory, in the same building as their shabby apartment, but more like the fancy homes in Antwerp.

First he showed them Flo and Millie's room. "Twin beds," he said and Shayna marveled at the rich fabric covering each bed that matched the curtains on the big window. "All new appliances," Ulkeh said as he directed them to the kitchen. "Four door ice box. Nothing but the best for Clara." Another beautiful bedroom for Ulkeh and Clara and a separate room for eating. The table was already arranged with white China dishes and silverware that matched. "I saved the best for last," Ulkeh said, as he opened the door to a private water closet and pointed with pride to a toilet, a sink, and a bathtub for them alone.

"Shvitser," Manya whispered to Shayna when Ulkeh's back was turned. "Modest, he's not."

As soon as they sat down at the table, Clara served chicken soup with matzo balls. Shayna's seamstress eye noticed Clara wore a different dress, this one gold. Cut on the bias which should flatter her full figure, but it was sewn at the wrong angle and made her look lopsided.

No one said a blessing, not even over the bread. Flo and Millie began to eat immediately. Yussi stared and motioned to the girls to wait. Ulkeh wore no yarmulke; Clara's hair was still uncovered. No awareness of God's presence.

"Don't forget to always thank God for your food." Yussi chanted the blessing.

Flo and Millie looked at their father, who shrugged and raised a spoon of soup to his mouth. He slurped it, smiled, and said, "No one makes better soup than your mother."

Shayna squeezed Yussi's leg under the table to send a message to him, to remind him to be grateful for a safe place to live, for food, to remind him God would judge her brother, he didn't have to. Yussi filled his spoon with soup but paused before he brought it to his mouth.

"The chicken? It's kosher?"

"Sure. Sure," Ulkeh said as he dipped the bread into the soup and ate. "You can eat in our home. Clara likes to keep kosher, but for me, I don't give a damn."

No one else spoke. Yussi finished the soup. He even took a second helping, but he said nothing more while Shayna talked about the ship that brought them to America and the girls fussed over Dovid and told him about school. They spoke Yiddish to the family, but between themselves, Shayna recognized the girls spoke English. Maybe they would teach her. The girls cleared the table. Shayna wanted to drop her head down and sleep. Dovid's eyes were almost closed. Although they had slept most of the day, she believed it would take weeks to feel rested.

"Now, maybe you'll tell us about the family, about how you reached the ship." Clara rested her elbows on the table in preparation for a story.

Ulkeh never asked a question about his sister Perl, or even how his parents died. Shayna didn't want to bring it up now. She would not bring those sacred memories to this table, as if she were serving Ulkeh and Clara a dessert.

Before Shayna could say anything, Ulkeh pounded the table with his fist. "These stories are the past. This is a new world. Terrible. Terrible what happened. But this is America. A new world. No need to cry over what's past. Worry about the future." He looked directly at Dovid. "You, little one, time to forget whatever you remember. This is your home now."

Dovid looked at Shayna for guidance but she was too startled to do anything but rise from the table, to get far away. But Ulkeh raised his hand, signifying he had more things to say. He addressed his comments to Yussi.

"You're a yeshive *bokher*, no? You spent years studying the Torah, Talmud, everything."

Yussi nodded.

"In the old country you prepare for the world to come, if there is such a thing, or maybe the *meshiekh*." He rubbed his hands together and smiled. "The Messiah will come to save you. Right?

"More or less."

Manya interrupted, "He also worked. He worked hard, making furniture, always from the day his father died."

Ulkeh ignored Manya. He paused, pulled a handkerchief from his vest pocket, dabbed at a few drops of sweat collected on his forehead, then carefully folded it and replaced it. Shayna could see him take a deep breath. As he leaned forward, he pointed his index finger at Yussi and pronounced, "Here in America, *boytshik*, a man saves himself."

Yussi's hands clutched the sides of his chair as Ulkeh continued to talk. She knew he resented being called little boy, an insult to grown man who had once been a yeshive *bokher* and studied with learned rabbis. Everyone knew that although rich men were honored in the synagogue, the true honor came to those who studied the holy books.

Again Manya interrupted, "My son knows about work."

"Nu, so he worked a little. I mean no disrespect, but here in America, you can't wait for God to help you. You must help yourself. Like I did. No one helped me. You have it easy now. When I came here in 1910, I carried a bundle of *shmates* from door to door from dawn to sunset. I knocked on every door. I climbed stairs and I went into basements to find customers. I finally saved enough for my first sewing machine. I worked day after day, from dawn until after the sunset, week after week. No one helped me. You, you're lucky. You've got me to help you. But don't kid yourself, *boytshik*, you'll have to work. No time for Torah here. In America you must work. Six days a week."

"Tea? Jack? Shayna? Manya? A glass of tea?"

"Clara, don't interrupt. Yussi needs to understand how it works here in America."

"Jack, look, they're tired. There's time." Clara smiled at Shayna. "Right? Time to rest now."

"OK, OK, Clara. Bring tea now. Give them some of the sponge cake too." Ulkeh pursed his lips and shook his head but continued, "I'm an American success story. I have people who work for me. I'm the boss. Do you know I own this building? I do. And I own the factory. A businessman. The boss." He tapped his chest. "I work seven days a week. You're lucky. You get Sunday off. You'll pay a little rent, not much, and you'll all have jobs. So lucky. A job right off the boat." He turned to Dovid and motioned him to come closer. Dovid looked at Shayna and shook his head.

"I see the boy's spoiled. We'll change that. He'll learn to listen to what I tell him. He'll get a good education. He's my nephew. Maybe I'll adopt him. Later he can work with me in the factory."

Manya tried to make eye contact with her son and daughter-in-law, but their eyes were downcast. She ignored Ulkeh's comments about Dovid, and before Shayna's brother could continue talking, she interrupted him.

"Sunday there's no work?" Manya asked, "Do you mean the factory is open on Shabbos?"

"Shabbos, shmabas, there is no Shabbos when you have to make a living, right Yussi?"

"I don't work on Shabbos." Yussi looked up when he spoke but quickly turned from Ulkeh to Shayna, who might understand.

"Fine. You don't work on Shabbos. You're special. Maybe you should remember that baby." He pointed at Shayna's belly. "That baby wants to eat every day. Simple. No work. No pay. But the work must be finished. Shabbos or no Shabbos." Then he looked directly at Yussi and added, "No disrespect."

As if Shayna needed a reminder, the baby chose to kick her at that moment. As if she could forget. Ulkeh was right. The baby would want to eat and she would have to feed it. They would all need food. She thought of the dingy, small apartment upstairs with no trees in sight, no birds, and no ability to see the sky. From where she sat at the table, she could see the shiny new ice box, knew it was likely full of fruits and vegetables, probably meat as well. Ulkeh's daughters giggled together at the end of the table, their hair shiny and clean, tied with beautiful ribbons.

They had no knowledge of hunger. Her family, her husband, her mother-in-law, and Shayna herself would have to find a way to work with Ulkeh, with Jack, to make money at least for the present. Here there were no corners to plant vegetables or sheds to keep a cow. They were no longer in the *shtetl*.

She should be grateful to her brother for sending tickets to America and for providing for them. She was, but now as she sat at her brother's abundant table, she struggled against her disappointment. In Ulkeh, she saw a hollow man, a son her father, a man of learning, would not respect. A man who valued only money. A man full of his own importance. He did not want to hear about the death of his parents, his sister and her family, or their frightening journey across Europe. She understood that the only value she, Yussi, Manya, and even Dovid would have for him would be about how much they could help him make money. Her intuition told her he would never be like a father to her, would never respect her husband and therefore would not respect her. She couldn't bring herself to think about his plans for Dovid. What did he mean about adoption?

"A little bit of cake left—Millie, Flo, want a little more?" Shayna saw Dovid turn and watch the girls as they giggled and gobbled their second helpings.

She feared that they had traded one trap for another. Hope traveled with her across Europe and across the ocean. Beyond her hopes for their safety, she prayed that the stories about America were true. That they could live with dignity and freedom. In her deepest self, she prayed for her dream, a dream given more substance in Antwerp at the home of the *rebetsn* and her friends, a dream of a future designing beautiful garments, the dream of making a living doing something she loved. She lowered her hand to her belly, where she feared she carried a further trap. She knew Yussi dreamed as well, dreamed of study, prayer, and a deep connection to God. This sustained him, but it would not add food to their table.

"Wait. Before you go." Clara rushed after them carrying a bag. "I forgot. I have a gift for you. Some beautiful dresses I don't wear anymore, for you and Manya. You'll have something nice to wear now."

Chapter 23

Winter 1919 – 1920

Ulkeh assigned her to a machine in the third row, still close enough to the window for light to penetrate. She and the other women in her row sewed seams, seams on cheap navy skirts. Seam after seam. Seams she could sew in her sleep. Each movement imprinted itself on her muscles. Reach, line up the edges, lift and lower the presser foot, slide the fabric forward, cut the threads and reach again. In the beginning she sewed as fast as she could. Maybe Ulkeh would see how skilled she was and give her something more challenging to do. Ulkeh himself never noticed. But her speediness irritated the workers around her, forcing them to speed up, which added to the bias they already had against her as Ulkeh's sister. Their dislike of the boss easily spread to her. It wasn't as if being his sister brought her a penny of benefit.

Of course, there were always the *tukhes* lickers, the ones that tried to make friends with her because she was Ulkeh's sister. No real friends for her in the employ of Jack Rifkin.

She kept one foot slightly forward on the treadle to keep the rhythm steady. The careful movement of her feet, back and forth, back and forth, not too hard, not too hesitant, keeping the stitches even, allowed her mind to roam back to Antwerp where she'd sew in the *rebetsn*'s sun room, next to a window above their lush garden. No view here, only the heavy rounded back of Bayla who sat in front of her, intent on each seam she sewed. Shayna wondered how many skirts would pass through her hands. How many hours would she sit before her back rounded? How long before she would scarcely be able to stand straight.

If she drowned out the sound of the machines, the smell of sizing and of the heavy perfumes some of the women wore to mask their infrequently bathed bodies, she could take herself back to that sunroom, to glancing at birds splashing in the large fountain, red poppies swaying in the breeze, to the sun warming her through the window. Take herself back to when her stitches meant something, her designs, her work, and her creations.

More and more she took her mind to the dresses she'd designed for the *rebetsn* and her friends, to the magazines the *rebetsn* let her study, the pictures of gowns, suits, and even slacks for women, the pictures that ignited her imagination and nourished her dreams. She still had the sketchbook Bluma had given her, but the pages remained empty, no ideas in her head, no hope in her fingers to hold a pencil.

All of them worked now. Employed in America. She could see Yussi's back as he stood next to the irons. A presser in Ulkeh's factory. Steam rose around his body, gluing his shirt to his thin back. Shayna couldn't see Manya from where she sat, but she knew her mother-in-law sat deep in the back of the long airless room in the corner, where she and several other women sewed buttons on finished garments.

Sometimes Ulkeh walked along the space in front of Shayna, or behind her, but she never looked at him. Over and over she reminded herself that without the tickets he'd sent, they'd all be hiding in barns, or dead. He'd saved them. Safe in America. She should be grateful. And she was. Grateful.

The few skirts she brought with her to America as well as the dress she sewed before her arrival no longer closed around her waist, and her breasts fought daily to escape from her blouse. This thing in her belly flourished in America and had every intention of seeing daylight. From each pay envelope they tried to save. Food, ice, rent, electricity, repaying Ulkeh for the tickets, only pennies were left. None to buy cloth. None for a down payment on a sewing machine at a cost of only four dollars, as far away as the moon. She'd studied the clothing Clara gave her. Although the designs were cluttered, ostentatious with too much ornamentation, the colors weren't all horrible, and the fabric was of good quality. She could take apart each dress and put them together in different ways.

She would make something for herself that fit, and something special for Manya as well.

She often thought of her sketchbook, nothing in it since Freide had put it in her hands and invited her to fill it up. "Show my sister what you can do. Take this to her in New York." She had nothing to show. She wasn't really a designer.

No familiar faces in the room, yet a very familiar smell. Cigarette smoke and old, musty books. The books of the Talmud lay strewn across the table. In the shtetl, the kerosene lamps left a smoky smell, different than the scent of cigarettes, nastier. Yussi remembered the taste of it on his tongue. No smell of kerosene here in this study room, no pale light, rather the brightness of electric lights hanging from the ceiling.

"*Borukh-habo.*" A warm welcome from the ancient rabbi who hosted this study room greeted Yussi. He introduced himself as Rabbi Schkrab and pointed to an open spot on one of the benches beside the table. "*Zetsn zikh,* sit." Cohen, from the Broadway shul told me to expect you—says you're a learned man for one so young, yah?

"Only a man hungry to learn."

"Come sit." The men around the table nodded as he joined them. All but one with white beards. Why in America were the young men not studying? Where were they? One by one they introduced themselves until they reached the other end of the long table, where a man of about forty sat, clean shaven, although he wore a yarmulke. He introduced himself as Mike Shor. Such an American name. He had no Talmud open before him but paid careful attention as the others began to read and discuss *Nashim*, Wives, the third section of the Talmud, was open before them, open to *Nedarim*, the tract about oaths, promises that must be fulfilled. He pictured Shayna, her belly stuffed with a baby, not his own. Her breasts growing, a wife, but in reality, no wife. He remembered lying in his bed in the shtetl, imagining her breasts, dreaming of their fullness filling his hand, imagining her face alight with pleasure. Now, when he even thought of touching her, she flinched, as if she could read his mind.

The voices droned around him, marriage and repudiating wives, abandonment of wives, widows. He couldn't tell who said what. So hard to concentrate. He straightened his back, tried to sit erect, but only wanted to lay his head on the long table and sleep. The sweat smell after a day pressing skirts in Ulkeh's factory lived on his clothing. Muscles sore from lifting the heavy iron. So tired. Not the America he'd dreamed about.

It had taken him weeks to find this place of study a few blocks from their apartment, not a real yeshive but a place where a *mensch* could sit with his brothers and take sustenance from the holy books. He stayed away from Jews from Obodivka and the surrounding areas. The marriage, the pregnancy—he feared any information might lead to the discovery that the baby was a child of rape. Or maybe they would think Shayna was pregnant before marriage, a *shande*, a shame on the whole family. And maybe his fear grew from his own shame, shame that people they knew might learn how deeply he'd failed his own wife.

Maybe here in this room filled with holy books he could find the missing threads that used to bind him to God, to make himself whole again.

Yussi looked around the table, the old men, with their long beards, dressed in black, their faces gray. Their eyes spoke of suffering, their fingers trembled as they turned the pages and read the ancient words. The man at the end of the table, Mike Shor, who Yussi learned was the rabbi's son, but with an American first name and a different last name. He sat smiling with his back straight, and although he wore a yarmulke, there were no other signs of observance. An American. Yussi wondered about him, about how old he was when he came to America. He must have been raised to be observant, but clearly he didn't follow all the laws. Yussi wondered how he himself would look at Mike's age. He tried to concentrate on the Talmud, ashamed of his vain thoughts yet unable to channel his mind into the holy books.

Clack, clack, clack. Clack, clack, clack. The incessant sound of five dozen sewing machines in constant motion surrounded Shayna, filled her mind with noise that vibrated through her body and left little room for thought. Her big pregnant belly smashed against the edge of the machine each time she leaned forward to guide the skirt seams, one after another, hour after hour. After more than three months working for Ulkeh, she could not feel more trapped if manacles locked her to the machine. She tried to find a position to reduce the ache in her lower back, but the need to maintain a steady speed and consistent treadle rhythm made that impossible.

Sometimes Ulkeh opened the door to allow fresh air into the stifling room, but after a few moments, January's icy air forced him to close the door. From the beginning, Manya complained of exploitation, "He pays us next to nothing. Every week he takes off for rent, for the tickets, for the right to sit at one of his machines, like slaves for Pharaoh."

Shayna remembered their first Shabbos, only days after their arrival. Truly like slaves, since Ulkeh hadn't paid them anything yet, not until the shop closed at six o'clock on Saturday. Torn between hope they would earn enough money to live and the reality of their meager pocketbook, they bought only a quarter of a chicken, plus extra chicken feet, leeks, a few carrots, and celery for soup. With an added couple of potatoes, they would have enough.

Manya's candlesticks had their own place of honor alone on a shelf by the door, polished and ready for Shabbos in the new world. Shayna remembered dragging herself up the four floors after work that first Friday. No fresh challah waited for them; always in the shtetl the aroma of freshly baked bread filled their home. Although they had tried to clean as was required to prepare for Shabbos, they couldn't totally rid the apartment of an underlying musty smell, probably from years of neglect.

But still it was Shabbos; Manya had covered her head with her black shawl and lit the candles. Shayna stood to her left, her arms around Dovid, while Yussi stood on the other side of his mother as Manya moved her hands gently above the flames, inviting Shabbos, peace, and harmony to their home, and covered her face as she chanted the blessing. If Shayna closed her eyes she could see her mother in the same pose, uttering the same words. She opened her eyes and glanced at Yussi, who smiled at her, a smile of his lips, not his heart. Always they had been drawn together like magnets. No longer, not since the pogrom. The invisible bond that had nourished them both, that filled them with hope for their future, hovered now just beyond their reach.

That was the first Shabbos, and as the weeks passed, they had more chicken in the soup, but less and less to say to each other. Manya filled the emptiness by constant muttering and name calling about Ulkeh. *Paskudnyak* was her favorite, the best word to describe a totally despicable person. Then she would direct her irritation to her son.

"I didn't raise you to be a fool; you're not a *nar*. God blessed you with gifts. There's gold in your mind. Be a teacher." She shook her fist in his face. "Gold in your hands, you're a carpenter. I didn't raise you to sit like a *golem* in this *farshtunkene*, stinky apartment. You weren't born to be a presser, a slave to an iron."

But Yussi refused to listen. His differences with Ulkeh didn't change his belief they owed Ulkeh loyalty as well as the cash taken from their weekly pay envelopes to repay him for their tickets. He refused to listen to Manya when she urged him to find other work.

After weeks, Shayna had only one thought. Get through the day. Give birth to this baby. Push it from her body.

She waited every afternoon for the sound of Dovid's voice, *"Tante, tante,"* he would call as he ran into the factory after school. Kindergarten. On his first day, Shayna walked him to the school and watched as he joined scores of children enter the big brick building. Millie and Flo took him after the first day, and soon Shayna was happy to see he made friends with other children his age who lived in the neighborhood. He'd run into the factory as soon as he came home and try to climb on Shayna's lap for hugs. Her pregnant belly made these hugs more and more of a challenge. She also knew Ulkeh frowned on wasted time, as he called it. She kissed his forehead, made sure his jacket was buttoned all the way to the top, and wrapped the scarf carefully around his neck before he ran outside to play with the children of the neighborhood. He was no longer the child she'd found curled up behind the curtain in Obodivka. Although Shayna wanted him to remember his family, a blank look filled his eyes and he looked away when she showed him the family picture. Maybe Ulkeh was right, maybe it was better for him to forget.

Dovid often played with his cousins after school, and Clara gave them a *nosh*, but he didn't like staying there after Ulkeh came from the factory.

"They yell all the time," he told Shayna. "Ulkeh yells at his wife. Hollers at her and at the girls. Clara yells back at him."

"Does he yell at you?"

"No. It's fun until he comes home. They have logs, to build little houses. Clara gives us cookies, sandwiches with peanut butter and jelly. As soon as Ulkeh comes, the girls go into their room. He eats alone at the table and wants me to sit with him."

Dovid liked coming upstairs and telling them about school. He already spoke some English with Millie and Flo and loved to pretend to be a teacher. With his index finger pointed at objects in the room, he pronounced the words carefully and made sure Yussi, Manya, and Shayna repeated after him. Bed. Table. Chair. Dish. Knife.

Shayna was often too tired to play and moved to the bed she now shared with Yussi, although nothing conjugal passed between them since their wedding night. Shayna didn't know what Yussi thought. Didn't know what he wanted or desired, if anything. She wondered if the pregnancy repulsed him. Through the months, as the nausea disappeared and she began to feel movement in her belly, combined with the hellish work in Ulkeh's factory, her exhaustion knew no limits. Any personal conversations between Shayna and her husband disappeared.

Manya and Dovid shared the sofa bed now. Soon after a dinner of soup, or bread and herring, Yussi left for the synagogue, or to study Torah with other men.

His once ruddy complexion now gray and drawn. He insisted he was grateful to her brother, but he barely spoke to anyone. At night she heard his teeth clench and the stirring of his body as it twisted and turned. In the day, he no longer played with Dovid nor smiled at Shayna.

Soon his every free moment was either at the shul or buried in a book. Shayna didn't know what book, she only knew Yussi began returning from the study room with thick volumes of old learned texts. A pile of them now filled a corner by their bed.

As tired as Manya was after a long day sewing buttons, boredom also became a problem for her. First Dovid would drift off to sleep, then Shayna. Yussi was usually out, either at shul or the study room. How long could she look at the four walls? In the shtetl, she could go out her door, talk to Rifka or Sima who lived close, or just go into their homes for a glass of tea. Or someone would visit her. Or someone needed her help, to care for a child, to sit with a widow, or needed to talk about their *hartsveytik*. Who didn't have heartache in the shtetl? Always someone needed something.

A few days after they arrived, Raizel, who lived at the end of the hall, a widow from Kiev, welcomed them with a honey cake. After her husband died, a heart attack at fifty-one, there was no way to pay the rent, she told them. Yussi left for shul a few minutes after she started to talk and Shayna excused herself to take a nap, but Raizel didn't stop telling her story. She had Manya as her audience.

"I had to make a place for boarders; I put mattresses wherever I could put them."

"They sleep on the floor?"

"They're just off the boat. They'll sleep anywhere. I put Max, the short one, in a closet, a big closet, room for a small mattress, but he liked it. Max, with red hair, not so tall himself, got a real bed, because he was the first. But they come and go."

"Where do they go?"

"They find a job, save a little, then move to a room, or they find some lady, a lonely one, a widow, or even divorced, and they marry her. Some it takes a week, some a month, but they leave. Move up in the world. I forget the names, so I call them all Max."

She reached into the big pocket in the flowered apron covering her housedress and pulled out a pack of Lucky Strike cigarettes, looked to Manya for permission to smoke, then lit her cigarette. She took a deep drag and sighed. "No one to stop me from smoking now that he's dead. May he rest in peace." It wasn't often that Manya had seen women smoking, not decent women anyway.

"So like I was saying, Max this and Max that. But as long as they pay the rent, I'm happy and they're happy. They have a clean place to sleep and eat. I make them a little something in the morning and at night some supper. You should come to me. Play cards. Have a glass of tea. Max, the Litvak is older, so what if he's from Lithuania and you're a Galitsianer from the Ukraine. Big deal. You may like him. You never know."

"What? You're shopping him around? Buy him yourself."

"I buried two husbands—do I need more *tsores*, more aggravation? I got someone to talk to when I want, but they don't bother me, if you know what I mean."

Every time Manya saw Raizel, in the hall, on the steps, at the bakery downstairs, anyplace, Raizel talked about her boarders.

Sometimes on nights when Yussi didn't run out the door as soon as he ate and Shayna didn't fall asleep, the words not spoken in the apartment were louder than if someone was hollering. They talked about this and that, but never about the baby that was coming. Manya remembered their engagement party. They'd been so young, glowing with happiness. She remembered her own envy to see such joy in her son and Shayna. Not the kind of envy that wanted to destroy their happiness, but more like sadness, sad that she'd never experienced such love, not from parents she never knew, not from her husband, not really. But the tension between Shayna and Yussi now was uncomfortable for her. What could she say? What could she do? What can a mother-in-law do?

There were some nights when Manya's disgust about Ulkeh burst from her. But the young people didn't want to hear her opinions or even hear the gossip she heard in the back of the factory.

But the evenings when she sat alone at the kitchen table tapping her fingers on the wood, looking down at the floor she could never get clean, her *shpilkes* were the worst. Those times her irritation and restlessness sent her down the hall, where she discovered, in Raizel, a friend, and someplace she could have some laughs and always good pastry, not only honey cake, but often strudel or, better yet, a rolled poppy cake.

Occasionally, when she sat with Raizel and a Max or two, she had to pinch her forearm during the conversations to remind herself to be careful about what she said. Manya learned her lesson in Antwerp when Shayna was mad at her for asking the rabbi for his help to get Shayna an abortion. Oy, was Shayna mad—and Yussi too. Again she opened her big mouth on the ship. Her daughter-in-law got mad when she discovered many of the women knew she was pregnant. They knew because Manya told them. "Talk about yourself as much as you want," Shayna told her, "but not about me. If I want someone to know something, I'll tell them."

Even before they arrived in New York, Manya began to talk to Shayna about the need for a midwife. Although Manya was still convinced Shayna would miscarry, she nevertheless began conversations about the need for a midwife with "just in case."

In the shtetl, when Shayna's sister Perl was pregnant with Dovid, there had been no confusion. Their mother was still alive, and everyone knew Sara Rokhel, the midwife, and if she was busy, her sister Yetta Bella would be available to deliver babies. Sometimes babies died. No matter how many prayers, how many blessings from the rabbis, no matter how much money someone had, babies died. Maybe instead of a miscarriage, this baby would find life out of her body and then die. God would take this child, conceived in violence, and rescue it from life's pain.

More and more as her time neared, with her hand on her stomach, her side or wherever she felt movement, Shayna shut her mind to how the child was conceived. She thought about the revenge she wanted after the pogrom. She began to believe the greatest revenge she could take on the Cossacks, on all the anti-Semites of the world, was to survive, to live and to give life to Jewish children, to create life to replace those who had been sacrificed. Shayna began to pray that she would not lose the child at its birth and that she would not die in childbirth. She could not abandon Dovid, nor could she abandon this new child who clung to life so tenaciously, who like Shayna herself was a survivor.

There must be midwives in America, probably many doctors as well, but when Shayna tried to focus on the actual birth, her mind filled with smoke and she could not find a direction to her thoughts. Although Yussi had found a doctor in Antwerp when she was sick, he sat mute whenever the issue surfaced. Shayna had no energy to talk with him, to break the silence that filled the space in their room. She was embarrassed to ask her brother about female concerns. Her belly grew and her back ached. She felt the baby move around within her, a constant irritation. It kept her from good rest, from deep sleep. And when she managed to close her eyes and find a comfortable position, she saw row after row of skirts, of zippers and seams, and heard the clack of the sewing machines. She suffered most from needing the water closet so many times in the day, she felt only shame as she rose from her treadle machine and found her way to a toilet in the back of the factory. She kept her eyes averted, but knew her brother watched.

"Ask Clara," Manya said. "Your sister-in-law had two babies. She'll know about midwives or doctors here. She'll tell you what to do." But Clara rarely came to the factory. Ulkeh seemed proud that his wife did not have to work. She always smiled when she passed Shayna in the hall, leaving a trail of Le Jade, but asked no questions, offered no advice. The few times they were invited to dinner, Ulkeh dominated the conversation and there never seemed to be a moment when Shayna could seek help. She felt invisible in the face of their indifference. She wanted to cry, to scream at Ulkeh, to ask him to explain how a young man who had left a loving family in the Ukraine had turned into such a selfish person. His escape from the Russian army came at the expense of her grandfather. It took most of *Zeyde's* money to ransom Ulkeh from being drafted into the Russian army, to rescue him from twenty-five years of servitude to the Czar, the same money that had been saved over decades of hard work, saved for the whole family. All of it went to save Ulkeh. There had been no question then, but now, she felt the accusations grow in her mind. She stopped herself each time she wanted to speak. Their livelihood came from him, the very roof over their heads.

It was actually Manya who found a solution, or at least the information that might lead to a midwife or a doctor. The women in the back of the factory, who sewed buttons and completed other handwork, were able to talk while they worked. They didn't have to concentrate on the machines, and if they met their quotas, Ulkeh ignored them.

"Maternity center," was the response to Manya's question about midwives. It came from Zelda, a woman whose bottom was big enough to fill two chairs, a woman who acted like an expert on everything. A real *yente*, a know-it-all, but Manya had to admit Zelda knew about a lot of things.

"Shayna needs to go to the maternity center on Henry Street, the settlement house there. I read it in the *Forward*. You read the *Forward*? It tells you everything you need to know."

"The *Forward*?"

"I can't believe you never heard of it. Oy, excuse me, I forget you just got off the boat."

Manya hated Zelda's superior attitude but waited to hear the woman's information. She usually knew what she was talking about.

"The Yiddish newspaper. You can read, can't you?"

"Of course," Manya answered. She didn't say she only knew how to read the woman's prayer book in Yiddish. What else was there for her to read? Who had time to read?

"You don't have to remain ignorant here in America," Zelda continued.

A few other women looked up from their sewing and joined the conversation to talk about the *Forward* and its most popular feature, the *Bintl-Briv*. The advice column appeared daily in the *Forward* and was read by thousands of Jewish immigrants in the United States. Within seconds, the conversation turned to a recent controversial letter. "Can you imagine, their fifteen-year-old daughter ran off with a *goy*, with the man who delivered coal? They can't show their face in the neighborhood."

Manya eventually brought the conversation back to her question about midwives and learned that since so many babies died on the Lower East Side where they lived, and in other poor areas of the city, the government decided to set up maternity centers to educate and help pregnant women.

"The government?"

"The city government. Helps them get votes. They're going to give the vote to women. New York agreed last year. All the states have to agree. I read about it in the *Forward*, but first you have to be a citizen. I'll be able to vote. Only in America." Zelda herself had become a citizen and loved to tell the tale of how she studied and learned everything so that she could take the test.

"The maternity center?" Manya reminded Zelda.

"A nurse will come and explain everything to Shayna. They'll send a midwife or a doctor or whatever she wants. Very smart nurses. They'll speak English or Yiddish or whatever someone needs. I walk right by the settlement house on my way home every night, so I'll tell them about Shayna."

No matter how much Zelda annoyed Manya, she was true to her word. The very next day, in the eighth month of Shayna's pregnancy, there was a knock on their door and Manya opened it to discover a tall lady in a heavy winter coat wearing a wide-brimmed gray hat with an odd flat top. She reached out and shook Manya's hand. "Bessie Lessin, from the maternity center." She looked over Manya's head into the room. "Is there a Shayna Edelman here?"

"She's asleep. So tired."

"Let's wake her now."

Chapter 24

Spring 1920

Sounds from the street filtered up to where Shayna sat near the only window in the apartment, the baby now asleep in her arms. They'd washed the window as best they could from the inside, then opened it and reached up to clean away years of grime that stuck to the outside. Usually a heavy curtain covered it to contain the chill that seeped through the cracks in the wooden frame, but today Shayna drew it back to let in the light. She tightened the thick shawl around her shoulders and sipped from the glass of water Yussi left for her when he came up to check on her. So far he hadn't asked about the baby or held the baby, although that morning Shayna noticed he stopped before he left for work and stared at the child as she slept in the basket. Shayna said nothing as she watched him and wondered if ever he ever could see this tiny being as his child.

After months of listening to the incessant clack of sewing machines, the muted sounds from the street were like silence to her ears. With her eyes closed, sometimes she could imagine herself back in Obodivka by the window in her house and hear the whoosh of wind through the silver birch trees, the sweet coo of the doves, and the yammering of geese as they flew up from the river. All this before the pogroms, lost to her forever, replaced by the sound of automobiles and streetcars.

She felt the baby stir in her arms, whimper and begin a sucking motion. Shayna shifted the baby across her lap, caressed her soft hair, and moved the infant toward her full breast until Shayna felt tiny fingers clutch at her and then a stab of pain on her nipple. She tried to relax as the baby began to suck. The midwife said the pain of breastfeeding would diminish soon. Nothing compared to the pains of giving birth.

Shayna rocked in her chair as she listened to the soft sucking sounds. Four days since the birth. Four days and three nights since she believed she would die.

She'd felt a massive fist enter her and twist and pull every organ within her body, squeeze and coil each muscle until she could no longer breathe. Through each contraction, pain in her lower back ripped through her. While she waited for the midwife, she believed the pain would kill her, there in her own bed in a strange city, in a new and foreign world. Her screams must have filled the street. The women in Ulkeh's factory, four stories down, certainly thought she was dying. Dovid, who had been waiting in the other room, ran out and stayed at Ulkeh's house since then.

The midwife continued to reassure her, but as her pain increased her screams grew louder, and with each scream the image of the bald man tearing through her filled her mind, the smells of his drunken body smothered her. She believed the *Malakh-hamoves*, the angel of death, had come for her and the God-forsaken child. Manya placed cool damp cloths on her forehead, whispered soothing words. It was as if her own mother was by her side.

She heard Manya say, "You're close. Shaynaleh. Push. It will be over soon. Push." The next thing she remembered was a sharp stinging sensation and then the sound of a baby's cry.

"Breathing perfectly. A girl. A beautiful baby girl." Shayna heard the midwife and struggled to see over her belly, still large and in her way. She reached to hold the baby.

Thank God. Dark curly hair covered her head. Hers. Her baby. A girl. Shayna studied the tiny hands, counted the fingers. Was this child filled with her blood and the blood of her forefathers and mothers? How much belonged to the beast? So far from the fiend, maybe his blood was too thin to touch the baby. Shayna feared in the years to come her baby's innocent face could grow to resemble the monster who attacked her, that evil might emerge. Yet in spite of Shayna's questioning mind, her heart felt no doubt, confusion, or fear. She knew something within her had shifted, as if a chamber in her heart had been waiting to open, to welcome this tiny being, which was hers forever, to protect, cherish, and love.

Shayna believed that maybe Manya had been right when she'd said, "The memory of the pain will fade. It happens to all mothers. And to fathers too. When the men hear their wives scream, they swear they will never seed another child, but he forgets and the mother forgets. You begin to love the child and the memory of pain slides back into the past."

She wondered if there would be other babies. If she and Yussi would ever be truly married, as man and woman. Her eyes drifted toward their bed. Clean sheets now covered the thin mattress, and the blanket lay rumpled near the foot of the bed where she'd pushed it when she arose to feed the baby. Their bed. Where, at night, Yussi rolled toward the wall and covered his head with a pillow. Never yet a marriage bed.

Darkness came early in March. Shayna didn't move from the chair near the window as the light in the room dwindled. She could scarcely see her way to the small chain that pulled the light bulb, so she sat in the dark with the sleeping baby in her lap.

She never doubted growing up that she would have children, but now holding this unexpected, unwanted, helpless infant in her arms, she thought of her childhood best friend, Mirtzeh, and wished there was some magic that could bring her to this room. Children together in the shtetl. Every day they walked to school together until they were twelve and no longer went to school. Every Tuesday, on market day, Mirtzeh helped her mother in the market, selling onions, potatoes and turnips. Shayna, in a booth near them, helped her mother sell clothing, the skirts Mamme herself made along with blouses, often decorated with her beautiful embroidered designs. Everyone wanted her mother's embroidery. She could never fill the orders until the time when Shayna's fingers were coordinated enough to follow the patterns her mother drew on the cloth. From far away it didn't look that different. She and Mirtzeh practiced to be women in the shtetl.

Mamme made them dolls. Mamme said playing with dolls was important to teach her to care for babies. May she have many. While Mirtzeh often entertained her with chatter, Shayna took the dolls and with her tiny careful stitches and the remnants Mamme gave her she sewed new dresses for both dolls, but no baby clothes. Shayna remembered the gowns they'd seen in the bookseller's magazines, so she created long gowns in the boldest colored scraps and decorated them with a row of embroidery, not too much, the thread was expensive and Mamme would get mad.

She tried not to think about Mirtzeh. No one knew what happened to her. They never found her after the pogrom, not dead or alive, only her parents with bullets in their heads. Did she run away? Where? Did the Cossacks take her? Maybe Mirtzeh ran to relatives somewhere, but Shayna left the shtetl so fast, she had no idea how to find her best friend.

She brushed her fingertips along the baby's arm, softer than the richest silk. Shayna leaned down, kissed the baby's head, and smelled softness. She never knew there was such a possibility, that softness, a baby's softness, had its own precious scent. As she held this tiny, fresh little girl, she understood she knew nothing. Making clothes for dolls taught her naught about being a mother. Was she a mother? The baby came from her body, no matter how it got planted there, she nourished and cared for it in her belly and now it wanted to eat all the time, or sleep. There was more to do than sew her clothes. She wanted to write Mirtzeh a letter, tell her what happened, but she had no idea where to write.

The baby should be named soon. Yussi needed a name to give the rabbi. Maybe she would name this baby after Mirtzeh, alive or dead, here or gone, always her dearest friend. But another idea came to her mind as she watched the gentle movement of the baby's chest, one breath after another. Her first child, not what she envisioned, yet already she couldn't imagine her life without the baby.

When he and Manya came upstairs after work, Yussi pulled the chain to turn on the light, then sat at the table, his shoulders slumped, his shirt still damp against his body. Manya sank into the sofa, her face gray with exhaustion. Soon Shayna would go back to work and Manya would stay with the baby. Ulkeh agreed to give her buttons to sew on garments. Here in their room she would have a daily button quota. Sewing on the machines paid pennies more than hand sewing, so it was clear to them all that Shayna would soon have to leave the baby to go back downstairs to the factory. Ulkeh would dock her pay each time Shayna went upstairs to nurse the baby.

"I have to treat you like I treat the others," he insisted.

Since the baby's birth, Dovid stayed away from their room as long as he could. He ate at Ulkeh's house and stopped coming upstairs to sleep. He said he liked playing with his cousins, but Shayna wondered if he might be jealous of the new baby. Perhaps, she had to acknowledge, Dovid might be better off with his uncle, live a more comfortable life.

Shayna placed the baby in her basket and began to prepare supper, reheated potato soup, sliced bread, and herring.

"You must tell me her name soon," Yussi said as she served them supper. "On Shabbos, when they read the Torah, we must have a name for her, a name to announce to the congregation. Already people ask me." Before she could respond, he muttered, "They think they ask the father. I feel like a fool." Shifting to look at his mother, he added, "I am the father of a baby not my own. At least she should give it a name."

Shayna noticed Manya looked down at the floor. Neither she nor Shayna spoke. Yussi's words drifted around the room like a fog over the river at home.

In the silence, Shayna lowered her body to a chair, her elbows resting on the table. The swelling in her legs made it hard for her to remain standing, and the steady cramps continued to distract her. The midwife told her what to expect, but she never believed her. Shayna expected to be back to normal immediately after giving birth. She could not imagine sitting at a sewing machine for ten hours in her current condition.

"Name her after your mother, your sister," Yussi broke the silence. "Perl's baby. I don't care, just give her a name."

Yussi's eyes simmered with emotion Shayna couldn't identify, maybe frustration, anger, defeat, and confusion. He looked at Shayna as if giving the baby a name would change something in their lives. He had promised to accept her. On the ship, he'd promised, but this was not the America they'd dreamed about. He'd promised when it was easy to promise. Now everything was about the pennies they earned. The nickels. The dimes. The pennies he didn't earn when he went to shul instead of the shop.

She thought about her time in Antwerp, the joy she felt designing clothes for the *rebetsn*, the delight she felt holding, draping, and molding silk, the sense of pride she felt. A reason to live beyond survival. Shayna didn't know exactly what drove Yussi, what made him sullen, irritable, maybe he was repulsed by her now, by the baby, by the constant evidence of her shame. Or was it his shame at not protecting her? She didn't know because he wasn't talking. She pictured them in five years, in ten years, hollow empty shells, all of them barely surviving to feed themselves and two children. No longer living in the fear of Cossacks, of violence, instead living like beasts, like yoked oxen without the strength to free themselves. Maybe it was time to move beyond gratitude to Ulkeh. To take her own steps in this new world. At least, time to write to Bluma, the *rebetsn's* sister. She looked at the meager food on their table, the peeling paint, and saw clearly she had little to lose.

Shayna had postponed writing to Bluma. Certainly not when she was pregnant. Not when she couldn't speak English. Not until the baby was older. Maybe these were just excuses. She would fill the sketchbook, then write to Bluma. No point in waiting longer. No point either in not giving the baby a name. She needed a name.

"*Khava* will be her Hebrew name. The first woman, Adam's helpmate, mother of us all. *Khava*, to live, to have life, to give life, to nourish. It's Eve in English, Eva, but still a name from the Torah. Eva Edelman." She straightened her back and smiled at Yussi and Manya. "Tell them at shul."

She watched Yussi's face for a reaction to this unwanted baby bearing his name. A grunt from him and a nod from his mother would have to satisfy her fear that they might reject her baby.

"This is the shul?" Shayna inhaled the musty smell as they entered a tenement much like their own, just a block away. She studied the mailboxes and found thick Hebrew letters, *Beys Emanuel*, the house where God is with us, and under those letters she recognized the words in English: Rabbi Rabinowitz.

"It's where the rabbi lives," Yussi answered as he lifted Eva's carriage and carried it to the second floor. "Three rooms," he said as he opened the door and handed the carriage over to Shayna.

Against one wall, shelves above the sink and stove were filled with dishes, pots, and pans. The smell of chicken soup lingered in the room. Chicken soup and stale cigarettes. Wooden chairs clustered around a tall table, which must serve as the *bime,* the surface that would hold the sacred Torah scroll.

Yussi pointed at a faded curtain along the other side of the room. "The *mekhitse,*" he said. "The women's section. There are chairs there for you. The rabbi's wife is always there."

Where else would she be? Shayna thought. Her home was a shul.

"I'll take Dovid with me," Yussi said as he quickly took Dovid's hand and walked to the front of the room, where he joined old men who looked as if they'd just walked from their homes in the shtetl, the fabric of their heavy black clothing faded and shiny from wear.

Shayna didn't recognize anyone she saw in this shul. Yussi thought there must be a shul with *landslayt,* a congregation from their own shtetl, but he didn't have time or energy to look. These people were mostly from shtetl near Kiev; the *davening* was the same. Here in this little shul or in the beautiful synagogue in Antwerp. Always the same prayers.

Behind the curtain were a half-dozen wooden folding chairs. Wrinkled and stooped, a woman in black opened her arms to Shayna. "*Mazel-tov. Mazel-tov.* You must be Shayna, and this must be the baby who we will welcome today. *Mazel-tov.*" Before Shayna could stop the *rebetsn,* she reached out and tweaked the sleeping baby's cheek, surprising Eva and shocking her into frightened screams.

"*Zol zayn shah.* Shut up," Shayna heard a man yell from the other side of the curtain, but Eva continued to cry, so the rabbi's wife opened a door that led to a room with three beds.

"Maybe the baby's hungry," the rabbi's wife said. "Sit." She pushed Shayna down on one of the beds and handed her a heavy woolen shawl. "Cover yourself. Feed her," She watched as Shayna released her breast and brought Eva to her nipple. The rabbi's wife stood over her and smiled.

"Such *nakhes*, such pride you must feel. An American baby." Shayna nodded and tried to disguise the pain she felt as Eva began to suck.

Here she was hidden behind a curtain and behind a door with the baby whose name would be announced by all the men in the other room. Dovid, her five-year-old nephew, could be there, but the baby and the mother of the baby could not. Not near the holy Torah. Somehow back in Obodivka, Shayna hadn't felt anger about this. Maybe because she was the aunt. She remembered the small shul, not a fancy one, but a separate building with an *orn-koydesh*, a holy ark, draped in a cloth her own mother had embroidered. Real benches and a real *mekhitse*, a wall of lattice that separated the men and women. She had sat with her mother and her sister and all the women from their village in celebration at Dovid's birth and again at Sarah's, *zikhroyne livrokhe*. Blessed be their memory. A congregation of loved ones. Even Manya wasn't with her now in this shul. They needed the few quarters Manya could make sewing buttons on this day. No time to spare.

The *rebetsn* had returned to her seat behind the curtain and Shayna continued to sit in the room of the strangers as Eva slowly stopped sucking and her eyelids closed. She studied Eva's face as she did daily, looking for signs of the baby's brutal father. Not father but something else, some beast that had planted this precious child in her belly. But each day as Shayna followed the delicate hairs of Eva's eyebrows down across her plump cheeks with her index finger, and traced the outline of her tiny lips, exactly the same shape as Perl's baby Sarah's lips, Eva became something separate, less and less linked in her mind to what happened back in the Ukraine.

The *rebetsn* had left the door partially open so Shayna could hear the *davening* from the other room. She heard Yussi's voice, strong and clear as he chanted the blessings before reading the Torah. The new father had been given the honor of an *aliyah*, to reach into the Torah scroll with the holy y*ad*, the hand that touches the words of God. His voice full and rich, the way it used to sound, the way she had forgotten he could sound.

Borukhh atah Adonai, notein ha-Torah, Blessed are You, Adonai, who gives the Torah.

She saw Yussi as he was in her brother's factory, his shirt damp from the steam iron and sweat on his brow. His eyes hollow. His voice, on the rare occasions when he talked as they sat at the rickety table in the apartment, devoid of life.

Not only her life had been torn into shreds—his had as well. All of them tossed by his God, or worse yet maybe, no God. Tossed into the wind. Without thought her mind went to prayer, her custom, although she believed all the prayers in the world evaporated unheard into space. Yet, here in this strange windowless bedroom, still she prayed. She prayed that they could find a way, that this new life would by some miracle infuse them with the hope they needed to continue, that they could and would find a way to feel alive again, to find purpose, to find a way to make a life for themselves in America.

Only after she heard the words of *Adon Oylam*, the closing prayer, did Shayna leave the small stuffy bedroom. Eva still asleep in her arms. Lord of the Universe, the congregation sang. Chants to an absentee lord. Never there when He was needed. And when He was there, was there a place for her, a woman, a mother? The bitterness of Shayna's thoughts surprised her, more biting than her usual irritation.

She was accustomed to life in the shtetl, it was what it was, like the leaves changing their colors in the autumn or rain turning the roads to mud. Women were this and men were that. But everywhere here in New York there was change. The muddy roads were covered with cement. She could go days and never see a tree. For years she'd lived with a silent annoyance, shared by her friend Mirtzeh. Certainly by her sister Perl. Probably her mother as well. Were all women irritated? Did she want to find a different path for herself in this new world? Shayna made a flicking motion with her hands and pushed away such thoughts. She didn't need this aggravation now.

Waiting near the door, Shayna watched as all the men in the congregation shook Yussi's hand. "*Mazel-tov*," they said, not suspecting that he had nothing to do with Eva. Only his name tagged on to make her legitimate, as if a baby could be illegitimate. And Dovid. Little Dovid there among the men, learning his place in the world. They left the synagogue together, a family. Yussi led the way down the crowded street, followed by Shayna pushing the baby carriage and holding Dovid's hand.

"Like a fool," Yussi muttered. "Just a fool."

Shayna heard but didn't respond. His stride was longer than her own, as he maneuvered between people on the sidewalk. Even though it was Shabbos, carts and shoppers filled the street. The smell of unwashed bodies and *shmuts*, filth, surrounded her. He suddenly turned to look at her, his jaw tense. He spit out the words, "Nothing to say now?" and continued to walk away from her. Dovid tightened his hold on her hand as she tried to push the carriage and catch up with Yussi.

"What should I say? What are you talking about?"

Yussi stopped, the carriage nearly bumping into him. "Before God I lied, Shayna. With the Torah open before me, I claimed the baby as mine. A lie. For all times."

"Yussi…"

"Shah, don't say anything. There's nothing to say."

"You agreed. No one forced you."

He turned and hurried away from her. The carriage tipped as she hurried along. She struggled to right it. The sidewalks filled with cracks and bumps made catching up with Yussi impossible. The last bump woke the baby, who began to cry.

Yussi disappeared. She tried to see through the crowd, waited for him to return, but he didn't. She had no idea where he'd gone or when he would come home. She couldn't remember seeing Yussi this angry before. He'd transformed before her eyes. Dovid's hand gripped her own. She tightened her hand around Dovid's while the other rocked the buggy. She never knew if she should hold the baby or let her cry until she slept again. Manya always picked her up, but Perl had let her babies cry a little before she picked them up. She saw herself stopped in the middle of a busy sidewalk in this new country, alone with a crying baby and a frightened little boy.

She found her way back to the apartment where Manya sat sewing buttons on ugly, cheap clothing. The *"goldene medine"* the golden place, this new country, full of buildings, people, and a thousand kinds of businesses, but as empty as a desert to her.

Yussi abandoned Shayna on the sidewalk near their apartment, with the baby carriage and Dovid. He walked and walked without direction, without a thought to their welfare. The thin soles on his shoes provided no protection from the ground, still damp from melting snow. Late in the season snow, they said, but snow nevertheless. He kept his hands deep in the pocket of his overcoat. A used *shmate* his mother bought for him for twenty-five cents, too thin for any warmth. He should go back to the apartment where hot soup waited for him, but he continued to walk, ashamed of his own behavior.

He agreed to be the father of this baby. From the beginning he should have said no. Give the baby to someone for adoption. Instead he lied, pretended to be a *mensch*. Do the right thing. Doing the right thing made him a liar. Maybe not the right thing after all. How was a man supposed to know?

He walked under a massive carved marble arch, imposing like some of the buildings he'd seen in Antwerp, into a large open round space. Barren trees bordered the edge of the park and benches spread out along different paths, empty now at the end of winter. He wanted to remember to return to this park in the spring when the benches might be full, when he might sit somewhere and have a conversation. He'd find someone wearing a yarmulke, someone who spoke Yiddish, a stranger. But what would he say? The secret that choked in his throat must always remain a secret.

In the shtetl Shayna's eyes used to light up when she saw him. Now she was a stranger to him. He imagined she would cringe if he reached for her at night. Regularly in the *Forward* he read the advice column, *Bintl-Briv,* where men complained about their wives or women complained about their husbands. So many cases when one or another would simply leave, walk out of the door and never come back. Men left their children with no support. Could he leave her and disappear, make Shayna an *agune,* an abandoned woman? His imagination didn't stretch that far.

Nor could he abandon his mother. And if he did, where would he go? These thoughts rolled around in his mind, chasing each other. He used to find contentment, peace in prayer, in simply reciting the words imprinted on his heart, but lately the stillness God used to settle on him was out of reach.

Like an ox pulling a plow, he was not free and could not free himself. A beast of burden now chained to Shayna's brother. Chained to two children that were not even his own. Chained to a woman who used to love him and now did not welcome his touch. Wicked thoughts had dug their way through him, burrowed into the secret places of his soul, inhabited now by *Yeytser-hore*, the inclination to evil. The day he first began to stare at the Irish girl in the factory, to watch her breasts as she stretched, and feel his body heat with desire, Yussi knew his soul was threatened. The strength the Torah gave him was dwindling, his soul at risk and he didn't know if he cared. He needed to talk to someone, to unburden his heart to a trustworthy soul.

Yussi leaned against a massive oak tree; his thin coat was no protection against the rough bark. Pushing against it, increasing the pressure, rubbing his back against the tree bark reminded him of the confusing pictures he'd seen of religious mystics who whipped themselves. For the first time he understood the quest for pain, for absolution. The chill soaked into his body. Yet he remained there, his eyes closed. Maybe he fell asleep, maybe it was a dream, maybe his father came to him from the afterlife, but there he stood with open arms to enfold Yussi with warmth and love. The smell of his father's tobacco, the scratch of his beard, so tangible, as if he truly had come to this park in America to embrace his son. Memories flooded Yussi's mind, but not of happy times, only of the frequent arguments between his parents, always about him.

"We must dedicate his life to Torah. He must go to the yeshive," his mother would cry. "My son will be a scholar, a rabbi, a loyal servant of God." She always sobbed and spoke of their three little sons, who had died, taken by God for himself, and the vows she made to God if he let Yussi live.

And his father's retort: "Superstitious nonsense. Let him be a free man. Let him study mathematics, science, history of the world. What good is Torah and Talmud to a man who must make his way in the world? Would God love our child less if he doesn't perform all the *mitzvos*, all the commandments? That's a slave to old superstitions, not a free man. Live in this world and not the next."

And when his father died, and they grieved, Yussi couldn't fight his mother. Nor did he want to. God came into his heart. Gone now. Here in America, he was lost.

In actuality, as he looked around, truly lost. Yussi had pulled away from the oak tree, left the park from a different direction, and wandered along streets he didn't recognize. The cold seeped through to his bones. He would have to find his way home soon before he froze. He found his way back to the park, located the oak tree, and retraced his steps to the path he knew, smiled when he realized he had only discovered it that day. It hadn't taken long for it to become familiar.

As he walked, his thoughts turned to the man he'd met at the yeshive, not a real yeshive, yet a place where men came to learn, to study and to absorb the words of God. Shor, Mike Shor. The son of the old rabbi who ran the place. The son who supported his aging father. The son rich enough to pay his father's rent, buy his food, allow his father the freedom to immerse himself in Torah and ignore the rest of the world, as if he still lived in the shtetl and was married to a woman who worked in the market to honor his scholarship. His son now willingly carried that burden.

Yussi had witnessed an argument between father and son. The rabbi, his face red, eyes boiling over with irritation, mumbled *"apikoyres,"* atheist, non-believer as his son spoke. Yussi didn't remember the question or how it started but this man, Mike, spoke to the assembled old men, like he would speak to children, without anger, with warmth and kindness.

Mike Shor told them a Jew in America should adapt, go to public schools, and leave off the garments that separated them from others. Learn English. Become citizens, become a part of the country, not separate from it. Move forward. Change.

"I'm not any less a Jew because I don't wear *tsitses*, don't let the knotted ritual fringes dangle from my waist, that I don't pray three times every day, don't study Torah all day, and don't keep the Shabbos."

Yussi remembered how the man, Mike, such an American name, looked straight at his elderly father and said, "It doesn't mean I don't love God, don't hold him close." Yet, despite their arguments, Mike seemed welcome.

His words stayed in Yussi's mind. Mike, even with such a crazy American name, without the *tsitses*, without *peyes*, without daily prayers, was still a Jew, still loved God. So different than the arrogance of Ulkeh, his brother-in-law, a foolish man who thought he could cleanse God from his soul. Yussi wished his father still lived so they could talk. Mike wasn't old enough to be his father, for sure, but Yussi had a strong feeling he'd be a good older brother.

Chapter 25

"Did you see Dovid after school?" Manya asked Yussi as he climbed the dark staircase behind her up to their fourth-floor apartment. Manya hated the stairs, hated the dank smell in the dim halls. But every day she had to pick up more work and give Ulkeh her finished garments. She stopped at each landing to catch her breath.

"I saw Ulkeh talking with him. They walked out of the factory together."

Manya could barely hear Yussi's voice over the sounds coming through the thin doors as they climbed the stairs. She must remember never to raise her voice. Everyone knew everyone's business. She missed the privacy of her home in Obodivka. Always there were neighbors, but she didn't hear every word they said.

She stopped at the next landing. "He's hardly here since the baby was born. Shayna said he sticks his head in the door to tell her he's going to Ulkeh's."

Yussi continued up the stairs.

"Stop a minute. Listen to me. I'm worried about him."

Yussi waited for his mother to keep moving up the stairs. They heard a scream, a door slam. A young man pushed by Manya as he ran down the steps and almost knocked her over. Maybe one of Raizel's boarders. She thought about yelling, swearing, anything to let the idiot know he needed to pay attention.

Manya leaned against the wall, "Who was that?"

"No one I recognized."

"Another pitiful boarder with no manners." The stranger could have broken all her bones. Raizel wasn't the only one in the building who rented mattresses on the floor to bachelors fresh off the boat. Anything to make an extra penny, even from poor immigrants with no relatives. Maybe they should have a boarder too. If only there was extra floor space. Maybe a boarder with manners. She grabbed Yussi's hand before he continued up the stairs.

She couldn't stop thinking about why Dovid didn't want to spend more time with Shayna, with the new baby, with all of them. From the beginning, Ulkeh had tried to lure him away from Shayna, but she remembered Dovid didn't like him, didn't like to be at his uncle's house. He said there was hollering. Ulkeh always yelled and they all walked around on their tiptoes. Why was he going there now?

Yussi was lost in his own thoughts, indifferent to the little boy. She wished he would open his mouth, say something about what was in his heart, but he rarely spoke. Maybe Yussi talked to people at shul, or to this Mike person, but not to her, his own mother, or to Shayna, his wife.

Tsores. Troubles. She knew it in her bones. Yussi and Shayna barely spoke, and Dovid decided to stay away with an uncle he didn't like. Manya pinched her arm to remind herself to stay out of it. Not her business. But if it wasn't her business, whose business was it?

At the third floor landing, she saw Yussi had stopped to light Sophie Silverman's cigarette. The *zoyne*, the tramp, blew out smoke from her mouth, her lips covered in red lipstick the color of blood. She leaned against the door of her apartment, smiled at Yussi, like he was a dish of ice cream. She should be careful how she moved in such a tight dress; one wrong move and it could split. The girl couldn't keep her eyes from Yussi, who stood there like a fool. The woman claimed there was a husband somewhere but no one ever saw him. Who paid the rent? She probably traded her *farshtunken* body to Ulkeh and God knows who else. Manya pushed Yussi forward up to the fourth floor.

Her thoughts drifted back to Dovid. Such a good boy before the new baby, now invisible. She'd asked him why he stayed with Ulkeh and he'd mumbled something about playing with his cousins. But Manya remembered Dovid standing in a corner when Shayna's labor pains started. He covered his ears when she screamed. There was a frightened look on the little boy's face, so she tried to pick him up and hold him, but his little body stiffened, harder than a board. Soon, Shayna's screams filled the halls and he pulled away from Manya and ran downstairs. Everyone was too busy with the baby to follow him or pay attention, but in her bones, Manya knew. At least she guessed what might be happening in his mind.

She wouldn't say a word to Shayna. No need to give her more worries. And Yussi was off in his own world. Manya didn't understand much about grown men, but she had plenty of experience with the thinking of little boys.

"Yussi, wait. Do you remember the time a hawk flew down and grabbed a little rabbit?"

"Mamme, what's the matter with you today? What kind of *narishkayt* is in your head? Hawks. Rabbits. Foolishness. I need a sandwich. Mike's waiting."

Maybe Yussi forgot the rabbits and the hawk, but she certainly didn't. Maybe he just refused to remember. They used to walk in the forest together, maybe when he was Dovid's age. If she closed her eyes, she could still feel his hand in her own. He liked looking for rabbits and hopped after them. He raised his little fingers counting, one at a time, each time they saw a rabbit. One day a big hawk dove near them, so close Manya could see the bird's claws reach out as it dove for the rabbit Yussi had just counted. She felt the rush of wind as he flew straight for the baby rabbit, whose struggle ended quickly. Yussi never wanted to look for rabbits again. Never.

Manya couldn't stop thinking about Dovid. She didn't know exactly what Shayna found at her sister Perl's house after the pogrom, only that Perl and her baby were dead and Shayna discovered Dovid curled up and hiding behind a curtain. Did the little boy see his mother murdered, maybe raped? Did he see his baby sister murdered? Or did he only hear the screams? She could imagine his little body hiding, curled up in a ball, maybe with his hands over his ears, maybe in shock from his mother's screams. Sometimes, from her own childhood, pictures flashed before Manya's eyes: people she couldn't name, places she couldn't recognize. Each time one of these scenes flitted through her mind, she felt a strange chill, like no other feeling. Manya didn't know what happened to her as a child, what she saw in the days before the Russian soldiers found her, a little girl, wandering alone on the road outside of Odessa. She knew Dovid must have memories, or shadows of memories. Flashes of his mother and his baby sister still lived in his mind. Did Shayna's screams summon them?

Just before Yussi left the apartment, she said, "Listen Yussi, maybe you should talk to Dovid."

"He's fine. Maybe you should mind your own business."

The wheels on the baby carriage wobbled as Shayna maneuvered it along the slippery, crowded sidewalk to the dry goods store to buy paper, envelopes, and stamps. Eva slept despite the street noises, hawkers shouting out their wares, automobile horns, and the voices of people. More people lived on her street than lived in all of Obodivka. All she'd seen of New York so far was the walk from the ferry through the park and a few streets around Ulkeh's building. Even the shul, where Eva was named, was only a few blocks away. If she stayed on these streets, there was no need to learn English. Everyone spoke Yiddish—a transplanted shtetl without Cossacks. But these people hurried everywhere. They pushed, argued, and fought.

Blessed Eva continued to sleep. A good baby, no colic and healthy. The midwife complimented Shayna when she visited, on her breastfeeding, on her skill in making sure the baby's tush was clean. Sometimes Shayna thought the midwife, a real American, even though she spoke Yiddish, was shocked that Shayna was competent at all. Had she not helped Perl care for her babies? Shayna knew how to read and write in three languages and she would learn English as well. Her dream of America was more than these crowded, dirty streets, more than subtle servitude she experienced living under her brother's thumb.

Shayna kept one hand on the carriage handle and the other holding on to a folded paper in her pocket. Shayna was sure she could copy the address in English; she'd already learned the alphabet. The letter could be in Yiddish.

"Write to Bluma. Don't be shy. Write to my sister." Shayna could still hear the voice of Freide, the *rebetsn* in Antwerp, her unintentional insults and compliments braided together.

"She'll be in New York when you get there. Bluma liked you. You remember how much she liked your designs. The suit you made my sister impressed her. She was as surprised as I was. No one expects such talent from simple country Jews, no disrespect intended."

Two cents for the stamp and a penny for the paper and envelope. Shayna rolled Eva's baby carriage through the narrow aisle in the store to the back and stopped at a table piled with books. She slid them aside to make room for her paper, pushed the carriage back and forth slowly to make sure Eva continued to sleep, took a deep breath and asked Bluma for help, for an opportunity. Ignoring the echo of her mother's warnings, Shayna stretched beyond the edges of her imagination. Not only for her dream but for the chance to catch a better life which flickered in the distance. She would reach out, and if she was ignored, humiliated, or fell on her face, she would get up. She would not drown.

As she dropped the letter into the blue mailbox on the corner by Ulkeh's factory, she prayed that God would have compassion on her, and on Yussi, and help them find a way out of their bondage, for it felt like bondage.

Chapter 26

She rocked Eva in the carriage outside the factory and could see the women at their sewing machines. Bayla, Leah, and Irene, the Irish girl, sat hunkered over their sewing. Behind them, three more and then three more not visible to her where she stood.

She could see Yussi in a haze of steam off to her right, no expression on his face, unaware she watched him. He must be bored, exhausted by the heat, the monotony, the total lack of interest in the tasks that occupied his life. Each day that passed it became more and more difficult to watch his spirit fade.

Shayna saw Ulkeh where he stood by the cutter's table. She didn't often see him actually working, but she knew he could do every job in the factory and probably had at one time. Her brother suckled at the same breast as she. Until Eva's birth, she'd never thought about the act of an infant clinging to a mother's body, nourished by her, protected by her own strength. She reached for Eva now and brought the warm bundle to her chest, inhaled the sweetness of her daughter's hair as she pressed her lips to Eva's forehead.

The heat of the factory enveloped them when she entered. Shayna got Yussi's attention and nodded. He lowered the steam iron to its plate and left to carry the baby carriage up to their room. She felt a hand grab her own as she left and turned to find her brother behind her.

"Starting tomorrow you'll earn money again. You won't have so much time with the baby." He smiled and glanced at Eva. "Lots of work to care for a baby."

She wondered if she heard him correctly over the din of the sewing machines. Shayna watched the women at their machines, frowning in concentration as they guided the fabric through the presser feet, their legs pumping the treadle with a rhythm matched by the surrounding machines. *Clack, Clack, Clack.*

Ulkeh thought caring for her baby was a lot of work, oddly, now a work of love. Suddenly without much thought, she said, "I have an idea. What if I work upstairs? We'll take the machine upstairs and you'll give me quotas. I'll be able to watch the baby." She watched his face as she talked, watched his eyes transform from surprise to a conniving look she'd come to recognize. A big smile grew on his face, although he didn't really look at her.

"Hmm, hmm. I'll have to think. Maybe. We'll see."

"Thank you, Ulkeh, you know how much we appreciate your help."

He pulled a handkerchief from his vest pocket, wiped the sweat from his forehead, and looked out over the large room.

"Maybe I can help you. After all, we're family." He concentrated on folding his handkerchief carefully while he continued to talk as if the ideas just flew into his head. "Why don't I ease your burden? Take Dovid off of your hands. It's a big responsibility to take care of an orphan. Not to worry. The uncle should also be responsible for a nephew. Not only the aunt." He replaced the handkerchief in his pocket and patted it down.

Shayna's hand trembled as she adjusted Eva's blanket. Did he think she was stupid? An idiot? Maybe she just got off the boat, but she wasn't fooled by his lies and his manipulations. She wanted to grow taller, as big as a giant. She imagined shoving him to the floor, but she stood still, her knees weak and hoped he would stop speaking soon.

"No need to worry about Dovid anymore. Clara always wanted a son." He leaned toward her and whispered, "But she can't have more children. She wants to take care of him. He should just stay. Clara would be thrilled and my girls too. It would help you, help Dovid. Maybe we could adopt him. Such a good idea." His eyes challenged her to disagree.

"Adopt?" Shayna hugged Eva closer. This wasn't the first time her brother mentioned adoption. Could he take Dovid away from her? Was there such a law? If there was a law, he would have done it already. She didn't want to push him.

His eyes roamed across the factory, "I'm busy now. We'll talk. Think about it."

"What?"

"Later, Shayna. We'll talk later."

Soon Manya and Yussi would come upstairs, their work day completed. She should get up, pull herself from under the blanket, and warm the soup for their dinner. Eva was already fed and asleep, at least for a few hours. Shayna hadn't been able to nap after her walk, to sleep while the baby slept. Ulkeh's words rattled in her mind. She knew her brother was selfish and maybe a bit of a *ganef*. There were rumors in the shop about him, about promises made and not kept, about short-changing workers on their hours, about lying to vendors. Her brother wanted Dovid, no question, wanted to take Perl's son. Like a thief, just pretending to help her, pretending to help Dovid, when he only wanted to help himself.

She was so young when he left. Other families got money or at least letters from their children in America. Mamme and Papa never said a bad word about him even though he only wrote three times in all the years. They never asked him for help. Only when she was older did she learn the whole story. The only kindness came after Perl wrote about the dire situation and begged him for help.

Maybe she was the selfish one, wanting to keep Dovid with her and deny the boy the comforts she could never provide. She hadn't thought of Dovid as an orphan, only her beloved nephew. It didn't take a *khokhm*, a genius, to sense in Ulkeh the worst selfishness, a man who would manipulate and use people for his own profit. If he wanted to adopt Dovid, it wouldn't be for the boy's benefit. Her sister Perl would not want this for her son. She couldn't give Dovid away, like a pair of shoes. Shayna wouldn't trade the boy for an easier life for herself. Never. But would it make Dovid's life easier? Ulkeh would not give up. If he wanted Dovid, he might find a way. They were totally dependent on him.

No use praying for miracles. They had all survived the massacre in the Ukraine. Dovid had survived the murder of his family. She'd survived the rape. The horrific journey across the ocean. They used up their quota of miracles. Survival was more than continuing to breathe. Shayna didn't know how or what; she only knew she would not live under Ulkeh's fat thumb. She needed to restore her strength. She stretched but couldn't make her body rise from the bed. Instead, she rolled over and must have dozed.

Voices woke her, whispered voices, but she didn't move. Yussi and Manya back from work. She didn't hear Dovid and knew he must have gone to Ulkeh again.

"Ulkeh wants Dovid," Manya whispered. "He told Shayna today. I heard him."

"Dovid?"

"For his own. He wants a son."

"What did Shayna say?"

"She only listened."

She heard Manya light the gas flame to warm soup and then, after a moment, Yussi's tired voice, "Maybe it's a good idea. Ulkeh can afford another child."

"What's the matter with you? Dovid's like an *eynikl* to me, my own grandchild."

"You have real grandchildren already. Remember? Your son Gershon's children in Palestine?" The bitterness in Yussi's voice stung. Shayna knew Manya would react and she did.

"You think I'm an idiot. That I don't remember. Every day I think of them. What's the matter with you? I don't recognize you anymore."

Yussi mumbled something and then all Shayna heard was the clatter of plates. Ice box opening. Closing. The sound of a flame.

"You're like a boarder here. Not a husband, not a son to give an old lady more grandchildren."

"Nu, Mamme, so if I'm like a boarder, where's my dinner? I'm hungry."

Shayna could barely hear Manya muttering, "Poor thing, she gets no rest, waking up for the baby every few hours. You're lucky, you don't hear when the baby cries."

"I hear."

"You never get up."

"For what?"

Shayna pictured Yussi as he sat at their table, likely with his head in his hands. His skin gray, his eyes sunken like a starving man. His beard had grown back. He still wore *peyes* and *tsitses* every day. But he no longer lay *tfilin* every morning, nor rushed to morning services. Some days, few words came from his mouth, only words of annoyance and irritation.

"If she wants to work here in the apartment, he'd let her, but only if he would take Dovid." Now Manya's whisper was louder than a shout, but still Shayna did not move. "It's my turn now, the *mamzer* told her, the bastard. You've done enough he said, the big *makher*. Big Shot. Like he really wants to help."

A chair slid across the floor, then footsteps.

"Yussi, you haven't eaten."

The door slammed. Eva cried and Shayna pulled herself from the bed to tend the baby.

Shayna watched her brother, sometimes as he worked alongside the cutters, or sat high at his raised desk and made telephone calls, or marched up and down the aisles of sewing machines. Sometimes when she was deep into the deadness of monotonous work, she'd see him across the room and her mind would play tricks. He resembled their father from across the room, but as he neared, she saw the calculation in his eyes, the suspicion, not the warmth and kindness that lived in her father's face. The same bushy eyebrows, which on her father were endearing, but on Ulkeh's face seemed menacing. Everyone was afraid of him. Afraid for their jobs. Afraid of insults. Afraid of humiliation.

He began to walk by her sewing machine, to lean over as she sewed, his body like a cloud covering her and he would whisper, "We should make it official. Between your work and the baby, you're tired. Clara's already taking care of him." Shayna held her breath until he finished. Then without looking at her, or waiting for an answer, he straightened his back, adjusted his vest, and continued across the floor of the shop.

She could feel Chana, who sewed on her right and Faigl on her left, lean in, try to hear what he said, but they never said anything to her. Even Bayla leaned back in her chair to catch a word. Here in the shop everyone looked for an advantage. It wasn't safe to make a friend, to talk to anyone about the things in her mind.

Sometimes as she rushed out of the shop to feed Eva, he caught her by the door, grabbed her arm, and leaned in close, close enough for her to smell whatever he'd eaten for breakfast or lunch, "Just to help you and to help the boy," he said. Or he would say, "The girls love him, teach him English. He could learn the business. He'd inherit it. It's for a son, not daughters. Why do you deny him the chance for a better life?"

Her breasts ached. She knew Eva would be crying by now and Manya would be torn between walking and rocking the baby and trying to meet her quota of sewing buttons. Worrying about the pennies. They all worried about the pennies. Twelve cents for bread, thirty-three cents for milk, two cents for a cabbage, and after their rent and a payment for the tickets he sent, so little was left.

Yussi found extra work, some carpentry, from Mike, the American. The man owned apartment buildings. A few days a week, after Yussi finished pressing for Ulkeh, he worked extra hours repairing apartments. He no longer went to shul every day. Now he brought in extra money. Like a boarder, he slept, ate, and hardly talked.

Shayna had stopped waiting to hear from the *rebetsn*'s sister. She wondered if she had written the wrong address, or if maybe Bluma moved or even died. Not a word. She thought about showing her designs to Ulkeh. She thought she might suggest a new line for his factory, but Manya swore her to secrecy.

"He's a *ganef*," Manya said. "A thief. He doesn't pay you a fair wage. He would steal your work. I can smell it from him, the rot in the man, like gangrene of his soul."

Day by day Shayna's strength returned along with her energy for life. Time heals. A message she'd heard her entire life. She didn't know what healing was exactly. She doubted grief could disappear like a cold or a headache, or her memories could be erased like a spelling mistake.

But as the months passed, the shadow that had embraced her slowly began to fade. More now of a living, breathing being, Shayna had found the courage to write to Bluma, to reach for her dreams. Each day she felt her limbs more connected to her body. Her eyes began to want to see, her mind to learn, even her appetite was returning. And her hands wanted to touch.

At night she felt the heat of Yussi's body next to her and remembered the evenings in the shtetl after they were engaged, hungry for each other as they walked along the river. Now, like strangers, they tightened their bodies and never touched. No words came, no anger, no warmth. She often felt him awake, breathing next to her. She imagined reaching out toward him, her fingers caressing his cheeks but feared he would turn away in disgust. Words should be spoken, but Shayna couldn't find them.

Chapter 27

Yussi lit his last cigarette, crushed the empty pack, and threw it into one of the big metal garbage buckets Mike left in each empty apartment. This one overflowing now with the debris from Yussi's work remodeling this unit in Mike's building—twisted nails, shredded wires, shards of glass from broken windows, and bits of lath and plaster. His cigarette smoke mingled with the scent of fresh wood and paint. Soon Mike would come to pay him for his hours.

A union construction crew worked in the building during the day. They'd fumigated the derelict building, cleared years of trash and neglect, basically demolished whole sections and rebuilt them. Mike explained he had some deal with the city to restore the building and provide decent low-cost housing.

Yussi leaned out a window into the dark night sky and took a deep breath of the fresh air. He knew it was spring, but mainly by the calendar, not by any tiny buds on trees, or crocus peeking through the earth. Not here in New York. Not what he saw every day. As he closed the window he admired his own woodwork. The perfectly mitered corners and flawless stain work would have pleased his father. Surrounded lately by the smell of fresh wood after over a year, he felt at home. He remembered his father's fingers, testing Yussi's sanding, testing his corners, proud of his son.

His arms reached high as he stretched, easing the ache in his muscles, exhausted by such long workdays. Yet grateful. Grateful for the opportunity do something useful and deeply grateful for the extra money that came his way when Mike's father, Rabbi Schkrab, discovered Yussi was a carpenter. When the men in the study group started to ask Yussi personal questions about his wife, his children, his parents, and his education, he avoided responding. They weren't hard questions, but anything that connected to Shayna and the baby rattled his mind. For that very reason, he'd stayed away from his own *landslayt*. He didn't want to answer personal questions.

He wanted to protect Shayna. No one needed to know that she'd been raped, nor could he let anyone think the baby wasn't his or maybe that he took advantage of her before they were married. When he thought about it clearly, he knew there were ways to answer the questions. He could have twisted the facts, no one would know or care. But when Yussi was honest with himself, he realized he was hiding his own shame, shame that he hadn't been able to protect Shayna, to save her. Shame that the baby who bore his name was not his child. Shame that he worked like a slave for Shayna's brother. Shame that, day after day, he considered abandoning the rituals that bound him to God. He decided work was a safe topic, so he talked about his father's cabinet shop.

"I made furniture," he told them. "After my father died, *zikhroyne livrokhe*, blessed be his memory, I left the yeshive to help my mother, to work with her in the business that fed us. Chairs, tables, cabinets. My father sent me to yeshive, but he insisted I also learn to use his tools, to be ready to help if he needed me."

Yussi heard the other men murmuring appreciation for him. "A good son, a *mensch*, your father would be proud." The rabbi's thoughts went in a different direction.

"Oy, Mike will be happy to hear this. My son the businessman. He always needs help with his buildings. You have *seykhl*, common sense, always worth a million. I'll tell Mike right away. He'll find you work. You need work? Who doesn't need work?"

He told the rabbi he already had work. He worked for his brother-in-law who had helped them come to America.

"This is work you want?"

Yussi remembered the eager look on the rabbi's face and his own hesitation. He had nodded, which was a lie. He hated lifting the heavy iron all day. Hated the sweat that poured off his body. Hated the monotony. But they owed Ulkeh loyalty, gratitude for providing them a way to escape.

"So, I'll talk with Mike. Maybe a few hours. Won't hurt. He should have around him men he can trust."

Three nights a week, after working in the sweatshop and instead of going to shul, instead of studying Torah, Yussi now earned extra money and helped Mike remodel apartments. Mike paid him less than union wages for a carpenter, but much more than the forty cents an hour that Ulkeh paid. Yussi had come to understand how much Ulkeh exploited them. Straight off the boat they knew nothing. He hadn't told Shayna yet. She didn't need more reason to be disappointed in her brother. He said nothing to his mother who, always quick to judgment, would want to take a knife to Ulkeh's throat. Already his mother thought the worst of Shayna's brother, maybe deserved. Yussi tried to keep gratitude in his thought, for now, even though he knew Ulkeh was a *shmuck*.

After checking the lights in the two bedrooms were turned off and the windows closed, Yussi used the water closet and washed his hands in the clean sink. He ran his fingers along the smooth, shiny white porcelain. Maybe someday they would have their own washroom, one that didn't stink with years of *shmuts*, layered with filth so thick it couldn't be cleaned.

He heard the entrance door close downstairs and Mike's quick steps reverberating through the empty halls as he climbed up three floors. Yussi gave the place a quick look. Everything straight and even. Crisp paint lines along the ceiling. This was the seventh apartment where he'd finished trimming all the windows and doors, painted the rooms and installed new baseboard everywhere. He could be proud of his work.

"Sorry I'm late," Mike's words echoed as he came through the door and looked around. "Slow down, I'm paying you by the hour." He smiled and reached to shake Yussi's hand. "Hard to believe how much you accomplish. You sure you don't want full-time work?" He walked through each room and yelled back to Yussi, "And you clean up after yourself."

"Who would clean my work if I didn't?" Yussi gathered the few tools he carried with him from his father's carpentry shop. Mike wanted him to commit to a full-time job, but Yussi wouldn't leave the sweatshop yet. Maybe he should talk with Shayna about Mike's offer. But as much as he wanted different work, he couldn't erase the idea that they owed Ulkeh at least a year to thank him. Now, he needed to be home, in bed, asleep, but he couldn't hurry Mike.

After he handed Yussi his pay envelope, Mike drew a pack of cigarettes from his jacket, leaned against a wall, and lit up. "Have a minute? Have a Lucky?"

Yussi wanted to go home but instead joined Mike and inhaled the rich tobacco. Close to midnight now and no one else was in the building. An odd quiet lived in the space, like an echo of silence through the empty halls and vacant rooms. He wasn't superstitious but imagined the spirits of all the impoverished people who once inhabited the building still lingered.

"You remind me of my baby brother." Mike's voice came quietly out of the silence.

"I didn't know you had a brother."

"Three brothers. We were four sons. The rabbi's sons."

Yussi didn't know what to say, what to ask because Mike's eyes looked blank, focused on something above Yussi's head. He waited for Mike to say more.

"I'm the oldest," Mike said, "then Eddie. He married a girl from Cincinnati. Lives there now."

"Cincinnati?"

"Maybe Cincinnati, maybe something else, west somewhere, near the Mississippi."

Yussi watched the ash on Mike's cigarette grow longer as he talked. He thought about saying it was late, that he needed to get home. Instead he sat on a saw horse and waited.

"Then Benny, Benjamin. He's somewhere in New York. We think. Sick of the rabbi's lectures. Disappeared. No one talks about it. No one really left to talk with about it."

Yussi wanted to learn about Mike but he wanted to go home more. His head ached from the paint smell. Maybe he should open the window again. Instead, he asked, "And your baby brother?"

"You remind me of him. Samuel. We called him Sonny. He loved Torah. Loved studying with my father. He never worked in the candy store. That's what we had. A hole-in-the-wall candy store. Father studied Torah while Mamme and I and the boys worked the store, sold newspapers, *shmates*, and peddled stuff, whatever made a few pennies. Sonny was the smart one, the scholar like you."

Yussi raised his eyebrows.

"Yah, my father says you remind him of Sonny. Smart. Told me to be good to you."

"Where's Sonny now?"

Mike flicked the long ash to the floor, then pinched the butt and tossed it into the garbage bucket. "Dead. Seventeen years old. Just getting ready to go to college."

"Died?"

"The flu epidemic. Spanish flu. Killed my mother too. Two days later. The rest of us escaped. Just the two best ones, that's what my father likes to say. The *malakh-hamaves* only took the best ones. The angel of death knows who to take."

Mike ran his fingers through his hair, rubbing hard, as if pushing out the memories. "Come. I'll drive you home. It's late."

Neither of the men talked over the noise of the truck's engine. "Sit a minute," Mike said when they reached Yussi's building. "It'll take weeks, maybe a month or two to get the occupancy permit from the city before we can rent the building, but still you'll have to decide in the next week or two."

"Decide? What am I deciding?"

"You know the staging room on the first floor, the one full of wood, tools, all the supplies?"

"Sure."

"You know that's the main room of a full apartment, one that's never been cleared of all the trash?"

"That's what I thought. It stinks around the doors in the back."

"Never cleaned the whole place and I need it now. Super's apartment. For the guy I need to manage the building."

Yussi rolled down the window in the truck, hoping the fresh air would keep him awake until Mike stopped talking.

"My dad thinks I should give you the job. You're smart, a hard worker and honest."

"Job?"

"I need someone I trust." Mike turned toward Yussi, "Someone to manage, collect rents. Fix things. You up to it?"

Yussi didn't know what to say, just looked at Mike and tried to keep his eyes open.

"The apartment's free," Mike continued. "Part of the super's salary. But I'm running short of cash now. The whole place needs to be cleaned and fixed. I was a fool to ignore it. The inspector won't certify the building until all the apartments are finished. Listen Yussi, I can't pay you much, not until the rents start coming in." Mike lit another cigarette and offered the pack to Yussi. The words "free apartment" and "can't pay you much" wrestled in Yussi's thoughts while they smoked in silence and looked out at the few stragglers on the street. Most of the lights were off in the buildings around them.

"Let me know in the next week or two. Needs to be done soon." As Yussi got out of the truck, Mike added, "You'll need to keep working on your English."

"I'll stay here in the apartment with the baby. Maybe Dovid will stay with us." Manya kept her eyes on the newspaper while she talked. She read the *Forward*, likely *Bintl-Briv*, Yussi thought, the advice column, which was his mother's favorite section of the paper. Plenty of troubles for new immigrants and many sought advice from the *Forward*.

"Mike invited all of us." Yussi almost said the whole family but caught himself. A mother, a wife, two children, not his own. Was this a family? "Mike invited everyone, so we will all go."

"Is his home kosher?"

"What do you think? I would go to someone's home, to a Seder that's not kosher?"

"So, you asked him."

"Mamme, stop with this *narishkayt*. Don't be foolish. We'll all go."

Manya sipped her tea and continued to read, her eyes glued to the paper. Yussi paced back and forth until his mother looked up and said, "They're strangers," as if she'd discovered that fact in the paper.

Yussi leaned over his mother's chair. "You'll meet them. They won't be strangers."

Manya removed her glasses and looked up at Yussi, "What about the baby? Does he know you have a baby?"

"I don't have a baby. Shayna has a baby."

"What got into you?" Manya folded the paper, put in on the table, and stood. "What happened to the *mensch* I raised?" She must be shrinking in her old age, Manya thought. He was so much taller now, but still her baby. "You act like a spoiled child. You promised her, we promised her, on the ship. You don't remember? The baby would be an Edelman. Our family. To me, Eva is already my grandchild. Take your head out of your *tukhes*."

"Listen Mamme, I don't have time for this." Yussi's lips were thin and tight. Manya hated that look on his face. "I've got work to finish for Mike now." Yussi sliced a few pieces of cheese and looked around. "Where's the bread?"

But Manya wasn't listening. She'd sat again, picked up the newspaper and studied the front page. "Sometimes I don't know why I bother to read. The words run together, like a line of ants across the page."

"Mamme, where's the bread?"

"Oy, Shayna ran to the bakery. She'll be back in a minute." He left before Manya could warm soup for him, or cut herring, or prepare something to put in his stomach.

A doorman wearing a red cap stood outside of the building with Mike's address. Must be where he lived, with a doorman. A doorman.

"What's the matter with him, he can't open his own door?"

"Mamme, shh. *Genug*, enough complaining," Both Shayna and his mother checked their clothing, picked at invisible threads, adjusted their collars, their sleeves, their skirts, patted and straightened before they were ready to enter the building. Yussi let them take the elevator to the sixth floor because another man with a red cap would push the elevator buttons. It worked on electricity, and it was forbidden to use electricity on the first two days of Passover, just like on Shabbos. Yussi knew about the elevator because the men in the study group discussed it after Mike's invitation. If someone else pushed the button on a holy day, they could use the elevator. Although only a few of the men had ever been in an elevator, Mike's father, Rabbi Schkrab, explained it to everyone. Dovid held tightly to Shayna's hand, while Yussi put his arm around his mother. The baby slept through her first elevator ride.

Most of the strangeness disappeared when they walked into the apartment and saw the dining table with a Haggadah placed by every plate. The book guiding the order of the Seder, including the tale of the Exodus from Egypt, rested alongside the traditional Seder Plate with shank bone, bitter herbs, eggs, and greens, all familiar symbols of Passover that minimized the strangeness of the fancy china, silverware, and elegant furniture.

Yussi knew the men and he quickly joined them. Mike seemed to be a *mensch* and his wife, Lillian, welcomed them in Yiddish—Yiddish with a strong American accent. She wore a sunflower-colored dress with a dropped waist, no headscarf, and her red hair was styled with waves around her face. When she smiled and welcomed them with great warmth, Manya immediately relaxed. Dovid was invited to join the other children at what they called the kid's table. There was never room in the shtetl for another table—plenty of children, but never a separate table. Eva, still asleep, stayed in her carriage, off to the side. Such a big room and they could see many rooms beyond.

Shayna sat at the opposite end of the table, with Mike's wife, Lillian, her mother, and the wives of the men from the study group. Maybe a table for thirty people. Yussi's glance often left the text and drifted toward Shayna more and more as the Seder continued. After months of living with her, day after day, hour after hour, strangely Shayna was more visible to him, clear to Yussi as the girl he loved in the shtetl, the girl he always wanted to marry. Although he watched her, she didn't glance his way. She looked down at the Haggadah and followed the ancient texts as the men read. Or she talked with the women seated around her.

Yussi kept his eyes on her now. Watched her delicate fingers turn each page, slowly, thoughtfully. Watched her eyelashes as they fluttered along her cheeks each time she blinked, watched her smile as she sipped each glass of wine. Four glasses required during the Seder, symbolizing freedom in every generation since the Exodus. Shayna took pleasure in each sip. He saw her big smile, the one where her dimples emerged as she laughed with the woman sitting near to her. Most of these people were strangers to them, but Shayna had made friends. She never looked his way once. Why should she? Who was he to her now? A husband. A husband in name only.

As the Seder neared the end, they came to the traditional recitation of the Song of Songs, a love song, the love of a people for God, as well as the love between man and woman. *Your lips are like a scarlet ribbon, you are altogether beautiful, my darling; there is no flaw in you.* They read and Yussi listened and saw Shayna before him, as if she had been lost in a cloud, almost invisible and now tonight, at the home of people they barely knew, she rose before him like a beacon calling to him. Maybe she hadn't been lost—he had.

The baby had slept through the whole Seder, but now she began to cry. Loud cries. Hungry cries attracting everyone's attention. Everything stopped while Shayna rose, lifted the baby from the carriage, and followed Mike's wife to another room.

As the baby's cries slowed and then faded, Yussi was surrounded by comments and questions. "How old is your baby?"

"A boy or girl?"

"May you have *nakhes*, pride in your child."

"So wonderful, born here in America?"

"Such a quiet man, who knew you had a baby and such a beautiful wife. Mazel-tov."

Yussi's lips pulled back into what he hoped was a smile and not a grimace. He looked around the table, smiles everywhere, on the faces of the old men from his study group, the younger men who must be friends of Mike's, and the wives at the other end. He knew he should be happy to be invited to a Seder, happy to be making a life here in America, but instead he was trapped in the big lie. Shayna would never let go of the baby, and he could never have his wife without the baby. They had all prayed for a miscarriage, tried to abort the child, and now Shayna smiled each time Eva reached for her. He remembered his promise on the ship before they landed in America. "I will be the father, as if it was my own child." A promise he hadn't kept.

Lillian led Shayna down the hall to a large bedroom, big enough for two upholstered armchairs as well as a bed and dressers. She directed Shayna to sit in one of the chairs and then plopped herself down into the other one. The wall across from them had two broad windows. In the darkness, Shayna could see shimmering lights spread out for a great distance. The only light in the room came from the hall until Lillian switched on the brass lamp between the chairs.

"I looked forward to meeting you. God, I need a break. Seders are so much work." She kicked off her high heels and wiggled her toes. "My feet are killing me. Five minutes and then back to the company." She leaned back in the chair, closed her eyes, and continued. "According to my husband, your husband is the best, so me, always nosy, wants to know his wife." She opened her eyes and gave Shayna a look that reminded Shayna of her friend Mirtzeh from the shtetl, especially when Lillian said, "Tell me everything."

Shayna smiled and wondered how to respond. Simple conversation had never been easy for her. She liked to speak the truth of her heart, there was so much to say, but she didn't even know the woman. She wished Lillian would leave so she could feed the baby, but the baby didn't want to wait five minutes. Eva's hungry cry, her little red face and sweaty forehead told Shayna that any minute she'd start screaming. She didn't have a shawl or anything with her to cover her breast as she nursed; she couldn't tell the woman to leave her own room, so she simply unbuttoned her blouse, twisted to the side, and began nursing the baby. Shayna turned her eyes to Eva and felt a melting warm sensation when her eyes met the baby's.

"Oops. Are you embarrassed?" Lillian didn't wait for an answer but charged ahead. "Sorry. No need to be embarrassed. I sat in that same chair with all three of our kids. Seems like a million years ago."

"Three? How old are they?"

"Hannah's the oldest, she's fifteen, then Esther, thirteen and our little guy, Ronnie, will have his bar mitzvah in two years. Did you meet them when you came in?"

"So many children, so many people, I don't remember."

"Not to worry. You'll meet them again. When Yussi takes the job as super, you'll live much closer and we'll see you more often. Hannah can even babysit for you."

Shayna nodded but didn't understand what Lillian said.

"He'll manage the new building. It's not too far from here, an easy walk."

Yussi hadn't said anything to her about a job, about managing anything.

From down the hall, they heard a loud voice calling, "Lil, Lil, where are you?"

"You'll love the neighborhood," Lillian said as she struggled to get her shoes on before returning to the Seder.

Chapter 28

After sitting through a lengthy Seder, the walk back to their apartment seemed twice as long as the walk there. Manya's feet ached and she leaned heavily against Yussi. Dovid trailed them and Shayna followed with the baby buggy. As they neared their own neighborhood, they passed other people dressed in holiday clothes leaving Seders. If it weren't for some shops still open and an occasional car, it would feel like the holiday atmosphere in the shtetl.

Shayna lifted Eva from the carriage, kissed the baby's cheek, and looked to Yussi to carry the buggy to the fourth floor.

"Let me help my mother up the steps first, then I'll get the buggy. Stay here and watch it."

"Dovid will keep me and Eva company, right?"

Dovid looked away. "Millie and Flo want me to tell them about the Seder. Never went to one. I'll tell them about the *afikomen* I found. Mr. Shor gave me a whole quarter for finding it. I have to tell them no one can finish the Seder until someone finds the hidden matzo."

"After you tell them, you'll come upstairs?"

He shook his head. "Uncle Jack bought me my own Lincoln Logs. I can build houses. I want to stay and play. Please?" Without waiting for permission from Shayna, he rushed toward Ulkeh's apartment.

"Wait. Dovid. We miss you. Don't you miss us?"

He shook his head. "I'm going to stay here. You said I should know him. He's my uncle."

"I never thought you'd stay there so much." Shayna's voice dropped as she saw her brother open the door and let the little boy in.

Ulkeh came outside, walked very close to Shayna, so close that she could smell the cabbage he must have had for dinner.

It was no surprise to Shayna that Ulkeh pointed his index finger at her even before he opened his mouth.

"You see, you see, he wants to stay with me."

"You bribe him with toys. He's a child." Shayna kept her voice low. Neighbors sat along the stoops across the street and on the steps of the building next door. She heard a hum of voices, some loud, and hoped no one would pay attention to them.

"What bribe? Since when can't an uncle buy his nephew toys? I can afford to buy him toys. A child needs toys." Ulkeh wasn't actually yelling, but his natural voice filled the air around them.

Bitter words flowed through her mind, things she could never say. You disgust me. Perl would never want her child to come near you. You are a man without principle. Father would be ashamed of you. But she said nothing, only held Eva closer.

"Shayna, Shayna I don't remember that you were a selfish child. I remember you were kind. How did you become so selfish?"

She stepped back, rocked the baby back and forth as she glanced across the street at the neighbors. No one seemed to be paying attention. Don't argue with him, she thought, but words she should never say pushed through her lips and came pouring out, "Selfish? I'm the selfish one? I'm glad Mamme and Papa didn't live to see your selfishness." She caught her breath, tried to stop the words, but instead, her voice got louder, "Why did it take you ten years to send money for tickets? Mamme worried that you didn't have enough. Other children sent money to their parents all the time. Not you."

"Shut up."

Ulkeh's face was red now, deep red, like a ripe tomato that would split, Shayna thought. She closed her mouth, but it didn't stop him.

"What are you? Some kind of a *makhsheyfe*? Not fit to take care of the boy. A witch. The authorities should know."

Shayna glanced across the street. People on the stoops were watching, listening now. She saw some windows open and people leaning out, likely curious about the noise. Ulkeh's fists were clenched, his loud voice carried. Shayna lowered her voice even more, "Me? Not fit?" She didn't know what he meant by authorities but couldn't stop her words. Her stomach clenched, and she shivered. "They would all still be alive if you weren't so selfish. Dovid would still have a mother and father." Tears blurred her vision, but she couldn't stop. "Only after the horror of the war, the Bolshevik revolution, chaos in the Ukraine, and only then because Perl beseeched you did you do something. And then just tickets. Not enough to buy a piece of bread. Selfish? Me?"

"*Klafte*. How dare you?"

Eva began to cry. Shayna turned away from her brother, just as he grabbed her and turned her back to him. Without letting go, he raised his other hand to slap her. She tried to move away, but before his palm connected with her face another hand grabbed his arm and pulled it back away from her.

"Let her go. Now." Yussi's voice was calm, but there was an edge to it, like a sharp knife. Yussi took a step toward Ulkeh. For the first time she saw Yussi enraged, and she wasn't surprised when Ulkeh backed up.

"I tried to be nice to her," he said to Yussi. "We helped you, but no more." He made sweeping motions with his hands. "You're strangers to me now," and then he backed away from Shayna without saying another word. He didn't go into the house, but stood close, his arms folded across his chest, a malevolent presence, poised near them.

"I need my handkerchief. Yussi, take the baby." Shayna handed Eva, who was still crying, to Yussi, who held the baby away from his body. She reached into her pocket for her handkerchief and tried to dry her eyes, but the tears kept coming, like a river flooding over its shores.

Yussi brought the crying baby closer to his body. "*Zay shtil*, Sh, quiet, sh." He began to pat the baby's back.

Ulkeh watched without speaking until Yussi handed Eva back to Shayna and lifted the carriage to go upstairs. Then Ulkeh yelled, "You owe me. You still work for me. You owe me." With his index finger waving at them, his voice loud, he hollered at them as they started up the stairs. "I'll treat you like everyone else. No more special favors. Show up for work. You'll pay me what you owe for the tickets."

Shayna no longer heard the voices of neighbors. They must be listening to everything. She refused to feel ashamed. She imagined Ulkeh was well-known in the neighborhood.

Manya had tea ready for them when they came upstairs. Shayna settled Eva in her basket and tried to avert her face from Manya, to no avail because Manya noticed her teary eyes immediately.

"What's the matter? Your eyes are swollen, red. What's the matter? What happened?"

Shayna adjusted the light blanket over Eva and began to prepare a diaper for the baby. She knew Eva would need it in the next few hours.

Manya repeated her question. "What happened?"

"Nothing."

From across the room Yussi said, "Nothing? Nothing? It's nothing to you if your brother tries to hit you."

"He didn't hit me." Shayna kept her face turned away while she smoothed the blanket on their bed and fluffed the pillows. She did not want to have this conversation, or any conversation. Ulkeh didn't actually have to hit her for Shayna to feel the blow. No way to escape from the ache of disappointment about her brother, the shame of him, the recognition that she and Dovid were alone, without family. They were truly without *mishpokhe*.

"Nu, what happened?" Manya looked to Yussi.

"He would have hit her if I hadn't stopped him. He was ready to slap his own sister. Slap her while she held the baby."

"No, couldn't be," Manya said. "Such a shmuck he's not."

"Please, let's get ready for bed. I don't want to talk about it."

Manya approached Shayna and put her arms around her, "And why not talk? Have a glass of tea and we'll talk. Don't let it sit on your heart."

"Please," she pulled away from Manya. Shayna wanted to say it's none of your business. She hated that they knew her own flesh and blood was rotten. "Please, he's all I have. He's my brother. If it wasn't for him, we'd still be in Obodivka, probably buried there." Even as she said these words, she knew she could no longer think of him as a brother.

"What do you mean, all you have? What are we?"

"Manya, no disrespect. It's hard to explain. Ulkeh's my flesh and blood, my brother, even if he's a selfish *mamzer*."

Shayna saw Yussi watch from across the room, his lips like a straight line across his face. Maybe she shouldn't have said Ulkeh was all she had. She wasn't surprised when he walked toward her and yelled, "And me? What am I to you? Nothing? Your husband is nothing to you?"

She wanted to calm herself. She'd wanted to wait for a quiet time to ask Yussi about what she had learned from Lillian. Instead, the rage she felt about Ulkeh came pouring out and landed on Yussi. "And what am I to a husband, a husband who keeps secrets, who doesn't tell me the truth. What kind of a husband?" Her voice cracking. "You, you are a liar."

"A liar? What secrets? What are you talking about?"

"You lie," she poked her finger toward him, "when you don't tell me the truth."

"What truth?" Yussi raised his hand to his head, rubbed his forehead.

"Your son fooled us both, Manya. Mike offered him a job. And an apartment." Shayna poked him in his chest. "Were you planning to live there and leave us? Or maybe just leave me and the children?"

Manya turned to Yussi. "What is she talking about?"

"I had to hear this from a stranger. Mike's wife told me tonight."

"Yussi, what's she talking about?"

He reached for his smokes. Shayna watched him grab the pack of cigarettes left on the table, then stop himself, reach again, pick it up, put it down. It was the first night of Passover—forbidden to smoke, just like on the Sabbath. When Shayna saw him begin to chew on the nail of his index finger, she knew he'd lost his argument with God, or won it maybe. He took a cigarette out of the pack, lit it, and inhaled deeply.

"Nu, sit down. The tea must be cold already," Manya said. "Talk to us."

He looked around their dismal home, the peeling paint, the chipped and stained sink, their clothes hanging from hooks because there were no closets, and tried to remember why he'd thought it was a good idea not to mention Mike's offer.

Shayna watched him from across the table, her face blotchy from crying, her shoulders hunched, and her eyes wary.

"Give him a chance, Shayna. My son doesn't lie."

Shayna sipped the now lukewarm tea and waited.

Yussi searched for the right words, among all the unspoken words cluttering his mind since Mike talked with him. "I was going to tell you." He flicked the ash from his cigarette into a saucer.

"Were you waiting for the *meshiekh*?" Shayna asked. "Waiting for the Messiah to drop down and let you know it's time to tell us your secrets." Shayna put her empty glass in the sink and went into the bedroom.

He stubbed out his cigarette and followed her. "I needed to think before I told you. Eventually it's a free apartment but now it's a mountain I don't think I can climb. I'd have to manage the building. How do I do such a job? Do I even want such a job?" Yussi's fingers raised to lightly cover his lips, but his words didn't stop. "A person walks through one door and can't find his way back to where he started, to who he was, to who he wants to be. And even if I took the job, we wouldn't have enough money to live."

"What are you talking about?" His words made little sense to Shayna.

Manya pushed aside the curtain that separated the bedroom from the main room. "I can hear you talk but I don't know what you're saying." There was barely room for the three of in the room between the bed, the baby's basket on small table, and the chair.

Shayna watched Yussi's eyes shift between her and his mother. His hands flexed into fists, then opened, and flexed again.

"I don't know if I can do the job. I don't know if I want the job. The apartment's free, but I probably have to quit working for Ulkeh to fix it. There will be no wages."

"No wages?" Shayna looked down at Eva who kicked under her blanket. "Why would you work for no wages?"

"Until it's fixed. Until Mike gets the permit to start finding tenants and collecting rents."

Eva began to kick harder at her blanket, a blanket too warm now in the spring heat. Shayna removed it, raised her index finger to her lips, and signaled the others to leave the room.

"Shayna, if I took the job, worse things could happen. You could suffer. I can't do it. I played it all out in my mind. If I quit and we moved, Ulkeh would fire you. Fire my mother. Your brother wouldn't speak to you. He would believe you betrayed him, that we wouldn't pay him back for the tickets. Who knows what else? You would suffer terrible guilt. I couldn't do this to you."

"You decided all of this yourself? All of these ideas you leave swimming in your own head. Never tell anyone. Don't I get to decide too? You think I don't have a good head? What about your mother? A son talks to his mother. A husband talks to his wife. Why don't you trust me? Trust her? This is not a marriage, not a *mishpokhe*, not a real family."

No one spoke. They stood frozen. Shayna shocked herself giving voice to the words that shouldn't be said. Could they pretend they'd never been spoken?

"I need fresh air," Yussi said, and he slammed the door on his way out, followed immediately by the noise of Eva screaming. Manya, who was closest to her basket, picked up Eva and soothed her for a moment, then averted her eyes as she transferred the baby to Shayna's arms and turned away. Manya's slumped shoulders and heavy step spoke louder than any words Manya could have said. In that moment, that one single moment, Shayna heard her mother's voice, "*Der seykhl iz a krikher.*" Understanding comes at a snail's pace; it crawls along. Awareness had come to her slowly, so slowly, along with shame at her own blindness. She wasn't alone at all. She did have a family, a struggling family now, but still she was a part of a *mishpokhe*, a *mishpokhe* that cared about each other, protected each other, and cherished each other.

The drawers are empty. Of course they're empty. Mamme's dead. This drawer is full of brassieres. Papa will be home soon and he'll bring Mamme with him. Maybe someone knows where they are. Shayna wandered into a room she didn't recognize and down some stairs to a deep basement, very dark and damp. Someone said she could find Papa there. Ulkeh was there too, only he was a little boy with a beard, sitting in a chair with a glass of shnaps and laughing, she didn't know why. The dresser drawers were empty. She looked next door, sure that her mother would be there. She wanted to tell them Ulkeh was laughing and they had grandchildren. The room was full of furniture. There was Papa's pipe, lit on the table. He would be back. She should wait, but maybe she'd missed him. More furniture piled up in the room. Somebody was throwing things through a window. She tried to move out of the way but couldn't find the stairs. "Papa," she called, "Papa. Papa!" She could hear Ulkeh laughing while chairs came toward her, higher and higher. "Papa! Papa!" Shayna screamed as the chairs crashed over her.

Hands held her down. She struck out but couldn't move.

"Sh, sh. Shayna, sh. You're dreaming."

Shayna shook her head and looked around the dark room, could barely see Yussi next to her in their bed, his arms wrapped around her. "Only a dream. Shayna. A dream."

"The chairs kept falling around me. There's was no room for me to run. I couldn't find Papa," she mumbled.

"Sh, Shaynalah, it was a dream." He pulled her closer and kissed her forehead, as she curled against him, wrapped her arms around him, snuggled into his chest. His fingers brushed her hair back as he moved closer, so close she could taste wine and cigarettes on his breath. She leaned toward him, felt his lips against her own. Soft. Only a hint against her lips.

"Shaynaleh?" She heard his whispered question. Her finger drew an outline around Yussi's lips, touched his beard, then caressed his cheeks and traced his thick eyebrows, so furrowed lately. She pictured them lifted as they often used to be when he laughed and teased her. Before he became a sullen, silent man. Here in the dark now no arguments or tension existed. He was her Yussi, the man she loved and the man she knew loved her. Shayna felt his heart beating beside her own, loud in the silence of the room. She welcomed his hand, calloused and warm, against her cheek and turned to reach her own hand into the opening of his night shirt. Her fingers explored the hard planes of his chest, its bristly hair and heat. Yussi slowly, tentatively, raised her nightdress. Shayna lifted her body, allowing him to remove it. She held tightly to his body trembling over her own. Awakened now, as if they were transported back to the river in Obodivka where they used to walk in the evening. Hungry to taste. To feel. To possess. Joining together in the stillness of the night.

Night after night, Eva's soft whimpers woke her. Shayna knew in a few minutes Eva's hungry cries would begin in earnest. This night she awoke to find herself wrapped around Yussi, her arm across his chest and her head nestled on his shoulder. She felt the gentle rise and fall of his breath. It was harder than usual to make herself move, hard to disengage from Yussi. Always careful not to wake him and yet maneuver off the bed before Eva's hungry cries woke them all. Since Eva's birth, whenever she cried at night, Yussi had raised his head for a moment, rolled over, and continued to sleep. On this night, she felt his arm tighten around her shoulder. Then, before she could move, she found herself lying beneath him. In the dark, she couldn't make out his expression. Shayna wanted to see his eyes—see the story in his eyes. In the darkness, he couldn't see her blush.

"I've dreamt of this," he said as he kissed her eyes, her nose, her lips. She wiggled to free herself. "Eva needs me." She pushed against his chest and reached Eva's basket before the baby's cries woke Manya.

Shayna had grown to love these moments in the silent darkness, Eva's warm body next to her own, the tug, the tiny sucking sounds, and the relief when the milk in her breast began to flow. Usually she turned away from the bed when she nursed the baby but as she unbuttoned her nightdress, Yussi whispered, "Don't turn away."

These moments had been private—between her and this tiny baby girl. Her daughter. Yussi watched and she wondered what he felt. Was it her breasts that drew his eyes? Did he resent Eva, this child who was not his own?

"Does she have teeth?" Yussi whispered. "Is she biting you?"

"No teeth. Not yet."

"When does she get teeth?"

"I'll ask her, *Mamele*," Shayna teased, turned toward Eva but stopped herself just before she said, "Papa wants to know when you'll have teeth." Instead, she adjusted the blanket over Eva and said, "She doesn't know." Shayna knew that Yussi didn't see himself as Eva's Papa. Yet just as her own understanding came slowly, maybe his would as well, *der seykhl iz a krikher*. Shayna believed the day would come when Yussi would love Eva, cherish her. Wait until Eva began walking and reaching toward Yussi, she thought; he would never close his heart to her.

"Ask my mother, she'll know," Yussi mumbled, rolled over, and must have slept.

As she transferred Eva to her other breast, Shayna kissed the baby's cheek, softer than a flower petal. Eva latched on and looked up at Shayna, a look that stopped Shayna's heart. To see into another soul, to be the source of sustenance for that soul, filled Shayna with gratitude for the gift of Eva. In truth, she didn't know much about teeth, although she remembered Dovid suffering with baby teeth. But she wasn't sure what was normal for a baby—things she would have learned from her mother or Perl or even Sara Rokhel, the midwife. Things she must learn, answers she must seek.

She thought of the four questions recited at every Seder, *Mah nishtanah*, how is this night different, Jews ask. Tonight, she had her own answer to the question. Definitely not the traditional answers from the Haggadah, but her own answers on this night, a night she would never forget. This Passover night, she met Lillian, maybe her first friend in America. This night, she and Yussi truly became husband and wife. She felt her face flush as she let herself remember. And this night she accepted that her brother was rotten and she owed him only the money for the tickets. Nothing else. No loyalty. No obligation. And strangely, this night, she understood that she wasn't alone. She was part of a family.

They must have a real conversation about the job Mike offered. About a free apartment. Maybe this was a gift reaching out from the darkness. They had to find a way to separate Dovid and themselves from Ulkeh's poison.

Chapter 29

Often when Yussi walked by the barbershop near the corner of their block, he'd stop, lean against the brick wall, light a cigarette and watch the commotion on the street. Men, women, children, old and young competed with push carts that crowded the street, making it a challenge for the few cars or trucks that came through the neighborhood. Since warm weather arrived, the barber kept his door open. A sweet aroma hovered around the entrance, giving some relief from the stench of the street, a talcum powder scent, maybe mixed with the woody smell of aftershave.

On this evening, after work, when Mike wasn't expecting him and neither the synagogue nor the study group drew him, he looked through the window into the shop. The barber was busy cutting a man's hair, while a young boy, who looked like he'd already had his haircut, maybe the man's son, waited in a chair bouncing a ball. Another chair was empty—a big red leather chair that called to Yussi.

He wished Zecil, the barber, had given him time to think and hadn't wrapped his face in a warm towel as soon as Yussi asked for a shave. He wished Zecil had started immediately with him, taken scissors and razor to his beard, never left him reclining in the barber chair, giving Yussi time to change his mind. Nothing cut yet, nothing shaved. He could still remove the towel, say thank you, and leave intact, the same man who left Obodivka, observant and deeply bound to God. Not the man that rested here on this comfortable chair ready to…ready to what? He didn't even know. Change. To make himself a man who could walk down the street without announcing who he was. Was he ashamed? Did he love God less? Did God care if he wore *peyes* and a beard?

This evening felt different to him than the memory of shaving his beard before they crossed the border, pretending to be a goy, hiding who he was. Only when Inge insisted, did he consent. Proud to be a Jew, hating to hide it in order to survive. Now he willingly put himself in the barber's chair. In Eastern Europe, there was only suffering for the Jews, here Jews suffered the way all immigrants suffered as they found their way. Here in America, for him, being a Jew didn't have anything to do with *peyes*, or a beard, or *tsitses* or anything but only what was in his heart.

Yussi continued to recline in the barber's chair and tried to listen to Zecil, who talked with the man in the next chair, a man of about forty, no yarmulke, but he clearly understood Yiddish. The young boy had gone outside. Music from a piano filtered into the small shop. Maybe it came from in the back or upstairs. Yussi couldn't see anything but heard what he thought were cheerful American tunes played one after the other. Almost like klezmer, yet it wasn't klezmer; the rhythm was different. It still reminded him of weddings and other *simchas*, times of joy, dancing, and laughter. He could feel the music, light, happy, and free. It flowed through his body, alive now, his limbs loose, almost wild. Could he get out of the chair and dance, raise his arms to his side, twirling with the memory of Shayna in his arms, the ecstasy? Probably not, but he could and would remove his beard and ease the path for Shayna's fingers to caress his face. Yussi laughed out loud, such crazy thoughts.

"How about a haircut too?" Zecil asked as he lifted the wet towel.

"How much?"

"Thirty-five cents for both." The barber leaned back and studied Yussi's head. "It wouldn't hurt you to get a haircut. I'll cut it. It'll feel good."

Shayna draped one of Eva's just-washed diapers on the rope that ran across the room. She needed to make space for one more diaper but stopped when a man walked into their apartment.

"What did you do with my husband?" Shayna asked the man who resembled Yussi but looked much younger than the Yussi she'd seen in the sweat shop all day. "Manya, come look at the stranger at the door."

"Do I look like a stranger?" Yussi turned his head to the right and then to the left, "a dangerous stranger?"

"Yes, a very dangerous stranger. My husband is a *frume yid* with a beard and *peyes*."

"Yussi, my beloved son," Manya gestured toward his face, "What does this mean?"

"It means now I'll have to shave every day, or let the beard grow back."

Shayna hung the last diaper, wiped her damp hands on her apron, and caressed Yussi's cheek. "So smooth." She realized that no longer was there a beard to scratch her when they kissed. Lately, they had kissed more and more and did other things as well. Now a different kind of marriage.

"A very handsome man, my son, with or without a beard," Manya said. "But really, Yussi, what does this mean?"

"Mamme, with or without a beard, I'm still *frum*. Here in America, God tells me that he cares what's in my heart, not on my face. A man without a beard can still love Torah. Nu," Yussi looked toward the stove. "Can this stranger get a glass of tea here?"

The tensions of the last many months seemed to have dissipated, at least for now. Shayna wondered if a man's character changed when he had marital relations. Someday she would ask Yussi. Maybe it was influencing her good mood as well.

Shayna finished hanging the laundry while Manya prepared tea. Since the moment Lillian mentioned a new apartment, Shayna had grown increasingly irritated by Yussi's ambivalence, his fears. She understood fear. Between stuffing herself into a tin box as the shtetl burned and being torn in two by a drunken renegade, she knew fear. She was tired of it. The hope of a new apartment, no matter how much work it entailed, would not leave her mind. Yussi was afraid of the risks. She wondered if he would have stayed in Obodivka rather than face the unknown. She watched from across the room as he helped his mother reach for glasses on the shelf above the sink. Kindness, gentleness, and an appetite for learning were his qualities, not *khutzpah*.

"Shayna, there are a couple of pieces of Raizel's strudel left. One for Yussi. You want to share the other one with me?"

Shayna laughed. "Is this a serious question?" She joined them at the table.

Yussi cut a small section of the strudel with his fork, raised it, and inhaled the sweet apple smell. "Mamme, it smells almost as good as your strudel from home."

"If I had an oven here I would make it for you."

"Nu Yussi," Shayna asked, "would there be an oven in this new apartment?"

"Eventually. Now it's a garbage can."

Shayna cut only slivers of the strudel, taking her time between tastes, savoring each mouthful. "Garbage can?"

"Squatters, homeless people, bums, all manner of desperate people lived there even after the building was condemned. *Farshtunkenen* garbage covers the floors."

"Garbage can be cleaned," Manya said.

"That's the least of it. Like animals lived there. Everything is broken, half the kitchen sink is on the floor, big holes in the linoleum, in the walls." Yussi pushed away the empty plate and finished his tea. "Even if I could quit Ulkeh's *farkakte* job, it would take weeks, working twenty-four hours in every day." His chair creaked as he pushed away from the table and began to pace.

Shayna picked up the empty glasses and rinsed them. The pressure in her breasts told her that Eva would be hungry soon. Yussi was not born to be a presser, chained to an iron all day. Nor did Shayna want to imagine sewing seams for her brother for the rest of her life. Manya wanted what was best for all of them. No response from Bluma to Shayna's letter yet. Yussi was lucky to have this offer. Maybe not luck, rather hard work and honest character brought an opportunity to the whole family. He should be proud. Wasn't it a sin to look the other way when good fortune came their way?

"You don't have to do it alone," Shayna said. "We'll help you."

"You think I don't know how to use a hammer?" Manya asked. "Who put together the chairs that you sold?"

Yussi came back to sit at the table. "Listen. Facts are facts." He pointed to the line of diapers and underclothes strung across the room. "Soap costs money. So does bread. Rent. The electricity. Without my wages, even the *drek* that Ulkeh's pays me, we could lose everything."

"Or we could end up with a decent place to live," Shayna said. "Maybe even a chance to save some money. Find better work."

Yussi ran his hand down his cheek. Shayna sensed he looked for his beard, for something to hold on to. "I don't know why Mike thinks I can do the job. I need to know more English. Manage other workers sometimes. Fix plumbing. Show apartments to strangers. So many things I've never done."

"It's obvious. Mike trusts you. He's no fool."

Shayna slid her chair closer to Yussi and took his hands in her own. Her father's hands had been soft, the hands of a teacher. Yussi's rougher, the hands of a carpenter. Now in addition to callouses, she felt what she knew were scars from the daily small burns he experienced using a hot iron all day.

No words were spoken for a few minutes. Shayna listened to the constant jumble of sounds in the background, sounds so constant in the building they were barely heard. Doors slamming in the distance. Voices raised. Toilets flushing. It was clear to Shayna that no one was standing in line to save them. They had to reach out, stretch themselves. America was about taking chances. And Mike was offering them a chance.

"Yussi," Shayna said. "You'll take us to see this garbage can."

Both Shayna and Yussi were always exhausted, tired from days in the sweat shop, from the long walks to and from the disgusting job before them. The shovel got heavier with each lift. Shayna squinted to avoid seeing clearly as she began to empty the last corner. The first desiccated rat she'd found had been a shock, now just another piece of garbage. Dirty blankets, too dirty to wash, torn clothes, broken dishes, broken bottles of whiskey and beer. Broken chairs. Broken glasses. Rotten food scraps. Chicken bones. Newspapers. Moldy books. Dried animal feces and the enduring smell of urine. There were fresh droppings, so the rats were still coming and going. Yussi had blocked one hole near a lot of the droppings and set up two traps.

The need to regularly nurse Eva became a problem because none of the temporary solutions to Shayna's longer absences worked. Eva screamed whenever Manya tried to feed her the formula the midwife recommended. Then Manya tried cow's milk with light Karo syrup, but Eva remained cranky and Shayna's breasts leaked and hurt. No end to the list of Shayna's complaints, but she kept them to herself. As soon as there was a clean room, Shayna would bring Eva and nurse her as usual.

Now there was enough trash removed so Shayna could see the wood floor in this room, which must be a bedroom. Yussi had collected empty galvanized trash cans from the rest of the building and made a path through the equipment in the main room to this one so they could carry the filled cans out to the street for collection.

Three other rooms remained to be cleaned. And then the washroom, which looked and smelled like a dozen drunken Cossacks had been locked in there for a month.

Chapter 30

With each block Shayna walked, the air lightened around her. Fewer people crowded the streets, and they didn't push and shove. There was room to walk, room to breathe. The store signs gradually changed from Yiddish or Hebrew to English. On some streets there were no signs, only buildings with clean windows and automobiles parked along the sidewalk. Her back straightened and her steps eased as she walked, street after street. No end to all the streets.

"You'll get lost," Manya warned. "You can't go alone. After a few blocks, no one will speak Yiddish. What will you do if you're lost? You don't know enough English. You'll disappear down a hole somewhere and the baby will never know her mother. Yussi, forbid her to go."

Shayna shrugged and focused on feeding Eva.

"Mike wrote directions. A long walk but only a few turns," Yussi told his mother. "She will not get lost."

Shayna listened to them go round and round. Since Bluma's letter arrived it had been the major conversation. Although Manya didn't stop swearing about Ulkeh, nor complaining about her swollen fingers, she focused on what she saw was the new danger—the danger of expecting good things.

Manya surprised Shayna. At first she'd encouraged Yussi to take Mike's job. She'd helped clean the apartment. She'd told Yussi not to worry, yet as each day passed and the need for Yussi to quit working for Ulkeh came closer, Manya grew more and more agitated.

"We already have jobs with Ulkeh. Already he's mad about Yussi working extra hours for Mike, without even knowing about the apartment. If Bluma gives you work, he'll throw us to the street. How will we live? On Mike's promises. Promises don't buy food."

"Mamme, you yourself said not to borrow trouble. You convinced me. Stop making me crazy."

"Shayna should wait to meet Bluma until we know for sure." Over and over, Manya repeated the successes they'd already experienced: "Dovid is in school, learning English, and eventually he will come back to us. Thank God, the baby is healthy. You're already earning extra money. Why make trouble, Shayna? What if Ulkeh finds out you are looking for other work? You should wait. You can't bake a cake before the chicken lays the eggs."

Yussi's and Manya's voices drifted in the background along with muted sounds from the street. She barely listened to their words. She'd heard them all before.

Shayna raised Eva to her shoulder and patted her back, listened for the sweet burps and soon the easy breathing of her sleep. Three months old now and according to Manya, a perfect baby. No colic, not too much crying, eats well. Shayna watched for telltale signs of trouble, for signs of evil. Crazy, she knew, but each day she watched the baby for signs, for markers, for hints of her fearsome origin. She saw nothing. It was as if God sent Eva to make amends, to heal Shayna's wounds, to mend her scars.

"America is a lie," Manya said. "I work harder here than in Obodivka. No time for *simchas*, no celebrations, no time for Shabbos. Rush. Rush. Work and work more. Nothing left of me. No energy even to talk with a neighbor, no energy to put my head on a pillow."

"So you'd rather be murdered by the Cossacks? Maybe have an arm or leg cut off?"

"Eventually the pogroms would have stopped. What do we have here in this little room? Slaves to Shayna's brother."

Shayna heard the irritation in Yussi's voice and knew his mother's constant worry aggravated him. "Stop with your complaining," she heard him say and then felt his hand caress her shoulder. "*Zol zayn mit mazel.*"

He wished her luck, kissed her forehead, and slammed the door as he left to work on Mike's building,

The coming meeting with Bluma Silver, the *rebetsn*'s sister, absorbed Shayna's thoughts. Maybe there would be an opportunity for her, a chance for her to design clothes, to build a better life for herself and her family. Ulkeh didn't know of this meeting. Maybe he would think she betrayed him, abandoned him, or failed him as a sister. Shayna could no longer allow herself to be concerned with what her brother thought.

She slid all of the designs she'd created in Antwerp into a large envelope. The women there wanted suits to wear to the synagogue and dresses for weddings and fancy parties. Bluma had already seen some of these designs when they'd met in Antwerp, and besides she had commissioned a suit for herself. Shayna also added the sketch book she'd gotten from Bluma to the large envelope, each page now full. Her pencil had flown across the paper, no limits on what she could draw. She simply played on paper with embroidery designs, collars, cummerbunds, and long jackets with belts. Ideas flowed, maybe influenced by the dresses she'd seen in the French magazines or on the streets of Antwerp—or maybe the designs were born in her mind. It often seemed that way to her—captured from the air. She imagined shirtwaist dresses for girls who worked in offices, middies with skirts, and elegant gowns for wealthy women to wear to the theaters she'd heard about.

Shayna inspected the suit she'd designed for her meeting with Bluma for loose threads. With two dollars, she took a risk to buy wool to create a beautiful suit, a light wool for spring, the color of the irises her mother loved. Shayna scrutinized the hem and every seam, then reinforced the silver button on each cuff. Each button cost as much as a dozen eggs. Bluma invited her to come to her department store Monday through Friday, any time between nine in the morning and five o'clock in the afternoon. She waited one week. Two weeks. Three weeks. She didn't know what would happen if she didn't appear at her sewing machine as expected. She couldn't afford not to be there.

Good news and bad news came together. The government of New York City fined her brother for bad ventilation and forced him to close the factory until he added enough ventilation to air the room. An official told everyone to leave the premises immediately until further notice. Manya saw Ulkeh try to give the official an envelope, but the man shook his head and put a big sign on the door. Although Ulkeh said no one would be paid until the factory opened again, at least Yussi could go to work on the apartment in Mike's building and she could meet Bluma without missing work.

Shayna walked for over an hour, worried the whole time that she might have made a wrong turn. In the letter Shayna finally received, Bluma apologized for the delay in responding. She'd been out of the country, in Paris and London, ordering the latest fashion for their store, Silvers, the fashion capitol of Manhattan, at least that's what Bluma wrote. Again she visited her sister in Antwerp, who didn't stop singing Shayna's praises. Hard worker. Such an imagination. So sweet. Magic in her hands. In her letter, Bluma listed all the compliments as well as her approval for the suit she'd commissioned. Shayna blushed each time she read and reread the letter and dreamed there might be work for her.

At each corner, she looked up at the signs and knew she was on the right path when she continued to see 2nd Avenue. On 14th Street she turned left for a few more blocks until she was captivated by the models behind a long window—not living models but statues, like she had seen in Antwerp. All were dressed in different shades of blue, from the palest sky blue to shades of indigo and navy. Evening wear in one window, then dresses for the daytime, and in the last, she saw two of the statues of women dressed in men's trousers. This must be Bluma's store. Shayna ran her hands along the sleeve of her own suit and admired its deep blue tone, pleased to know that she had chosen a current fashionable color for her own ensemble.

Well-dressed women walked in and out of the store. Shayna compared her clothing to what they wore. Her head was covered as was required by Jewish tradition, but she wore only a simple crocheted hair net. These women wore wide-brimmed felt hats decorated with long feathers and silk flowers. Some wore velvet or dramatic bright-colored silk cloches. She studied their shoes, high heeled with delicate straps, many with silver ornaments on the toes, or shoes with three or four colors of leather sewn together. Skirts were shorter; their ankles showed. She knew her brown laced shoes with short, worn heels made a mockery of her attempts to look elegant.

Shayna reminded herself she wasn't there to be a model or to shop in Silvers. Bluma wanted to see her. Clutching the envelope with her designs, she pushed open the door and entered an American store for the first time. The stores in her neighborhood resembled poor shtetl shops. Shayna remembered finding stockings for Eva in a dark corner of a store next to tin pails, a colander for noodles next to towels, underclothes for Yussi piled under a stack of magazines. Things fell on top of each other with nothing organized and everywhere she smelled pickles. This store was full of light. The ceiling reached up many floors with a window across the top. Balconies lined the sides. Two or three or even four people could walk between the aisles. The display cases were all glass. Cosmetics. Sparkling jewelry. Perfumes. Sweet scents mingled with spicy fragrances. So intense she had to hold her breath as she walked by. From where Shayna stood, it looked like this first floor was as large as the whole block where she lived. She didn't know where to find Bluma.

"May I help you with something, Ma'am?" asked a young women dressed in a black skirt and white middy blouse.

Shayna stood mute. She wasn't sure what the woman asked. The young woman spoke English quickly.

She shook her head, then said, "Bluma?"

"Are you looking for Mrs. Silver?"

"Bluma Silver," Shayna repeated.

"Is she expecting you?"

Shayna smiled and nodded, although she wasn't sure what the young woman asked. Maybe if the salesperson spoke more slowly, Shayna knew she would have understood. She'd been trying to learn phrases, but making sense of a sentence in a book was very different than hearing words fly out of a native speaker's mouth. The salesgirl left her standing next to the hat counter and then spoke with an older thin man in a dark suit. He nodded and disappeared into the crowd of shoppers while the girl smiled at Shayna as she walked away.

Although she'd fed Eva shortly before she left the apartment, Shayna felt a heaviness in her breasts and prayed milk would not leak. She needed the water closet as well. She looked around for a familiar symbol, something she had seen at Ellis Island. She saw nothing familiar and was afraid to move from where she stood. In her mind it had been simple, walk a long distance and she would find Bluma Silver, the *rebetsn*'s sister, and she would find help and a friend. Instead she came face to face with her own ignorance. Without language, without words, she was a simpleton. She knew Bluma spoke Yiddish, but she would never succeed in America without English, not if she ever wanted to leave the American shtetl. Nothing was simple. Alive, but lost.

"*Borukh-Habo.*"

A welcome. Simple Yiddish words that warmed Shayna's insides like a glass of wine. Warm hands clasped her own. She blinked several times to keep the tears from flowing as the woman's smile eased her fears.

"Bluma Silver," the woman continued in Yiddish. "Remember? Freide's sister." Her hair was uncovered, no *sheytl*, no scarf, her white hair pulled back into a chignon. More beautiful than her sister, large, dark eyes with wrinkles at the corners, narrow nose, and high cheekbones. Even the wrinkles on her face and her neck did not diminish her beauty.

"New York agrees with you," Bluma said as she studied Shayna. "So lovely. Such a beautiful complexion—and your eyes. Such a clear blue, a wonderful contrast with your black hair. So pretty."

Shayna felt heat rise along her neck and she looked away.

"Don't be embarrassed. It's an asset in this business. Looking good. I'm sorry it took me a long time to answer your letter. But you're here now." She took Shayna's hand, "Come with me," and led her to a moving staircase.

Shayna managed to step quickly on as it moved upward. Bluma held her hand and continued to talk. She barely heard the words as the stairs moved upward. She thought she might pee her pants. But within seconds, Bluma pulled at her hands and led her away from the moving steps.

"An escalator," she said. "We had it installed last year. Isn't it wonderful?" They followed a marble path through thick pale-gray carpet lined with statues of women like the ones she'd seen in the store windows outside. A few racks of clothing were scattered around. She wanted to look more closely, but Bluma urged her forward toward an archway, which led to a room with upholstered chairs and long sofas.

"Take some time to freshen up." She pointed to a door, sat down, and said, "I'll wait for you here."

No amount of Shayna's imagination could have created this washroom. A stupid word for this room with sinks and water closets that looked like a palace. Marble floor, crystal chandeliers, and embossed wallpaper. More impressive to Shayna than the room was the fact that Bluma realized she might need a water closet.

Shayna looked for clues, a raised eyebrow, a smile, anything that would give a hint about Bluma's response to her drawings, but Bluma's face remained impassive, without expression, as she studied each of Shayna's designs. They sat across from each other at a round wooden table in Bluma's office. Shayna could see her own reflection in the patina of the wood, as if it were a mirror. She thought of how proud her mother would be to see Shayna sitting in such an important room. She wished her mother was alive so she could describe everything to her. No sound in the room except the regular tick of a gilt clock, which sat on a sideboard along one wall. Bluma finished the stack of drawings, tapped the sheets together to form a neat pile, and slipped them back into the envelope.

"You never studied design? Never apprenticed for a designer?"

Shayna shook her head.

"Where did you learn?"

"I sewed with my mother."

Bluma rose from her chair and began to pace. Her footsteps silent on the thick carpet. "Tell me about the embroidery designs. They're like paintings. So artistic. Ethnic. Primitive. Lovely."

Shayna wasn't sure what Bluma meant by these words, and again she felt heat rise up along her neck. She took a deep breath and then another to still her heart. She wondered if Bluma could hear it.

"I don't know what to say. I think of the flowers in my mother's garden. She loved the irises, the color and the movement of the petals. And then I think of the beautiful designs I've seen on Ukrainian festival costumes. And then something else happens. I don't know what."

"Very ethnic," Bluma repeated. "Very popular these days."

Shayna lowered her head. She wanted to ask Bluma exactly what that meant but didn't want to appear stupid.

Bluma returned to her seat at the table and took Shayna's hand. "Freide told me your situation, your marriage, and your nephew. And by now you must have a baby as well."

Shayna nodded, although she wasn't sure why Bluma asked. Actually, she hadn't asked. She described Shayna's life like she was reciting facts. Bluma rose again from the table and walked to a large desk against the wall.

"This is your lucky day," she said. "Better yet, it's my lucky day. I will write to Freide and let her know we have a plan."

"Plan?"

"Let me explain," Bluma said.

Her full breasts demanded attention. Likely, Eva cried on Manya's chest now or chewed on a cloth dipped in sugar water. Still, Shayna decided to stop at a bench in a small park, only a block from Silver's department store, and watch squirrels run across tree branches, just like the squirrels in Obodivka. Up and down, celebrating warm weather, drunk on the sun. Buds on trees would soon open and shade the benches and walks. No time now to sit, to absorb the sun, but still she sat. Not quite a year since Perl's murder. Since she'd was violated. Here she sat now in America, a wife, truly a wife now, and a mother. Her eighteenth birthday passed with scarcely a mention. No father to kiss her forehead. No mother to answer her questions. For the thousandth time she wondered why God had not let her suffocate in the box, why Perl had been slaughtered. Why? Why? There were no answers. No reason for her to be sitting in a park in America while her family lay buried underground. She'd like to believe they were all in *Yene velt*, watching over her, protecting her from above. This was the magical thinking of a child, or maybe her own husband. God's will. He still believed. Bless him. Dust turned to dust and they were gone. Yet still she hungered for her mother, for sheltering arms.

She didn't know which way to turn. Bluma would help, but she was not her mother or her grandmother, someone who would reach out and hold Shayna, cuddle her and sing a lullaby, rock her until she fell asleep, let her rest for an hour or two. She was no longer a child. Eva waited to be fed. Manya would be irritated, walking back and forth with a crying baby. She should hurry home, change clothes, and go to help Yussi. The inspector might come soon. Now there was a clean room and she and Manya could bring Eva. Yet she continued to sit.

She gathered stillness around her, remembered her parents as they sat at the Shabbos table, the lights of the Sabbath candles flickering over their faces. She recalled the peace on their faces, in spite of what they knew about the pogroms, about the massacres, about starvation. She wished she could find that peace in herself, but the old world was lost, as lost as the last winter's snow. Nothing remained. Only memories, and they were not enough to sustain her.

This was a new world, a new family now. She tried to concentrate her thoughts on the good news. She had a little extra work now and a plan.

"You have a future," Bluma told her. "Real talent. But you are young. So much to learn. Start with English. You must learn to speak English if you want to succeed in this business." Shayna remembered the big smile on Bluma's face when she talked about what Shayna could accomplish. "I'll try you out with an order for a couple of styles." Bluma sorted through Shayna's designs and selected two. "Let's start with these. Can you make half a dozen of each for me? I will advance you seed money. Just this time."

"Seed money?" Shayna had asked.

"Money to get you started. Don't worry. I'll get it back. You have a machine at home? No, no machine? You'll get one. You'll have money for a down payment. We'll meet with Agnes, my buyer. She'll work with you and come up with a budget for fabrics, notions, and other supplies you'll need for this project. She'll advise you on sizes. You'll learn a lot from her. She speaks some Yiddish, but very little. Where can you learn English?"

It seemed to Shayna that Bluma said all of this without taking a breath. She thought it might take her a few days to sift through all of Bluma's words and understand what she meant, but she did know where she could take English classes. "The settlement house on Henry Street. They have classes there."

"Start right away. In a year or two, when you have enough English, we'll see if there's a place here in the store for you. You have much to learn. We'll see. There is no future for you if you don't learn to be an American."

Bluma wanted fine fashion. Not the *shmates* Ulkeh made. A small order to start along with the connection to someone who knew the business, but enough to give Shayna hope for the future, for a time she could be free of Ulkeh's sweatshop, any sweatshop.

She should be happy. Her parents would be proud. Although the weight of grief still clung to her as she rose from the bench, she knew a better path lay ahead. She must turn away from her brother, walk away from her blood. Rescue herself and the children and, with Yussi and Manya, somehow build a new life, a better life, a life where they would be safe to create new memories.

The *Shehechiyanu* prayer came to her lips, the prayer of gratitude to God, the prayer to celebrate special occasions. She wondered why old prayers came to her when she no longer believed, yet she recited the words, like an incantation. *Borukh atah Adonai, Eloheinu Melekh haolam, shehekheyanu, v'kiy'manu, v'higianu laz'man hazeh,* Blessed are You, Lord, our God, King of the Universe, who has granted us life, sustained us and enabled us to reach this occasion.

Chapter 31

Manya moved the basket with the sleeping baby from the dark corner in the bedroom to a stool near the window. She sat trying to finish her quota of hand sewing, close enough to hear Eva's tiny snoring sounds, close enough to inhale the unique baby smell, that intangible essence she knew from her own babies. Manya spent her days alone with Eva, with only very quick visits from Shayna, who rushed up from the shop to nurse the baby. Sometimes Raizel, from down the hall, came for a glass of tea and some gossip, but mostly Manya did her work and talked with Eva. There was so much to tell the baby: all Manya's sorrows, her dreams, and her fears. Eva never once said, *genug*, it's enough. Never said, *zol zayn shah*, be quiet.

"Oy, Evaleh, look at my knuckles." She held her hands over the basket to show the sleeping baby her gnarled fingers. "So big, even if I had a diamond ring, I couldn't put it on. So much rain this spring, it twists my fingers so I can barely hold a needle. Soon you'll be old enough to thread it for me. You know, I used to thread needles for the old ladies who worked in the orphanage. Maybe I was four or five. No one knew how old I was. They only guessed when the soldiers found me. Some said I was undernourished and must be older than I looked, maybe even five. And Gittel, the big boss, said I must be three. They made my birthday the day they found me.

"You don't need to hear my sad story. You yourself have *mazel*. Your mother didn't send you to an orphanage. No one knew if my mother threw me away. You shouldn't know such loneliness in your life. Maybe she died and I got lost. Maybe she's waiting for me in *yene velt*. Maybe all these years she watched over me from heaven."

Eva whimpered in her sleep, raised her arms and legs. Was she dreaming?

"Sh, *mamele*." Manya placed her hand on the baby's chest, a light presence to calm her. She resisted the impulse to lift the baby from her basket and hug Eva to her own heart.

No time. She had work to complete. Her fingers no longer worked like fingers should, certainly not for perfect stitches, but since Ulkeh switched her from buttons to basting, she could still make money. Not much, but something.

Raizel had brought her a remedy for arthritis, "Better than anything a doctor would give you. Rub it in good," Raizel told her, "just a little. It loosens the joints."

Manya left her sewing to find the small jar and heated a few spoonsful. Maybe it would soothe the ache in her hands. She turned her head from the sharp smell of mustard oil and garlic as it warmed, a smell strong enough to scare her fingers into working. She walked around the apartment as she rubbed the *farshtunkene* medicine into each finger.

"So Eva, what do you think of your home?" Manya looked back at the sleeping child and lowered her voice. "Lucky you're living in a basket. There's room here for a basket, but not much else. Maybe by the time you outgrow this basket, maybe, maybe Yussi will finish his work and Mike will have his permits. Maybe Shayna will have more work from Bluma. We'll have another place, a place where you can have crib. And Dovid will come back to us. For sure he'll have a bed of his own."

Manya stood in the middle of the room, their only room, except for what they called the bedroom, which was really only a little bigger than a closet, just big enough to hold a bed and a chair. Their kitchen, dining room, living room, her bedroom, all in one room. Clothing hung from hooks, and cluttered shelves covered the walls. Only her Shabbos candlesticks stood alone on their shelf near the door, polished and shiny. She forbade anyone to put something else on that shelf. Every week she tried to make Shabbos.

"Eva, you missed our first Shabbos here. We bought a quarter of a chicken. Our first meat since we left the shtetl. Kosher chicken. I made a soup with leeks, potatoes, onions, carrots, as much as the pot would hold. We bought candles. Oy, Evaleh, never like Shabbos in Obodivka. There the air filled with holiness, here never enough time to prepare, to cook, to clean, to make Shabbos like we should. Sometimes I don't even light the candles anymore. Don't tell anyone."

She looked down to the street from their one window. The morning sun reflected off the store windows across the street. Sounds coming from the pushcarts were muffled by bits of cardboard stuffed into the spaces between the warped window trim and the wall. So many people, always rushing someplace. Manya pinched her forearm. She wouldn't make a penny looking out of the window.

America. Finally America. She'd dreamed about America. Who didn't dream about America with gold lining every street? Fool's gold. Who dreamed about a *mamzer* like Ulkeh? May leeches suck him dry.

"This I can't say out loud to you Eva. He's your uncle. You won't hear it from me."

Manya stretched her fingers, curled them into fists, and opened and closed her hand. Maybe a little better, she thought, and wiped away the residue of poultice before returning to her sewing.

Soft snores still came from Eva's basket. Hopefully she'd sleep longer.

"Now we've got Mike, *Mamale*. You met him at the Seder. You probably don't remember. A man full of promises. Yussi trusts him, my Yussi, the boy with his head in the clouds. Your Papa, surely one day he'll pull his head out of his *tukhes* and you'll have a father. *Mirtse-Hashem*, all in God's hands."

By the time Yussi finished work and got back to their apartment, the streets were almost empty. His footsteps echoed on the street. He was often alone here in this country full of people. Each in their own corner. The staircase was dark, no light from the one window on each landing. He heard muted voices as he passed the doors on each floor. As he turned to climb the last flight before their apartment, he heard a whimper, a sniff somewhere along the staircase, but he saw nothing until he came across a dark heap of something. At first he thought it was a pile of clothing someone dropped, but a sound came from the pile. He stopped and leaned down, so difficult to see in the dim light. A child, his head hidden between his knees.

"Are you hurt?"

No answer. Gradually he recognized who it was, maybe the small bare toes sticking out, maybe the ears that were visible. What was Dovid doing here on the staircase crying in the middle of the night? He'd been with Ulkeh for the last few months. It was what he said he wanted.

"Dovid?"

No answer.

"Dovidel, it's me, Yussi. What's the matter?" He sat next to the boy and placed his palm on Dovid's back, waited a few heartbeats, then slid the boy's trembling little body closer to his own.

Should he just pick him up and carry the boy upstairs? His mother would know what to do. Shayna too. They would be sleeping now. Should he wake them to get help? Instead, he sat quietly with the boy's body touching his own. He reached to God for guidance, for the words to soothe the heart of this child, for wisdom to know what to do. He was not a father.

They sat in silence broken only by an occasional sniff from the boy.

"Does Ulkeh know where you are?"

No answer at first. Only a whimper. And then, "I sneaked out."

"Sneaked out? Why did you sneak out? Why are you sitting on the steps? Why didn't you go to Shayna?"

Dovid sunk his head deeper between his knees.

"It's okay. You can always go to Shayna. She'll help you."

The boy's back quivered. The whimpers changed to quiet sobs. Yussi rubbed his hand along the boy's back. "Shh, tatele, it'll be okay."

Dovid shook his head and said something Yussi couldn't hear. He leaned down, placed his head next to Dovid's and heard him whisper, "Bad. I was bad. He hit me."

"No. Dovid, what happened? You're a good boy."

"Made my shirt dirty. Spilled juice."

"You made your shirt dirty and he hit you?"

"Said sorry. Slapped me, another time. Threw me on the bed. Slammed the door."

Yussi lifted the boy on to his lap. "Shh, tatele. It's okay. We'll find Shayna. She'll fix it."

Dovid clung to his shoulders. His whimpers turned to deeper sobs.

"Shayna loves you. You don't have to go back to Ulkeh's." Yussi rubbed his back. Tried to calm him, but the little boy's body shook with his cries. Over and over Yussi whispered words of comfort, but the boy continued to cry. Yussi didn't understand why Dovid didn't want to go upstairs to Shayna and then he remembered what his mother had said. Maybe Shayna's screams during childbirth frightened the little boy.

"Are you afraid Shayna will be mad at you?"

Dovid shook his head.

"She would never be mad at you."

Yussi lifted Dovid and started up the stairs, struggling to contain the little boy who wiggled and tried to free himself.

"No. Maybe she'll be dead," Dovid pleaded.

Yussi wanted to rush upstairs and hand the boy to Shayna, to his mother, to someone who knew what to do. He had no idea what fear drove the child. Maybe his mother was right. Maybe Dovid did stay at Ulkeh's because Shayna's screams while giving birth sparked memories of his mother's screams during the pogrom. Who knew what crazy thoughts lived in a child's head? The wiggling stopped but the cries did not. Dovid's body was hot, sweaty, Yussi's shirt damp from holding him. Only a few more steps to their door. He paused for a moment to wipe the sweat from Dovid's forehead and kissed his warm cheek.

Dovid tightened his arms around Yussi's neck and whispered, "Papa, Papa, Papa."

Yussi faltered but held the boy more tightly. He felt an opening in his chest, as if his heart broke apart, opened wide and filled with light, with love that brought tears to his eyes. Nothing in the long journey from their home in the Ukraine until this moment awakened his spirit like Dovid's words. Not all the prayers, the rituals observed, or the study of holy books brought him this peace. It came to him as a gift, the gift of Dovid's love. He'd been blind. A fool. Ignoring what lay before him, searching hollow places while this little boy waited for him to see. He never thought Dovid needed him. Never thought maybe he needed Dovid. Not a son of his loins, but a son of his heart.

"Sh *tatele*. I'm here. No one will hurt you. Papa is here."

Yussi woke surrounded by the heat of Dovid's still sleeping body. Without waking the little boy, he maneuvered to his side and saw Shayna, seated near the bed, holding Eva against her breast, her eyes closed. In repose he could see traces of the girl she'd been, a girl without strain in her eyes, without the tension that thinned her lips, lined her forehead. In her relaxed face he saw again the girl who hid behind a curtain so she could study, the girl who even now was full of the same courage and curiosity. In his sleep, Dovid adjusted to fit more comfortably against Yussi, who gently threaded his fingers through the boy's curls, careful not to wake him.

No light came through the curtain, must still be before dawn. Soon this stillness would disappear. Dovid must be ready for school. Manya would make them *kashe*. He and Shayna must leave for the factory downstairs. In the past, Yussi would have pushed the boy aside, hurried to wash, quickly recited first prayers, and left for shul to find a *minyan* for *sharkharis*, formal morning prayers before he came to the factory. Always late, always losing pennies each day. Leaving his family each day to perform these rituals. He always believed he would have a family. At the yeshive he learned a man could not be complete without a wife, without children. A man needed to be complete, whole. He felt as if the pieces of himself, his dreams, his love for Shayna, his love of study, his faith, indeed his whole identity, everything about himself had scattered after the pogrom, and all these pieces were now coming together in new and unexpected ways.

He leaned in and kissed Dovid's head. If the boy saw him as Papa, he would be Papa, a father. His son. Not only to support, but to guide as his own father had guided him. Yussi raised his eyes and saw Shayna watching him. His wife, with Eva at her breast, blameless. Shayna pointed at Dovid and raised her eyebrow.

"I found him on the steps," Yussi whispered, then grinned. "We'll talk later." His eyes drifted closed as he heard Shayna humming to Eva, "*Sheyn Vi Di Levone,*" pretty as the moon, a lullaby he remembered from his own childhood. At Dovid's age he was already studying Torah at the yeshive. Yussi felt the softness of Dovid's curls, saw his fingers almost white against the boy's black hair, curls so much like his own. Surely now his son. Did he want a life immersed in Torah for Dovid? It seemed to Yussi that the desire he always experienced in the shtetl for Torah faded into the background of his mind, replaced now by the challenges of building a decent life in America.

Here in the darkness, in the warmth of the boy cuddled into him, Yussi was surprised by the memories that came to him from the yeshive. Of sitting with many other young boys and absorbing the words, the laws and traditions of his people. Then, he'd been sure about his path in life. Now, clean shaven here in America, he didn't rush to shul, or to study Torah. He no longer wore *tsitses.* He'd abandoned the outer symbols he had cherished. Never an *apikoyres,* he believed the God who lived in his heart would understand these changes. Nothing was as he expected. He was a married man now, with a family. A family.

Shayna had fallen asleep with the baby in her arms. Eva, born under a cloud, yet an innocent child. Maybe his own mother had been born under such a cloud; no one knew her history. And to be honest with himself, Yussi remembered the one time Shayna handed the baby to him for a moment; when Eva's eyes connected with his own, he wanted to continue to hold her. Maybe like Dovid, Eva would need him and he could love her. He could see now, as if cataracts were lifted from his eyes.

Yussi thought of his father more and more and understood his father had seen into the future. "You need to prepare for life in this world, not for the next," his father liked to say. Then he liked to pose the question, "Who survives in this *farkakte* world, as shitty as it is?" Then he'd nod his head, shake his index finger, and make his pronouncement, "The man who can change. That's the man who survives." Time to truly be a *mensch.*

He hugged Dovid, kissed his forehead. "*Gut-morgn,* sleepyhead, time to get ready for school."

Surely Clara was awake and would open the door so Shayna could just ask for Dovid's shoes. He couldn't go to school without shoes. Maybe she could avoid her brother. She would get the shoes Dovid left when he sneaked out, hurry upstairs, get the boy off to school, and still have time to get to the shop on time. But Ulkeh opened the door, still in an undershirt, unshaven.

Shayna wanted to say *gut-morgn,* but before she could open her mouth, Ulkeh barked, "Where is he? Where did you take the boy?"

"I didn't take him anywhere. He came upstairs. He needs his shoes."

"He left his shoes. He should come and get them." A small piece of cottage cheese clung to Ulkeh's upper lip and bobbed up and down when he talked.

"Let's not argue," she said. "He needs his shoes." She tried to move forward into Ulkeh's apartment, but he blocked her way.

"If that little shit wants his shoes, he'll come and get them. He has no respect. Clara bought him beautiful new shoes and he runs away and leaves them. He doesn't deserve new shoes."

"Don't give me the new shoes. Give me his old shoes."

Ulkeh raised his index finger and shook it in front of her face as his voice got louder and louder, his face redder. "The old shoes? Why do you think Clara bought him shoes? Why? You have no answer. I'll give you an answer. He couldn't even tie his shoes. Too tight. Too small. The boy is growing."

Shayna stood less than a foot from her brother. She saw his tongue reach up and snap the bit of cottage cheese into his mouth. Nothing escapes him, she thought, while she put out her hand, palm up. "Give me some shoes for him. Old ones. New ones. I don't care. Just for today. I don't want to be late for work. We'll argue later."

Shayna forced herself to look directly at her brother, not to hide, run away, or apologize. Dovid needed his shoes. She would not be afraid. She kept her eyes directed toward his. She did not hide her anger.

"You think I don't know that you look down your nose at me? You think you're better? Your husband, the dreamer, taking extra work, too good to help his brother-in-law with extra work? Don't look surprised. I know about it. Does he think this American boss will treat him with kid gloves? Out of the goodness of my heart I am trying to help you. What do I get? *Bubkes*. Nothing. *Drek*, shit, all of you. All of you. Disloyal. Selfish."

Shayna stopped herself from laughing in Ulkeh's face. What a fool he was. What did he think would happen when he didn't pay a worker enough to live on, when he charged them an outrageous rent, when he demanded repayment for the tickets other brothers gave as loving gifts to their families? Instead she kept her face resolute, waiting for Dovid's shoes. She refused to lash out or cower, only prayed that soon they would be free of him.

"Can your dreamer husband take care of the boy? Can he buy him shoes? A jacket for the winter?" His face moved closer and closer to hers. She tried not to turn away from the strong smell of herring.

From behind him she heard Clara's voice. "Enough, Jack. Stop it. Stop yelling. You're scaring the girls." She pushed Ulkeh aside and handed Shayna Dovid's shoes, but he grabbed Shayna's arm before Clara could close the door.

He tightened his fingers around her. "He's my nephew and I want the boy. Full time. Do you understand? I can provide for him. You can't." He pushed her away from the door and slammed it in her face.

Shayna tightened her lips around all the angry words rushing to get out, locked them out of her mind, and rushed upstairs to give Dovid his shoes. She still didn't know why she woke to find Dovid curled in Yussi's arms. No time now for questions. Ulkeh would dock pay if she was minutes late to work. She was grateful her parents hadn't lived to witness what had become of their once beloved son.

Chapter 32

Summer 1920

Shayna came upstairs from work to find Raizel teaching Manya to play pinochle. Eva was focused on a tiny pink stuffed dog, a gift from Raizel. She clutched it in her little fingers, brought it to her mouth, then bounced her arms up and down until the dog flew from her hands. Sometimes it landed at the end of the basket, but more often outside of the basket. Dovid picked it up each time, wiggled it over Eva until she grasped it, and the game would begin again. She watched Dovid paying attention to Eva, playing with her. She'd seen him play the same way with his baby sister Sarah. Did he remember? Shayna wondered if Ulkeh had ever played with her or Perl. She had no such memories. Of course, Eva would never remember this moment either. Shayna wanted to pick her up, hug Eva's softness close, but she was conscious that Dovid was old enough to make his own memories. He was home again, away from Ulkeh, and she was hungry to spend time with him, to let Dovid know he was important.

After weeks of cleaning the new apartment with Yussi, Shayna no longer went there in the evenings. Mike was actually helping Yussi install the windows and get the apartment ready for the city inspector. Unable to pay Yussi a full-time wage until he got some rents, Mike decided to help. Now, every evening, Shayna had something special for Dovid, and Eva wasn't crying to be fed yet.

"Nu, Shayna, do you want to eat first?" Manya placed her cards on the table. "I've got a good cold borscht. Or do you want to feed the baby first?"

Shayna shrugged, washed her hands and face, and drank a glass of water.

"Dovidel, come here, just a minute." The boy walked toward Shayna, a suspicious look in his eyes. Justified suspicion, because he guessed what she wanted. As soon as he got close, she grabbed him and swung him up over her head.

"It's time for your special treatment. Doctor's orders." She tossed him down on the sofa bed, knelt by his side, and began to tickle him. Shayna loved to hear his giggles, as he struggled to escape, but she held him down, her head on his belly as he tried to roll away.

"Bubbeh, help me. Bubbeh!" Dovid giggled.

Shayna looked to Manya, who shrugged her shoulders and whispered, "Calls me Bubbeh now." She wondered why he started to call Manya grandmother after so many months together, but she was grateful for Manya's presence in their lives, in Dovid's life. Every child needed a Bubbeh. Manya certainly qualified. Maybe it was going to school all day with so many other children, maybe it was the simple passage of time, or a miracle from God, but Perl's son was again recognizable. Life danced in his eyes again. It was as if he had returned from a long absence. He'd been like a shadow in his own life. Maybe that was true for all of them.

"Bubbeh's not going to help you, you little *mazek*. Little rascals need their daily tickle." Shayna pulled Dovid's shoes off and, holding both of his legs with one hand, she got to work on his feet. She reached for one of his hands and kissed his palm with loud smacking kisses. His giggles turned to cackles as he yelled, "Mamme, stop! Mamme, Bubbeh, help!"

Shayna released his legs, and before he could escape, she lifted him into her arms, held him, kissed his forehead. She pictured him as he lay curled in a fetal position, hiding after the pogrom. His mother dead in the same room. Mamme? She was *Tante*, only his aunt. He had a mother, a beautiful, loving mother. She couldn't let him forget Perl. She needed to think. Clearly Dovid thought of her as Mamme, at least to escape a serious tickle. Would Perl want her beloved son to call Shayna Mamme?

"Nu, *tatele*, tell me what you learned in school today?"

Shayna wiped the sweat from her forehead. The light wool suit she'd made to meet Bluma was far too warm to wear in the summer heat, but nothing else seemed appropriate to attend the end-of-year concert at Dovid's school. Inside the building, the heat only increased. There were no windows in the auditorium, no fresh air. They found places to sit near the back of the already crowded assembly hall. The seats went downhill toward a stage where wooden boxes of different heights were organized like steps. Shayna noticed some women wore lightweight cotton dresses with flowing sleeves. But even they had sweat on their brows.

Last week Dovid had rushed home to deliver the invitation. Shayna studied the paper but could only make out a few of the English words. Dovid explained the rest.

"We're going to sing. Want to hear?" Without waiting for an answer, he began. Shayna and Manya had to lean in to hear his soft voice sing about a farm, a word Shayna recognized, but she didn't catch much else until Dovid mooed like a cow. She wished Perl was alive to witness her son's joy.

"We practiced getting on the stage. Climbed on the boxes. Sammy and Angelo are in the back, too tall for the front. That's where she put me. Far from them. Except I stand next to Molly. They don't." Dovid clapped his hands, "You'll come? Papa too? The teacher says all the parents should come."

"If Yussi leaves work early, he'll come. For sure I'll be there and Bubbeh too."

"No, not me. Somebody has to stay with the baby. She doesn't need to go someplace with a lot of people. Eva could catch something." Manya glanced into the basket where the baby now dozed, "Anyway, Eva would rather stay with her Bubbeh. You'll tell us all about it."

Shayna squeezed Yussi's hand when she got a peek of Dovid marching up the steps with the other kindergarteners. She had to shift her head between the people seated in front of them to get a better view of him, his floppy curly hair making him easy to identify among so many children. Maybe it was time for a haircut. Shayna studied the other children's clothing. Some boys wore long pants, others dressed in short pants and long stockings. Some little boys wore miniature suit jackets and ties, like grown men. Dovid's white shirt looked yellow from too many washings. Shayna hadn't noticed that the long pants that fit him in the shtetl now ended above his ankles.

He needed not only new shoes, but new clothes as well. Now that she had a sewing machine, it wouldn't take her long to make a pair of shorts for the summer and a couple of shirts. She'd received the seed money from Bluma and immediately put a down payment on a Singer sewing machine. Now, after work, Shayna was focused on making the dresses Bluma ordered, finishing that order, getting paid, and hopefully getting another order from Bluma. Never enough time, never enough money.

Shayna took off her suit jacket, ignoring her worry about perspiration stains. The children's voices filled the auditorium, but she couldn't make out the words, only the animal sounds they made, the sounds that made the whole audience laugh, including Yussi.

She looked around the assembly hall and wondered if Ulkeh and Clara were somewhere in the crowd since Flo and Millie would likely perform with the older students. As Shayna fanned herself with the paper program, her shoulders drew together with the thought her brother might be in the auditorium. Even if he wasn't there, even the thought of him made her tense. Shayna wished Perl sat next to her, that Perl was alive and here in New York with her.

For months, since the pogrom, almost all memories of her sister had been overshadowed by the moment when she found Perl strewn across the bed, almost naked, blood covering her legs. It was as if a photographer had taken that picture with a big camera and sealed it into Shayna's brain. A picture, like a bomb, so horrifying, so powerful it destroyed all other memories of Perl. That picture might be fading a little because as Shayna sat with Yussi through the remainder of the program, memories of her sister came to her, each one a comfort. Perl holding her hand when they were children as they walked to shul. Perl laughing at her husband, Avrom's, bad jokes. Working with Perl to set the table for Shabbos. Perl with her eyes closed at baby Dovid's *bris*.

Shayna wished she could talk with her sister, tell Perl they registered her son to attend public school in New York with his own surname, Goldfarb. David as his first name, not Dovid, because since Ellis Island David was now his legal name. Why not? Of course. But they received letters addressed to Mr. and Mrs. Goldfarb, parents of David. Did that matter? Shayna wanted to talk with Perl about their brother, who was greedy and selfish but who said he wanted to adopt Dovid and give the boy more opportunities. Would Perl want that for her son? Dovid was now calling her Mamme. Calling Yussi Papa. And to Dovid, Manya was Bubbeh. Would Perl want them to be guardians of her son, or parents? What was best for Dovid?

Shayna's thoughts were interrupted by loud clapping. The program must be over and she realized she'd missed most of it, lost in her thoughts. It took her a moment to clear her head, stand, and join Yussi and the other families in the room in a standing ovation. All the children were coming off the stage now and running through the aisles to join their parents. She heard Dovid calling, "Mamme, Papa," as he ran toward them and jumped into Yussi's arms.

Shayna saw Manya pacing back and forth in front of their door when she returned from work. Something must have happened to Eva, she thought. Manya never waited outside the apartment for her.

"Where's Eva. Is she all right?"

"No, No. She's fine. The baby's sleeping. But I was waiting for you. I must talk with you right away before I change my mind. Promise me you won't tell Yussi what I'm going to tell you."

"What are you talking about?" Shayna rested for a moment against the wall, catching her breath after climbing four flights of stairs.

"I sent Dovid to Raizel's. I gave him supper first. She'll play cards with him. I have to talk with you."

"Okay, okay," Shayna said as she walked into the apartment, checked on Eva first, then washed her hands and face and drank a glass of water. Manya followed her.

"Nu, Manya. What are you talking about? You want to tell me something, something you want to hide from your son?"

"Maybe I shouldn't say anything. I should mind my own business. But Dovid is my business."

"What are you talking about? What does this have to do with Dovid? With Yussi?"

"Yussi knows I grew up in an orphanage, but there are things I've never told him, anyone really—no one. I never had the words. I was ashamed."

"Told them what?"

Manya placed a bowl of hot soup in front of Shayna and buttered a slice of pumpernickel for her. "It would only cause Yussi *hartsveytik* to learn how I suffered. He doesn't need the heartache."

"Were you sick?"

"No. Healthy. Strong. Always. Strong like an ox. By the time I was nine I worked, cleaning, carrying wood, whatever the older orphans did, I did. You know what Manya means in Russian? Bitterness. That's the name they gave me. For my bad fortune. But I never showed them bitterness."

"So, are these the things about being in the orphanage that you haven't told Yussi?"

"Yah. Wait. I've been thinking all day. I have to tell you about being an orphan, so you'll know." Manya poured herself a glass of water and sat down at the table across from Shayna. "I was about Dovid's age when the soldiers found me walking alone on the road. Before they took me in the orphanage, they passed me between Jewish families, because I only spoke Yiddish. Maybe someone would want me. But no one wanted me, Shayna. No one."

Manya wrapped her hands around the glass of water and stared into space. Shayna waited.

"I understand Dovid in a way no one else can. At least he knew his parents. Maybe I did once too. But by the time they found me on the road, I couldn't remember anything. You wondered why he stayed with Ulkeh—maybe he doesn't want to be close to you, and maybe he thinks you'll leave him too. On the outside I behaved one way, but on the inside…" Manya reached into her apron for a handkerchief and wiped tears from her eyes. She glanced at Shayna. "On the outside I was always strong, polite. Did what I was supposed to do with a smile. But on the inside, on the inside I stood alone, in a big empty field. Always windy and cold. The weather never changed. All alone in a big empty field, barren land. Nothing is there. No mother. No Bubbeh. No Papa. Nobody."

Manya finished the glass of water and took the empty glass to the sink. She moved to a chair next to Shayna and took Shayna's hand. "The worst thing is I thought maybe I did something, that I caused it. I didn't understand it wasn't my fault."

"You mean that you were alone? How could it have been your fault that you were alone? You were just a child?"

"That's why. Because I was a child. I didn't have the words. I didn't understand. Dovid is not the same as I was, but I beg you, don't let him be an orphan. Don't let Ulkeh have him either. Give him your name so he'll belong to you. When he's older, you'll tell him about his parents. Then, if he wants, he can take his name back. Let him know he belongs somewhere. That you want him. And you won't leave him. Let him say my aunt and uncle took me in and made me their son because they loved me so much. Let him not think everyone would be happier without him."

Chapter 33

Almost every evening on his way to Mike's building, Yussi passed women surrounded by children. They sat on curbs, tears in their eyes, huddled around their belongings, rolled up mattresses, a trunk or two, sometimes a few suitcases. Sometimes there was a man sitting with them, mostly not. At first, he'd stop to offer help, but there was little he could do. Evicted. Lost jobs, evicted. Sick child, not enough money for rent. Evicted. As the weeks passed, he stopped any efforts to help. What could he do when his own world teetered? Any day the permits would be signed and he'd leave the misery of Ulkeh's sweatshop. He'd make an enemy and soon after Shayna and his mother would do the same, break ties with Ulkeh, the man who gave them a lifeline with jobs and a place to live. Ulkeh would never forgive them.

Hopefully just another few weeks until Ulkeh would learn that they were all leaving and taking Dovid with them. If Yussi failed at the job of super, not only would he lose that job, but they would lose the apartment that came with the job. Then they would be no different than the families he saw huddled outside with their belongings. No place to lay their heads to rest. He pictured Shayna and his mother on the street curb. Eva in Shayna's arms and Dovid clinging to his mother. *Mirtse-hashem*, that wouldn't happen, God willing.

Yussi waited until Mike got the actual occupancy permit before he gave Ulkeh a week's notice that he was quitting. He also waited until payday, always on Saturdays, to give Ulkeh that news. From the beginning, Shayna and Manya had worked on Shabbos and after a few months Yussi joined them. He couldn't afford not to.

He tried not to dwell on the *aveyre*, but Mike insisted it wasn't a real sin. Mike asked him, "Would God prefer to have your family starve? You think your mother or your wife can make enough money to support you while you study Torah and also raise a family? This isn't the old country."

Just as his father always said. He must be a *bal-takhlis*, a practical man, not a *bal-torah*, not a scholar. Yet he missed the light that shined from the holy books, missed the quiet of study, and missed the freedom of his mind to explore, but now there was no time. Maybe someday. Someday he would continue his study of Torah and Talmud or maybe even go to a secular school, even to college. Here in America, Jews were allowed entrance.

In the late afternoon on a Saturday in July 1920, after he received his pay envelope, Yussi handed it to Shayna as she left the shop to go upstairs, and waited for all the other workers to leave. Only then did he approach his brother-in-law who was inspecting the sewing machines, checking to see that the needles were all raised. Leaving them down might cause breakage.

"Nu, Ulkeh."

"Jack, my name is Jack." Ulkeh waved his index finger at Yussi. "Are you too simple to remember? I'm going home. It's late."

Ulkeh walked away to where his suit jacket hung. As his brother-in-law raised his arms to put it on, Yussi noticed huge patches of sweat and smiled to himself when he saw the boss suffered from the heat like the rest of them.

Yussi followed him and began again. "Nu, Jack, I want you to know I am grateful for all you have done for us. Thank you." Yussi thought about shaking his brother-in-law's hand, but Ulkeh's arms were now folded across his chest. "I was offered another job and I'm going to take it. To be a carpenter. What I was trained to do." Ulkeh's lips curled into a sneer, but Yussi ignored the potential response and continued, "I won't leave for a week. You shouldn't have a problem finding someone to take my place."

Ulkeh was shaking his head, his sneer more marked as he reached for his handkerchief, patted sweat from his brow, and turned away from Yussi toward the door. Just before he opened it, he changed his mind and walked back to Yussi, stood so close Yussi could see the hairs in his nose. "You'll give me a week? Don't do me any favors." Ulkeh poked Yussi's chest with his index finger. "You're a *nar*. I don't need anyone to replace you. You're worthless."

Yussi stepped back to avoid spit from Ulkeh's mouth. He thought to defend himself, to talk about how hard he'd worked for many months, but knew it was a wasted effort. He'd said what he had to say and moved toward the door. Ulkeh grabbed his arm before he reached it. "If it wasn't for my beloved sister I would have fired you on the first day."

Yussi pushed him back with his free arm, but Ulkeh grabbed it as well and yelled into Yussi's face. "This is the proof I needed to keep my nephew. You're unstable. A bum. Can't keep a job. Not a decent father. The government is deporting bums like you, anarchists and other trash." Yussi looked down at Ulkeh; he was taller and stronger than his brother-in-law. There would be no contest if he used his height and strength to have the last word. But Shayna and his mother still worked for the man. Instead, without too much effort, he freed himself, pushed Ulkeh out of his way, and resisted slamming the door on his way out.

The waiter's warm smile as he approached the table disappeared when Shayna and Yussi ordered only one slice of cheesecake to split between them and two glasses of water. Ratner's was busy. She'd heard from Raizel that it was always busy. A *milkhik* restaurant serving only dairy foods, where all the waiters spoke Yiddish, totally kosher right on Delancey, not far at all.

She'd never been in a restaurant before, neither in New York nor in Europe. Manya had insisted Yussi should celebrate his freedom— freedom from ironing. "I try to save a few pennies every time I buy groceries. I save them just in case," Manya said and pressed a quarter into Shayna's hand. "You go celebrate. I'll take Eva and Dovid with me to

Raizel's. She's making blintzes. Don't worry. I won't say a word to her about anything."

Manya refused to listen to Shayna's excuses. "The dresses for Bluma will wait a few hours. Go enjoy. Don't worry, it's only enough for a dessert, not a whole dinner."

Yussi lit one cigarette after the other after they ordered cheesecake. Knowing her brother, she guessed Yussi's conversation with him must have been aggravating. She looked around all the tables she could see a few families with children, but mostly young couples and some tables with only young women, maybe office workers or teachers. They looked prosperous, wearing bright stylish clothes in reds and yellows. Tables full of people who looked relaxed, comfortable dining in restaurants, away from their homes.

Yussi interrupted her thoughts. "I know he's your brother, but how did such decent people like your parents give birth to such a shmuck?"

"I don't know. I was only seven when he left. What did he say to you?"

Yussi paused for a moment. "The usual. Angry. Empty threats about Dovid and the authorities, deporting me. A bully like always."

Ulkeh had also threatened Shayna with authorities. She had no idea what authorities or why Ulkeh had mentioned them, but she knew only months before scores of immigrants, even citizens, were deported. She read about it in the *Forward*. A terrible thing. She knew her brother could be a threat to their future in America. Maybe the threats weren't empty. They weren't citizens. Hardly spoke English. Shayna wanted to prepare herself if there was a danger, but she had no idea how to prepare. They needed to get away from him as soon as possible.

The waiter didn't hurry to bring their cheesecake. Shayna wasn't used to just sitting, waiting with nothing to do, not hurrying to do laundry, cook, take care of Eva, or sit for hours like a prisoner chained to Ulkeh's sewing machine.

"At least he sent the tickets," Yussi said, trying to find some redeeming quality. "Enough tickets for the whole family. Maybe not a complete shmuck."

"*Bubkes*. Nothing to him. Salve for his guilty conscience." Shayna quickly realized she'd opened the door to a conversation she didn't want to have.

"Guilty? Why guilty? Because he escaped the pogroms?"

"Maybe." Shayna folded her hands together on the table. "Maybe guilty about what happened to the family when he ran away from the Czar's army."

Laughter from the table next to them drowned out whatever Yussi said, but the surprised look on his face reminded her she never told him about Ulkeh's history. Long before they arrived at Ellis Island, Shayna had decided not to talk about Ulkeh. She wanted Yussi and Manya to meet him without prejudice.

"Was he conscripted?"

She nodded, but didn't go on.

"Nu, so what happened to the family?" Yussi lit another cigarette. "Don't make me pull the words from your mouth."

"Leave me alone. I don't want to talk about it."

Yussi leaned back in his chair, pulled away from Shayna. "So why did you bring it up?"

"I shouldn't have brought it up. I was only seven when he left. I didn't understand much, but I know his name was on the conscription list."

"Most boys never came out alive, not after twenty-five years in the Czar's army," Yussi said. "Everyone worried about conscription."

"I'm not sure exactly what happened. You never knew my zeyde, did you? He was a *makher* in the shtetl. I think he managed to get confidential information from the authorities. Ulkeh's name was on the list."

"Nu?" Yussi raised an eyebrow.

"I think Zeyde bribed somebody to put another name on the list, instead of Ulkeh. The authorities took every ruble Zeyde had down to the last kopeck to save his grandson. My parents had little, but they arranged for Ulkeh to leave the country." Shayna noticed a button on her sleeve cuff hung by a thread. She wiggled it off, wrapped the button in her handkerchief, and put it in her skirt pocket.

"So your parents had enough to get him out of Ukraine?"

"They must have. I think Ulkeh promised he would send money from America, but he never sent anything. Not until the tickets."

"Why did I never hear this? Why didn't you tell me?"

"Why? So you could think even less of him? It was so many years ago. I wanted to give him a chance. I wanted you to give him a chance."

Shayna noticed Yussi's leg was bouncing up and down. She wished the waiter would come with the cheesecake. She wondered if they could just walk out, but Yussi motioned to another waiter, who apologized after Yussi asked him about their dessert and said he'd bring it soon. They wouldn't be able to leave now.

"Shayna, all these months you didn't talk about what was really in your heart. Even when he didn't meet you at Ellis Island, even when he put us in such a *farshtunkene* apartment. And dinner at his house, the way he talked to us. Now, for the first time, you tell me Ulkeh escaped conscription and your family suffered."

Shayna didn't have to respond right away because the second waiter brought a large piece of cheesecake, two glasses of water, and a small piece of paper with twenty cents written on it. She let Yussi take the first bite. His eyes opened wider as he tasted the cheesecake, then licked his lips. He filled his fork with more and raised it to Shayna's mouth.

"Eat," Yussi said. "You've never tasted anything so good." Within minutes the cheesecake disappeared and Shayna rose to leave. "Shayna, wait a minute. Tell me why in all these months you never told me the truth about Ulkeh."

"Why are you making such a big *tsimes*? No need to make fuss."

"It is a big *tsimes* to me." Yussi kept his voice low, but its tone was loud. "Who am I to you now? Someone you used to know, someone from your childhood, a friend, sort of husband, one you share your body with now, but not someone you love or trust. Don't you understand I married your *tsores* as well as your *simchas*? You're hiding from me."

For a moment Shayna thought about arguing with him, denying, getting mad. Foolish. She needed to make him understand so she sat again. "Hiding? Who's hiding? I don't know what you want."

She looked around the restaurant for the waiter, then pulled the quarter from her pocket and placed it on the bill. A nickel would remain from the quarter. A tip. Shayna knew about tips because one of the women in the sweatshop had been a waitress before Ulkeh hired her. Shayna didn't remember her name, only her chatter about the five-dollar tip she once got from a man in a silk suit and a diamond ring on his pinkie finger.

"When we decided to marry, I was seventeen. Seventeen. You were twenty. I thought I understood marriage. I said I loved you. I knew we could have sex if we were married." Shayna's face reddened when she added, "I wanted that."

Yussi tilted his head, nodded, and smiled.

With her elbows on the table, Shayna leaned forward and stared into space. "We would have children. We could make a living. All in our little shtetl. I knew nothing. *Der mensch trakht un got lakht*, man plans and God laughs. We lived through the war, through poverty, pogroms. I didn't understand, not really. I still don't understand." Shayna covered her face with her hands for a moment, then looked directly at Yussi, "My parents were murdered on the street in front of our house. Perl was raped. Murdered in her bed. You know what happened to me. So now I'm eighteen and have two children. Next month I'll be nineteen. What is love? What do you want from me?"

The waiter came to the table, picked up the bill and the quarter, and walked away. She wondered if waiters just kept the change.

"I want us to be as we were in the shtetl," Yussi said. "You smiled when I walked into a room. We laughed together. We had dreams." He raised her chin and lowered his voice even more. "I want you to trust me, be close like we were."

"Yussi." Shayna pulled back. "How can it be like it was? I'm a different person." Shayna brought her hands together for a moment, as if in prayer, and stood. "I am responsible for two other human beings." She rested her hands on his shoulders. "You think you haven't changed? The boy I married carried God in his heart. He was observant, he wore *tsitsits*, he *davened*." Shayna turned and walked out of the restaurant, Yussi just steps behind her. He guided Shayna to a quiet spot near the wall of the building.

"All of a sudden that matters to you?" Yussi took a deep breath. "You tell me you don't even believe in God. What does it matter to you if I *daven*?"

"But I knew that boy."

"I'm the same person."

"No you're not." She rubbed the back of her head. "We've both changed." Shayna looked up and down the street. Delancey was a busy street, still full of pushcarts and people shopping. No one was paying attention to them. These thoughts had been rolling around her head, but she tried to follow her mother's example. Since the pogrom she did only what lay in front of her. The next thing and the next thing. But Yussi was right. They needed to talk.

"Things have happened. Do I have to remind you what's happened to me?" Shayna looked down, picked a tiny piece of lint from her skirt. "I'm not the same person. We're no longer children. We'll continue to change." Shayna folded her arms across her chest. "I thought a person grows up and then they're an adult. Finished. Like a person's height. But now I see, growing up, being an adult, is more like baby teeth coming in, endless baby teeth."

"Baby teeth?" Yussi looked confused.

"Yes, baby teeth. They hurt. They pierce your skin, tear a hole and push out. This causes great discomfort. That's what it means to grow up. To be an adult. Yussi, we're in a new world, with two children, growing baby teeth."

Yussi's hand covering his mouth gave him away. He was laughing and mumbling, "Baby teeth. Baby teeth."

"Don't laugh." Shayna unfolded her arms and moved away from the wall. "You're laughing at me. Why do I bother talking to you when you laugh at me?"

"Shaynaleh," he nodded. "I am laughing. Laughing because I adore you. I love the little girl you were behind the curtain, the girl who stood with me before the rabbi and became my wife, my partner, the woman you are now, working so hard to make a life here in America."

Shayna relaxed back against the wall of Ratner's.

"Baby teeth hurt. But they don't hurt forever," Yussi said. "You get new teeth." He tapped his finger on her front teeth.

"New teeth, huh?" She laughed, "I bet they hurt too."

"Probably. Then they fall out and we lose all our teeth."

"So that's the time the wife makes mush for the old man to eat." Shayna ran her fingers along his cheek. "I suppose you'll want me to feed you mush."

"Of course, and when you're an old lady, without any teeth, I'll make you mush. That's the job of the husband." Yussi placed his hand on the wall and leaned toward Shayna. "Before we lose our teeth, tell me the truth, if you just met me today, would you still marry me?"

Shayna stopped smiling and looked up at Yussi. Warmth went through her body, not the warmth she felt when he made love to her, but more like the warmth of the kitchen on Shabbos. A deep fullness filled her heart as she recognized hope in his eyes. She imagined her eyes carried the same message. "Yes," she said. They were bound together, *bashert*, from the beginning. Who knew why?

Chapter 34

Yussi was finished with the sweatshop. Never again would he pick up a steam iron. Never. Never would he lock himself into such a job, standing on his feet all day doing the same thing over and over.

Mike didn't have to teach Yussi much about the handyman part of the job as super, but he did have to teach him about renting apartments, how much to charge, getting deposits, the rules, how to get references, and who to get them from. Often there were no references, no one to vouch for someone new to the country. Mike told Yussi to trust himself—trust what Yussi's own eyes told him. Don't rent to someone who might be a *ganef*, or a *shiker*. Trust yourself.

Yussi worried more about communication problems than judgment concerns. Yet he already spoke Yiddish, Hebrew, Russian, and Ukrainian, the languages of many on the Lower East Side. Mike taught him several basic sentences in English, and soon he would start classes. Among the workers still finishing details in the building, there were eight different languages spoken. Even a man from Sweden, but so far no Swedes had come looking to rent. Yussi collected deposits from the first people to move in, filled in the receipt forms Mike left for him, and locked the money in a safe in the super's apartment.

On this day he supervised day laborers hired to wash all the windows in the building, inside and outside, and directed the delivery of appliances, stoves, and ice boxes to each unit. Yussi liked to keep busy; it kept his mind from drifting. Often it drifted even when he was busy. As the afternoon grew into evening, just before the sunset, he sometimes pictured himself among a *minyan* davening the afternoon prayers. Sometimes his mind wandered to the now dusty pile of holy books stacked in a corner of their apartment and he would feel a gnawing, a hunger for the past, for the days before his father's death when he sat for hours in the yeshive. There he could study detached from daily concerns and be nourished by the spirit of God in his heart.

Just before he left the building, he checked to confirm the door to the super's apartment was locked. Already there were a few furnishings. Lillian, Mike's wife, had collected things to give them: a child's bed and toys for Dovid, things her children had outgrown. She also collected cooking utensils, dishes, and baby things from her friends, and Mike brought over a table, a few chairs, and a bed and dresser abandoned by someone in another building Mike owned. There would be a bed for his mother and Shayna while Yussi would sleep on a mattress he bought from a peddler for forty cents, at least until they bought or found another bed. Likely they could find a good used bed with a mattress for a couple of dollars.

In a few days, his family would move in. He wasn't sure exactly when he started thinking of them all together, as a group, not just a collection of people he knew traveling together, not just his mother and a fiancé who became a wife, and the little boy, Shayna's nephew. And then Eva. Born of Shayna's own flesh and blood. What was hers was his too. It was now visible to him, clearly. His family. His family would be together in this new place.

Shayna sat without moving on a bench in Seward Park, a park in walking distance from their apartment, while alongside Eva slept soundly in her buggy. Raizel had told them about the park, otherwise they may have never discovered it on their own. Shayna leaned back, raised her face to feel the morning sun, and spied a hawk high in one of the large cottonwood trees lining the path. Back home, she loved to watch them soar through the air above the shtetl, their wings spread flying free in the sky. Maybe this hawk was hunting his breakfast. Raizel told her to be careful walking in the park, that it was full of rats, rats the hawks liked to eat. Raizel also told her sometimes these birds swooped in on the tiny dogs Americans seemed to love. The first time she saw a man in a suit, walking a tiny dog on a leash, she had to cover her mouth so the man wouldn't hear her laughing. Now she was accustomed to such things.

Coming to the park was a necessary first step in their plan. Shayna wanted to start the day surrounded by trees and flowers, away from the dreariness that hung from the walls of their apartment. From the park they would take Dovid and Eva to Mike's house, to Lillian and her children, until the move was finished. Shayna and Yussi would then go to Ulkeh's home, and she would tell her brother she was quitting. They were moving. Taking Dovid with them. It was up to Ulkeh if he wanted to be an uncle and a brother in more than name only. Shayna had seen little evidence that her brother had a *neshome*, a soul, or a heart that could be generous and loving.

Manya waited in the apartment with their things and waited for Mike, who would come with his truck, help them move their meager belongings to the new apartment and drive them all away from the sweatshop forever. They packed the colander, two sharp knives, the breadboard and a half-dozen new glasses they'd bought from peddlers on the street. What Ulkeh gave them they'd leave behind.

Shayna took several deep breaths, inhaling the sweet lemony smell of honeysuckle coming from a cluster of blooms near her bench. She felt the scent flow through her body, touching each nerve, each muscle, and bringing her peace. She thought of Obodivka, in the times before the pogroms. Always her mother filled a vase with flowers from their garden for Shabbos. Shayna thought of her favorite prayer, the *Shehekheyanu*, a prayer of gratitude. She sent it out to whatever God might be listening, gratitude for the loving family she once had and a prayer for the future, for her new family, and for a time when there would be flowers on the table again.

In spite of the summer heat, Shayna chose to wear her blue suit, the one she made to meet with Bluma about a job. She insisted Yussi wear his best shirt and slacks. No longer just off the boat, maybe her brother would treat them with respect.

"Nu, there's a party somewhere?" Ulkeh said when he opened the door. "Or maybe a funeral. What's the occasion?"

"I've come to talk with you," Shayna said. "Can we come in?"

Ulkeh waved them into the house, sat down in his big chair, but did not invite them to sit.

"Ulkeh, Jack," Shayna corrected herself and pulled an envelope from her pocket. "Here's money for next week's rent. We're moving out, so this money is for the one-week's notice. Also in the envelope there's the money we give you every week for our tickets." Ulkeh said nothing but took the envelope and put it next to him on a small table.

She could hear her own voice quiver and paused before she continued. "We need a bigger place. I have another job. Manya will come with us. She asked me to quit for her." Still her brother said nothing. Yussi took her hand, and as they turned to leave, Shayna said, "Thank you. We appreciate all you did for us. But you'll no longer have to help us."

"Not so fast. Not so fast." Ulkeh stood. "Just like that. Like a slap in the face. After all I've done for you. Poor refugees. I took you in, fresh off the boat, and gave you jobs and a place to live." He took a few steps toward them, "Go. Good riddance." He motioned them toward the door. "But David will stay here with us…"

"David?"

"He'll use his legal name, his Ellis Island name, not a name from the old country. He'll have a better life. I don't want my nephew living with a janitor and a cleaning lady."

"Janitor?" Yussi asked, "Cleaning lady? What are you talking about?"

"You think something happens in this building and I don't know about it? What do you think a super is? A janitor for all the people in the building."

Shayna tried to figure out how he knew Yussi was going to be a super in Mike's building. Manya must have said something to Raizel.

"And you, Shayna, big shot you, when water leaks all over, who will clean it up? When someone vomits on the steps, who cleans it up?" Ulkeh took out his handkerchief, patted the sweat that always seemed to live on his face, and settled back into his chair. "I should send my nephew into such an environment? Never. I already talked with a law-yer."

Yussi tugged on Shayna's hand, urging her to leave, but Shayna re-sponded. "Jack, let's talk about this quietly. We must think about what's best for Dovid."

"I'll tell you what's best for David, best for him to have every ad-vantage. As my son, he'll have money to go to college, to learn how to run the business and inherit it someday. What can you promise him? *Bubkes.*" He poked the air with his index finger. "Already I've started with a lawyer, to make sure the uncle gets custody of David."

"There's no point talking to him, Shayna. Let's go."

Shayna shushed Yussi, walked toward her brother and said, "Jack, Dovid wants to stay with us. He is more at home with us."

"He'll get over it. Learn to appreciate what he has here."

"He doesn't want to be with you, Jack," Yussi said. "He told me."

"Stay out of this. This doesn't concern you. Don't you understand, you janitor you, I need a son. Clara can't have more children. For what am I building this business? For sons-in-law to steal?" Shayna could see spittle fly from his mouth across the room.

At that moment Clara came into the living room, drying her hands on her apron. They hadn't seen her very often, nor thought about her. With her arms folded across her chest, she said in a quiet voice, "Stop Jack. Stop this."

"Go finish lunch." Without looking at her, he added, "You should mind your own business."

"Jack." She walked deeper into the room, took off her apron, and stood in front of her husband's chair, blocking his face from Shayna and Yussi. Although she spoke in a low voice, Shayna and Yussi clearly heard what she said.

"Mind my own business? You're telling me to mind my own busi-ness. Jack," she shook her head, "Jack, don't make yourself a bigger fool than you already are. Stop this now. I told you once. I told you fifty times. I don't want the boy. I don't want more children. I should do laundry and feed someone else's kid? Are you deaf, Jack?"

Ulkeh stood and pushed Clara away from him. "Clara, this is a man's business. Go make lunch. The girls will be hungry. They'll be back from the park soon."

"Did you just push me? I think you pushed me." She turned to Shayna. "Did you see him push me?" She didn't wait for an answer. Instead, she shoved Ulkeh back into the chair. "Something my father would want to know about, don't you think? Don't ever push me."

"A man needs a son. You didn't give me a son."

"Maybe not a son, but my father bought you a business."

"*Oy yey*," Shayna muttered.

"You're surprised? This genius, your brother, was a poor peddler when I met him. Where do you suppose he got the money to start this business?"

"Nu, big deal." Ulkeh folded his arms across his chest. "Every month your father gets his money. He made a good investment. You think he'll stop the money coming to him. Leave me alone. I can still give the boy a better life."

"You can't give him a mother to love him," Shayna said. "That's what every child needs, more than anything." Shayna looked at Clara, who ignored her.

"My father may like the money he's earned, but you know, Jack, he's a very strict man. You think he wants to hear his son-in-law is *shtuping* a whore on the third floor? You want I should tell him? You think he can't run the shop himself. Don't test me. Don't test him."

Ulkeh's shoulders slumped. His face paled. Clara glanced at Yussi and Shayna and walked back into the kitchen.

Without a word of farewell, Shayna and Yussi left. Everything had been said. The door opened inward, and when they pulled it toward themselves to leave, they discovered Flo and Millie, Ulkeh's daughters, standing outside, as pale as their father. They must have heard everything. These were Shayna's nieces. Family. She hardly knew them, even after all these months. They'd been good to Dovid from the beginning. Maybe they weren't like their father.

"You'll come and visit us. Dovid will love to see you. I'll make sure you get the address."

"Wait here," the older one said. She rushed into the house and ran by her father, still frozen in his chair. She returned moments later and handed Shayna a red and green box with a picture of a wooden house on the top. Lincoln Logs was printed on the outside. Shayna could make out the words.

"These are David's. He loves to play with them."

Ulkeh now stood behind them. He put a hand on each girl's shoulder. "Take a look," he said to his daughters. "Take a good look. Don't be fooled. These people were kicked out of Russia. No one wanted them there and no one wants them here. Ignorant refugees. Let's go inside. Stay away from them."

Chapter 35

In a classroom again after many years, Shayna no longer hid behind a curtain because she was a girl. Here she could feel the warmth of Yussi's body next to her own in this crowded room of strangers at the Henry Street Settlement. They'd walked together from the new apartment to their first official English class.

Each of them had picked up words and phrases here and there as their lives stretched out to the world around them. Shayna worked with Agnes, Bluma's major buyer, who had a limited knowledge of Yiddish, forcing Shayna to learn more English. With Dovid's help or by consulting with her Yiddish-English dictionary, she and Agnes understood each other enough to order fabric and notions to complete Bluma's first order of a half-dozen dresses in two different designs. Agnes also arranged for Shayna to have an adjustable mannequin torso, which enabled her to create different sizes. The dresses were ready for transport to the store, and soon Shayna would know if there would be more orders. If not, she'd have to find a job in another sweatshop or take piece work to finish as Manya had done.

The new apartment had four rooms, two bedrooms, a kitchen, and a living room, plus their own washroom. Each bedroom had a window, and even though they faced the brick wall of the building next door, there was enough space between the buildings so that light entered the rooms. Above all, the windows could be opened for fresh air. The living room was now also Shayna's design studio and sewing room, housing her machine, a cutting table, and an ironing board.

So far, Shayna hadn't cleaned up anyone's vomit or had to clean anything in the building. She spent most of her time sewing or designing while Manya attached buttons for a coat manufacturer. Both took care of Eva. As super, Yussi was prepared to clean whatever needed to be cleaned but learned Mike had what he called an arrangement with a cleaning company for all of his buildings. He told Yussi it had something to do with protection. If the company did the cleaning, there would be no problems. Yussi knew enough not to ask questions.

He picked up English from Mike and the other workers, but both Shayna and Yussi didn't want to sound like greenhorns for the rest of their lives. Lillian found a class for them, one that would be very simple in the beginning, but over time would give them a good foundation to learn. Two nights every week they would attend classes, get books and exercises to do at home. To Shayna it seemed like it would take forever to sound like an intelligent person in English, to sound like an American. Yet she knew every time she stared at a blank page waiting for a design to come to her or she studied a bolt of fabric to imagine dresses that could emerge, she was forced to admit that everything takes time. In making a garment, a beautiful quality garment, she couldn't take shortcuts. Yussi was even more committed to studying.

A tall blond woman stood and greeted each person as they walked through the classroom door. Men and women. Tall and short. Old and young. Some men dressed in well-worn suits, the fabric shiny from too many washes. Other men sat, their eyes downcast, still in work clothes coated with wood shavings or paint smears. Fresh-faced young women wore skirts and middy blouses. Their long hair, uncovered, hung loose around their shoulders. Stout, wrinkled women wore black, some with colorful head scarves, others with heavy black hair twisted tightly back into thick knots. Around them they heard not only Yiddish, but languages she could only guess. Italians, Germans, Poles—everyone here to learn English, to become Americans.

The smell of vinegar lingered in the room, likely used to clean the gleaming huge windows. When they first arrived, foot traffic outside on Henry Street was clearly visible but had slowly become indistinct as the sun set. Soon Shayna could only see blackness beyond the windowpanes, giving her a sense that they were enclosed in a secret cavern and embarking on an important journey.

The blond woman moved from the door and took her place at the desk in front of the room. Shayna had never imagined there would be a woman teacher. She knew Dovid's teachers in elementary school were women, but she'd never imagined a woman teaching adults especially one so young and beautiful. Shayna studied the woman's clothing carefully, filing away the design of an ankle-length skirt, with pockets, wide at the hips and tapered to the hem. A shape Shayna had never seen. Nor had she seen anything like the fine yarn of her knitted sweater. Both garments in a soft cream color. Not a spot on it anywhere. Shayna adjusted her own skirt, sewn originally from Clara's discards and altered now as she lost weight after Eva's birth.

The teacher motioned to the class to open their books to the alphabet. She began to sing the letters, A, B, C, D, each letter sung in a clear, strong voice, and then invited everyone to join her. Titters and groans crossed the room until gradually everyone joined, some in full voice, others at barely a whisper. They sang once and then again and again. Yussi's full, rich voice clear among the others.

"My name is Miss Evans. What is your name?"

Around the room they practiced. Some already had American names. To those without such names, the teacher often made suggestions.

A wizened woman, dressed in all black, spoke in a clear loud voice, "My name is Chana."

"In English that's often Anna." The old woman simply nodded in acknowledgment. Miss Evans looked at the man wearing a white shirt and wine-colored vest seated next to Chana.

"Velvel, my name is Velvel."

"William?" Miss Evans suggested. The man responded in Russian, "I always hated the name Velvel. So maybe I'll be William now." Those in the class who understood Russian, including Yussi and Shayna, laughed and someone tried to explain it in broken English. But Miss Evans smiled, shrugged her shoulders, and moved to the next student.

She came to where Shayna and Yussi sat. When Yussi introduced himself, the teacher paused and suggested, "Joe?" He thought for a moment, shook his head, then mumbled so only Shayna could hear, "Maybe someday."

"My name is Shayna." When the teacher suggested Sharon, Shayna smiled, cocked her head, and repeated, "Shayna." She wanted to become an American with the name her parents gave her. Dovid was already David at school, but Shayna's mother's voice lived somewhere in her mind instructing her, guiding her, reminding her, always Shayna this and Shayna that. She could remember her father's loving kisses on her forehead and hear him say, "*Zise, Shaynaleh*. Her name would remain her own.

††††

GLOSSARY

This novel adheres closely to "YIVO-Standard" Yiddish, but exceptions were made for words with more known American or Hebraized spellings

Az och un vey	Too bad, such sorrow, intense grief
Agune	Deserted wife
Akshn	Stubborn
Aleyem-hasholem	May they rest in peace
Aliyah	Rise, call to read from the Torah, call to immigrate to Israel
Apikoyres	Non-believer
Aveyre	Sin
Bal-takhles	Practical man
Bal-torah	Man of learning
Bar Mitzvah	Coming of age and assuming religious responsibility
Barukh-hashem	Blessed is The Name
Bashert	Destiny
Bime, bimah	Platform in the synagogue from which the Torah is read
Bintl-briv	Advice column in Jewish newspaper, *The Forward*
Borukh-habo	Welcome, Bless those who come
Boytshik	Young boy
Bris	The Jewish ceremony of circumcision
Brokhes	Blessings
Bubbeh, (Bobe)	Grandmother

Bubbeh-mayse	Old wives tale
Bubkes	The least amount, nothing
Daven, davening	To pray, praying
Der mensch trakht un got lakht	Man plans and God laughs
Der seykhl iz a krikher	Understanding comes at a snail's pace
Drek	Rubbish, Excrement
Eishes khayal	Woman of valor
Es	Eat
Es, tatele	Eat good little boy
Es tut me vey	I hurt
Eynikl, eyniklekh	Grandchild, grandchildren
Eyns, tsvey; dray, fir, finef	One, two, three, four, five
Farkakte	Crappy
Farshtunkene, farshtunkenen	Stinky
Fleyshik	Meat, meals containing meat
Frum	Observant
Frume yidn	Observant Jews
Galitsianer	A subdivision of the Ashkenazi Jews of eastern Europe, originating in Galicia, western Ukraine and SE Poland.
Ganef	Thief
Genug	Enough
Get, ghet	Jewish religious divorce
Goldene medine	The Golden State/country, America
Golem	A clay figure brought to life by magic – Jewish legend
Gotenyu	Dear Lord
Goy/Goye/Goyim/Goyeshe	Gentile m, f, plural
Guter mensch	Good man
Gut-morgn	Good morning
Gut-shabbos	Good Sabbath

Hartsveytik	Heartache
Ikh darf pishn	I have to pee
Kaddish	Mourner's prayer
Kashe	Porridge made of buckwheat or other grains mixed with water or milk
Khevre kadishe	Burial society
Kheyder	First educational setting for Jewish boys, sometimes girls
Khokhm	Smart
Khutzpah	audacty
Kidish	Blessing over wine
Klafte	Bitch
Klezmer	Traditional eastern European Jewish music
Kneydlakh	Matza balls in soup
Kokhlefl	Cooking spoon, busybody
Koykhes	Strength
Krie	Making a tear in one's clothes, ritual of mourning
Libe ken brenen un nit oyfhern	Love can burn and never end
Lokh in kop	Hole in the head
Landsman, landslayt, Landsmanschaften	A person from the same village or nearby, benevolent societies organized by people from the same village or region
Litvak	Jews from Lithuania, Belarus, Latvia,
Lokshn	Noodles
Makher	Big shot, influential person
Makhsheyfe	Witch
Malekh-hamoves	Angel of Death

Mamele	Term of endearment for child
Mamme	Mother
Mamzer	Bastard
Mayse	Story
Mazek	Mischievous child
Mazel	Luck
Mazel-tov,	Congratulations
Mekhaye	A pleasure, what you live for
Mekhitse	Partition to separate men and women in the Synagogue
Mensch, (mentsh)	A person with integrity and honor
Meshuge, meshugene meshugas	Crazy, a crazy person, craziness
Mezuzah	A parchment scroll in a case affixed to the door post of Jewish home. Religious texts are inscribed on it.
Mikve	Ritual bath for purification
Milkhik	Dairy food
Minkhe	Afternoon prayer
Minyan, (minyen)	Quorum of ten required for Jewish prayer
Mirtse-hashem	God willing
Mishpokhe	Family
Mitzvah, mitzvos	Good deed
Meshiekh	Messiah
Nakhes	Pride of another's accomplishments, usually parents of children
Nar, narish, nariskayt	Fool, foolish, foolishness
Neshome	Soul
Nosh	Snack
Nu	Well, a word with various meanings depending on intonation, and context from exasperation to questioning, to scolding

Olev-hasholem	May he rest in peace
Orn-koydesh	Holy Ark container the torah
Oy vey	Woe is me
Paskudnyak	Despicable person
Patsh	Smack, gentle slap
Peyes	Sidelocks worn by the very orthodox males
Pisht	Urinated
Pogrom	From the Russian 'destruction' An organized massacre of a particular ethnic group, in particular that of Jews in Russia or eastern Europe.
Prost, proste	Common, vulgar
Puptshik, du bist mayn lebn. Ikh hob dikh lib	A song, You're my life, I love you
Rakhmones	Compassion, mercy
Rebetsn	Rabbi's wife
Reboyne shel-oylem	Master of the Universe
Rozshinkes mit mandlen	Lullaby - Raisins and almonds
Seder	A ritual dinner on the first two nights of Passover
Seykhel	Intelligence, smarts, common-sense
Shabbos	Sabbath
Shadkhn	Marriage brother, match maker
Shah	Quiet
Shande un a kharpe	Shame and disgrace
Sharkharis	Morning prayers
Shayna, sheyne	Pretty
Sheyn vi di levone	Song, pretty as the moon
Sheytl	Wig worn by very orthodox women
Shiker	Drunk

Shiva	Mourning ritual lasting seven days
Shlong	Penis, vulgar usage
Shmate	Rag, anything worthless
Shmuck	Contemptable person, vulgar for penis
Shmuts, shmutsik	Dirt, dirty
Sholem aleykhem	Greeting, peace to you, typical response is Aleykhem Sholem
Sholem-bais	Peace in the home
Shoykhet	Kosher slaughterer
Shoymer	Guard
Shpilkes	Needle, on pins and needles
Shtark, shtarker	Strong, powerful
Shtetl	Small town in eastern Europe with large Jewish populations, pl
Shtup, shtuping	Vulgar slang for sexual intercourse
Shul	Synagogue
Shvitser	Braggart, literally someone who sweats
Siddur, (sider)	Prayer book
Simcha, simkhe	Joys, celebrations, happy occasions
Takhlis	Practical matter, goal, end or limit
Tagelakh	Pastry dipped in boiling honey
Talis	A Prayer shawl, plural
Tante	Aunt
Tate mame makt mir khasene	Song, Father, Mother make me a wedding
Tatele	Toddler, m, good child
Tfilin	Phylacteries- Biblical mandate- keep God's words in mind
Treyf	Not- kosher
Tsayt	Time, menstrual cycle

Tsimes	Fuss, uproar, from cooking term for mixed fruit, veggies.
Tsores	Troubles
Tukhes	Butt
Tsadik	Righteous man
Tsedoke	Charity
Tsitses	Specially knotted ritual fringes attached to the four corners of a tallis or special undergarments
Tumbalalaika	Russian/Jewish folk song in Yiddish
Vayb	Wife
Yad	Literally hand, a ritual pointer when reading from the Torah
Yakne	Annoying nag, gossipy, trouble-maker
Yarmulke	A Head covering worn as a reminder that God is above
Yene velt	The world to come
Yente	Gossipy woman
Yeshive	Jewish religious institution focusing on religious texts
Yeytser-hore	Inclination to evil
Yeytser-tov	Inclination to good
Yid, Yidn	Jew, Jews
Yikhes	Status
Zay shtil	Be quiet
Zets zikh	Sit down
Zeyde	Grandfather
Zikhroyne livrokhe	Blessed be his memory
Zise	Sweet one
Zol zayn mit mazel	Wishing you luck
Zol zayn shah	Be quiet
Zoyne	Whore

Hebrew

B'sham Hashem	In the name of God, a prayer before going to sleep, a lullaby
El Malay rakhamim	God, full of mercy, prayer for the departed, sung a funerals.
Mah nishtanah	What is different (From the Passover Haggadah)
Mi Shebeirakh avoteinu,	May the source of strength who blessed our ancestors, prayer for healing
Nashim	Tractate of the Talmud, Women/Family law
Nedrim	A Section of Nashim, Oaths/Vows
Shema Yisroel	Hear, O Israel, the LORD (is) our God, the LORD is One
Shehekheyanu	Special Jewish prayer to celebrate special occasions
Y'hi ratzon milfanekha	May it be Your will – prayer for journeys
Yis'gadal v'yis'kadash sh'mey raba (Aramaic)	An ancient prayer recited for the dead - May His great Name grow exalted and sanctified